A CRUEL HARVEST

❧ ❧ ❧

PAUL REID

PUBLISHED BY

amazon encore ≋

Published by AmazonEncore
P.O. Box 400818
Las Vegas, NV 89140

ISBN-13: 9781935597070
ISBN-10: 1935597078

This book is for my parents, Nicholas and Breda.

PROLOGUE

1790 – Northwest Europe

A weary hulk. Cliffs visible through the mist. Men's eyes strained from rigging ropes.

The sea was the colour of dulled steel, capped with spume tossed up by a spiteful wind. It was not yet midday, but the sky was darkened by clouds that thundered above the hills beyond the beach. The ship, under assault from swollen waves, heaved desperately on her anchor like an animal with its leg in a trap. The crew were unable to seek sanctuary in the inlets because the coastline here was treacherous, jagged rocks and hidden reefs lurking like sea predators, aching to snarl their teeth on the light vessel and disembowel her. If disaster befell them, death would swiftly follow, for something as frail as a man's body could last only a moment in these murderous, churning waters.

Captain Al Abbas al-Zaki balanced himself against the larboard rail, searching the shore with hooded eyes. He grunted in contempt. The island looked as if it must be eternally grey, devoid of even a single ray of sunlight to lift the pallor of the weather-beaten landscape. They called this place Ireland. Rain-sodden expanses of bogland cast adrift beyond the fringes of northern Europe—what people could live in such a place? No doubt a people as barbarous as the environment, uncultivated infidels and swine-eaters, worshippers of idols and false gods. Al-Zaki crinkled his mouth in distaste and turned away.

'Fetch me the boy.' He snapped the order, and two crewmembers went below decks, returning some moments later with a pale-skinned youngster of about eleven years. He was shivering, both from the Atlantic air and the intimidating presence of the Arab captain. Captured from a fishing skiff just days before, he had begged that he be released back to his family, promising in return to direct the ship to a village on the southern Irish coast which al-Zaki had been searching for but was so far unable to find.

His scarred face betraying his displeasure, al-Zaki addressed the boy in English: 'The further you take us into this hellish place, the worse the weather gets. Have you lied to me, *weld*? I think you have lied. I think I must deal with your lies right now.' He put his hand on the hilt of his broadsword, and the boy let out a squeal.

'No, my lord!' He pointed desperately to the headland situated off the larboard bow. 'Around that, my lord, and there sits the harbour. You will see the little boats at anchor. That's the village of Dromkeen for you, my lord.'

Dromkeen: a coarse, offensive sound, a spawn of the savage native tongue. It was a fishing village of some two thousand souls, according to al-Zaki's intelligence, but the directions given to him had been inaccurate, for he had expected to find it further east, nearer to Youghal. Youghal—another disgusting, scarcely believable sound. If the boy was not telling the truth, then this would prove a wasted journey, which was a sore prospect. The voyage southwards, back to the heat-baked plains of his homeland, would be a bitter one if his quest did not bear fruit.

'I do hope you are right, *weld*,' he said ominously.

'On my life, my lord!' the boy declared, striking his breast to demonstrate his sincerity.

'It will certainly come to that if you are wrong.' Al-Zaki's eyes flashed, tempests brewing, for he was running out of patience. He said a silent prayer that Allah might bless the enterprise, and then he turned back to the rail.

He had never journeyed this coastline before, confining his travels instead to the places of memory that he had visited on so many successful voyages over the last forty years, from Sicily and Spain to Portugal and France and the Cornish coast, once even as far as the continent of America. Months of hardship in stormy seas—eating damp, weevily biscuits and with the threat of naval vessels always present—were made worthwhile by the acquisition of a commodity which was as enriching in its trade as it was bountiful in its supply.

Slaves.

He shipped human cargo to the teeming markets of North Africa and sold it to merchants and sultans, where it was pressed into lifelong servitude. Unlike gold or diamonds, humans were easily acquired and unlimited in their numbers. Seaside towns, fishing villages, ports—the corsairs of the Barbary Coast would descend like the wind in the night and depart with their ship-holds crammed with a resource that would never lose its value. The European governments, desperate to stem this plague on their lands, despatched emissaries clutching truces and treaties for the Arab rulers to sign, but the trade thrived nonetheless. No matter where he found them, be they English, Spanish, French, or Irish, al-Zaki could win a reward for every unfortunate creature he managed to snatch from the shore.

They weighed anchor, and the crew fought the storm for the rest of that morning and afternoon. When evening came, the wind had lost much of its vigour, and the waves settled into a more leisurely rhythm. Following the boy's directions, the ship steered around the headland and slipped discreetly under the cliffs. Through the fading light of dusk, al-Zaki spied with his glass tiny Dromkeen nestled by a sandy cove. Its houses were in shadow, its roads quiet.

With the lamps on the deck extinguished, the darkness of the night would cloak the crew's approach. The villagers would be asleep by that time, tucked into their beds and oblivious to the menace sweeping across the harbour.

CHAPTER ONE

Orlaith had only begun the walk to the village when she sensed that she was being followed. She heard nothing, and there was no one in sight, but she had an unsettling feeling as though someone watched her, was keeping pace with her. Carrying a basket of eggs in one arm and holding her baby son Sean in the other, she was unable to hurry. Instead, she stopped and listened. It had been raining all morning, and the droplets made an incessant sound as they dripped from the trees. Bushes rustled. The wind, she thought. She shivered and went to walk on.

Behind the hedgerow at the roadside, a branch snapped. The sudden noise startled her. She heard movement in the ferns.

Footsteps.

'Who's there?' she demanded in a shaky voice. No one replied, but the footsteps stopped. She peered into the hedge and then became aware of the shadowy outline of a man on the other side. She put the basket down and clutched Sean to her chest.

'Who is it?' she asked. 'Please, what do you want?'

'You,' he answered. His feet swished through the grass, and moments later he emerged into view. 'Or I'd settle for a kiss, if needs be.'

'Oh!' Orlaith exclaimed, her face flushing with anger. 'Are you not the great big fool, Brannon Ryan!'

He grinned. 'And I thought you'd be glad to see me, Orlaith.'

'Glad, indeed. What are you about?'

'You should have told me you were going to Dromkeen—I would have helped you. Give me that fellow.' He reached across and took Sean from her arms; the youngster gave a whimper of protest, but then he nestled into Brannon's chest and went back to sleep.

'I can manage the walk to the village well enough,' she berated him, 'if the local rascal wouldn't be bothering me.'

He laughed. 'I'm a thick Cork lout, am I not? But you love that.'

'I certainly do not—' she began, but her voice was silenced when he pulled her forward with his free arm and kissed her. She immediately raised her fists to fend him off, but they remained in the air for a moment, unmoving. She gave a small inward sigh and surrendered, one hand lowering to touch his face. He thrust himself against her, and she could feel the firmness of his body, his urgent advance making her legs weaken as her own arousal flared.

Then, remembering Sean, she recalled her resolve and pushed him away. Her skin was flushed as she swept the strands of hair from her face. 'This...' she breathed, 'will not do at all. What would the neighbours say—'

'They'd say, "There goes that awful Mrs Downey again, harassing that poor, God-fearing, and terribly handsome Brannon Ryan."'

'Stop it,' she warned. 'I don't like it when you call me that.'

'Sorry, Orlaith.' He remembered that she did indeed find 'Mrs Downey' an uncomfortable title. But everyone in the village called her that, even though her husband had been dead over a year now. Brannon was the only one who addressed her by her Christian name.

He gestured to the basket of eggs on the ground. 'I see the hens are being kind.'

'Oh yes,' she said, brightening again. 'I have more every day than me or Sean can eat. I'll sell these at the village, and my purse will be jingling on the road home.'

'You're a proper farmer at last. I'm relieved to see it.'

'And whom might I thank, I wonder?' she said with a smile. 'For a rogue, you're still a handy fellow to have around at times.'

'Then marry me, Orlaith,' he said seriously. 'Marry me tomorrow, and let's be together at last.' He raised an eyebrow and said, 'Unless—you don't love me?' He let the question trail with a knowing look in his eye.

'Oh, Brannon,' she sighed, reaching out to embrace him. She kissed him and said, 'I do, you wicked man. God help me, but I do.'

⊕ ⊕ ⊕

They walked to Dromkeen together, where Orlaith sold her basket of eggs to the fishermen, and on their return a shy sun peeked through the scudding clouds. On the track the pools of rainwater sparkled, and they made a game of trying to dodge them, much to Sean's amusement. Orlaith delighted in the burgeoning relationship that was developing between Sean and Brannon, for they were not blood-related. Sean was the offspring of her marriage to Seamus Downey, a man she barely knew, who was befriended by her father one day after they fell into conversation in a tavern and spent several hours drinking porter and damning England. Seamus had lived only until the bleak, difficult autumn of 1788 when he received a retaliatory kick from his long-suffering donkey and made Orlaith a widow. A widow with child, as it soon transpired.

'I don't like the look of that.' Brannon's voice distracted her. He gestured across the bay to where a bank of dark clouds had dimmed the horizon. 'That'll be knocking on our doors soon, I reckon. Could have a rough night of it.'

'You'll fix the leak in the cabin?' she asked. Her tiny cabin, mud-walled and thatched with woven reeds, was susceptible to bad weather.

'I will.' He handed Sean back. 'Let me go on ahead. There'll be a warm fire when you get home.'

'Thanks, Brannon.' She smiled as he moved up the road. Without Brannon she would never have coped after Seamus's death, not as an eighteen-year-old girl who knew nothing of furrowing fields and sowing crops. Brannon had spared some hours each day from his own farm to help out, and she liked him from the start. Three years her elder, he was tall and strong, blond-haired and blue-eyed, and their neighbourly co-operation lasted only a month before it caught flame and became a love affair. She teased him, being unforthcoming with a definite answer to his frequent marriage proposals, but this month she intended to give her consent. She knew he was growing impatient for her, as indeed she was for him, but she was also wary of her Catholic obligations, and thus it must be the church before the bedroom.

A brisk wind was whipping up the waves by the time she reached home. The clomping of hooves interrupted her, and she saw a horse and rider in the trees near the roadside. The rider spotted her, waved his hand, and steered the animal closer. Orlaith took a step back.

'Mrs Downey.' He beamed and climbed down from his horse. 'How are you this morning?'

'I am very well, Mr Whiteley,' she answered, giving a curtsey. Concerned, she said, 'Perhaps I have made an oversight, sir, but I thought the rent not due for another two weeks?'

He laughed. 'Don't fret yourself, Mrs Downey. I'm not here for the rent. I was simply riding in the area, and when I saw you, I thought I might say hello.'

She nodded, unsure of what to say. Randall Whiteley was her landlord, as he had been her husband's before his death. She knew little of him but for the few details that Seamus had relayed to her. A single man, he'd been married years before to a beautiful young woman who had subsequently eloped with a lover and left Randall pining in misery. According to Seamus, Randall changed after that. He was known to treat women badly now. It seemed his wife had robbed him of his decency along with his innocence.

He saw the empty basket in her hands and said, 'You were at the market this morning?'

'Yes, sir. I thought to sell the eggs, sir.'

'Splendid. But it must be a long walk for you with the child?'

'It's not so bad, sir.'

'Of course not,' he said. 'After all, you had Mr Ryan to help you, had you not? He helps you often.'

'Yes, sir.' The realisation that Whiteley had been watching her movements was discomfiting. 'He's a kind neighbour, sir.'

Randall didn't reply to that. He was no longer smiling. Orlaith fidgeted anxiously and stammered, 'Begging your pardon, sir, but I have much to do.'

'Ah, yes.' The smile returned to his face, but there remained a coldness in his eyes. 'I'll not keep you any further then, Mrs Downey.'

She almost broke into a run as she carried Sean up the track towards the cabin. She knew Whiteley was still standing on the road and watching her, and she kept going until she reached her door. She pushed it open, bustled inside, and locked it behind her, too frightened to look back.

The following morning Dromkeen was shaken by storms from the east. The clouds loosed a stinging rain which swelled the small lakes and ran in rivulets of water through the fields towards the beach. From his cabin on the hill, Brannon watched the heaving sea. The waves were monstrous, big living beasts that made a tremendous sound as they pounded the shore. There would be no work done this day.

In the afternoon, he braved the elements and sprinted down to Orlaith's cabin. The grass was thick with moisture, and the mud spattered under him as he ran, staining his linen breeches.

'Are you mad to be out in this weather?' she scolded him as he stepped inside, dripping wet. 'You will have a cough in the morning.'

'It's a dirty one, right enough. How's the little fellow?'

Sean bounced excitedly when he saw Brannon. He was sitting on the earthen floor, listening to the boom of the thunder and clearly enjoying himself.

'I was trying to boil the potatoes for us, but the wood's too wet,' Orlaith lamented. 'It's cursed weather.'

'Let that alone for now.' Brannon turned her away from the damp kindling in the hearth. 'Get your hands on the carrots and the cabbage, and I'll see about this.'

He got the fire going some minutes later. Orlaith stewed the potatoes and vegetables, and the three of them ate together. By evening time, when the light outside was fading to dusk, she was starting to yawn. Brannon heaped more turf on the fire and went to kiss her goodnight; she pulled his body down to hers, and the goodnight kiss lingered on for several minutes before he could finally make his way home.

The rain had eased, the worst of the storm having passed them over. He trudged through the grass and climbed the shadowed hill towards his cabin. Before approaching the door, he glanced out to sea and saw that the waves had calmed. He strained his eyes—a tiny object in the far distance caught his attention.

A ship.

He stared at it for a while, its shape and sails unfamiliar to him. It was too big to be one of the local fishing boats. Moving along the shoreline, it tacked skilfully against the wind until eventually it disappeared under the cliffs.

'Poor beggars,' Brannon said to himself. They must have come for shelter from the weather. Often such ships slipped into the harbour when the seas were bad.

He went inside, giving no more thought to the strange vessel. It was too late to light a fire, and so he went to bed soon afterwards. He was tired, and he looked forward to a night of untroubled sleep.

⊕ ⊕ ⊕

Several hours later, he awoke. The ceiling was in shadow, but there was a blunt blue light rimming the shutters. It was almost dawn. He yawned, wondering what had disturbed him so early.

A sudden bang made him jolt. Swearing, he scrambled from the bed and grabbed a shoe in defence. 'Who's that?'

Again someone hammered the door, as if trying to break it down, and the bolt rattled in its rusting lock.

'Who is it?' he demanded.

'It's me!' a voice cried. When he opened the door, Orlaith stumbled inside, Sean whining in her arms. Her face was white.

'What the hell is going on?' He grasped her shoulders to steady her. 'Tell me!'

'There's people coming,' she spluttered, glancing back in fear.

'What?'

'They're coming to get us, Brannon. We must hide!'

'What are you talking about?' Her words made no sense. 'Let me see.'

'No, don't go out there!' she pleaded, trying to block his way.

'Calm down, Orlaith,' he barked. 'Stay here. I must take a look.'

Outside, the morning air penetrated the cover of his shirt as he ran barefoot through the frost. Stars twinkled above while to the east a pale light was rising above the sea. He was panting by the time he climbed the hill on which his farm was set, and from there he had a view that reached into Dromkeen.

A view that made the breath catch in his throat.

Hordes of figures with bare arms and dark skin were swarming through the village, smashing their way into the houses along the road. They were armed with swords and pistols, and three dead locals lay on the ground. The thatched roofs had been torched to drive the occupants out, and the flames now bathed the whole scene in an eerie amber glow. As Brannon cast his eyes further up, he saw at least a dozen villagers being dragged away and then bundled and beaten down the sloping path towards the beach.

'Dear God,' he whispered in horror.

'Brannon, come inside!' Orlaith cried from the cabin.

The sound of her voice pulled him from his trance. When he hurried back down, she was ready to lock the door behind him, but he said, 'We can't stay here. Take Sean and come with me.'

'But who are they, Brannon?'

'Damn it, we're not waiting to find out.'

He led her across the windy slopes into the meadows and woodland. It was still dark there, and the noise from the village was only a dull hubbub. They climbed over a tumbled fence, where they found themselves on a path that led through quiet groves of pine before winding downwards along a fold in the terrain.

'You know where this goes?' Brannon asked her.

She nodded. 'To the west strand.'

'Go down there and hide in the smugglers' cave. You'll be safe there.'

'But where are you going?' she protested in alarm. 'Don't leave us!'

'I'll follow you, but I've forgotten my pistol.'

As a Catholic, Brannon was forbidden by the Penal Laws to own a weapon of any kind, but this pistol had been given to him by his father, and it was still in working order. He kept it hidden inside his cabin with a pouch of lead balls and some powder. He had taught Orlaith how to use it—she was actually quite a good shot—and he was glad he had never surrendered it to the authorities, for tonight was a night when he might need to use it for the first time.

'Don't be long,' Orlaith begged him. 'And don't let them see you!'

'Go now, Orlaith.' He waved her away. 'Go to the cave and wait for me.'

She looked at him forlornly, moonlight glistening in her tears. 'I love you, Brannon.' Taking a firm hold of Sean, she turned down the path and disappeared into the darkness.

Brannon ran in the opposite direction, wishing he had remembered the pistol earlier. But he had to have it. He stumbled down the hillside, the cold air stinging his lungs, and made straight for the cabin. Once again he could hear the terrifying sounds of the horror unfolding in the village.

Something made him hesitate before entering the cabin, a sixth sense warning him of danger. He took a step back. There was a growl from the bushes, and suddenly a dark shape sprang from the shadows. Brannon ducked instinctively as a weapon was swung at his head, but the force of the attacker's charge knocked him over. He rolled to the side, scrambling to his feet while the man roared some indecipherable foreign battle cry and lashed out at him again. Brannon jerked his head and dodged the blow, but now their struggle had drawn attention.

Two more of them appeared from the cabin door. They had ransacked his meagre belongings, and now their teeth gleamed in the dawn light when they saw him. Wielding iron-studded cudgels, they advanced to form a semicircle, entrapping him against the potato cart. He reached to the ground, searching for a weapon of some kind. His fingers closed around a rock, and he flung it. The rock struck the first attacker in the forehead, splitting him open and taking him out of the fray. Brannon looked for another stone or some heavy object and faced the remaining two.

A fourth attacker had slipped behind him without his realising. He crept up quietly and, using his cudgel, gave a light but precise tap at the base of Brannon's neck, and then he stepped away.

Brannon felt the seemingly innocuous blow as if it had been driven home with a mallet. His vision started to blur. He grabbed for the cart to balance himself, but then his legs buckled under him, his eyes rolled in his head, and he collapsed. He was already unconscious when his body slumped into the wet grass.

CHAPTER TWO

Captain Al Abbas al-Zaki stood at the cove as the foamy tide lapped around his ankles. Dawn had arrived in full now, transforming the sea from oily black to pewter grey. A weak sun crouched above the horizon, the faint promise of a brighter day. It was time to be leaving.

He had ordered that the captives be arranged on the beach, using steel chains with manacles for wrists and ankles. The captives were too weak and confused to resist. They were forced to sit on the ground so that those still lying unconscious could be manacled to them, and then they were herded in groups to the longboats which would ferry them out to the ship. Al-Zaki estimated that there were well over a hundred of them, and he was satisfied. Despite the darkness and the unfamiliar terrain, the crew had performed at a rapid pace. Raids like this they had carried out more times than they could remember. Three of them had been shot dead at one house over the hills, but they were the only losses that al-Zaki suffered.

The ship was an Algerian-built xebec carrying twenty-four guns. Its shallow draught and light hull made it fast and easy to handle under sail, ideal for the corsairs when pursuing a target or evading an enemy. Xebecs, however, were more at home in the blue waters of the Mediterranean rather than the cold and volatile Atlantic. The seas here had given the crew a rough time.

When the last captive was aboard, al-Zaki went to the foredeck, the anchor was weighed, and the crew unfurled a square sail on the mainmast. The long journey south began.

⊕ ⊕ ⊕

As the vessel cleared the harbour, the chained villagers were led through a hatchway into the confines of the main hold. The hold was layered with tiers of decking so that they could be arranged in rows, each deck placed no more than fifteen inches above the lower one. Under this system a surprisingly large number of bodies could be accommodated. The space between each tier was so narrow that a person was unable to turn on either side but was forced to lie flat. Every available portion of room was utilised, and the captives were squashed together, their manacled arms and legs overlapping.

Brannon had only regained consciousness a while earlier; he was tottering shakily on his feet, and now his stomach heaved when he caught a whiff of the stench inside the hold. It was vile, like rotten meat, and he fought to suppress a wave of nausea. Behind him one of the other captives vomited; he heard it splashing near his feet, and immediately the insufferable smell worsened.

It was difficult to see in front, the hatchway providing the only means of light. They were pushed along a narrow aisle by the decking and one by one allotted to a space. The crew worked diligently, securing loops on the chains through rings bolted to the bulkheads. Brannon was desperate to avoid this fate, being shackled down like a dog, but with the manacles restricting his hands and legs there was no chance of him mounting a fight against the brawny Arabs. As if to remind him of this fact, one of them cuffed him hard in the ear and shoved him on to the decking.

He found himself bundled beside two other men and could only squeeze his long frame between the tiers with great difficulty. There was barely enough room to lift his head, much less to move his body. He feared suffocation and took deep breaths to steady himself, though that was difficult in the foul, torpid airs of the hold.

'Looks like we're to be bedfellows,' the man next to him grumbled.

Brannon recognised him as Pat Browne, a retired sailor who rented a farm near Dromkeen. 'Who are they, Pat? What are they doing with us?'

'You don't want to know, young Ryan.'

With their prizes now safely stowed, the crew climbed out and shut the hatch, plunging the hold into darkness. A moment of silence passed. Then somebody began to sob in some corner, and this triggered off a clamour of wailing and lamenting. People wept and cried out to God, or yelled angrily, demanding answers. The cacophony of human anguish made it impossible to converse with anyone, and Brannon closed his eyes, trying to shut them out. He was dazed and confused, still unsure of what was happening or who the fearsome-looking foreigners were. This nightmare, however, was one he couldn't wake from.

The captives were kept below decks for a full day, and it wasn't until the following morning that the hatch opened. There was little sound from the villagers, for they had gone without water and sleep and were already in a weakened state. After the initial hubbub the day before, they had soon lost their voices and settled into their cramped positions, lulled by the sea's rhythm into a disconsolate silence.

Six crewmembers came below, their bellows filling the hold. They unbolted the chains from the bulkheads and hustled the captives towards the hatchway, lashing out with leather scourges to speed the process. The captives bowed their heads and hurried along, anxious to be spared a painful lick of the scourge.

Up on deck the morning light dazzled their eyes as they stumbled forward. The sun peered down between flecks of cloud, and the hull's timbers gleamed with sea spray. They were herded into formation alongside the larboard rail, where a keg of water had been placed between some casks of pickled meat. The captives stared at it, their tongues lolling between their teeth. They were now suffering from severe thirst, and the sight of water was cruelly tormenting, making them restless and agitated. But the crew made no attempt to fetch the keg.

Brannon searched the row of bodies with a sense of dread. He almost couldn't bear to look. But after he had checked each dour face in turn, he was hugely relieved. There was no sign of Orlaith. He felt sure that she had managed to hide in time and had escaped capture. She had to be safe—he couldn't stomach any other possibility.

Because they had been locked below decks all night, he had no idea of the ship's position. Many hours had passed since the raid, and he wondered how far they had travelled in that time. There was no sound of sea birds, which indicated that they were no longer near land. A full wind was filling the sails, and he could tell from the ship's motion that it was making steady progress. The thought of it was greatly discomfiting. Brannon had lived his entire life by the sea but had never travelled far enough into it to lose sight of the coast. Now every breath of wind was increasing the distance between him and home.

One of the crewmembers walked along the line of captives. He stopped in front of Brannon and regarded him keenly, impressed by the effect which years of farm work had had in building and strengthening his frame. He poked his finger at the ridges of muscle along Brannon's arms and flanks, testing and appraising like someone would a bull at the fair.

'Can I help you?' Brannon asked, his irritation flaring.

At his words the Arab's eyes widened. He raised his scourge and struck Brannon in the face, mouthing a torrent of abuse in his foreign tongue and bunching his fist. The twisted leather thongs raised painful stripes across Brannon's cheek; he drew a breath to growl his anger, but beside him Pat Browne hissed a warning. 'Keep quiet, you fool. They'll kill you.'

Brannon managed to check his temper. The big Arab continued his examination down the line, and when he was finished, he crossed the deck. Another man had appeared, and from the way the crewmembers made space for him, Brannon guessed him to be the captain.

He was tall with wide shoulders and big, callused hands, one of which rested on the hilt of his broadsword. He wore a turban and had a hawkish face with a dark, trimmed beard. He stepped forward, close enough for Brannon to see his eyes. They were black like charcoal, devoid of tone. The captives shifted uneasily before him.

The big one, who had carried out the inspection, came over in response to a question from the captain. In reply he indicated a number of the captives, and the captain spoke to him briefly before leaving the deck again. The big one then barked an order, and two crewmembers approached the villagers. They unlocked the manacles of three people, bidding them to step forward from the line.

Brannon recognised them. The first, Myles O'Mahony, was an unmarried farmer in his fifties. A quiet man who lived alone, he was a decent sort and friendly. He looked tired and nervous now. The person next to him, Margaret Clancy, was about the same age as O'Mahony and the wife of Dromkeen's blacksmith. Brannon knew her as a gossipy woman with a sharp tongue, though at the moment she was too frightened to open her mouth. Her hands were clasped across her bosom, her plump cheeks pale.

The third captive was also female, but much younger, about ten years old. She was one of the Murphy daughters from up the village—Tara. Like her sisters she had a head of bouncing blonde ringlets and could always be heard before she was seen. But today she was barely recognisable as that chattering young girl. She swayed on her feet, arms hanging listlessly by her sides, exhausted.

Brannon watched, confused as to why these three had been marked out. They were led forward together, across to the starboard side of the deck.

The remaining captives howled in disbelief when they saw what happened next. The old man, woman, and young girl were seized and lifted bodily over the rail. Even in their weakened state they battled, struggling and kicking once they realised the fate in store for them. But their efforts were feeble against the beefy arms that held them, and one by one they were pushed over the side.

There were three separate splashes as they hit the water. No further sound came from Myles O'Mahony and Margaret Clancy—their fatigued bodies couldn't resist, and they slipped quickly beneath the waves. But young Tara Murphy tried desperately to survive. She flailed her thin arms about and vanished for a moment as the swells submerged her. They thought she was gone, but she fought to the surface again, spewing out a mouthful of seawater. In between gasps, she let out a cry for help.

Her stricken voice carried to the captives on deck and sent them into a frenzy of anguish. They strained against their chains and begged the crew to pull the girl from the water, but they received only scornful laughter in response. The sound of Tara's pleas soon began to weaken as her energy deserted her. She gave a last keening cry, and after that there was nothing. When the captives looked back into the ship's foamy wake, there was no trace of her blonde curls. She had disappeared forever into the dark immensity of the ocean.

The captives were overwhelmed by grief. The women sobbed while the men tried to wrench themselves free, voicing vicious threats against the crew for what had just happened. The crew watched this show of emotion for a while and scoffed, but soon the noise began to irritate them and they moved to quell the disorder. With whips and kicks they laid into the row of people, quickly overpowering them and stilling their voices. The captives re-formed their line in despondency.

'They picked out the weak ones,' Pat Browne fumed. 'They knew they wouldn't last the journey.'

Brannon was numbed with shock at what he had just witnessed, and he stayed silent. But a few minutes later he picked up on Pat's words. 'Journey to where?'

'To wherever it is they mean to sell us. It's not likely that anyone will pay a ransom for us, which leaves only bondage.'

'Bondage?' The word sent a chill down Brannon's spine. 'You mean—slavery?'

'That's exactly what I mean. It's a thriving business with these Moors. I hope you're a praying man, young Ryan. You will need God's help now.'

Brannon struggled to take it in. It was too appalling. Only two days ago he had been tilling soil in Dromkeen.

'They'll be bound for North Africa is my guess,' Pat went on. 'After that we'll be cheap labour for grubby Arabs. A foreign land with foreign tongues and foreign gods.'

Brannon knew little of Africa, only that it was a savage place inhabited by wild beasts and cannibals and other hellish creations. He didn't like the thought of it.

'The devil knows what will become of us, but we've got dark days ahead. You mark my words.'

'Enough, Pat,' Brannon said bleakly, feeling sick again. 'I think I've heard enough.'

The captives were eventually watered and then banished below to the hold again, where they remained for the following week. On the seventh night of the voyage, the ship hit storms. Great winds drove mountainous waves over the sea, which created mayhem for the light vessel. It lifted up over each crest with tremendous zeal, as if it could break free and soar into the air, before plummeting into the following trough with a force that threatened to wrench their guts through their mouths.

Inside the hold there was chaos. Most of the captives had never experienced seas like these and were violently sick. Unable to move off their backs, they were spewing on top of themselves, covering their clothes with hot, stinking bile. Such copious levels of liquid were being produced that it was streaming onto the deck and sliding up and down with the ship's motion. As they hadn't been allowed outside for days, the captives had no means of relieving themselves in any dignified way. They were forced to empty their bowels where they lay, and the foetid stench was so thick that it coated their mouths and nostrils like grease. They were administered a daily ration of water, but in the heat this was not sufficient, and they soon became badly dehydrated.

At some point—they couldn't tell whether it was night or day—the storm abated. Their stomachs settled down, but the deck remained in wretched condition. The smell was like a physical thing, so appalling was its presence. They had been in total darkness for over a week now, and some were starting to babble to themselves, the first signs of insanity beginning to take hold.

Some days later, they were relieved to see the crewmembers climbing down and proceeding to unlock the chains. The prospect of fresh air was tantalising. They were ordered to their feet and directed towards the hatch, though this time it was a much slower effort. Their bodies were stiff from confinement, their skin blistered from the rough wood.

Up on deck, the first thing to catch their attention was the sight of land. They saw a rocky strip of coast and a row of sunburnt hills off the larboard side, the sky beyond flecked with multitudes of birds. The water here was clear blue, the sunshine penetrating its surface so that the shoals of fish glittered like silver trinkets. After the odorous confines of the hold, the ocean air was sweet. Mercifully, it went some way towards alleviating the stench of their soiled clothing.

Sixteen people had died during the voyage from dehydration and suffocation. Due to the oppressive heat within the hold, their bodies were decomposing rapidly. The crew had released their manacles earlier and were now dumping them one by one over the rail. Within minutes the waters below were churned white by packs of hungry sharks competing for the feast. On deck the survivors were subjected to an inspection like before, and Brannon was convinced that this time the lot of them would be tossed overboard, such was the miserable condition they were in. But they were spared.

'Where are we, Pat?' he whispered.

'The gates of hell,' Pat answered tensely, gazing towards the silver-sand beach that rimmed the coast of Africa.

They were allowed to sit on the deck to savour the air—al-Zaki wanted to preserve his cargo as best he could. Sixteen people from one hundred and fifteen was a trifling loss, but nevertheless, every dead body represented a further lightening of his purse. So he indulged them a while, the crew went about their work, the ship followed the coast, and all was quiet.

An hour later, the peace was shattered.

From the mainmast a crewmember yelled in alarm, gesticulating towards the larboard stern. Al-Zaki appeared in a heartbeat, glass to eye. He spotted the threat and uttered a gruff order to the first mate. The crew were galvanised into action, stations run to.

Pat dragged his body up, ignoring the protests of those chained to him. He stared over the rail and swore aloud. 'Christ, they've raised a sail. We're being hunted!'

They all gaped at him. 'Who is it?'

'A frigate, by the looks of her. She must have been hiding on the coast.' His face broke into a smile. 'I can see her flag—she's English! By God, our luck might have swung.'

His words brought a chorus of cries from the captives. But it was still early for sudden hopes.

'Where is she now?' Brannon asked eagerly.

Pat was able to remain standing while the crew were occupied. 'She's gaining. Jesus, she's a big one. There's got to be forty guns on her.'

'Can she catch us, Pat?'

'She can; she's a beauty. She'll catch us!'

The xebec slaver was outgunned by the English frigate, and clearly the Arabs knew it. They were working to instigate an escape rather than a fight, shaking all the reefs off the sails. The wind was coming from the land and to the English ship's advantage, pushing her out to the windward side of the xebec and narrowing the gap between them.

The chase continued along the coast for an hour, then two, then more. Al-Zaki used every trick he knew, slipping into coves and sheltered bays in the hopes of outwitting the English vessel, but to no avail. Several times the frigate fell out of view behind a headland, but each time it reappeared, refusing to let go of its quarry. The chase became evenly pitched, with neither ship able to alter the gap significantly. The captives were kept under close watch, but as yet there were no spare hands to secure them below.

Miles of rocks and sandy beaches streamed by as they surged south. Al-Zaki was desperate to find sanctuary somewhere. He kept one eye on his pursuer but was also monitoring the shore closely with his glass.

'If the Moors reach port, we've had it,' Pat warned.

But it was the natural elements which ultimately decided the day.

The fresh wind dropped off just as the xebec's lighter hull was starting to work in its favour. The billowing sails emptied of air and slackened to hang from the masts like wasted skin, and the crew were aghast. Their escape had failed. The English frigate tacked cleverly to utilise the dying gusts and swept abreast of the xebec, trapping the Arabs on the coast.

The chase was over.

'We're saved!' Brannon joined in with the excitement of the other captives. But Pat ducked below the rail and said, 'Not yet. We're in God's hands now.'

'But the English will rescue us!'

'They're not here for us, lad. They're here for these pirates.'

As if to elaborate on his words, the air above reverberated with the boom of cannon. The English fired a thunderous broadside, which ripped over the xebec, tearing away yardarms and strips of canvas. There were screams, and the captives cowered on the deck for cover.

More shots came, pummelling the Moroccan flank and blasting holes through the hull. The Arabs responded with counter-fire, inflicting their own toll, but from the outset the battle was one-sided. The English had bigger guns, and more of them.

After a twenty-minute barrage, the Moroccan ship was dappled with puncture wounds on its starboard side and was beginning to list ominously as its holds flooded with water. On the English front the damage sustained was minimal. The battle was almost over.

'She'll go down,' Pat warned Brannon. 'Be ready to swim for it.'

'But how are we going to—' Brannon's words were cut short by a massive crunching sound above their heads. A fluky shot from the English ship had struck the Moroccan mainmast, cleaving through its midsection and severing it. With a deafening clamour of grinding wood, the masthead came crashing down, sending an explosion of wooden shards and rigging across the deck. It landed on the larboard rail, crushing five of the captives and killing them instantly.

'Jesus, we're done for!' Brannon swore.

Pat didn't answer. He was focused on the deck as the crew rushed about, watching one of them intently. As the man passed, Pat threw his manacled hands around his neck and yanked him back by the chain. The stunned Arab fought to get free, choking as his air was cut off.

'Grab his key!' Pat shouted. 'It's for the manacles!'

Brannon quickly wrested the key from the man's hip. He unlocked his own hands and ankles and then Pat's. Between them they managed to shove the struggling Arab over the rail into the sea.

'Free us!' the captives beseeched. Working fast, Brannon went to them one by one, undoing their manacles and releasing each of them in turn. The crew were preoccupied with the English attack, so they missed the vital few minutes that it took Brannon to free everyone.

'Jump!' Pat roared at them. 'It's your only hope—swim for the shore!'

They stared at him in horror. The shore was still a considerable distance away.

'This ship is going to sink—and you with it if you don't jump!' he snapped.

Resigned to this one hope, they began to climb over the rail and leap into the sea. Some were too frightened to make the attempt and faltered on the deck, torn between a possible drowning and certain death on the doomed vessel.

A roar distracted them. Out of the tumult came Captain Al Abbas al-Zaki, the only one of the crew who had spotted the escape attempt. He thundered forward, raising his broadsword with bared teeth.

'Watch your back, Pat!' Brannon yelled.

Pat spun around. 'Come on then, you filthy Moorish bastard. Let's have you!'

He attempted to duck the sword swing and tackle the captain around the waist. But al-Zaki was a skilled swordsman and fighter; he halted his charge, anticipating Pat's move, and then whirled on his feet and sliced the sword into Pat's side, cutting deep across his belly. Pat froze before his legs gave way and he collapsed.

Al-Zaki turned his attention to the remaining captives still cluttering the deck. He was the captain of a foundering ship, yet the fanatical gleam in his eyes showed that he was determined to take as many of them with him as possible. They stood petrified before him.

Another shot roared across from the English ship. Brannon looked on in fascinated terror as the cannon ball clipped al-Zaki's head and tore it clean from his shoulders. The head disintegrated with the impact and threw a scarlet shower into their faces. The trunk stood for a moment, shuddering grotesquely before crumpling on the blood-slicked deck.

Brannon was almost paralysed with shock, but quickly he gathered his wits and turned to the rail. Most of the captives had plucked up the courage and taken their chances with the sea. Only a few remained.

'Go now or never!' Brannon gave them his last advice and then clambered over the rail and jumped.

The water was littered with bits of wood blasted away by the guns. Between the debris the swimmers tried to strike for shore, but several became entangled in the winding canvas and rope. Some of the crew had jumped too; they were attempting the swim rather than stay aboard the ship. Its stern was almost at the sea's surface, and it was listing heavily to the starboard side. It had only minutes of life left.

The swimmers were engaged in a race to the shore. Many were too weak and succumbed along the way. Behind them only the bodies of those killed in the fighting remained on board the splintered deck.

With a last mournful sound, like the groan of a dying old man, the ship slipped beneath the tumbling water, its bow pointing briefly towards the sky before it was dragged into its grave below.

Waves foamed over the white sand of the shore, carrying sails and timbers and bodies. The captives who made it were crawling onto the beach, breathless and shaken, while the crew's numbers were more or less intact, missing only those who had perished amid the bombardment. They were gathering themselves further up. They had lost their weapons, being forced to discard them in order to manage the long swim. Both groups of survivors appraised each other warily, unsure of where the balance of power now lay. The crew were unarmed and outnumbered, and they seemed reluctant to approach the captives. With their ship gone and their captain killed, they were in disarray.

Brannon kept an eye on them while simultaneously coughing the salty water out of his lungs. His limbs ached from the swim, but at least now they had a chance. Coming to his feet, he waved his arm out to sea. The English frigate had dropped anchor and was preparing to lower a longboat. One of the crew waved back to reassure him.

'They're sending a boat for us,' he said in relief. 'We'll be all right now.'

Within a few minutes the Arabs had deserted the beach and slunk into the rolling sand dunes. The wracked Irish villagers waited for the longboat, blinking their eyes against the dust blowing out of the plains beyond the shore. Brannon counted their numbers: the English crew would need to launch more than one boat to carry them all, unless they planned to make a number of trips. He was impatient to be off this coast. It had a taste and smell that he found unsettling, and he was keeping a nervous eye on the dunes. The sooner they were on board and setting sail for home the better.

Then a warning cry distracted him.

He looked behind, picking out a dark shape silhouetted against the blue bowl of sky. A camel. With a rider. They came over the crest of a sand dune and moved towards the beach. There the rider stopped the animal, making no attempt to approach the people at the shore's edge. He adjusted his dress and mopped his brow, watching them quietly.

'Who's he?' one of them asked.

Brannon waved to the ship again and shouted, 'Hurry up! Send the boat!'

The English crew had seen the mysterious figure emerge from the sand dunes and hesitated, but now at Brannon's voice they set to work again. The boat was manoeuvred down to the water. Three men sat inside, each armed with a pistol and sword. They began to row for the beach.

'Won't be long now,' Brannon said, calmly ignoring the presence of the intruder. 'The women first. Be ready to climb aboard.'

The muffled thunder of hooves startled everyone. All of a sudden, riding out from the interiors of the dunes, came a group of sword-wielding Arabs. They advanced on the beach, and the captives cried out in terror, some floundering into the water to reach the longboat. The lone rider they had first seen was now leading the charge across the sand. He gave an animal roar. There was nowhere to run to, and they circled like hyenas, blocking the routes of escape.

The three Englishmen in the boat stopped rowing. They were outnumbered by the wild Arab warriors, and to strike for shore now would be suicide. Fearful, they turned back for the safety of the ship.

More riders appeared, and the captives wailed in despair when they saw what they carried. The chain of manacles again, the same type used to restrain them on the slave ship. The riders had been due to rendezvous with al-Zaki to buy up his goods and had followed his chase along the coast, waiting with their chains and hoping for an opportunity. The opportunity came once the captives were stranded on the shore.

Aboard the English frigate, the crew were torn by indecision. They possessed a powerful array of guns, yet to open fire now would mean certain death for the captives. The earlier attack had been justified by the need to destroy the Arab slaver, but the situation had altered entirely.

Brannon watched them. He knew, too, that there was nothing they could do. The riders were blockading the beach and would easily thwart any further attempt to send a boat ashore. The ship might as well have been a thousand miles out to sea for all the effect it could have. The Arabs knew this, and they prepared the manacles.

The captives' brief fortune had ended.

CHAPTER THREE

The Moroccan ship had been driven far south of its original destination by the attentions of the English frigate, and now the Arab traders faced a trek up the coast to where the slave markets were. The route was a dangerous one. They could expect to lose more than one captive along the way, and for that reason they would have to bargain a little harder once the auctions opened. Misfortunes befell every long journey in this country—everything from banditry to snakebite. Losses were inevitable.

The sun beat down with bitter vengeance as the captives were pushed up along a beach strewn with mouldering kelp, passing blue channels and sparkling lagoons, crossing mangrove swamps and creeks that meandered and twisted their way inland. The shifting dunes baked underneath them, and the very landscape seemed to shimmer in the heat. The sand was so fine and insubstantial that they lost their footing frequently, and every time someone fell the line would be yanked to a halt until the person responsible was beaten back on their feet. Their white bodies were ill-equipped to cope with the African sun; it scorched their flesh, raising angry red blisters that stung at the slightest touch. They did their best to avoid provoking the guards, for the lash of a leather scourge on sunburnt skin was sheer agony.

Once they had negotiated the sandy littoral plains, they turned cross-country into slopes and hills, bleak wastes of land untidy with the remnants of recent nomadic camps and centuries-old, crumbling citadels. The track wound on between bluffs and rugged peaks, through semi-arid terrain coloured with scrub grass and other spiny vegetation. Brannon saw lizards in the shade of rocks, retreating from the sound of people. Once, when his foot moved a stone by the path, he saw a giant yellow scorpion scurrying out and disappearing into a hole nearby. It made him shudder.

Most of them were without shoes, so the pebbles cut their soles and they were soon hobbling painfully. Their clothing, already ragged, offered scant protection against the abrasive rock faces and the euphorbia, the nasty spiked plants that hid their moisture under poisonous sheaths and which now littered the way in brazen displays. As if in sadistic glee, the day seemed to become more insufferably hot. Soon not even a threatened beating from the guards could force them to go on, for the heat and cruel terrain were taking too big a toll on their parched bodies. The guards relented—it would serve no benefit to have the shipment die from exhaustion.

They were allowed to sit in the shade of a sandstone cliff, and a calabash of water was distributed among them. The rations were spared—barely enough to moisten their dust-filled throats. Even in the shade the heat continued to wring precious droplets from their skin.

Brannon could hardly keep his eyes open. He felt he had reached the limits of his reserves, and he wondered how the others had managed to last this long, particularly the women and younger captives. He wished he knew how much further they had to travel, yet asking one of the guards would merely invite another lashing.

Blinking against the swimming heat, he studied their surroundings. On one side of the track was a sheer vertical cliff, and on the other a slope strewn with boulders and stubborn desert plants. It was a savage place. The memory of Dromkeen's heathered hills and loamy soil was a million miles removed from this world of sun-baked rock and ochre ground and small scuttling things that hid in shadows.

He turned his thoughts to escape. To run for it now would be impossible—he hadn't the strength and in any case would never slip his manacles. But he would have to try soon. There was no other option. He had to get away, back to Ireland and back to Orlaith. The alternative—slavery in this hellish land—was too awful to contemplate.

That evening the march was brought to a stop, the Arabs being unwilling to travel through the uncertainty of the night. They made a camp out of brushwood, filled a copper kettle, and lit a fire to keep the insects at bay. The temperatures dropped sharply, and the captives had to huddle together to keep warm. The hills became so cold that their breaths were misted and a thin layer of frost formed on the ground. It didn't seem possible that this could be the same sun-blasted landscape they been travelling through only hours before.

Though exhausted, they found it difficult to sleep. In the distance there was a persistent howling, somewhere out in the darkness, an eerie sound that made their skin tingle. 'Wild dogs,' one of the guards told them in English. 'They hope you will try to escape—they wait for you.' And that was enough to quell any lingering thoughts of flight.

At daybreak they moved on again. The march was another gruelling one, followed by another night of tortured sleep. The days dragged by, and the sun was a relentless menace. They came out of the cheerless hills and into greener pastures, and at the end of the week Brannon spotted what he guessed was their destination: a fortified city, lined with battlements and watchtowers and brooding cannon. Outside the gates were vineyards and orange groves. Oxen laboured in the fields. Workers were gathering baskets of lemons and figs, and there was a tangy smell from the docks where young boys stacked slippery mounds of fish, big tunnies and rock-cod, turbot and bream. Guarding it all, the broad city walls emanated a golden-amber colour in the strengthening sunlight as the captives entered the gates.

The narrow streets inside were not so appealing. The roadways and buildings were splashed with human waste and animal droppings, and to Brannon's disgust, he saw a rat the size of a small dog emerge snuffling from a midden heap. The rubbish piles were covered with swarms of flies so thick that they seemed like a single entity, some brute black monster gorging on the putrefying filth. By the walls were the severed heads of criminals stuck on pikes, their tongues lolling from their grinning mouths. Even in death they looked terrifying.

The townspeople were no more pleasing to the eye. There were thousands of them, their skins a variety of shades brown, black, and bronze. They seemed keenly interested in the captives, for they were closing in around the line, filtering out of the alleys and back-streets like scavengers with the scent of offal. The guards made only a half-hearted attempt to keep them at bay, lashing out with the scourge, picking a random target. But the crowd had become a horde and was pressing in.

Brannon swallowed nervously, unsure of what was happening. And the mood soon turned ugly.

Almost in unison they began to curse and screech, berating the captives with snarling voices, hawking gobs of phlegm in their eyes and slapping their heads. From young boys to old women, they joined in the abuse, much to the amusement of the guards, who only intervened whenever there was a risk of a captive being seriously damaged by an overzealous local.

Brannon attempted to duck the blows, blinking against the jets of spittle. With his hands manacled, leaving him defenceless, his temper began to boil. In front of him a toothless beggar was cackling and raking his fingernails down the captives' cheeks. Brannon dodged his talons and then butted him hard in the face, knocking him into the crowd and earning a bellow of appreciative laughter from the guards.

Eventually the mob was dispersed. The captives were led through the town, past bustling souks and spice markets where rich aromas of cumin and coriander filled the air. The markets were loud with the babble of voices, the movement of bodies, and the slap of sandals on the cobblestone. Women balanced casks of water on their heads and drifted effortlessly through as though immune to the heave and swell. Traders peddled their wares—dried fish draped on racks next to pots of honey, hunks of smoked meat, and live hens. The captives came under a series of grated archways, reaching a courtyard fronted by cypress trees and armed sentries. Inside the courtyard were steps leading underground. Here the sentries unlocked the covering grate, and they were hustled in.

Below it was almost total darkness. The only light came from braziers by the wall. They continued down the shadowy passageway until they reached a small chamber, where the guards released their manacles and left them. When their eyes adjusted to the gloom, they realised that there were already people in here, miserable-looking creatures sprawled on the earthen floor. The air was hot and stale, and a trickle of light came through a grille in the ceiling. The captives stood in the centre of the chamber, unsure of what to do.

Brannon cleared his throat. 'Do any of you speak English?' They looked European to him. There was a mumbled response, but nothing he could make out.

The chamber was extremely cramped, almost as bad as the ship. There were mats on the ground, but they were filthy and speckled with maggots. In the corner was a row of slop buckets, their contents dribbling over the rims. It was a horrid little room.

'Scottish, I'm guessing,' a voice spoke up from the wall, with a harsh, clipped accent that Brannon remembered from English sailors back home. The speaker was a short, stocky man with an unkempt beard, about forty-five years of age. He had a smile on his face.

'We're from County Cork,' Brannon told him.

'Irish, then.' The man nodded. 'I'm from London, me. Peckham, to be exact. The rest of these are a greasy shower of frogs and dagos, from the sounds of their bellyaching.'

'How long have you been here?'

'About three weeks,' the Londoner grumbled. 'The Moors sank my ship off Gibraltar.'

'You were a crewmember?'

'I was the bloody captain, mate. Don't know what became of the rest of me lads—if they're alive, they're probably rotting in one of these dungeons too.'

Three weeks was a long time to spend in this dank pit, Brannon reflected gloomily.

'Daniel Jones is my name,' the Londoner introduced himself.

'I'm Brannon Ryan. Pleased to meet you, if that doesn't sound daft.'

Daniel chuckled at that. 'Do three weeks down here, mate, and nothing will seem daft any more.'

26

They endured a night in the airless cell and woke the following morning almost delirious with thirst. A keg of brackish water had been placed in the corner, its surface dappled with dead flies and two black beetles. The captives sipped from the brim, half-heartedly, having to drink in order to restore their ravaged bodies. Their hunger remained, however, gnawing at their bellies and leaving them feeble and hollow. For over two weeks now they had eaten nothing but the cakes of dhurra that their captors had given them, a cereal grain which wasn't sufficient to keep starvation at bay.

Brannon sat staring into a hole in the ceiling where a hairy-legged spider had cast a web. The spider was perfectly still, its body arched. An ugly thing. It watched the world below it patiently, as if formulating some dark plot. Brannon eventually couldn't bear it any more, convinced that the spider was watching *him*. He rose up, grumbling, and went to sit at the other side of the room.

No one disturbed them for some hours, but a little before noon, as Brannon was dozing softly on his side, he caught a smell that made him sit up and open his eyes. It was the scent of food—fresh meat and bread and fruit. He groaned aloud, thinking that he must be going mad. But the other prisoners could smell it too, and they were gazing towards the door in anticipation. Moments later it was unlocked and the guards appeared, directing along a number of servants in white robes.

The captives almost wept when they saw the platters of food being brought by the servants. There was warm lamb tagine, running with fragrant juices and served with couscous; chicken stewed in preserved lemons; fresh garden vegetables; bread and cinnamon cakes; jellies and sweetmeats. The servants laid the food on the ground and then left with the guards, locking the door behind them.

The captives were overcome with longing as they gazed upon this heavenly spread, but they were too afraid to approach it, fearing that it would vanish or that some other cruel trick would be played on them. But then Daniel Jones stood up and swaggered across. 'Blimey, if you lot are passing, I'm bloody well not.'

He took up a streaming fistful of the lamb stew and stuffed it into his mouth. The juices ran down his chin, and his eyes closed in ecstasy at the taste of it. This broke the others' paralysis, and they crowded forward, seizing with their grubby hands as much meat and bread and everything else that they could. They became frantic with hunger, overturning the plates and spilling the contents in their excitement. The food was soon scattered in clumps on the ground, and they went down on hands and knees, gorging themselves like pariah dogs.

The servants had provided more than enough, and long after, when the prisoners were lying on their backs with swollen bellies, there was still enough left to feed them all over again. Each had eaten more than his or her body could comfortably accommodate, and they could eat no more.

Brannon sat by the wall after the feeding frenzy ended, sucking contentedly on a sugared apple with the contents of the meal sitting warmly in his stomach. He glanced across at Daniel Jones, lying with his hands clasped on his midriff.

'Their consciences must be troubling them,' Brannon quipped. 'I can't think what else brought about this. Bloody handsome fare it was too.'

Daniel grinned. 'Here's the good news: there'll be another feed like it tomorrow, and the day after, and probably for at least another week or two yet.'

'But why?'

'Nothing to do with consciences. There's an auction coming up.'

Brannon stared at him.

'Yes, my friend, an auction.' Daniel sat up to explain. 'You were brought here with the flesh wasting from your bones. You'll have lost a lot of weight on the voyage. You're weak and skinny and pretty much useless. If I were a merchant looking for a strong worker, I'd hardly be dishing out bagfuls of gold for the likes of you.'

Brannon nodded warily, and an understanding dawned. It made sense. They would be fed to the gills so that they could be fattened up, and thereby fetch a higher price from the slave buyers. He swallowed uncomfortably. 'I don't feel too well.' Suddenly he wished he hadn't eaten so much.

'That's the truth of it for you, Irish. That's how they work. It's all about trade and profit.'

'And how come you know so much about all this?'

'Hah! I'm an unlucky fish, I am,' Daniel grimaced. 'I went through this before. Twenty-odd years ago, when I was a scrawny young bosun's mate, I was captured by Algerians when our ship left Venice. I went through the whole rotten business. I refused to change to Islam, fool I was, so I stayed a slave, but I managed to escape on a Dutch merchant ship after five years and eventually found my way back to London.'

'So you did manage it—to escape?'

Daniel nodded and said with a sigh, 'I did, only because the smiles of Lady Luck and the benevolent Lord happened to meet above my head at precisely the right time. But that doesn't happen very often. Out here, it doesn't happen often at all.'

'I don't need luck,' Brannon said stubbornly. 'I'm damned if I'm going to stay in this place. I'll escape.'

Daniel smiled. 'Then keep that faith, mate. By Christ, you're going to need buckets of it.'

Over the following days Daniel was proved correct, and the prisoners were treated to banquets every bit as splendid as the first. Despite his misgivings, Brannon couldn't help but feast on it. He would need his every ounce of strength if he was to mount an escape. After a week they had a visitor, a thin, balding white man with a nervous manner and peeling skin. He turned out to be the British government's consul in Morocco, a supremely difficult role considering that he was serving in a country whose citizens had been plundering his own nation with wild abandon for years. Dolefully he took the names of the captives but could only shrug when they asked him about their possible release, making instead the uninspiring promise that he would write home and impress upon King George the misery of their plight.

Eighteen days later the guards arrived, and once they had chained each prisoner, they led them through the passageway and out into the searing heat of the Moroccan morning. The captives' eyes were sensitised after weeks in the gloomy dungeons, and the sudden light was a torment. They shuffled across the tiled courtyard, blinking owlishly, into a square where a crowd of merchants and curious townspeople had already gathered. The manacles were unlocked.

To their consternation, they were then ordered to remove their clothes.

They protested at this, clasping their bodies defensively, but only drawing the wrath of the guards, who moved in with whips and fists. After a brief commotion, in which several captives received a painful reminder of who was running the proceedings, they were forced to obey.

Shamefaced, they began to strip. Within a few minutes they were standing naked in a line. The morning was extremely hot, and their sweating milk-white bodies gleamed in the sun like polished ivory, much to the crowd's mirth.

Brannon burned with shame. They didn't allow him to keep even the barest shred of clothing, and they made him stand with his hands by his sides so that he couldn't cover his dignity. He was aware of the scrutiny of a thousand foreign strangers over his body, and his face reddened at the humiliation of it.

But the real humiliation was yet to come. The captives were made to run around in a circle a number of times, to hop, skip, and roll so that their physical fitness could be judged. They were harried like cattle onto rickety wooden podiums, and a mob of men in flowing robes came forward. Brannon guessed these to be the buyers.

They were a boisterous lot. With rough, greedy hands they assessed the goods on offer, poking their fingers into ears and under tongues and counting teeth. Brannon's blood rose as four chattering Arabs groped his flanks and thighs. He swore and tried to bite one of them, and he received a clatter from a guard in retort. In the corner of his eye, he was sickened to see the children being subjected to every kind of lurid examination, boys and girls as young as nine. The boys were forced to bend over and display their bare buttocks for the benefit of several leery-eyed men, while the girls had to allow their most intimate regions to be fingered and probed so that the buyers could be satisfied of their virginity. His stomach turned as he imagined what lay in store for the youngsters, condemned to see out their childhoods as playthings for these lecherous brutes.

The captives were in varying states of well-being, some thoroughly emaciated, skin grey and limbs brittle, and the buyers quickly separated the quality from the substandard. Brannon found to his dismay that he was among the six or seven most highly prized in the group. They crowded around him, and the competition became spirited. They growled and spat at each other, gesturing wildly, rolling their eyes to heaven. There was a whiff of violence in the air. Yet somehow they were managing to reach agreements.

As deals were struck, hands were clasped and captives led away. Brannon was herded in with a large group of males and a smaller number of young women, a variety of nationalities and skin colours. A plump, sweaty-faced man in a gold turban and an embroidered robe emerged as their buyer; he was admiring them with a proprietor's avarice, his beady, suspicious eyes darting from one to another.

Once the slaves were secured, he began to speak, first in a language Brannon couldn't understand, then in English.

'Slaves and infidels, I am Abdullah El-Gharrouj. Today you are most fortunate, for you have become the property of His Royal Highness Moulay Yazid, Sultan of Morocco, may Allah's blessings be upon him forever. Now and for many years to come you will atone for your wicked lives, serving His Excellency in the great imperial capital of Fez. *Allahu Akbar!*'

The title of 'Moulay' before his name, El-Gharrouj later explained reverently, signified that Yazid was a direct descendent of the Prophet Mohammed. Brannon was not impressed, however. These people were madmen. He had to get away, and soon. Once they reached their next stop, an opportunity would surely arise. He could steal away somehow, flee to the coast, and signal a passing European ship. He had to try, at least. He desperately had to do something.

Instead of making the slaves complete the journey on foot, Abdullah El-Gharrouj packed them all inside mule-drawn wagons with tarpaulin covers. This was not out of kindness; he wanted them to be fresh when he presented them to Moulay Yazid, for the sultan had a ferocious temper. Punishment including torture and execution was frequently administered to those who displeased him, no matter how high their ranking. And anything could displease him. A bad smell, an ugly woman, a fly on his clothes, insufficient laughter to his jokes— even the merest antagonism would often end in bloodshed.

It was over a week's travel to the imperial palace in Fez, but being allowed food and water and rest, the slaves found the journey less taxing than what they'd grown accustomed to. The further they moved, the more fertile the land became. Instead of bland, arid plains, there were lush valleys and green forests, populated by myriad warbling birds and wild boars and leopards. The winding tracks were hushed, with no mark of foot or wheel. One of the other slaves, an African, told Brannon that these woodlands were known to be haunted by the *djinn*, malevolent spirits that changed guise to prey on the unwary. For this reason only those who knew the paths well would risk crossing the forest.

They came out of the wooded hills into low-lying pastures where olive trees swayed in the breeze. The drivers followed a track beside a river leading east. They eventually reached the outlying farms and hamlets of Fez, and in the evening they came to the city walls. El-Gharrouj waited until nightfall before entering—he knew the reception the townspeople would give the slaves, and he didn't want his precious cargo damaged.

Once inside, the streets were quiet and shadowed. Winged insects hummed around lanterns while armies of mice foraged in the alleyways. The wagons trundled into a guarded compound where the slaves emerged sleepy-eyed and were put inside a chamber for the night. There they rested in the few hours left before dawn, trying not to think about the coming day.

In the morning, they would meet their new master.

Abdullah El-Gharrouj's forehead was beaded with sweat as he walked, but the morning sun was not the reason. His stomach was in knots, his hands clammy, the way it always was before a meeting with Yazid. What would the sultan's mood be like today? Would he be jovial, indifferent, irritable? Angry? It was impossible to know, and El-Gharrouj sighed unhappily as he made his way along the shaded roads towards the palace.

He entered the guarded inner gateways, passing walled gardens and a domed mosque into a courtyard where a peacock was preening its feathers beside a marble fountain. Yazid's quarters were at the end of a tree-dappled walkway, its edges lined with gurgling lapis streams. The guards in the antechamber made El-Gharrouj stay put while they announced his arrival to the sultan's viziers. After a forty-minute wait, El-Gharrouj was told to remove his shoes and come inside.

The chamber smelled of hibiscus flowers and incense. Courtiers mingled with kaids along the aisles, and they peered suspiciously at El-Gharrouj. The room became still.

At the far end, reclining on a mound of brocade cushions, was Moulay Yazid. He held a thimble cup of black coffee between thumb and bejewelled finger, sipping it first and then swallowing delicately. Beside him a servant girl carried a brass tray of sweetmeats. To his flanks stood two massive, black guards.

El-Gharrouj hesitated until summoned, and then he immediately knelt on the floor, keeping his eyes down. 'Most Gracious Excellency, I am your humble servant. The sight of your pious face is like the sun on my heart. May Allah bless your every moment, may His benevolent smile warm your—'

Yazid grunted, cutting short the customary exaltation with a flick of his hand. He raised his body and fixed El-Gharrouj with a cold stare. His eyes were an amber colour, like faded sunlight, but with a dark, enigmatic depth. He had burnt-copper skin and jet black hair under a silk turban, and his trimmed beard gave him a predatory appearance, like a wolf. It was clear from his present manner that he was not pleased.

'You have business to discuss with me, Abdullah El-Gharrouj?'

'Most Gracious One,' El-Gharrouj said, nodding fervently, 'I have delivered a new batch of slaves this morning. I wished to inform Your Excellency of their arrival.'

Yazid stroked his beard in thought. 'Two months ago I sent you to the markets, Abdullah. Two months it took you to buy a handful of slaves. The task should have taken no more than three weeks.' He stood up suddenly, and El-Gharrouj trembled. 'You were stuffing your fat face in all that time, with my money. Eating and smoking your hookah pipe and lying with your women. Is that not so?' Yazid didn't wait for an answer but unsheathed his sword.

'Excellency, I...' El-Gharrouj was so overwhelmed with terror that he couldn't get any more words out. He began to pray, frantically aware that it was probably his last prayer ever. Tears welled in his eyes as he prepared himself for the sword-stroke above his exposed neck, and everyone watched.

Then, after a moment's silence, Yazid let out a scoff of contempt. He aimed a light-hearted kick at El-Gharrouj's shoulder and sent the frightened man toppling off his knees. 'Get up, Abdullah, you coward. I know we lost a ship to the British, and the auctions were delayed. Why didn't you just tell me? You think me so unforgiving?' He glanced at the courtiers to ensure they were enjoying this little amusement, and they dutifully erupted in laughter, bellies wobbling.

El-Gharrouj didn't dare to lift his head from the floor until Yazid grasped his arm and pulled him up. 'You scare too easily, old Abdullah. Not an admirable trait.'

El-Gharrouj gaped at him in bewilderment and then quickly gathered himself and forced a smile. 'Excellency, you are too clever for this humble servant. I am dirt in your presence.'

'Come!' Yazid led him towards the door and bade his guards follow him. 'Let us see what fine offerings my good friend Abdullah has brought me this morning.'

Brannon's body ached. It took a huge physical effort to remain standing and not to faint. Beside him the other slaves were in similar condition, heads bowed under the sun. If it hadn't been for the food they had received before the auctions, many of them would have died by now. The large square where they waited was eerily quiet, the only sound being the shrill of a carrion bird overhead.

Abruptly the square's gilded gateway opened, and their faces turned in its direction. A huge train of people emerged: scampering palace officials, obsequious servants, menacing armed guards. Near the top, half shielded by the throng, walked an Arab man dressed in colourful brocaded silks. He was flanked by bodyguards, and two servants waved palm fronds to cool the air. Though they had been warned not to look at him, Brannon couldn't resist taking a peek. He wanted to see the man responsible for having dragged them across the seas and deserts, far from their cherished kin and homes.

Yazid looked about forty years of age and was of average height, belying Brannon's image of a seven-foot-tall monster. His limbs and hands were slender, girlish even, with delicately tapered fingers. He wore a silk haik tucked inside a belt of gold filigree and a pair of wide saffron pantaloons. He almost looked something of a fop, yet there was an air of speed and ferocity about him, like a snake coiled to strike. His dark eyes never stopped moving, and Brannon, despite himself, felt a shiver of nerves in his presence. He quickly lowered his head again.

The sultan strolled past the line of slaves, pausing frequently to examine some in detail. The heat continued to plague the crowd, and the process drew on at length. At one point he stopped in front of a female, a pale-skinned woman with startlingly red hair. As she trembled, he reached out and squeezed the sensitive skin of her nipple between his fingernails. She blinked in pain, her cheeks turning a bright red that almost matched her hair. Yazid smiled after a moment and let go. Without saying a word, he carried on.

Brannon was near the end of the line, readying himself for when Yazid would pass. He hoped he could keep his temper in check.

But then there was an interruption. One of the slaves fainted, dragging down the men chained to him and throwing the line into disarray. There were angry roars from the guards, and they pounced forward to sort out the mess, laying into the fallen slave with cudgels and whips. The slave came round and tried to get back on his feet, but couldn't under the rain of blows.

'Let him be, you animals!' Brannon shouted, but no one heard his voice. The guards continued to beat the hapless slave and only stopped when another voice penetrated the clamour.

'Hser!' Yazid forced his way between them, ending the attack. The guards withdrew contritely and lowered their weapons.

The slave was on the ground, face streaming with blood. Yazid murmured something like a prayer and reached out his hand. The slave hesitated, terrified. Tentatively he took Yazid's hand and allowed the sultan to lift him up. Yazid gave him a nod, clasping the man's shoulder in reassurance. The brief chaos ended.

Brannon breathed a sigh of relief. At least Yazid had the sense to keep his mad guards in check.

What happened next was too fast for him to follow. Yazid stepped back, pulled out his broadsword, and whirled on his feet. The slave's head was severed from his neck and toppled off, bouncing on the stone like a ripened coconut.

It took a brief, awful moment for the crowd to comprehend the scene. There was complete silence in the square. Then, with uniform precision, each person promptly straightened up and held their chins as high as they could. Even the unfortunate two still chained to the corpse managed to bear its weight on their manacled hands. It was clear that Moulay Yazid did not like weak slaves.

Afterwards, Yazid broke them up into smaller groups according to their deployment. Brannon and at least thirty others were directed to work on a new barracks alongside the armoury. They envied those sent inside the armoury for they would have the benefit of shade, whilst Brannon's group was required to toil under the burning sun.

Their labour began that very morning. They worked on the half-constructed walls, carrying blocks, mixing mortar, and removing rubble. It was physically punishing and dangerous; a number of slaves were injured by falling stone, while one man was severely burned when he spilled a bucket of caustic lime over his legs and groin. His screams distracted everyone on the wall, but they were compelled to ignore him and carry on. The sharp-eyed guards scanned for idlers.

That day proved to be the longest of Brannon's life. He was allowed water only twice in sixteen hours, which he had to gulp down quickly before returning to work. There were no stoppages for rest. By the end of the day his lungs were thick with dust, his hands black and raw. Earlier he had caught his finger between two blocks and the nail was torn off, leaving an oozing mess of blood and lymph. The heat left him dizzy, and it was some relief when they were allowed back to their cell, there to rest the few hours remaining before the next day's shift.

The cell was underground, but in one wall there was a grate that filtered in the evening light. This wall was part of the city's north walls, and at the other side was a fifty-foot drop into a brown river. The river was lined by a bank topped with scraggly trees, beyond which were rough acres of wilderness, shadowy and uninviting. Brannon turned his eyes from the landscape and looked up at the darkling sky where a pale crescent moon had lit its beacon. Loneliness assailed him as he cast his thoughts across the forbidding terrain.

She was somewhere out there, he knew. Somewhere far beyond the hills and sea, thousands of miles away perhaps, but she was there. And yet would he ever see her again?

He remembered that fateful night, when he left Orlaith to find his pistol. 'I love you, Brannon,' she had said. He could remember her words clearly. But he couldn't remember if he had said it back. It was a source of torment. Had he told her he loved her? He desperately hoped he had.

He put his hand on the grate, as if she might somehow see this gesture, and he whispered, 'I love you too, Orlaith. With all my heart, I do. Please wait for me, my darling. I will come back.'

CHAPTER FOUR

Damp squalls chased sea fret across the harbour. On Dromkeen's cliffs the trees groaned under the wind's chastisement while the hills beyond were shrouded in a ghostly embrace of mist. Orlaith stared at the mound of potatoes she had dug from the pasture below her cabin. They had been planted too late and the crop had failed, rotted to mush in the ground. No potatoes, no meat, and no money to buy them. She felt tears coming. With effort she steeled herself. There were always the eggs—she could sell them to the fishermen in the village. Yet it would probably fetch pittance, even if she sold all the eggs and kept none for herself and Sean. It wasn't enough.

Again the tears threatened. Sean would starve. He was already undernourished, half the weight that an eighteen-month-old child should be. She could feed him today if she used the rent money, but the rent could not be missed. Homelessness was as tough a prospect as hunger.

Instead, she would gather what vegetables the ground had yielded and swap them for some pork from Jim O'Sullivan, a farmer she knew. O'Sullivan probably didn't need the vegetables, but he had taken pity on her in the past. Maybe he would do so again.

It was difficult, trying to survive. She wasn't strong enough for the work of the farm, though it could hardly be called a farm any more, more a patch of hard ground from which things occasionally grew. The constant worry about Sean's welfare was also taking its toll. She felt constantly tired, and she was becoming increasingly desperate. There seemed to be no way out.

And then there was that ache in her soul, that awful emptiness which couldn't be shaken away. It had been there ever since the day when they took

Brannon, when they had torn her heart in two. Even now she could not believe that he was lost. So many thousands of tears had been shed between that day and this, yet she felt that she had only scratched the surface of her depth of mourning. She wanted him back so badly. For a time, she had hoped that a miracle might bring it about.

Now, she knew with certainty that she would never see Brannon Ryan again. Some weeks following the raid, news filtered into Dromkeen from the naval base in Kinsale revealing that the Arab slaver had been destroyed by an English frigate, with the loss of all on board. Brannon had perished somewhere out in that deep, uncaring ocean, and Orlaith felt he had taken her soul with him. Without Brannon it was like the sun had set forever, the light had been snuffed out. There was blackness now, sheer and cold and total.

Sean had been sitting nearby, hands caked with earth as he played out some childish game. Seeing her distress, he toddled across the grass and wrapped his skinny arms around her legs, his eyes wide with confusion under his curling chestnut locks.

She forced a smile and bent to pick him up, kissing his cheek. 'You're all I have left, Sean. I won't fail us. I promise.'

Randall Whiteley slowed his horse to a trot over the humped roads until a large house loomed above a hill, an imposing structure faced with Portland stone and surrounded by a high demesne wall. The plaque at the gate read *Dromkeen Hall*. The avenue was lined with oak trees, and further on beyond the ordered banks of rhododendrons were orchards, goldfish ponds, a row of stables, and a sloping paddock fenced with pinewood.

A groom came to fetch the horse as he pulled up, and a servant girl appeared at the door. Kathy had been acting as his housekeeper ever since the previous lady had died. She curtsied and said, 'Your lunch is almost ready, sir. Shall I bring you tea in the meantime?'

'I shall take my meal in the drawing room,' he instructed her. 'And see that you're quick, for I have a beast gnawing my belly.' He mopped at the sweat on his brow and took a moment to breathe the cooling air of the grounds.

The foundations of this lavish estate had been laid by a distant ancestor, William Whiteley, not long after the English Civil War had ended. An act passed by the Long Parliament back in 1642 had allowed for the confiscation of millions of acres of Irish land to be handed over to Protestant investors who would fund the campaign against the Catholic rebels. Thus enriched, William Whiteley, a thirty-year-old native of Yorkshire, had joined the Cromwellian adventurers in crossing the sea to Ireland, where he was awarded fifteen thousand acres in County Cork. William was already a wealthy man from his involvement with the East India Company as well as his own shipping enterprises: African slaves to plantation owners in the Caribbean and the import of tobacco, sugar cane, and coffee to Great Britain. Upon arriving in Cork, he set to work on building his house near the ruins of a Norman tower, shipping the stone from Dorset at huge cost. It made a dent on his personal finances, but a newly acquired rent-roll allowed him to recoup at least some of the expense from his tenants. Over the decades, floors and extensions had been added, the gardens were expanded, and an artificial lake was created. Now, in Randall's time, it was one of the most impressive houses in the county.

With a grunt, Randall waved the servant girl away. 'Hurry along then, Kathy. Gawping at me won't speed the process.'

She curtsied again and disappeared to the kitchen. He glanced at her plump little bottom as she left, his loins stirring. Young Kathy had been a good sport in bed on the numerous times she was summoned. Her fear had made the experience all the more fun, though her freckled face and doughy body couldn't hold his interest for long. He had almost lost the poor girl last April when those Moorish apes attacked the estate, which would have been a considerable nuisance. Fortunately, Randall had a guard employed as security against the Whiteboys and other subversive groups. Vincent Barry was a tough, ex–British Army soldier who had fought against both Indians and American rebels back in the former colonies. On the night of the attack, he killed three of the raiders with a blunderbuss, spilling enough blood to scare the others away, and thus Drom-keen Hall suffered no casualties.

In the drawing room, he measured a whiskey and sat on a walnut chair by the fire. The room was nicely warmed, ample light provided by a cut-glass chandelier fitted with tallow candles. Kathy brought his meal on a salver of Sheffield plate: soup and stewed trout for starters, followed by turkey pout with mushrooms, onions, and Dutch cheese, washed down with a bottle of Chablis from the cellar. Afterwards he stretched out on the damask settee to rest.

There was a card game at the Campbells' tonight. But Randall was weary of it. Every night seemed to be taken up with some frivolity, be it here in Cork or in the brighter society lights of Dublin and London. Having been born into wealth, and receiving a healthy dividend from a number of joint-stock ventures operating out of England, Randall was thus not encumbered with a profession and could afford to pursue a more hedonistic approach to life. He liked parties, though the parties at the Campbell estate were usually quarrelsome affairs, with the local rakes drinking all night and ending up in duels by dawn.

It was not a day to think about parties. There was somewhere else he wished to visit.

After a second whiskey to buoy his enthusiasm, he called for the groom to bring him a horse. He rode by the thickets beyond the demesne wall, threading a narrow track past rolling meadows and tumbled fences, through wild, verdant acres of brambles and birdsong. The track led into the hills, and Randall steered the horse through the heather, coming down towards the cliffs on the far side. There he could hear the waves breaking on the rocks and the pining of seagulls in the air.

Following the shore towards Dromkeen, he met a few locals who saluted him deferentially with knuckles to the forehead, as was their manner with the gentry. He tipped the riding crop to his hat in acknowledgement and carried on until he reached the ragged cabins where the farms were. Here he slowed the horse, hoping for a glimpse.

She was in the lower field, digging something from the ground. She had on a white cotton dress, and her hair was tied in a ribbon. He felt his heart squeeze.

Even standing there in such ignoble surrounds, she looked beautiful, an angel giving light to the dreary world around her.

When Seamus Downey plucked her from some backwoods as his wife, Randall had been hugely jealous. She was artfully created, with raven hair over her shoulders and a creamy complexion that accentuated her soft brown eyes and full lips. The perfect spouse, Randall thought. Gentle and pure and incapable of the wickedness that other women were capable of. He had thought his first wife beautiful too, but she had coldly betrayed him. *Victoria*. It stung him to even recall that name.

'She might be your wife, Randall,' his brother Lawrence had warned at his wedding, 'but she's still a woman. And a woman cannot be a man's equal. Like a horse, a woman will respond to strict authority, will learn to be loyal and obedient. But if you indulge a horse, pander to its moods, it will never respect you nor do as you say. You must have a firm hand with a horse—you must dominate it and punish it and keep it in check. Remember this advice, Randall, and you will have a successful marriage.'

But Randall did not listen. He had been too besotted with her to even raise his voice in a harsh manner, and she had manipulated him effortlessly. She wheedled from him expensive clothes and jewellery and every other luxury that her whims demanded before she finally became bored and ran off with someone else, a charming young libertine from Dublin who bedded her in Randall's own house and then stole her away for good.

It was an important lesson, albeit a painful one. Randall resolved to treat women very differently in future.

There was no one else about now but for Orlaith's child, who was piping out some incoherent song. Randall dismounted quietly and tethered the horse. He walked up the lane, climbed over the stone wall, and stepped into the field.

Orlaith exclaimed in shock. She hadn't even heard him approach.

'Ah, Mrs Downey,' he said. 'Did I give you a fright?'

'Mr Whiteley, sir,' she said breathlessly, giving a curtsey. 'Excuse me, I didn't hear you come.'

'My apologies. No matter, I'm sure you don't mind a visit from a friend?' He smiled easily.

Orlaith was silent. His visits were becoming ever more frequent lately, always unannounced. She didn't like it at all. Yet she could hardly deny him access to his own land.

He peered down at the mound of carrots she had dug up. 'Oh dear. Not the year's finest crop, is it, Mrs Downey?'

'They're not as bad as they look, sir. There's good eating in them.'

'You are so brave, Mrs Downey.' He shook his head in sympathy. 'Truly you are. Most women in your position would have given up this pointless struggle.'

'I'm afraid I have little choice, sir. I have a child to feed and a farm to run.'

'Yes, but it must be so difficult, surely? On your own?'

'I can manage quite fine, sir,' she replied stoutly. 'It's the way I want it to be.'

'I don't know about that, Orlaith.'

That was the first time he had ever used her Christian name. It did not feel right to her.

He avoided eye contact and began to pace. 'I couldn't help noticing some difficulties with your rent. I understand, of course, and I dearly wish I could let it go for now. It's just that when one tenant falls behind, the rest inevitably follow. My hands are tied, I fear.'

'I'm aware that my rent is overdue, Mr Whiteley,' she answered. 'I will make amends as soon as I can.'

'Orlaith,' he sighed, 'it's not the rent that matters. Why can't you let me help you? Take you away from this squalor? You are a good, decent woman. You deserve better.'

She shifted her feet. 'I'm not sure what you mean, sir.'

'I think...' he began falteringly. 'I think you know how I feel. And I think it's a tragedy for you to live like this, especially when there's so much that I can offer. If only you would allow it.' He took a step closer. 'Do you understand what I'm trying to say?'

'Um, not really, sir.'

'We are more alike than you realise, Orlaith. You are alone; I am alone. Your husband is dead, and I have no family left, as you know.' Randall's mother had died a few months previously. His father and brother Lawrence had both perished on a voyage to France some years before.

'I think that binds us in a certain way,' he continued. 'Perhaps, in our loneliness, we might be able to find a mutual comfort. What do you think?'

Orlaith desperately wished he would leave. 'Sir, with every respect, I cannot accept whatever you are offering. It simply wouldn't be right. My place is here, with Sean, come what may. It is God's will.'

'But how long can you hope to last like this?'

'For as long as I need to, sir.'

'Well, we'll see,' he said primly. 'So be it.' He turned and began to walk off, but then he huffed over his shoulder, 'In the meantime, I should be obliged if you would deal with your rent arrears. Thank you, Mrs Downey.'

He stomped across the field and retrieved his horse, frustrated. There was a scowl on his face, and he cursed silently as he rode home. *The stupid girl*, he thought. She should have been thrilled by his advances, as a thousand others would be. She needed him—she just didn't realise she needed him. He had to make her realise it. Did she not know that Randall could make both her and her child homeless anytime he wanted? And perhaps he would…

Damn it, she'll learn sense, he fumed. *We are perfect together. She'll accept it, or she's finished.*

⚭ ⚭ ⚭

Unsettled by Whiteley's visit, Orlaith did her best to push it from her mind. There was work to do. She wheeled out the cart that Seamus had constructed for gathering potatoes and filled it with the healthiest-looking vegetables she had unearthed. Jim O'Sullivan's farm was about six miles away, on the far side of Dromkeen. Time to begin.

It was past midday when they set off. Sean insisted on walking himself, which would slow her considerably, but he was in a stubborn mood, and so she relented. Hauling the heavy cart was arduous work. Within a half mile she had to stop and rest, her strength already flagging.

'Wait for Mammy, Sean,' she called. He trotted onwards, content in his own imagination. With a sigh of resignation she picked herself up, took hold of the cart again, and began to pull.

It took nearly three hours to reach the O'Sullivan farm. She was exhausted when they got there, her cheeks flushed and her hair streaked in wet lines across her face. She took out a linen cloth to wipe her forehead, and then she tidied her hair and tried to smoothen her bedraggled appearance. Mud spatters clung to the tails of her dress, refusing to budge.

Sean had climbed into the cart further back, his short legs tired. Now he half dozed on the vegetables, face twisted in discomfort. She lifted him up, and he let out a bawl, flapping his arms to be released.

'Shush that now,' she scolded him. 'Stop your crying.' She planted him on the ground, and he blinked in bewilderment, lips quivering as he debated whether to wail or maintain a huffy silence.

'Come on. We'll go up there.' She pointed to the farmhouse to distract him; his eyes widened with interest, and he skipped eagerly ahead of her.

Two black dogs came out in a barking fury, but seconds later a roar scattered them. A figure appeared, a fleshy, ginger-haired man of middle age. He shook a fist at the dogs, and they slunk off, tails dropping.

'Mrs Downey, is that yourself?' He smiled.

'Mr O'Sullivan, sorry to trouble you this noon. You're well?' He was one of Dromkeen's few prosperous farmers, with several acres under grazing. A kind man.

'Won't complain at all, Mrs Downey. Nobody would listen, sure.' He chuckled. 'What has you out this way?'

'Well, I was wondering—' she began tentatively. 'I was hoping you would possibly...' Stuck for words, she gestured to the vegetable cart in explanation. The little cart suddenly looked rather pathetic.

'Ah.' Now O'Sullivan, too, ran out of words. He scratched his head and looked around.

'It's just that I've been down of luck lately,' Orlaith sighed. 'The potatoes are spoiled, and I've got no meat. I remembered you took some vegetables from me before.' She raised her eyebrows. 'For a cut of pork?'

'Ah,' O'Sullivan said again. He avoided eye contact, clearing his throat. 'The thing is, you see...'

Orlaith knew right then that she had completed a wasted journey.

'It's Mrs O'Sullivan, you see...'

At the mention of her name, his wife appeared at the front door. Her eyes narrowed when she saw Orlaith, and in a sharp tone she said, 'Jim?' It was a warning more than a calling.

'In a moment, love,' he answered. Then he turned to Orlaith. 'I'm so sorry, Mrs Downey. Times are hard for everyone. And Mrs O'Sullivan worries. She thinks we ought to keep what we have.' He was extremely uncomfortable, even more so when he saw the crestfallen look on Orlaith's face. 'Goodness, I would help you if I could. But my wife...'

Orlaith swallowed a lump in her throat. 'But you were glad of the few carrots and things before. Would you not like to have these? I can wash them for you.'

He glanced back to his wife, hoping for some sign of assent, but then he shook his head. 'I'm sorry, Mrs Downey. I'm afraid I just don't need the vegetables.'

She fought back the tears, taking hold of the cart again. 'That's all right, Mr O'Sullivan. I thought I should offer them to you anyway, in case you were wanting. But it's no matter.'

'Are you sure?' he asked. 'What will you do for meat?'

'I have a promise of some mutton,' she lied. 'So I'm well set. Come on, Sean.' She waved to O'Sullivan and trudged down the track, cart in tow.

He watched her for a moment, his heart heavy in his chest. He was about to go after her, but a voice interrupted. 'Jim!' This time his wife's tone was more forceful. Reluctantly, he walked back towards the house.

Sean slept when they arrived home that evening, much to her relief. She felt like sleeping herself, like she could lie down and never wake again—nor even want to. But instead she knelt on the earthen floor and joined her hands. She prayed, begging God to forgive whatever trespass she had committed, imploring Him to help her. She prayed with such passion that she expected to hear His voice answer, to seek her out in the darkness. But there was no such sound, only the cawing of crows on the thatch and the wind whistling under the door.

Tiredness weighed on her. She dragged herself up, ignoring the rumbling of her empty stomach, and began to arrange bits of kindling in the hearth. Once a fire was going, she boiled a pot of water and made a thin stew out of the vegetables. Without meat it lacked substance.

Sean slept longer than she intended, and when she called his name, there was no response. Alarmed, she went to his side and touched his face. 'Sean?' He made no sound, no movement. She shook him. 'Sean!'

He came awake slowly, blinking like a newborn. There were red rims under his eyes, his skin the colour of cold ashes. When she picked him up he whimpered, his frail body seeming entirely weightless. She knew he had not eaten properly in several days, and today's activity would have drained him out. She felt so ashamed. Carrying him to the fireside, she dipped a ladle into the pot and poured a bowl of stew. On her lap she gave him spoonfuls of the pale liquid, trying to coax it past his mouth. He refused the first few spoons but eventually acquiesced. After the meal he wanted to go back to sleep again, and she hadn't the heart to deny him.

She hated herself. Sean was starving, and she was unable to do anything about it. What a dreadful mother she had become.

Quickly she went to the corner of the cabin and scraped a layer of earth from the floor. Underneath was an old tinderbox. She opened it and counted the coins inside. Six shillings and three pence, money she was saving to clear the rent arrears. If she spent it, Randall Whiteley wouldn't be a happy man.

She held the coins in her palm, mentally weighing her options. Sean was sleeping quietly, but his waxen pallor was greatly disturbing. He was a sick boy. They simply had to eat.

She made her decision.

The following morning she purchased a slab of salt-pork and a satchel of potatoes in Dromkeen, and Sean ate his first good meal in weeks. He became a different person, demonstrating the amazing rapidity with which children can recover. There was a glow to his cheeks and a spark in his eyes as he bounced around the cabin, full of noise and chatter, and she was delighted.

For tonight at least she felt a return of optimism. There was always hope. Whatever she had to do, Sean would be taken care of. She was his mother—and that is what mothers must do.

⊕ ⊕ ⊕

One month later, Randall Whiteley was sitting amongst the tomes in his library with Percy Gray, the estate's steward and rent collector. Percy was going through papers on the desk, reciting figures and names and drawing frequent yawns from Randall.

'What do you think, Mr Whiteley?' Percy asked.

'Hmm…?' Randall was barely listening.

'About the O'Driscoll family, sir. They promised to clear the shortfall last time, but that was two months ago. Give them more time, sir?'

'More time?' Randall scoffed. 'I'm not running a charity, man. Put them out on the road. I'm surprised you let it go this far.' Getting rid of another family was ideal; he could demolish their cabin and outhouses and turn the land over to grazing, which invariably yielded a greater return than tenants did.

'With every respect, sir, might I remind you of our conversation last month?' Percy asked delicately.

'What are you talking about?'

'O'Driscoll's daughter, sir. The young lady who brings you the apples? You were fond of the apples, I recall.'

'Oh.' Randall hesitated. 'She's one of the O'Driscolls?'

'She certainly is, sir. You said you liked her, em, visits.'

'Really?' Randall chuckled as a sudden memory came to mind. 'You know, I once invited O'Driscoll himself up here, too. He was nervous as shit, and I had a taste for amusement. I gave him a glass of sour brandy from below, just to see his reaction. He took a sip of it, then bowed and thanked me. He hadn't the nerve to tell me it was rotten, the coward. Either that or he genuinely liked the stuff, which would make him a lunatic.'

'Indeed.' Percy coughed. 'So what course, sir? Eviction?'

Randall smiled. The young O'Driscoll girl had been bringing apples over the past two months, every Sunday as instructed. But he couldn't give a damn about her fruit—at least not the fruit she carried in the basket. Those afternoons were enjoyable ones to say the least, and he didn't want to finish them just yet.

'Let the O'Driscolls be for now, Percy,' he decided. 'We'll give them another month and review the situation. I'm a fair man, after all.' It was a wise move, for even though she wasn't beautiful, that O'Driscoll girl had a heavenly body inside her dress.

Percy returned to his work, concealing his disapproval. Randall's behaviour towards his tenants was shameless, but that was the lay of the land, as the Irish were wont to say. 'Right, then. That would bring us to the Downey widow, sir.'

Randall's interest quickened. 'Has she settled?'

'I'm afraid not, sir.'

'How far behind is she now?'

'Nearly three months, sir.'

'I see.' Randall sat back and stroked his chin.

'It must be tough for her without a man, though,' Percy remarked. 'She has a child.'

'Hah! You're becoming soft, Percy. In fact, I politely offered to help her some time ago, and she rudely threw it back in my face. She was downright offensive. That's the trouble with these sullen Irish. They can't help themselves, nor will they allow anyone else to help them.'

'So what will you have me do, sir?'

Randall mulled it over. Here was an opportunity. 'We'll evict her, Percy. Get her off my land. No rent, no land. That's the law.'

'Of course, sir. We'll see to the matter this week.'

'Wait,' he said. 'I want to be there when it happens. I want to come with you.'

'Are you sure, sir? These events can be unpleasant.'

'I'm not bothered by that, Mr Gray. It's my land, and I want to be there. Ensure that you inform me in advance of it.'

'I would think Friday morning, sir. Early is the best time. Less folk around to make trouble, sir.'

'That's fine by me.' Randall nodded smugly, relaxing back into his armchair.

So, Miss Orlaith, you'll be receiving a visit from us on Friday, he thought. *I hope you're ready. Perhaps on Friday you'll finally learn a few things.*

CHAPTER FIVE

The road west towards the Downey farm was slick with mud after the light showers. Muffled and gloved against the Atlantic wind, Randall rode between six other horsemen. Along with himself and Percy Gray was George Hindley, a bailiff from Clonakilty. He was a squat, pug-featured man who spoke very little. Four constables provided armed backup. The locals could be relied upon to kick up trouble, but a few pistol shots in the air usually scattered them.

They arrived at the farm after seven o'clock. There was no one else about, which was a relief. Randall dismounted, a smirk on his face.

'As you please, Mr Hindley,' he said as he gestured to the dour-faced bailiff. 'Let's have this business done with.'

Hindley clutched the eviction notice in his hands, a copy of which had been posted on Orlaith Downey's door. He read it aloud in a monotonous tone, and his voice echoed around the quiet farm.

No response.

Calmly, he folded the notice inside his pocket and moved to initiate the next step of the procedure—knock the door down and get her out.

'Wait, Mr Hindley, I'll do it.' Randall pushed past him. The door was a flimsy obstacle—one firm boot should be enough to burst the hinges. But just as he was readying himself, the door suddenly creaked open.

Orlaith appeared. She stared at the group of men, not shocked but with a strange, distant look on her face. As though she wasn't fully aware of their presence.

'Mrs Downey,' Randall began firmly, 'we'll not have trouble from you now. We're here to implement the law, that's all. You were given notice.'

51

She didn't speak, but tears welled in her eyes.

'Too late for that, I'm afraid,' he tutted. 'As I told you, my hands are tied. You should have been more sensible about the matter.'

She took an unsteady step towards him and stammered, 'He's, he's…'

Randall frowned. He had expected her to mount at least some resistance, but not this. 'What the hell's she saying?'

'Allow me, sir.' Percy Gray grasped her arm to steady her, and then he carried on into the cabin. He reappeared moments later, face white. 'Good God, it's the boy. He's—Christ, I think he's dead!'

'What?' Randall stopped.

'We haven't time for this, Mr Whiteley,' George Hindley intervened. 'Let's take possession—that's what we're here for.'

'You stay where you are, bailiff,' Randall growled, and then he marched into the cabin. In the corner was a wooden cot with a small, pallid-looking creature inside. His eyes were closed, his frail hands bunched over his face as if he were trying to protect himself. He looked utterly tiny.

'It must have been a fever,' Percy said in remorse. 'He was too skinny to fight it. We'll have to help her bury him, sir. Call off the eviction.'

Randall bent over the cot and touched the youngster's throat. He stood up. 'Belay the burying for now, Percy. This boy is still alive.'

'Alive?' Percy gasped. 'But he's cold as stone! Are you certain, sir?'

'Ride out to Courtmacsherry and fetch Arthur Jacob, the doctor. Bring him to my house. And send Mrs Downey back in.'

'Yes, sir.' Percy nodded and hurried outside.

Randall stood gazing down at the pitiful bundle in the cot until moments later when he heard a cry from outside. Orlaith rushed in but hardly dared to approach.

'He's alive?' She sobbed with relief and almost fell to her knees. 'God forgive me, he was so cold! I thought he was—'

'Almost,' Randall said. 'There isn't much time.' He gathered Sean in his arms and told her, 'You must come with me now. I've sent for a doctor. I only hope we can still save the lad.'

She followed him out, too frightened to speak. One of the constables took Sean while Randall carried Orlaith on his own horse. Then they rode with haste for Dromkeen Hall.

⊕ ⊕ ⊕

Arthur Jacob finished his examination, fixed Sean's clothing, and put his utensils inside his bag. They had given Sean a bowl of oxtail soup, which was bringing some colour back into his cheeks. Jacob gave Randall a reproachful look.

'Well?' Randall demanded. 'Will he live?'

Orlaith was the only other person in the room. She knelt beside the couch where Sean lay, murmuring quiet prayers.

'He'll live,' Jacob said. 'Nothing wrong with this boy that proper food won't mend. He's starving, just like every other child in this God-forsaken county.'

'Ah, excellent news. All's well then. Thank you indeed, Mr Jacob.'

'You're not listening,' Jacob said testily. 'I've seen a thousand children this month the same. It's not disease or injury—it's hunger. For a child to be dying from want of simple food is a sin, Mr Whiteley.'

'Aye, for certain. The times are cruel, are they not?' Randall was becoming irritated by the doctor's manner. 'Well, thank you for coming, Mr Jacob. Percy will see to your fee.'

'Mr Whiteley, your tenants are starving,' Jacob interjected. 'They have no money for food, yet you hound them for rent. Tell me, what is it you were doing at the farm in the first place? Before you happened upon this sick child?'

'Mr Jacob,' Randall answered darkly, 'the boy was at death's door. I was in the right place at the right time. Surely that's all that matters?'

'How fortunate for him, sir. If only every Irish tenant were so blessed.'

'My man will see to your fee, Jacob. He's waiting outside.' Randall's face had reddened, and Jacob relented.

'Obliged, Mr Whiteley. I'll do my best to see the lad soon. In the meantime, you might keep him fed. I know it will be taxing—the times are cruel, as you said. But I'm sure it won't beggar your entire estate to throw him a bread crust or two.'

Randall scowled as the doctor left the room. Orlaith hadn't heard the exchange; she was dabbing Sean's forehead and whispering quiet assurances into his ear. Randall stepped closer and laid his hand on her shoulder, expecting her to pull away. She didn't. He felt encouraged and almost dared to turn the touch into a caress.

But then Sean gave a murmur in his sleep, and Randall was put off. 'Anyway,' he said, clearing his throat, 'I think this boy needs a good meal. You look like you could do with the same, Mrs Downey.'

She lowered her head guiltily. 'I, um, I don't have any money, sir. I can't pay you.'

'Nonsense. Don't trouble yourself.' He headed for the door. 'I'll speak to housekeeping, and they'll rustle up some fare. Young Shane will be full of bounce before you know it.'

'Thank you, sir. And it's "Sean", sir.'

'Of course.' He left them and went to the kitchen.

Orlaith gazed around for a moment. There was an unsettling feeling in her stomach, a premonition almost. She blessed herself out of nervous instinct and then returned to nursing Sean.

How foolish she had been, she thought. The salt-pork had lasted only a few weeks, and after that Sean quickly faltered again, his strength fading and the shadow of death once more looming over their doorstep. It was her own fault. She felt so useless. In her most hopeless hours she had prayed to God, every desperate prayer that she knew. She even prayed that Brannon would come to her rescue and put everything right, as he always did. But Brannon never came. Only Randall Whiteley came. Randall was responsible for saving her son's life, and what that meant now, for her, she wasn't sure.

Over the following weeks at the estate, Sean made a solid recovery. Randall fed him on a nourishing diet of bread, fish, and meat with fresh vegetables and treats of raspberries and cream and cakes. Sean's strength returned. The flesh thickened on his bones, and as his health bloomed, so did his spirits. He was intrigued by his new surroundings, the labyrinth of corridors and vaulted rooms that made up Randall's house. The marble stairs, when polished, were ideal for sliding down on his belly; the tall library shelving could be climbed when the books were pulled out. He plagued the servants, yanked their dresses, and stole their brushes. In the drawing room, an antique Verdure tapestry had been damaged by one of his exploratory ventures. Yet, though the servants scolded him, each felt a joy at the youngster's presence in the normally dour confines of Dromkeen Hall.

Orlaith ate well too, and her body recovered. But her spirits did not match Sean's. She was aware of how they were imposing on Randall's hospitality, working themselves deeper into his debt. Sean's recuperation brought a fresh headache, for soon it would be time to leave. And what then? Return to their squalid cabin? Perhaps they wouldn't even be so lucky. There was still no money for rent, and Orlaith knew that Randall had been planning to evict her. He wouldn't tolerate them forever, not without some recompense. It was recompense she couldn't provide.

Homelessness, then, was what faced them. If Sean had starved before, he would do so again, but this time, without a roof to shelter him, he would surely die.

'For Christ's sake!' Randall lamented. 'Why didn't you watch him?'

Kathy clasped her head. 'I can't keep up, sir. I can't. He gets everywhere!'

Randall fumed at the damage. Sean had attempted to stoke the fire earlier, imitating the maids' work, but some embers had tumbled out and left ugly scorch marks on Randall's beloved Persian rug. Only Kathy's fortuitous visit prevented it catching flame.

'A fortune that cost, Kathy, and look at it now! Not fit for a dog to sleep on. Where is the little horror, anyway?'

Sean was sidling impishly by the door. 'Fire!' he announced, proudly indicating his handiwork.

'Fire is damn right, you scoundrel. Come here!' Randall went to grab him.

Just then Orlaith arrived, hearing the fuss. She exclaimed in dismay, 'Oh, Mr Whiteley. Did Sean do that?' She glared at her son. 'Did you? Answer!'

'Ahem, Orlaith,' Randall intervened, cooling his temper. 'He meant no harm. Only a fancy mat, easily replaced.' He forced a smile, awkwardly. 'Boys, eh? I'm sure he's sorry now.'

'Yes, he will be.' Orlaith turned on Sean. 'You are naughty, Sean Downey. Mr Whiteley's rug! Apologise to him.'

Sean took offence at this. Randall's scolding he shrugged off with a laugh, but his mother's was hurtful. He stared at his feet, giving an exaggerated sniffle.

'Enough of that nonsense, you,' she said sharply. 'Apologise!'

'Whoa, no need for that,' Randall chuckled, embarrassed now. 'Let him be. We'll be sitting down to eat soon.'

She smiled guiltily. 'You're very kind, Mr Whiteley. But he must be punished.'

'I won't have it. This business is over.' Randall nodded to Sean. 'Off you go, little scamp. It's time for your supper.'

Sean left the room with stomping feet.

'Thank you, Kathy, that will be all.' Randall turned to Orlaith, laughing. 'Young lads, terrors. I was the same myself.'

'Thank you for understanding, Mr Whiteley. He can be a handful.'

'Of course. I know it's difficult. A boy needs a man to discipline him.'

A shadow passed over her eyes, and he apologised hastily. 'I beg your pardon, Orlaith. That was insensitive. I do sympathise about the loss of Sean's father. Seamus, wasn't it?'

'That's all right, Mr Whiteley. It was a long time ago.'

'Mr Whiteley?' He shook his head. 'Goodness, Orlaith, will you call me Randall? It's my name.'

She shuffled her feet. 'I…I don't feel that would be appropriate, um, Mr Whiteley.'

'But we're hardly strangers any more, are we? I do hope we're not.'

'It's just—I just prefer to call you Mr Whiteley. That's all.'

He groaned. 'Dear me. Living in my home, and yet addressing me so stiffly.'

'I meant no offence, sir.'

'Sir? Good Lord, that's even worse. Don't be silly, Orlaith. You must call me Randall. I insist upon it.'

His countenance was stern, and she said quietly, 'Yes, Randall.'

'Much better!' He beamed. 'Thank God—now we can relax. Will you accompany me to supper, Orlaith?' He put his arm out.

She linked their arms together and allowed him lead her away. 'Yes, Randall.'

The day that Orlaith dreaded, but anticipated, finally arrived. She was finishing her breakfast when Kathy told her that Randall awaited her in the library. She knew why.

Randall had a novel open when she entered with Sean. He laid it down and smiled. 'Robinson Crusoe. Wretched fellow. Can't sail a league without a storm coming.' He gestured to the armchairs. 'Please.'

Orlaith sat down, but Sean went to the bookshelves and began pulling out titles, discarding the books on the floor when they lost his interest. Randall suppressed a grunt, but Sean sat quietly after a frown from his mother.

'Well, he's back to his best at last,' Randall said. 'I'm relieved to see it.'

'He has you to thank for that, Randall,' Orlaith said gratefully.

'Yes, I've been giving his situation some thought. I was wondering what it is you intend to do now.'

'You don't need to say it, sir—I mean, Randall. You've been more than kind, and we shan't impose on your hospitality any further. We will leave this very day.'

He sighed. 'That cabin of yours, Orlaith—do you really mean to take the boy back there? He will surely sicken again.'

She shrugged, thinking the question pointless. 'I don't have much choice—it's our home. And I will clear the rent as soon as I can.'

'Yet the winter will be long, the food scarce. Is it a good idea?'

'But I have no other choice—'

'Orlaith, it makes no sense. I can't suffer the thought of it. Not when there is warmth and good food right here.'

'But Randall, we can't possibly stay. Your tenants in your own house? Goodness, no.'

'Dear me, Orlaith.' She wasn't hearing him. He sat beside her. 'You wouldn't have to be tenants. Or guests. This could be your home.'

'But it's not our home, Randall. You're my landlord.'

'Now look, I won't hide behind subtleties any more. Please. I am completely taken with you, Orlaith. I want you to be here, with me, for good. I love you, Orlaith.'

The impact of this abrupt declaration made her splutter, 'Randall, good Lord. Do you know what you just—'

'Yes, I do!' He spoke defiantly. 'I love you, Orlaith, and I mean to marry you. Will you not see reason?'

'But I can't marry you, Randall! I have to go home!'

'Why? To watch your son starve, dying in a filthy bed? It would be a sin to let that happen to him, Orlaith.' This sparked guilt in her eyes, and he knew he'd gained an advantage. 'By staying here with me, you would be saving your son's life. Surely you could not refuse that...'

She couldn't answer. A turmoil of confusion swept her. Yes, returning to their cabin would doom Sean, probably them both. But what alternative? Marry Randall? That was an appalling prospect.

'I could give you a good life, Orlaith,' he went on sincerely. 'Sean too. All you must do is love me back. Devote yourself to me, and I will make you very happy—I swear it.'

It was happening so suddenly. Her mind raced. Randall put his hand on hers, and she almost instinctively recoiled. How could she possibly marry him? He might have wealth, and he might have land, but he wasn't a nice man. Acceptance might ensure a safe and healthy home for Sean, but it would also condemn her to unhappiness. What she really wanted to do was get away from this house as fast as possible.

'I'm flattered, grateful—I truly am,' she blustered. 'But my feelings, they just don't...'

Whose welfare mattered most? Hers? Sean's?

There was only one possible answer to that.

Sean always had to come first. The dilemma she now faced was enough to make her feel physically sick.

'I must think on it, Randall,' she stammered. 'Please.'

'Of course, Orlaith.' He lifted her hand and kissed it. 'I pray you think on it carefully indeed.'

⊕ ⊕ ⊕

Percy Gray stood in stunned silence, unable to believe what he was hearing. Eventually his voice stuttered to life. 'But…marry her, sir? I don't understand. She's penniless, she's—'

'Percy, I love her. We are to be wed. I thought you might offer congratulations at least.'

'But haven't you thought of the implications? No family or property, no dowry. She'll bring you nothing.'

'Haven't you seen her, Percy?' Randall chuckled. 'How could I ever let her loose for some other man to have? How could I *not* marry her!'

Percy cleared his throat. 'Sir, she is undeniably beautiful. But to marry a woman for the sake of a pretty face—folly in the extreme. I can suggest a dozen unattached ladies better suited, wealthy fathers, land to their name. You have your future to think about. This union will bring you nothing.'

'Bugger the money, Percy. I had such a woman before, you might recall, and I married her. And how did that end?' In fact, Orlaith's impoverished status was a positive in itself, as far as Randall was concerned. It meant she would need him more, unlike his first wife, making the marriage more secure. 'You think only of money, Percy. How mundane. There is more to life.'

'Sir, you would think differently if you were beggared in the morning.'

'Well, I won't be. I have money. So why saddle myself with some double-chinned frump simply to get more? Orlaith is the sweetest girl I have ever known. She would never let me down.'

'Sir, I understand that you suffered with your first marriage. And I certainly understand your desire to find happiness. But I don't feel you've thought this through. For example, have you forgotten the laws of this land? Orlaith Downey is a Catholic, you an Anglican. It is quite illegal for you to marry.'

'I'm aware of the law, Percy. And I've made a decision. Orlaith will convert to Protestantism. If *you* know the law, you'll know that we'll be then quite entitled to wed, with the full blessing of His Majesty.'

'She'll never convert, sir.'

'She has already agreed to it. We are very much in love, and Orlaith will do whatever necessary to facilitate our nuptials.'

Percy sighed. 'I can't attempt to hide my misgivings. She is beautiful, certainly, but there's no need to get carried away. By all means, sleep with her. Have some fun. But marriage? Good God, she's a peasant, an uncouth Irish native whose grandfather probably dressed in loincloths!'

Randall's face darkened. 'Careful, Percy. You are an acquaintance of long standing, and that is why I permit your familiarity. But there are boundaries, nonetheless, and I'd counsel you to be wise of them. Remember, this is my future wife you speak of.'

Percy was immediately contrite. 'Of course, sir. I do apologise. I withdraw those remarks.' It would be foolish to antagonise Randall, for the latter had a temper heedless of old friendships. Percy capitulated. 'What will you have me do, sir?'

'Firstly, I need to arrange her conversion. Visit Reverend Wheeler in Cork City. He was a friend of my father's, and I want him to conduct the ceremonies. Orlaith is ready, just as soon as the good reverend can make the journey. Send a coach for him—my expense of course. I want this business done with before the month is out.'

❀ ❀ ❀

Orlaith swallowed back tears, hearing the sound of her own words fall like executioners' blades.

'I, Orlaith Downey, do solemnly and sincerely, in the presence of God, profess, testify, and declare, that I do believe that in the sacrament of the Lord's Supper there is no transubstantiation of the elements of bread and wine into the body and blood of Christ at or after the consecration thereof by any person whatsoever, and that the invocation or adoration of the Virgin Mary or any other saint, and the sacrifice of the Mass, as they are now used in the Church of Rome, are superstitious and idolatrous.'

The Declaration against Transubstantiation was part of her conversion from Catholicism to Protestantism. The words in her mouth dripped with poison; their bitter taste seeped into the eternal resting places of her ancestors, for she had betrayed them all, her mother and father most cruelly. They had raised her to believe in the sanctity of the Roman Catholic Church, the pope, and the Virgin Mary. And now she was becoming a Protestant, the religion of the invader and the oppressor and the heretic. Had she damned her soul?

No, it was a necessary evil, she kept assuring herself. A means of saving her son. If the motive was entirely selfless, then surely God and his saints would understand. Would they look sympathetically on a decision made for the right reasons? She wasn't sure. But whatever she had to do, she would do it—conversion, marriage to Randall Whiteley, and anything else that fate might concoct. She had to do it.

The wedding three days later was a lavish affair. Those surprised at Randall marrying below his station relaxed upon introduction, finding that Orlaith was quite a pleasant thing with grace and manners, unlike much of her country brethren. And, of course, her face could hardly fail to impress. She was a rare beauty, and each of the married men secretly admired Randall's decision to ignore money and pick out this gorgeous creature for a mate. In a contest of looks alone, she was the choicest wife in the county.

Orlaith was too preoccupied with managing her layers of clothing to worry about gossiping guests. She had never seen such finery, and it took her several hours that morning to get dressed with the servant girls' help. She had to wear linen stockings secured above her knees with ribbon garters, hoops around her waist to give her slim body greater width, and stays reinforced with whalebone to enhance her posture. Her corset had several tight layers of fabric, and it forced her breasts up and together, forming a cleavage that made her face turn scarlet when she saw herself in the mirror. Her bodice, skirt, and petticoats were a teal green and decorated with pleated lace trimmings, while the stomacher and sleeves were of red taffeta. All at once she was wearing more items of clothing than one might possess in a lifetime.

The day passed too quickly for her to brood on her decision. In any case, it was made. Her inner conviction enabled her to maintain calm, even as she made her vows in the church. Randall's proud smile never left his face. He was warm and attentive constantly, which she appreciated. She could almost convince herself that perhaps this wouldn't be so bad.

Sean had been trussed up in an embroidered coat, coffee-coloured breeches, and polished silver-buckled shoes. His stiff attire made him agitated, and in mid-afternoon Orlaith put him to bed, fearing that the day's activity would overexcite him.

Randall had invited several families from Ireland and England, old acquaintances of his own family. There were the Fitzgeralds from Dublin, the Quinns from Waterford, the Wilsons from Somerset, and the Quigleys from Kent. The latter family had an unmarried daughter with them who happened to think that Randall was the most immaculate, awe-inspiring man she had ever met. It tickled him to see the dagger-eyed looks she gave Orlaith.

Then there were Randall's local friends—Percy Gray and his wife Joan, Willy and Charity Campbell, and the estate hands with respective partners. Vincent Barry, the big, balding security guard, stomped about with his usual vicious expression. Reverend Wheeler stayed for the post-wedding celebrations with his foreign houseguest, a French pastor named Devereux. The pastor had little English, but he shook Randall's hand vigorously while chatting away in his own tongue. He then made a gesture to Orlaith, and Reverend Wheeler translated.

'He congratulates you for rescuing this child from her popish ways. The unholy Roman doctrines no longer hold sway over her.'

Orlaith bit her lip in silence.

'It's a country of ignorance here, true enough,' Randall quipped. 'Half of them haven't learned how to lift their knuckles off the ground. If I can rescue but one, then I'm not entirely useless, eh?' He chuckled, and Devereux took the opportunity to launch into a blistering diatribe against the Catholic Church, which left Randall staring at him in hopeless confusion. He quickly signalled for a platter of food, hoping to plug the Frenchman's mouth a while.

The meal tired everyone, and they were content to lounge on the chairs within the great hall. But later the dancing began in earnest—halting, measured steps at first, then more spontaneous efforts as the wine was drained. Orlaith enjoyed the dancing; the unfortunate aspect was that the male guests became almost unruly in queuing for her dance card.

By midnight people were drunk. Wives had gathered in cliques to exchange disapproving mutters; their husbands sat at the long table boasting to each other and punishing Randall's brandy supply. Orlaith sat with them too, sensing unwelcome from the other women. Randall was next to Percy Gray, Reverend Wheeler, and a few others. The reverend relayed a story, for the fourth time that evening, about a grouse he had shot. The poor bird's head had come clean off in the event, and with each retelling the spurts of blood leaped higher and the destruction became more terrible. Randall then told a ribald joke about the pope's pointed hat, which produced great amusement. Orlaith did not like the joke and found it offensive. Devereux the Frenchman didn't understand a word, but when he saw the mirth on everyone's faces, he gave a roar of laughter and pounded the table with his fist.

'Gentlemen, I must thank you all for sharing this day and evening with me.' Randall rose to his feet. 'You have been most wonderful. But now, I'm afraid, I must retire.'

This brought a rousing applause from the men. They crowded around to wink and slap his shoulder. 'Good night, Whiteley, you lucky sod. Set the hounds loose, eh? Or will you let the fox into the hole?' The eruption of throaty laughter shook the chandelier.

Orlaith swallowed nervously.

Randall came around and waved to the wives in the corner. 'Ladies, a good night to you all.' They came away from their hushed secrets and smiled sweetly, wagging their lace-gloved hands. He took Orlaith's arm and led her from the hall. When they were at the stairs, he chuckled. 'Mrs Whiteley—I quite like the sound of that!'

She coughed. 'Yes, it's my name now.' She glanced worriedly to where the bedrooms were. 'Goodness, I'm so tired, Randall.' She hoped he might take this hint.

He laughed. 'Not to worry, my darling. I know something that'll keep your eyes open.'

Inside his bedroom, she was suddenly gripped by panic. She couldn't undo her dress—she didn't know where to start. She didn't even want to. She wanted to leave this house, now. What a terrible mistake, she realised. Where was Sean? She had to get him and go.

Sensing her nerves, Randall came up and clasped her shoulders tenderly. 'Easy now, Orlaith. You mustn't be afraid. I am here from now on.' He began to untie the strings of her gown and lifted it clear from her body. Calmly he opened her corset and sat her on the bed. With steady hands, he took off her shoes and released the garters above her knees, pulling the stockings below her legs. She was breathing heavily.

'Randall, I can't—'

'Relax, my love,' he whispered. 'I won't hurt you.' He leaned forward, kissed her lips, and gently laid her back on the pillow.

CHAPTER SIX

Orlaith woke late the following morning. A shaft of sunlight fell through a chink in the curtains, and fresh-cut flowers scented the room. The memory of last night chilled her flesh like the stab of winter, and she wanted to close her eyes again. But Randall was already gone. The bed-sheet bore the creased impression of his frame.

His snoring had kept her awake for hours, though he slept soundly himself after their love-making ended. She was a little surprised by his bedroom manner. Whereas Seamus had been rough and clumsy in the delicate art, Randall was a skilful lover, patient and tender. But if anything, this only increased the depth of guilt and revulsion she now felt.

The door opened; Randall appeared with breakfast, using the expensive tray of Sheffield plate that he had bought from the Cutlers Company in England. 'Good morning, dear. I wanted to surprise you. You're hungry, I hope?'

She was hungry. Yet she didn't feel like eating.

He put the tray down and sat beside her. 'You slept well, my darling?'

She was uncomfortable at this intimacy, lying in her nightclothes under his fawning gaze. Married or not, it felt very strange. 'I am fine, thank you—Randall.' She almost called him 'sir' without meaning to. 'I should get up.'

'You should not. Have some fruit.' He fed the piece into her mouth and slid his hand across her cheek, lingering on the pale skin. 'You are so beautiful, my dear. Truly I am the happiest man alive. You and I were meant to be.'

'Yes, Randall.'

He stood up. 'You may finish your breakfast, but I need to go out. I shan't be long.'

'Of course.' She was relieved by this.

'There's a hunt on, you see. It would be a shame to miss it with the fellows around. But I'll be back later—don't miss me too much.'

She smiled dutifully. 'I look forward to your return.'

He laughed with pleasure at her words, kissed her forehead, and left the room.

Randall didn't show for hours. Orlaith was left with Sean, unsure of what to do. She went without thinking to help the servants, but Kathy was aghast at the notion. The lady of the house did not demean herself with chores, she told her. It wouldn't do. The master would be displeased to come home and find his new wife polishing sideboards.

So she followed Sean for company. They went into the library, though the books were of little use to people who couldn't read. Outside they visited the stables to see the horses, watched the goldfish in the ponds, and peered around the draughty ruins of the Norman tower. In the evening she carried Sean up to bed as he protested between yawns. Still there was no sign of Randall.

When he finally arrived, it was dark outside and the servants had lit the candles in the hallway. Orlaith walked to greet him.

His face was red. A matted gash sullied his forehead, and he was blaspheming like a tavern lout. 'Where's Padraig Welsh, the useless whore-spawn? Christ, bring him out so I can boot his balls up his arse!'

Kathy arrived at the same time as Orlaith, alarmed. 'Sir, Padraig went home hours ago.' The stable groom lived in Dromkeen. 'What's happened, sir?'

'Damn it, girl, my saddle slipped clearing a wall. I was nearly killed. It's all Welsh's fault, the wheezing toe-rag. Someone should stick a uniform on that lad and bang him off to India before I kill him.'

'Randall, please calm down.' Orlaith took his arm, blinking at the reek of his whiskey-breath. 'Come, let's tend your wounds. Where else does it hurt?'

'Get off me,' he snapped, swiping her hand away. 'Find young Welsh for me, Kathy. And I want a gallows erected.' He spat ferociously, and both women were afraid.

'Sir, we won't find him at this hour,' Kathy protested, 'but we'll send for him tomorrow, God's truth.'

He grunted in exasperation. 'You're an insolent girl, Kathy. Bring me food.'

She went gratefully to the kitchen. Orlaith remained, uncertain. 'Randall, will I—'

'Don't bother.' He stumbled off for the drawing room.

Just then Sean appeared on the stairs, rubbing his eyes. When he saw Randall, he let out a whimper.

'Christ, that boy!' Randall fumed. 'Is he forever tormenting me with his weeping and nonsense? Remove him before I leather the brat.'

That physical threat punctured the fear swelling inside Orlaith. Maternal instincts roused, she stepped in front of Randall. 'You'll not lay a hand on him. You're drunk. Go to bed and sleep it off.'

He stared in surprise, thrown by her uncharacteristic aggression. For a fleeting, dreadful instant, an image of his former wife flashed in his mind.

Victoria. The wife who had trampled him into the ground, who had made him a cuckold, a pathetic weakling…

He made abruptly for the drawing room. Orlaith heard the clink of the whiskey bottle through the door.

'Now, young man,' she said to Sean. 'This is no time to be up and about. Come along.' She climbed the stairs, and within a few minutes she had him asleep in bed again. She went to her own bedroom, not wanting to sleep but anxious to remain out of Randall's way.

Some hours later, she was half dozing when the door opened. She saw a dark shape appear, and a blast of whiskey fumes filled the room. She sat up, unable to see his face. 'Randall? Are you feeling better?'

He spoke in a low voice. 'I did not like your behaviour earlier, Orlaith. I did not like it at all.'

'What behaviour?'

'You were rude. You addressed me in a disrespectful manner.'

'Oh, Randall, don't be silly. You were drunk—I only tried to calm you down. Sean was scared.'

He came closer and whispered, 'Listen carefully, Orlaith. This is my house. You are my wife. I am in charge always, of you and any runt of yours living under my roof. Do you understand?'

She clambered off the bed and faced him, temper resurfacing. 'And you won't ever threaten my son again. Otherwise I will leave this place and—'

His hand flew so fast that she was still speaking when it struck her. It spun her around, and she fell against the bed, letting out a gasp of shock. He grabbed her arm and forced her up.

'That,' he snarled, 'is what I mean by disrespect. You will never leave me, Orlaith. Never. Say that again and I'll shoot your bastard son in front of your eyes.'

She exclaimed in horror and lashed out at his face. He parried the blow and shoved her on the bed. With a strong arm he rolled her over and held her down. 'If you need to be taught respect, my dear, so be it.' His brother's advice now came rushing back. Dominate them, punish them, keep them in check. Randall was determined not to be fooled again.

Her screams were muffled as he forced himself inside her, his brute strength sending waves of agony into her belly until her eyes stung. He panted and groaned, and the ordeal went on as sweat dripped from his upper lip. When his rage-induced energy was finally spent, he slumped down beside her, coughing as he tried to bring his ragged breathing under control. Orlaith was too terrified to move. She remained still, her tears wetting the fabric under her face.

The following morning Randall woke first and nudged her awake. There was a tender smile on his face. 'Good morning, my darling.'

She stared at him numbly. Was last night a dream? No, her face throbbed now with a blunted beat. 'Randall—'

He nestled his head into her chest and said, 'I'm sorry I hurt you last night, Orlaith. But you needed to learn. I have forgiven you, and I'm glad you now understand. You must show me respect always—that's how a marriage works.' He grinned. 'We have such a wonderful future together. How happy we will be.' The smile on his face showed that he genuinely believed this.

'Yes, Randall.' They were the only words she could muster.

Like a seasoned drinker, he hadn't so much as a headache. He hopped out and said, 'You're hungry, I'll wager. Me too. Let's eat breakfast in bed.'

When he left, she rose up shakily. In the wall mirror she saw a cut and a purple bruise below her eye. Randall's handiwork. Had Sean heard the tumult last night? She desperately hoped not. Opening the french doors, she stepped onto the balcony. A cold morning breeze sifted through the pine groves and revived her senses a little, but it couldn't raise her spirits. She wept.

In the following weeks he didn't beat her again, and she did her best not to invite it. Resigned to life at the estate, she settled herself as well as she could and kept Sean out of mischief. Randall was mostly tolerable, if over-affectionate at times, but she learned to avoid him when he was drinking. Mildly drunk he was at his best, good-humoured and easy-going, but in the advanced stages of his binges he was to be feared, for that was when the devil possessed him and he would want to punish the entire world. Such nights were thankfully without incident, as Randall would drink away in the drawing room until he passed into a coma of sleep, and thus Orlaith would rest alone, in peace.

The weather stayed mild in October. They went on long walks through the wooded hills, ate picnics by the streams, and picked flowers from the meadows. Randall said they would soon go to his hunting lodge in Kerry where the air was clear and the fishing bountiful, where they would snuggle up by a turf fire and drink mulled wine all night. Orlaith remembered County Kerry. Her own birthplace. The beautiful west, the cosy hunting lodges with turf fires, built underneath hillsides on which wretched creatures scavenged for food and lay dying in the dripping grass.

One afternoon he decided to teach her about pistols, mostly for his amusement, and not realising that she had learned long ago from Brannon. He liked to be an authority, but when her first shot spun the target canister into the air, he huffily took the gun back and said such things were not for ladies.

Orlaith became accustomed to the same faces passing around the environs of Dromkeen Hall, and she noticed whenever there was a new arrival. This morning a visitor rode up the tree-shaded avenue, a young man in a greatcoat and a black cocked hat. In his hand he carried a roll of paper. Randall was in the library examining ledgers when Kathy opened the door. Words were exchanged for some minutes, and then Randall came inside the drawing room.

'You'll forgive me, my dear?' He held the door open, making it plain that he wished to speak to the visitor in private.

'Yes, Randall.' Orlaith scampered out.

In the hallway, she told Kathy, 'I'm going to take Sean for fresh air. I can't remember where you put his coat...' She stopped then, noticing the look of consternation on Kathy's face. 'What is it?' she asked.

'Ma'am,' Kathy began nervously. She glanced at the drawing room door.

'Kathy?' Orlaith said in confusion.

'Ma'am, I think you should know. That man has brought news from the Lord Commissioners of Admiralty in London.'

Orlaith looked at her, unsure of what she was saying. 'The who?'

'The navy, ma'am. About the raid.'

'The raid?' The very term made Orlaith swallow. She resisted the sudden welling in her eyes. 'Do they really need to be so cruel? We all know what happened.'

'But that's just why he's here, ma'am. It seems there's been developments.'

'Developments?' Orlaith became still.

Again Kathy glanced at the closed door. 'You won't tell Mr Whiteley I spoke of it, ma'am? He would be annoyed—'

'Kathy,' Orlaith pressed her. 'Please.'

'There were, um, survivors, ma'am. After the boat sank. It seems some are still alive.'

Kathy's words made Orlaith stiffen as though a thunderclap had resounded overhead. Her voice came out as a whisper. '*Some are alive?*'

Kathy lowered her head guiltily. 'I shouldn't talk so, ma'am. It's not my place. But I...I know you lost someone too.' She picked up her skirts and hurried to the kitchen.

Orlaith trembled.

Some are still alive.

Brannon.

She hardly dared hope. She had thought him dead all this time. She had mourned him; she had tried her best to bury him.

But was there a possibility?

She stared at the door. She had to know. If there was any chance…

Randall's voice sounded through the oak frame. 'But why are you telling *me*? What do you expect me to do?'

'Mr Whiteley, many of them were your tenants,' the messenger answered. 'Their loved ones still live on your land. It's your duty to inform them of this development, as captives can be ransomed if their families can raise money.'

'Ransomed?' Randall scoffed. 'Those miserable beggars out there can't even pay their rent, not to mind buy slaves in Africa.'

'You must tell them, Mr Whiteley.'

Randall sighed and grumbled. 'Very well, damn it. But this is a tiresome nuisance! I had thought that whole bloody show behind us.'

'I will read the list, then, if I may. It was forwarded to London by the British consul in Morocco.'

'Morocco, is it?' Randall sighed with disinterest.

'James Reilly,' the messenger began in earnest. 'William Hunt, Roger Buckley, Rachel White, Timothy O'Brien, Patrick McCarthy, Rose O'Dowd…'

Beyond the drawing room door, Orlaith waited in agony. Her hands were clasped, and she was praying desperately.

'Conor Fitzpatrick,' the list continued. 'Liam O'Shea, Charlotte Hooper, Ronan Galvin…'

Please, dear God, please…

'Brannon Ryan,' the man said.

Orlaith began to faint.

'What?' Randall barked.

The messenger paused at the interruption. 'Brannon Ryan, I said. Do you know him?'

Randall didn't answer. There was a brief silence, and then he grunted, 'No, I don't know him. Carry on.' He went to pour himself a drink.

The list went on, but Orlaith was no longer listening. Her legs had gone, her hands shook, and her mind spun with joy, shock, and turmoil.

She had thought him dead. But Brannon was alive.

Light sparked in the fathomless dark.

She had to hear what they said next.

'As you indicated, Mr Whiteley, your tenants probably have little hope of raising ransoms themselves. But there are people who can help. The government has already ransomed British slaves, and I understand that the Earl of Cork has arranged to ransom some of Dromkeen's captives. There are charities, churches, good men of means. In Dublin is an order of monks, the Mercedarians, who are carrying monies to Africa in person and negotiating with the slave owners. Your tenants do have options available to them, sir. They can at least try.' He closed the paper with a rustle and rolled it inside his coat.

'I'll inform them,' Randall said sourly. He went to open the door, and Orlaith hurried to the stairs. She turned about, making it look as though she had just descended.

'Orlaith, stay there,' Randall growled. 'I must speak to you.' He showed the messenger out.

'Randall?' Orlaith inquired, feigning surprise. 'Is everything all right?' It took an effort to make herself sound calm, her heart beating a violent rhythm.

'My dear, I need to tell you something,' he said. 'There's been news from the navy about that unfortunate business last year—the raid.'

'But I thought they drowned.'

'Ah. Well. It seems the first report we heard was inaccurate. Come here, Orlaith.' He took her close and placed his hands around her waist. 'Orlaith, I've been given a list of names. Survivors. Now I know, um…that is, I'm aware that you were once…friendly? With that Ryan boy?'

'Brannon,' she answered.

'Brannon, yes, whatever. Anyway, the point is, Brannon Ryan…' He hesitated. 'The point is, Brannon Ryan…is not on the list. He's dead, Orlaith. Sad business, terribly sad. I thought I should tell you so you can put him out of your mind for good.'

'Thank you, Randall.' She wasn't surprised by the lie. She tried to look suitably distressed. 'Poor Brannon, he didn't deserve to die like that.'

'So you'll do that?' Randall asked cautiously.

'Do what?'

'Put him out of your mind for good?'

'I will, Randall. But I will pray for his soul.'

He looked at her. 'You don't seem so upset, my dear. I had thought you fond of him once. His death doesn't pain you?'

'Randall, I believed him dead months ago. We believed them all dead, what we were told. I did mourn then. But now I am here, with you.'

He visibly relaxed, smiling. 'That's good, my dear. You're right—you're with me now. Poor Brannon Ryan, a misfortunate lad, but it can't be helped. We have each other.'

'Yes, Randall.'

And even as he leaned down to hug her, Orlaith's mind was already racing. Ransoms, the messenger said. There were ways. Brannon could be rescued.

He could be brought home.

She closed her eyes. Newly forged steel braced her body now as she faced a challenge that asked a bounty of courage. For the first time in many months, she felt strength within herself.

I'll find you, Brannon. I don't know how, but I'll find you. Be strong, my love. My true love, my only love, please wait for me. I'll find you.

CHAPTER SEVEN

The smell of murder was rank like gun-smoke. The stone slabs gleamed in the hot sun, bouncing heat into the faces of trapped, desperate men. They spat their defiance. The guards began advancing steadily, forming a ring of metal. Now the fight neared a bloody finish.

Heading the besieged group, Brannon stood with his chest bared, arms shining with sweat. A low breeze lifted the sun-bleached hair from his face and revealed the violence in his eyes. 'Stand your ground,' he snapped. 'Let them come!'

The young Spaniard next to him whispered, 'This is madness. We are dead men.'

Madness it certainly is, thought Brannon. Madness spawned by day after day of cruel treatment and wicked masters; the madness of men enduring horrific conditions, slave labour, brutal beatings, and starvation. Brannon had been a slave for many months now, toiling on walls and sleeping in damp, overcrowded pens with the flesh wasting from his bones and his spirits slowly dying. And he'd had enough.

After witnessing a particularly sadistic flogging earlier, the slaves had finally snapped and fought back. The guards responsible had their skulls bashed in with lumps of mortar, and though Brannon wasn't involved in the initial skirmish, he quickly joined the mini-revolt, lending his weight to the sudden flash-flood of anger. Within minutes the area became swamped with baying guards bent on vengeance, and now the slaves faced dire punishment.

'Let them come,' Brannon declared again. 'I'd rather die than crawl to these bastards any more.'

The first line of guards surged forward. A hail of rocks was directed down on them from the slaves on the wall, and several were injured by the flying missiles. Their charge disintegrated into shambles.

'Now!' Brannon yelled. He yanked on the chain linking the slaves together, and they attacked in formation. The wounded guards couldn't defend themselves and were quickly disarmed. 'Stay in line!' Brannon shouted. He picked up a scimitar and held it tight.

The onlooking guards were alarmed by the speed with which their comrades had been overcome. Uprisings needed to be crushed fast.

A second line of them attacked.

This time they were safe from the stone-throwers, who didn't want to hit their fellow slaves. Brannon's group were bunched together, their chains hampering their manoeuvres. The guards engaged them in the centre ground, and swords whined and clashed.

Seven of the ten slaves fell in that blistering assault. Brannon blocked a swing aimed at his neck, more through luck than effort. But he was unable to move, still manacled by the chain. There were just three of them left. Twenty more guards circled like wolves.

'Keep your guard up,' he grunted. Another line attacked, the guards' professional experience now tilting the battle in their favour. A sword cut through the air, half severing a head; an eighth slave fell. Six guards moved for Brannon. In desperation, he threw the scimitar. It struck bone and took one guard out of the fray. A cry of pain made him turn, and he saw his last remaining ally fall under a frenzy of hacking and stabbing.

He was on his own.

In this final moment, he was suddenly aghast at the prospect of death. He had not feared it, he had almost wished it, but now, as it closed its grip, he desperately wanted to live. Death wouldn't be a release. Death was a closed door, sealing off hope. He wanted to live.

They closed in, laughing at his futile attempts to break free. He edged away but tripped on the bodies and landed on his back. A fast-moving guard pounced, raising a sword between two hands and preparing to ram it through his heart.

Brannon closed his eyes.

'*Hser!*' A voice silenced the clamour. The guard stopped. The voice was not loud, but it carried authority, for the guard sheathed his sword and stepped away. Brannon blinked in bewilderment, still waiting for the blade to pierce his ribs.

A man had appeared, an Arab like the rest but wearing a different uniform. He smiled broadly, like a satisfied spectator leaving the gladiatorial arena. With his fists on his hips, he appraised Brannon.

'So, Christian. You are a fighter.' He spoke in the lingua franca, the mixed concoction of European languages and Arabic that enabled most nationalities in Morocco to understand each other.

Brannon stared at him but didn't reply.

'We will see.' The man smiled again, enigmatically. 'We will see.' He made a hand gesture, grunting an order to the guards. Two of them unlocked Brannon's manacles and then hauled him to his feet and led him away from the blood-stained plaza.

⊕ ⊕ ⊕

Moulay Yazid gazed dreamily at the richly painted cedar ceiling as he poured the cool water over his face and let it run down his sweating, naked flanks. The ritual post-coital cleansing required water over the head and shoulders first, then the genitals. After that he could soap the rest of his body, but not his genitals again. Once finished, he laid down the glass jug and dried himself before looking at the guard standing in front of him.

'How long do they wait for me?'

The guard knelt. 'Great One, they have been waiting since this morning.' He kept his eyes down until Yazid spoke again.

'I wish to see them now.'

The guard nodded and rose up. Sparrows fluttered from the window as a servant carried forth a tray of drinks for refreshment. Some moments later the guard returned; five manacled slaves entered, dusty and dishevelled, bringing a rank odour of sweat with them. The servant girls, who enjoyed daily perfume baths at the sultan's order, crinkled their noses in disgust.

Paul Reid

Yazid selected a drink from the tray. He saw that each slave was tall and wide in the shoulder, and more importantly white and European. The kind he'd wanted.

Brannon stiffened, struggling to conceal his hatred. Yazid: the man responsible for all his troubles and suffering, standing just inches away. If not for the presence of the guards, he could have killed him.

Yazid spoke to the guard, the guard replied, and their fast-flowing Arabic Brannon couldn't follow. But some words he'd managed to learn over the previous months of captivity.

'*Nagulizi?* I'm no Englishman. I'm Irish.' He spoke so abruptly that they stopped in surprise; then the guard reacted furiously, striking him across the head and knocking him down.

Yazid grunted an order to withhold the beating. He lowered a hand to help—a gesture Brannon had last seen moments before Yazid beheaded a slave in the square. 'Go to hell, you bastard,' he snapped, pushing the hand away.

The guard almost exploded with indignation. '*Kelb!*' He tried to attack him, but Yazid was now standing between them; he flicked his wrist, motioning for the guard to step back.

'I...speak English,' he announced with evident pride. 'Very good.' His words were faltering, not smooth enough to portray any level of fluency. But they obviously pleased him.

Brannon rose back on his feet. 'Your English sounds as good as my Arabic.'

'Please. More slow.' Yazid didn't understand that.

'I said, your English, superb.' Brannon winked.

Yazid nodded warily, suspecting mockery. But he remained placid. 'You strong, Christian. You *Irlandi?* Irish?'

'I am.'

Yazid bowed, hand on breast. 'I too. Irish.'

Brannon cocked an eyebrow. 'Hmm...'

'My mother Irish,' Yazid explained. He took a cup of mint tea from the tray, offering it to Brannon. 'You drink.'

Brannon was glad to take it. The mint was sharp and sweet on his tongue.

'Strong Irish,' Yazid said, seemingly reaching a decision. 'You no more slave.'

This time Brannon didn't understand. 'I'm what?'

'Come, Christian.' A voice hailed him from behind—the officer who had rescued him from the fight. He led Brannon outside the chamber and grasped his arm.

'So, Christian, our great sultan likes you. How fortunate. If he did not, I would be directing your execution.'

Brannon scowled. 'What's this business about? And who are you?'

'My name is Azedine Ben Hassi. I am a kaid in the sultan's army.' He was of middle age, with a trimmed beard and a gleaming bald head.

'A kaid?'

'A military rank. We wish to expand His Majesty's Imperial Guard, to train new blood, and the sultan's preference is for Europeans. Every new loyal European reinforces his reign against his foreign enemies, and I have been charged with the task of finding them.'

'Loyal?' Brannon scoffed. 'I'd not lift a finger to help that rogue.'

Ben Hassi smiled. 'Then you die, Christian. I merely need to raise my right hand and it will be done.'

Brannon peered nervously over his shoulder. 'But why me?'

'You did well against those guards this morning. And I've noticed you before. You're stronger than most.'

'I'm no soldier, damn it. I used to be a farmer.'

'Be a farmer still,' Ben Hassi encouraged him. 'Sow loyalty, harvest reward. Refuse, and I can simply find others. It would be foolish to die out of stubbornness, however.' He lowered his voice. 'I could see that the sultan liked you. And Irish blood helps. You would be wise to use this little advantage, for you shall not enjoy many of them.'

'Anything for a fellow Irishman,' Brannon replied gloomily. 'Not that I believe such nonsense.'

Ben Hassi shrugged. 'He spoke the truth, Christian. His mother was from Ireland, the wife of an Irish soldier sent here by the British government. After his death she was taken into the harem of Sidi Mohammed—Moulay Yazid's father.'

'And where is *he* now?'

'Ah. It is best you do not ask too many questions about him, Christian. Sidi Mohammed is gone, and that's all you need to know.'

'Sits fine with me. But what do you want me to do?'

'You chose wisely.' Ben Hassi clapped his shoulder, pleased. 'Now, you simply wait. You will see me again soon.'

The guards accompanying Ben Hassi took Brannon's arms and led him outside the palace walls. To his relief, they didn't put his manacles back on. Instead of returning to the slave pens, he was ushered through a marketplace where camels were being sold and a crowd watched a noisy cockfight. They climbed a dusty hill of chipped paving, grass growing between the cracks. This led through a series of narrow streets. Brannon looked up: high above were balconies where veiled women peered down at him, big fawn eyes behind flowing silk scarves. Up there were private worlds open only to the imagination.

A half hour later, they reached the proud but crumbling Merenid tombs. A sacred spot, this was where Moulay Idriss had founded the city of Fez and Morocco's first Arab dynasty a thousand years before. A quarter mile from the tombs was a large compound with a front wall of russet brown, broken in its centre by a rounded archway. Two stout wooden gates guarded access beneath the arch, and Brannon found himself being passed from one set of hands into another.

Bloody wonderful, he thought.

He slept that night on a mat in a roofless corridor, wedged between the snoring, sweaty bodies of his fellow recruits. By dawn he was struggling to breathe in the stale air, his skin aflame with insect bites. A sharp, piercing pain stung between his toes, from where he dislodged a red ant. Someone's piss had trickled along the ground.

This wouldn't do. He would never last.

They were fed later on, and then they had to wash themselves under one of the rusting pumps. A bench behind a wall was provided for those who had to relieve themselves, four men at a time sitting next to each other and emptying their bowels into the fly-infested latrine below. It reeked like corpse-meat, and Brannon waited until they were all finished, having no interest in listening to the groans of constipated Arabs.

Once done, he pulled his breeches back in place and went to follow the others. And then he stopped.

The guards, unaware that there was still someone at the latrine, had left a small gate open to admit a donkey hauling a cartload of mouldering fruit. Near the latrine wall, barely ten feet away, it led directly to the street outside. Brannon stared at it.

Ten feet to freedom. He could sprint for the city, follow the river, disappear into the hills, and head for the coast. His route to liberty was open. Yet if caught, they would kill him.

He had only seconds to decide.

He took a step forward. It was a chance.

Another step. He was walking for the gate.

Five feet to go—he would be free.

And a shadow fell across his path.

The guard glanced over in surprise and then growled a challenge. He shut the gate and put his hand on the hilt of his sword.

'Urgh!' Brannon abruptly doubled over and clutched his stomach, pointing to the latrine in explanation. The guard stepped back in alarm. He gulped and waved Brannon on, keeping a cautious distance.

And quick as it came, the chance was gone.

'You're still alive then, Irish?'

Brannon came awake to the voice, blinking and disorientated. He had fallen asleep during the afternoon, and the long corridors were in shadow. In the courtyard, crows picked at the ground. Rats were scuttling around the latrine.

'Is that you, Jones?' He turned to the familiar face.

'I didn't realise you'd wound up in Fez.' Daniel Jones grinned, his hair like burning wire in the evening light. 'Our paths touch again.'

'Well, I hadn't quite planned it,' Brannon grumbled. 'And I don't intend to stay for long.' He lifted himself from the rough bench of cedarwood and yawned.

'That's good, Brannon, but I wouldn't recommend doing what you did earlier. I saw you heading for that gate. Damned risky. You're lucky the guard was a dullard.'

'I almost made it, Dan. Next time I'll be quicker about it.'

'And how far will you hope to get? The hills out there are patrolled day and night, and deserters are killed on the spot. Sultan's orders.'

'They wouldn't catch me,' Brannon said, though he didn't feel so confident now.

'Maybe they wouldn't. But there are safer ways of escaping Fez, you know.'

'Such as?'

'This,' Daniel said, gesturing to their surroundings. 'It's a blessing, the army. Slaves in chains no more. Become a soldier, Brannon; pray for a posting near the coast, then jump on a ship and sail for home. That's what I'm going to do.'

Brannon picked a twig from the floor and attempted to remove a splinter embedded in his foot. The effort was unsuccessful, and he sighed. 'I don't know, Dan. Why us? I thought the sultan's army was a Muslim one.'

Daniel smiled. 'It is. And we will be too. We've got to convert before they'll allow us to serve.'

Brannon scowled at the idea. 'Come off it. I'll be joining no Islam.'

'You'll bloody have to, Brannon. It's only a ceremony—it means nothing. Agree to it and preserve your hide.'

'I will not,' Brannon retorted. 'I'm Catholic.'

'Devout Catholic, are you?' Daniel shrugged. 'You must be devout if you'd rather die than indulge a Moorish whim.'

Brannon knew he was anything but devout. He barely thought about God at all. But religious scruples weren't the reason for his opposition.

'It's just,' he began, 'I had a friend back in Ireland. A girl—a woman, that is. She's a believer, and she'd never forgive me for turning Muslim. It's something she would never do.'

'She would understand, Brannon. Means to an end.'

'No.' Brannon shook his head. 'She wouldn't understand.' He sighed unhappily. Orlaith had always been firmly devoted to her faith—what would she do in this situation? She would hold strong, no doubt. And if he did otherwise, she would think him a coward.

Daniel smiled patiently. 'God bless you, lad. You're young, and you don't like to listen to sense. But right now you must.'

'I won't do it,' Brannon declared.

'If you don't, they will execute you tomorrow. You'll be no further use. Say goodbye to everything you hold dear, in that case. Say goodbye to hope—and to that young lass you left behind in Ireland.'

That stung him. He couldn't say goodbye. God knows, his chances of seeing Orlaith were small at best, but refusing to convert would probably doom them entirely. Daniel was right. He had to go along with whatever the Moors desired.

He closed his eyes. Dromkeen. How he pined for its emerald beauty. It was probably raining there now; Orlaith would be brushing her hair by the fire with Sean toddling about, his little button nose sniffing out mischief. So many afternoons Brannon had spent in that cabin, the three of them soporific from turf smoke, lying under cosy blankets, ensconced in fairytales. What he would give for those days again.

'Oh, damn it all, I never believed in God anyway,' he decided. 'Very well, Dan. We'll wail some songs and burn our Bibles, or whatever it is they mean us to do. Anything to get out of this place.'

She would understand. She loved him, after all. She had told him so, many times. She would understand.

⊕ ⊕ ⊕

The recruits were bellowed out of their beds early the following morning. On the road outside they were assembled under the shade of the cypress trees, where a tally was taken of their numbers. To Brannon's relief, no manacles were produced. Marching through the city they presented a motley sight, a mixed rabble of foreigners, and the guards had to beat away the idle townsfolk who stopped to gawp. Moulay Yazid must not be kept waiting.

Emerging from the jumbled streets of the Fez el-Bali, they were directed under a portal of palm trees into an open ground where a tarpaulin-covered platform had been erected for the sultan's comfort. Yazid was listening impassively to the whispered words of a vizier at his ear. He looked up when the recruits were herded into the ground and dismissed the vizier with a jerk of his head. He wanted to observe the conversion ceremony in person.

Once the recruits were neatly gathered and a respectful quietness was achieved, one of the mullahs addressed them.

'Infidels! Raise your finger in the air.' The recruits acquiesced, and each man pointed his index finger towards the sky. The single digit was a refutation of the Holy Trinity, the concept of Father and Son and Holy Spirit, which Muslims considered blasphemous.

Brannon pressed his hands to his sides until Daniel poked him in the ribs. 'Do it, Ryan.' Grudgingly he raised his finger.

Once the mullah was assured of their willingness, a hand-painted picture of a crucified Christ was produced, and the converts formed a line before it. At the head of the line was a pile of rocks. In turn, each man had to hurl one of the rocks at the picture. The purpose of this was to reject the notion of Jesus Christ being the Saviour of the World, for although Muslims recognised Jesus as one of God's prophets, they did not believe him to be the Son of God.

Brannon, in a weak attempt at rebellion, purposely missed the picture with his throw and struck a guard in the ankle. The guard cried out and grasped his foot, while Brannon received a thump in the shoulder and was told to throw again. This time he hit Jesus straight on.

Finally they recited the Islamic creed: 'I believe there is no god but Allah Almighty, and I believe that Mohammad is His messenger. I believe in Allah, and in His angels, and in His scriptures, and in His messengers; and in the Final Day, and in Fate, and that all things are from Allah, and that Resurrection after Death be truth.'

Moulay Yazid enjoyed the spectacle. Each European convert was a triumph, a victory over his enemies in the Christian governments. '*Bono!*' he cried enthusiastically, clapping his hands. After the ceremony, he had them dressed in bright fabrics and bejewelled turbans and led on horseback through the streets with the blaring of trumpets to announce their conversion. The converts found it a humiliating experience but were forced to indulge him. Behind walked soldiers wielding bared swords, a reminder to the converts of what would happen to them if they were to recant their new beliefs.

Later, when the ceremonies were over and Moulay Yazid had retired to the palace, the converts were led back to the compound. Their fine clothes were taken away.

'What now?' Brannon asked, disgruntled.

'One more step.' Daniel cleared his throat nervously. 'If I had told you of this yesterday, you wouldn't have gone through with it.'

Brannon stared uneasily at him. 'What?'

'Not something pleasant, I'll warn you, but be brave. Stay the course, endure it—'

'For Christ's sake, Dan, will you not tell me?'

'We are to be circumcised.'

Brannon frowned. 'Circumcised? What does that mean?'

Daniel pointed to his groin and made a scissors motion with his fingers. Brannon's face went white.

'Christ Almighty! Are you serious?'

'Not the whole thing, you clown. Just some skin.'

'No way. No damn way!' Brannon proceeded to offer a colourful selection of his vocabulary, and Daniel let out a sigh.

'Now look, matey. You can keep your head or else your foreskin, but not both. What's it to be?'

Brannon was in almost physical pain as he thought about it. 'Nothing's worth that, Dan. Nothing!'

'Not even that pretty little friend you talked about? You wouldn't endure a bit of pain for her sake? Maybe she's not worth that much to you after all.'

He had thought he would endure any pain to see Orlaith again. But this? This was barbaric. 'Jesus…' he stuttered weakly. 'Jesus, Dan, I couldn't.'

'Of course you could. A small snip and it's over. And you're still alive.'

He closed his eyes, trying to banish the awful image from his mind. At this moment, Dromkeen had never seemed so far away. 'I'm not as strong as I thought I was, Dan.'

'None of us are,' Daniel agreed glumly. 'But will you do it?'

'I will,' Brannon said, and he shuddered. 'A knife in the nether regions—why should I be surprised? To these Moors it's probably as normal as buttering bread.'

A tent had been set up in a walled courtyard within the compound, a flap covering the entrance. Inside was a holy mullah mumbling prayers and a physician to carry out the procedure. There was also a black slave girl to assist them; she was not Muslim, and therefore her presence was permitted. A Muslim female could never touch the intimate parts of a man, not unless she was his wife or otherwise his property.

Brannon felt a cold sweat as his turn approached. He saw the other men being led inside the tent, and each was kept only about two minutes. It was swift and efficient. Some made no sound whatsoever, though a few times he could hear gasps of pain. At one point someone let out a piercing scream, which made the hair stand up on Brannon's neck, but from the muffled conversation that followed he gathered that the man hadn't actually been touched yet—it was merely the sight of the knife that had sent him into a panic. Each patient was eventually led out the other side of the tent, stiff and bowed, and brought into the recovery chambers to lie down.

Finally they summoned Brannon. He braced himself. His breathing was rapid, and he tried to stay calm.

Don't let me faint, he prayed.

Inside the tent it was dark but for the physician's paraffin lamp. His instruments were laid out in a row. He motioned for Brannon to sit on the stool, the legs of which were slick with blood. Brannon felt his throat go dry. It was stiflingly hot. He wanted to run.

They eased him down. The slave girl removed his tattered breeches, but she didn't meet his eyes. She looked neither pleased nor uncomfortable at having to carry out this task. She took his penis in her hand, and he almost choked.

'Easy now, girl! What are you doing?'

The physician cautioned him with a raised finger, and the mullah barked a rebuke. Brannon closed his mouth, burning with embarrassment. The girl began to massage him while the two men watched, and he had never felt so ashamed. Yet his body was unable to resist the rhythmic caress of the girl's hands, and subconsciously he became aroused. Once he was bigger in size, she stretched out the foreskin between her fingertips. The physician knelt, and the blade of his knife flashed in the lamplight. Brannon stuttered, 'Wait…wait a minute—'

With guillotine speed the knife flicked down, and the foreskin parted; Brannon felt a hot sting that brought every foul curse word he knew bursting to the tip of his tongue.

'In the name of Allah!' the mullah exclaimed as a flow of bright blood sprinkled the ground.

Again the physician thrust the knife, again the searing pain. Brannon bit his lip so hard that it almost split. But still he kept quiet. The small piece of skin that the physician cut away was discarded somewhere. Brannon didn't look, afraid of seeing the blood pooling at his feet.

As the mullah intoned a prayer, the slave girl diligently applied disinfectant and wrapped a thick bandage around the wound. The ointment seemed to stoke the pain like a furnace, and Brannon staggered as he rose up. Balancing himself on the girl's shoulder, he took a deep breath and allowed himself to be led through the flap at the far end.

'Can't see what all the fuss was about,' he stammered in a weak show of bravado. But there were beads of sweat running down his flushed cheeks. They brought him to the recovery chamber and laid him down just in time, before his strength went completely and he passed out.

The following morning the pain hit him the moment he opened his eyes. He forced himself to look, and the sight was nearly enough to make him cry. His manhood lay like a decapitated lizard between his legs, the bandage encrusted with blood. A male nurse came to clean the wound, which had swollen aggressively and was covered in pus-leaking scabs like leeches gorging on his privates. The nurse dabbed the wound with a strong-smelling disinfectant to prevent it festering and bound it up in a fresh bandage. Later Brannon was given a hot drink mixed with acacia resin, which eased the pain and made him drowsy. After a second cup, he fell asleep.

For the next few days they nursed the wound and soothed him with the painkillers. By the end of the week the burning had faded, though it was another few days before he was able to move about without discomfort. After two weeks he was fully healed and the scabs had shrunk away. Most of them recuperated just as fast, though in some the wounds had corrupted, and the chamber reeked with the cloying stench of wet gangrene. Circumcision always carried a greater risk when the patient was in adulthood. Those unlucky souls were still lying on their mats, thrashing about in waves of agony and delirium. Brannon didn't know what became of them. All the fit recruits were eventually summoned from the recovery chambers and despatched to the cloistered austerity of the soldiers' barracks up the road. There the drill instructors waited with bated breath for their latest crop of recruits. Young and old, Arab and European, these recruits would be broken down and lashed into undying submission, made soldiers worthy of Yazid's army, where service was for life and death a blessed reward.

CHAPTER EIGHT

The recruits spent several months at the barracks, where they received instruction in swordplay, firearms, hand-to-hand combat, riding, and Arabic. Before long the tough fitness routine, combined with a protein-rich diet, was adding substantial bulk onto their long-suffering bodies. Brannon enjoyed the training, though his stomach was frequently turned by the fare on offer—the pickled eel fillets or the boiled stag-beetles or the ugly *el babbus*, a fat Moroccan snail fried in oil. Yet his health flourished as his body adapted; his arms became bigger, his legs ran faster, his mind quickened. The swordplay, shooting, and wrestling he mastered, distinguishing himself from his fellow recruits. Even the Arabic he displayed a flair for, and he was able to expand on the already useful vocabulary he had acquired. The riding, however, proved something of a disaster.

He had assumed it would be horses, and horses he could manage. But the Arabs chose camels. They were cantankerous old beasts, grumbling and moaning and even spitting whenever the inclination took them. On the first morning, Brannon spent an age just trying to get on his camel's back. Each time he tried to climb up it would move slightly, enough to ruin his balance, and enough to earn its way towards becoming his mortal enemy. The others were already mounted as Brannon struggled, and it didn't take long for his enthusiasm to sour.

After an hour he had managed to plant both his legs on either side of the saddle. He squirmed about, blaspheming furiously, trying to get the balance right. Holding the reins, he uttered the command for the camel to go: 'Hut! Hut!' The camel dashed off with unexpected speed, and the depth of Brannon's foul language increased tenfold. He stayed on by digging his heels into the camel's flanks, which brought it to a stop again; it let out a bellow and pranced about in agitation. He calmed it by patting its neck while simultaneously whispering vicious threats into its ear.

It was a long day. By its end, after a number of tumbles, he was able to ride at low speeds without falling off. But he was far from proficient, and the disapproving looks from his instructors let him know that he was amongst the worst in the group. He was in bitter humour when he tramped back to the barracks that evening.

⚜ ⚜ ⚜

'You'll get used to the camels,' Daniel said in consolation, slipping a glass of smuggled wine across the bench to Brannon. Alcohol was strictly forbidden for the recruits, but that didn't prevent its clandestine trade.

Brannon took a sip and concealed the glass. 'I hope so, before I strangle one of those bastard animals. Why can't they use horses like civilised folk?' He grimaced at the acidic aftertaste of the wine.

'A horse is no good in the Sahara. That's why they teach us camels.'

'You think we'll end up in the desert?'

'Who knows?' Daniel shrugged. 'There are rumblings of rebellion. The sultan's brothers have been doing a lot of sabre-rattling. He might send us to sort them out.'

'Not for me,' Brannon said. 'I'm going to the coast. Give us some more of that awful stuff, will you?'

Daniel recharged his glass. 'I want the same as you, lad. But those brothers of Yazid's are mad bastards. Hisham and Maslama—they'd be a match for him any day. There's another called Suliman, but he keeps his head down. Perhaps a wise choice.'

'They sound like a respectable family.'

'Peas in a pod,' Daniel sighed. 'I heard that Yazid had a dog executed the other day. A dog! It snapped at his horse, apparently—an instant death sentence. Its head is stuck on a pike outside the palace to make an example.'

'It does sound like Yazid all right,' Brannon chuckled. 'I've seen him behead a servant just because her shadow fell across him. Jesus, if his mother had been pregnant with twins, he'd probably have strangled the other one inside the womb just for sitting too close.'

'God save our noble sultan,' Daniel agreed.

After a meal of boiled mackerel with pumpkin and egg-sauce, there were the evening prayers, part of Islamic daily worship. This was something Brannon found difficult to embrace. Praying five times a day was quite a shift for a young Irishman who hadn't even been to a Catholic Mass since he was a child, the Masses being illegal under English law. These Muslims he just couldn't identify with; all this bowing and kneeling and getting up and getting down was as bewildering as it was tiresome.

He was weary when he lay down that night. The coming months worried him, like a skulking threat in the shadows. He knew that unless he managed to win his place in the sultan's army, he wasn't ever likely to see home again. And if they returned him to the slave pens, he would never survive. In desperation he prayed—he wasn't sure to whom—for the strength to carry him through. He felt weak.

Orlaith's image appeared in his mind's eye then, like a sunbeam through the clouds. He felt himself relax a little, even though the thought of her face and the memory of her serene beauty and sweet fragrance caused an aching in his heart. Yet his courage slowly returned, seeping through his tired limbs like water to parched soil, bringing life to his spirits and putting steel to his resolve.

They won't beat me, Orlaith. Not ever will I stop until I hold you safe in my arms again. You are my light. Be my light and guide me home.

In mid-spring the toughest recruits who had survived Yazid's draconian training methods were brought together at the place where they had been converted to Islam the previous year. Moulay Yazid was present also, swathed in glittering regal dress and assuming his most imperious air. He had come to receive the pledge of loyalty from his new warriors, to be assured of their undying devotion.

He sat in a diamond-studded chair on top of a raised platform with a canopy to block the sun and four servants swatting off flies.

Brannon stood firm in the swelling heat. Months of exercise in the sun had bleached his hair to light blond and gilded his skin to a smouldering bronze. His body was honed by endeavour, his arms ridged with muscle, and his stomach taut and flat. Like the other recruits, he wore a white cotton haik, loose-fitting pantaloons, and buckled sandals, as well as a newly forged scimitar at his hip. The garb was ideal to the climate, a substantial improvement on the rags he had been wearing all along.

His step was confident as he presented himself before the sultan. He knelt first, prostrated himself for a suitably submissive length of time, and then rose and declared, 'To His Most Royal Highness, Sultan Moulay Yazid, I pledge my life. *Allahu Akbar!*' With this protocol complete, he turned to move on.

The solemn ceremonial atmosphere was abruptly pierced by a male cry. '*Vengeance, in the name of Allah!*'

A soldier broke from the ranks and unleashed his sword. Yazid's platform was ten yards ahead; he charged at it, eyes dancing in rage, weapon raised into attack poise. The response of the bodyguards was instantaneous. They swarmed over Yazid like ants, forming a square and presenting their bare backs to absorb the stab of a blade.

Brannon stopped, caught off guard. Unfortunate timing had meant he was still positioned between the attacker and the platform, but when he saw the demented soldier charging forward with a bared sword, he mistakenly thought it was his own life under threat. The assassin bounded on; Brannon dropped his shoulder and swung his scimitar, performing the move exactly as trained. The man gasped as a deep rent opened across his belly. He dropped his sword, aghast at Brannon's intervention. Slowly he slumped to his knees, grasping the lips of the wound and trying to stifle the blood.

'What did you do that for?' Brannon roared, keeping his scimitar raised in defence.

There was no time for explanations. The sultan's bodyguards arrived in a pack, one of them neatly lopping off the assassin's head with the flick of a broadsword so that a jet of blood spurted into the air and the body wilted into the dust.

Brannon shuddered.

The rumpus died down, and astonished silence filled the square. The bodyguards peered among the recruits, ready to hack down the first man who even looked suspicious. They made ready to move the sultan back to the palace, but Yazid forestalled them.

Clambering out of his chair, he stormed towards the decapitated corpse and kicked it, mouthing a furious tirade until spittle flew from his lips. This was the second time recently that someone had tried to kill him. Outraged, he hopped and pranced around the body, looking for all the world as though performing an impromptu Highland jig for the crowd. Brannon backed away nervously.

'You!' Yazid blurted, and he let loose some wild exclamation which Brannon didn't understand. Fearing for his life, he went down on his knees until Yazid grasped his shoulders and proceeded to plant kisses on both his cheeks. It became apparent that the sultan was thanking him, and he groaned inwardly.

That poor bastard wasn't attacking me, he realised in dismay.

Recognition dawned in Yazid's face. 'Ah, I remember you! Irish?' Now he was hugely pleased, convinced that Brannon had bravely tackled the assassin to save his life. He pointed to the dead body and said, 'This is a dog. But you are a man. My brother in blood, I will not forget this.' He kissed Brannon's cheeks again and began to walk away, taking time to spit on the body and curse it. '*Kelb!* Dog!'

As a precaution, the ceremony was suspended. Brannon, however, had now officially graduated to the ranks of the army and was ordered to fall in with his new unit. Several officers cheered and patted his back as he walked, Brannon having risen immeasurably in their esteem with that single act of courage. He now had a name and a fledgling reputation. Whether that would bode well for him or not, only time could tell.

'You are either shrewd or lucky,' Kaid Ben Hassi said, pouring out a cup of green tea. 'His Majesty had already decided he liked you, and now you have proven your worth.' He paused. 'I saw what happened the other day. A more suspicious mind might reckon that you were protecting your own hide, not the sultan's.'

Brannon smiled, conceding nothing.

'But it matters not.' Ben Hassi shrugged. 'His Majesty wants you promoted to captain and assigned appropriately, rather than sending you off to roast in the desert. You will guard his harem, here in Fez. Only those held in personal trust by the sultan are given such a duty. You should be thankful.'

'The harem?' Brannon's mouth dropped.

'Something's wrong?'

'No.' Brannon coughed. 'I thought, um, I thought I might be posted elsewhere. Why the harem? I wouldn't be any good there.'

'Guarding the harem will probably save your life. You could easily be posted elsewhere and be sent to your death, hacked to pieces by rabid tribesmen on some cursed mountainside. Yet you're unhappy?'

'Not at all—I am privileged,' Brannon huffed.

'Indeed. Just remember this—Moulay Yazid does not like to be disappointed.' Ben Hassi waved a hand to end the meeting. 'Go now, soldier. Soon your work will begin. Go and thank Allah for your good fortune.'

❀ ❀ ❀

Brannon stomped through the dust of the parade ground, cursing his luck. The harem? His whole aim in joining the army was to escape Fez, to escape Yazid. Yet this posting had practically landed him right at the sultan's feet. He cursed again and kicked at a flag-post in anger.

Damn him, he thought with fury. *Damn Yazid, if only he were dead, I would be free…*

A dead Yazid. Quite a concept. But impossible, of course. Yazid would probably never die. He would probably live a thousand years and plague people for every hour of it.

But what if he were *dead?* Brannon suddenly thought. What would happen? The death of a monarch in Africa was usually a trigger for bloody mayhem to commence, relatives and politicians turning on each other with guns and blades, chaos ensuing across the land until, finally, someone managed to climb atop the pile of corpses and claim the crown for himself.

And what an enticing scenario.

If a man were to keep his head down in such a bloodbath, no one would notice him. They would be too busy grabbing for the scraps of power, and Brannon could run for it. It would take months for the dust to settle, and he could be home in half that time.

His pulse quickened. The seeds of a plot were beginning to take root, though it still made little sense. Yazid was protected by soldiers constantly; he slept inside a palace with a dozen walls shielding it, each wall manned by a score of zealous guards who would willingly sacrifice their lives for him. Surely even God could not kill Yazid.

Brannon worked it over in his mind. There had to be some way. Killing Yazid—he felt a shiver at the cold terror that the very concept gave him. But it wasn't impossible. No man was invulnerable. There had to be some time when Yazid was exposed—a fleeting moment perhaps, but enough to capitalise on. But when?

He had a thought.

Once a month, Yazid liked to invite one of his wives into the gardens of the harem where a bathing pool offered tranquillity. Brannon knew that Yazid had to be escorted each time, the guards patrolling the surrounding corridors of the garden so that an effective watch could be maintained over his safety. None of the guards were allowed to see inside the garden, however, as Yazid's wives were taboo commodities. If a man were to have a few seconds in there, beyond the guards' eyes, he could make use of that time wisely.

And then, Brannon had a plan.

Over the following days he had little chance to rethink his sudden urge to murder the sultan of Morocco. He was ordered to report to the harem, where a young African soldier joined his command, and together they made a nervous coupling at their station outside the last of a series of doors that led into the chambers of one of Moulay Yazid's wives.

The harem itself was a massively elaborate structure fronted by marble columns under beautifully engraved stucco cornices. Beyond its studded gates was an expanse of tiled courtyards and ornamental gardens, scented with damask roses and jasmine and soothed by the pleasant gurgling of a dozen sculpted fountains. Moulay Yazid's four wives had their own lavish quarters within the building, with the concubines housed in single-room chambers. A constant stream of slave girls worked at bathing them, feeding them, and pandering to their whims, while eunuchs provided them counsel on matters such as medicine and astrology and politics. The harem was kept swept and polished, for the sultan liked to be in attractive surrounds whenever he was with a woman. His visits were always preceded by a fever of activity, with his wives and concubines screaming for slave girls to braid their hair or apply their make-up or perfume their bodies.

Brannon saw nothing of the inner workings of the harem, however. Under pain of death, he was forbidden to lay eyes on any of the sultan's women, the slave girls being the only females he saw coming and going. He wasn't allowed to open the door he guarded but had to ensure that no unauthorised persons gained entry either. Guarding the sultan's wife from intruders wasn't something he could afford to slip up on.

The first few nights passed without incident. Slave girls and eunuchs passed through, but he saw no one of import. Attending the harem by night and sleeping by day, the routine became tedious. But by the end of the week, he had his first incident to deal with.

On that night an almighty row erupted on the other side of the door. He heard screams and the sounds of a struggle taking place, and then the angry shouts of a eunuch echoed within the chamber. Brannon hesitated. He knew he couldn't open the door, not even to investigate. He remained where he was. The other guard looked as mystified as he did.

'Ignore it,' Brannon warned him.

The door suddenly swung open. A eunuch appeared, grappling with a slave girl who had blood staining her clothes. She was fighting viciously, clawing at the eunuch's face like a wildcat and trying to wriggle free.

'Treachery!' the eunuch cried. 'This slave has stabbed my mistress Halima, His Majesty's wife! I fear she has killed her!'

'What?' Brannon swore under his breath. Suddenly the sultan's undying trust in him was an unwelcome honour. He had no idea what to do.

'Take her!' the eunuch snapped, barely able to hold the girl.

Brannon seized the girl's arms to restrain her. 'Calm down, you,' he grunted. 'Quieten your mouth, and we'll resolve this.'

He didn't notice her hand slipping inside her black haik. She produced a tiny blade, no more than an inch in length, and plunged it into Brannon's side. The pain made him gasp, and he twisted her arm to make her drop the knife. She screeched in fury.

'Help me with her,' he barked at the other guard. Between them they managed to subdue the crazed girl and bundle her down the corridor into a cluttered storeroom. They locked it behind them and listened while she pounded the door and screamed like a banshee.

'Charming behaviour,' Brannon huffed. He checked the wound in his side; it wasn't deep, but the blood was leaking steadily. He pressed his woollen djellaba against it to staunch the flow. 'Little vixen is in need of a finishing school.'

They returned to their posts, where the eunuch was waiting. 'One of you must fetch a physician. My mistress lives, but she requires treatment immediately.'

Brannon could hear the faint wailing of a woman in distress, coming from somewhere inside the harem. He nodded to the other guard. 'Go on. Call one of the palace physicians.' The guard scampered off obediently.

'And you stand close by this door,' the eunuch told Brannon. 'I may want you before this night is out.'

'I'll stay here at the sultan's orders, not yours,' Brannon answered stiffly. He didn't like the eunuch's tone. The eunuchs were servant-slaves, beneath the level of an army captain, but many were personal favourites of the sultan's wives and therefore needed to be treated with a wary respect. It could be dangerous to make an enemy of one.

'Call on me if you need me,' he added as a hasty afterthought.

The other sentry brought a score of physicians to the harem. They tended to the victim, stitched the wound in her neck, and plied her with painkillers all night. Halima's loud and unending complaints led Brannon to suspect that her injury was probably not so serious after all.

A while later, the door opened and the eunuch reappeared. Brannon turned to him. 'The women fighting again?'

'No.' The eunuch beckoned behind him. 'I am sending a girl out with the soiled clothing. There is much blood spilled, and the sight of it upsets my mistress. A devilish night's work that slave has made.'

Brannon shrugged, standing back to make way for the dark-haired girl to pass. She carried the clothes outside, but when he saw her face, the breath seized in his throat.

He stared, dumbstruck. He couldn't believe his eyes. It was the same face that he had seen in so many of his dreams, the face that haunted him—a face that carried him all the way back to Ireland, to a tiny thatched cabin on the windswept Cork coast.

'Orlaith?' he almost blurted out.

The eunuch frowned. 'What is it?'

'Erm, nothing,' Brannon stuttered awkwardly. But the resemblance was astonishing.

The slave girl stepped past, not seeming to notice the reaction she had stirred in him. Carrying her bundle on her shoulder, she walked down the corridor and disappeared into the passageways.

The eunuch gazed at him.

'What?' Brannon asked.

'You're hurt.' He looked at Brannon's knife wound. 'It bleeds still. You should have told us.'

'It's not the wound,' Brannon answered gruffly.

'Go into the room three doors down the corridor—it's a surgery. I'll send someone to help you.'

The wound was indeed bleeding and in need of some attention. Brannon acquiesced. 'Very well.' He told the other guard, 'I'll stick a dressing on this; I won't be long. Watch the door.'

There was no one inside the surgery. It was a gloomy room, half illuminated by lanterns affixed to the clay walls. There were shelves containing an array of ointments and other concoctions inside bottles with waxed stoppers, along with splints, dressings, needles, and scalpels. Brannon spent several minutes browsing the display, not entirely sure what he was looking for.

A warm fragrance soon lifted the air. She entered so silently it was as though the breeze had carried her in. Brannon stepped back in surprise. Again, she made him think of Orlaith. They were roughly the same age, had the same fine facial structure, the same soft lips and glossy black hair. But now, as he looked closer, her coffee-coloured skin and feline emerald eyes dispelled the similarity. She had a smooth complexion and high, regal cheekbones, her body as light and nimble as a woodland fawn. She wore a cotton haik, and her head was half veiled, but not her face. She was beautiful, and he cleared his throat in embarrassment.

'Forgive me. I didn't hear you come.'

She bowed to him. 'I will clean your wound for you, master.'

'I see. Thank you.' He stood in the centre of the room until she pointed shyly to the table.

'Please sit, master, so that I can begin.'

'Oh yes.' He placed himself at the edge of the table and lifted his djellaba. She fetched a bottle of ointment from the shelf and cut a strip of cloth. The wound would have to be cleaned and stitched. Brannon ignored the pain of the procedure and asked her, 'What's your name?'

She stopped, looking discomfited by the question. 'That is not important, master.'

He shrugged. 'I was merely being friendly.'

They remained in silence for a few minutes. She closed the wound with the needle and then bandaged it with a cotton dressing. Her hands were gentle, and Brannon soon forgot the sting of the disinfectant.

'You're very kind,' he said when she had finished. 'It feels much better now.'

She nodded deferentially and replaced the materials on the shelf. Just as she went to go, she looked at him for a moment. 'It's Asiya,' she said softly. 'My name is Asiya.' She smiled and then turned and left the room.

❀ ❀ ❀

It was foolishness, he knew, but her resemblance to Orlaith remained vivid in his mind after that meeting. In his own way he found it comforting, albeit a curious kind of comfort, one tinged with pain. It gave him both solace and heartache in equal measures, reigniting the fire of his love but also stoking the cruel memories of his loss.

He sought Asiya in the weeks that followed, and she appeared regularly. She looked after her mistresses in their chambers, mixed their drinks and broths, and ran their errands to the palace. Often she passed Brannon in the passageways, but she didn't speak to him. He noticed how her movements were always hurried, and he wondered what made her so nervous. If only she would talk.

Late one evening he spotted her inside the Fez el-Bali, hovering near the shadowy mouth of an alleyway. What he first thought was a large, heavy sack that she dragged along was in fact a person, a hooded assailant with his arm locked around her neck. Brannon hissed in dread; the alleys were infested with footpads and vagrants, watching always for soft targets to pounce upon. Asiya was hardly likely to fight them off.

He bounded across the street, outraged by the sight of her slender, feminine body being manhandled to the ground. He came up behind the attacker, seized his arm, and flung him aside. The man tripped over Brannon's foot and went down with a squeak. His hood slipped, and a mane of matted hair tumbled down over an unmistakably female face.

'What are you doing?' Asiya cried in shock.

'A woman?' Brannon stared in horror at the person sprawled on the ground. 'Oh dear, I thought—oh God.'

'I saw her take a fall; I was trying to assist her. What came over you?'

His face turned beetroot-red. 'I'm sorry. Let me help.' The old woman moaned in terror as he lifted her from the street and carried her to a boarded doorway. 'Here. Feed yourself with this.' He produced a Spanish dollar from his pocket, which she accepted after a brief hesitation.

Asiya's glares were almost audible. He shrugged in embarrassment. 'It was her hood. I thought—'

'In Morocco, we are accustomed to treating our elders with greater respect than that.' Her tone was harsh, but he thought he noticed a glimmer of amusement in her green eyes. He nodded.

'I'll not make a habit of it. I'm sorry.'

She smiled then. 'It's all right. You were acting for my benefit.' She went to ensure that the old woman had recovered, and then she picked up her belongings and resumed her journey. 'Good night.' He heard her snicker as she walked off, a noise that instantly inflamed the mortified glow on his cheeks.

CHAPTER NINE

He avoided her for a few days after that, out of bruised pride, but as the weeks went by, they would often meet by chance. She slowly softened towards him and even started to engage him in conversation. Bit by bit he began to learn more about her, and she about him. Now, whenever she passed his post, she would give him a discreet wave. It brought him a warmth of pleasure each time.

'Hello, Brannon,' she said with a smile, seeing him one afternoon standing watch outside the gates of the gardens. The sultan's concubines were enjoying a picnic inside, their squeals and frolics carrying out to the perimeter. Asiya winked slyly. 'So near, and yet so far away...'

Brannon tried to look aloof. 'My mind is on my duty, Asiya. Where are you going?'

'My mistress is unwell. She complains that there is a snake in her belly, but I think she ate too many sweetmeats last night. I'm going to mix a drink to make the snake disappear.'

'What a clever little nursemaid you are. We could have used you in the army.'

A shadow passed over her eyes. 'I've heard Yazid is sending men into the deserts. I've heard his own brother has risen against him.'

'Several of his brothers, in fact,' Brannon explained cheerfully. 'Our good sultan has a talent for treading on toes.'

'And you go too?'

'Not that I know of. But maybe that will change.'

She bit her lip.

'What is it?' he asked. 'You worry for me?'

'There is another man I worry for. Someone I love very much. He is a soldier like you, but I don't know where he is.'

'Your husband?' This revelation took Brannon by surprise.

She shook her head. 'I have never married. It is my brother I speak of. We have not met in a long time.'

'I see.'

'In his last message, he said that he became a soldier. But that was over a year ago, and I have heard nothing since.' She was noticeably distressed as she stared into the gardens.

'Perhaps I can inquire about him,' Brannon offered. 'I have a good relationship with most of the sultan's officers here in Fez. What's your brother's name? Where's he from?'

Asiya hesitated, and Brannon got the sense that she was holding back. 'His name is Ahmed,' she said eventually. 'We came from a village to the south of here.'

'What's the name of it?'

'The village? It's, em, only a small place. Not really even a village.'

'All right, what was your father's name?'

'Our father? Why do you ask?'

'His name would make my job of locating your brother easier, Asiya.'

'My father was a peasant farmer. No one would have heard of him. But I can give you a picture of Ahmed, if that will help. I can draw it from memory.'

'That will have to do, though all of you Moroccans look the same to me.' He studied her expression for a moment. 'Anything else? I can't help thinking that you're keeping something from me.'

'No, that's all. And it would be best if you were discreet when asking your questions. Please.'

'Why?'

'Please,' she insisted.

'Fine. Show me his picture later. I'll do my best to dig him out.'

'Thank you, Brannon. You are a good friend.'

⊕ ⊕ ⊕

Asiya was quite a talented artist with her charcoal; the picture contained a male of roughly twenty-two years with shoulder-length hair and a jutting jawline, but it also reminded Brannon of nearly half the recruits he knew. He kept his eyes open, searching for a closer likeness, but his investigations came to nothing. The trail was cold before it had even begun.

Then something happened which made him forget all about it.

He was given orders one day to report to the palace and supplement an escort for Moulay Yazid while he visited his wives in the harem. The sultan wanted to go into the gardens to enjoy the bathing pool, and Brannon instantly remembered his nascent plan of a few weeks before. This was the opportunity that he had been mulling over, the chance to strike at Yazid while no one was looking. The quiet sanctuary of the gardens could well give him that chance.

He felt a prickle of nerves. Was he actually brave enough to go through with it? Time would quickly tell.

He walked to the palace and presented himself in the antechamber outside Yazid's council room. But Yazid was not yet ready to leave. There appeared to be some sort of hearing taking place, directed by a vizier, which Brannon was able to observe from the back. Yazid was sitting on a pile of velvet cushions with a middle-aged man prostrated before him, next to a young girl barely above thirteen years. The man was clearly distressed. His hands were clasped as he pleaded with the sultan for forgiveness, though Brannon didn't know what for. He positioned himself discreetly and tried to follow the fast-flowing Arabic as best he could.

'Enough!' Yazid suddenly shouted. 'Enough of your poison!' He came rapidly to his feet—a sure sign of his anger, for it took a lot to make Yazid get off his cushions for someone. The girl burst into tears. She crawled forward and tried to kiss his feet, but Yazid recoiled in disgust and raised his hand threateningly. Slowly Brannon gathered the gist of what had happened.

She was a concubine in the harem; the man was her father, and he been caught attempting to gain entry there, intending to remove her from it. For most families, having a daughter in the royal harem was a great honour. Clearly this man did not think so. Brannon pitied them; they were terrified, in fear for their very lives. He prayed that the sultan would show mercy for once.

Yazid gave his judgement with a look of intense hostility. The girl must be punished, given fifty lashes of the whip and then returned to the harem. As for her father…

'Give him to Juwairiyah,' Yazid decided. 'She'll like him, I dare say.'

'Ah, inspired thinking, Your Majesty.' The vizier rubbed his hands. 'Yes, Juwairiyah will be pleased. She hasn't had a man in a long time.'

At his order, the soldiers advanced on the two defendants. They cried out in despair, and she threw her arms around the old man's shoulders in an attempt to shield him. One of the soldiers grabbed a fistful of her hair and yanked her clear. Her father knelt and begged the sultan, tears streaming down his cheeks. He spoke so fast that his words came out nonsensically. In any case, Yazid wasn't listening. He had turned his back and was selecting a syrup drink from a servant's tray.

They dragged the girl out, and her pleas echoed heart-wrenchingly down the corridor. The man was hauled to his feet; Yazid nodded to the vizier, who was grinning with excitement, and the entire company left the room.

Uneasily, Brannon followed.

Outside they crossed under the shade of the palm trees through the scented gardens to a long, wire-enmeshed building beyond. Inside it was roofless, the sun beaming down into pink-clayed corridors. The entire building was populated with animals: monkeys squealing at the visitors, birds with exotic plumages, a glass tank of spiders, and a restless leopard that snarled at them as they passed its cage. They reached a locked door at the end, which led into a gloomy room, a canopy blocking the sunlight. It smelled damp and feral, and the guards held torches to provide light.

Brannon wondered what they had in mind for the prisoner. With the torchlight, he noticed a line of iron bars in the centre of the room. A cage of some sorts, reaching from floor to ceiling with wire lattice closing the gaps. Beyond, at the far wall, was a large hollow by the ground. Not high, but it was deep. A sleeping place for something.

The guards opened the cage gate. They shoved the hapless prisoner inside.

'Juwairiyah!' Yazid called, his eyes hooded in expectation. 'Come out.'

The man grasped at the bars, begging for release, but the guards prodded him back. He turned about, frantically searching the cage. Nothing moved— but now the deep hollow in the wall caught his attention.

There was a hiss, an intense and callous sound. He heard a body moving, the rasp of its skin against the rough clay, its breathing intensifying as it detected man-scent. The prisoner backed away, but his eyes remained fixed hypnotically on the hole where the beast lurked. Something stirred in the blackness, large and sleek. The indistinct slide and coil of reptilian flesh. A diamond-shaped head rose into the light with glittering eyes and a pronged tongue. The man moaned in horror and dropped to his knees, babbling out a desperate prayer for deliverance. His movements made the snake stiffen; it snarled from its throat and reared up, a terrifying sight, and four hundred pounds of scaly flesh began rolling across the floor.

Brannon watched, aghast. He had heard of giant pythons that lived in southern Africa, snakes big enough to swallow a lion. This was the first time that he had seen one live, and his skin crawled with fear. It was hideous, as thick as a tree trunk, its head the size of a mallet. If stretched out it would probably reach thirty feet in length, a sheer monster of a thing. He swallowed in revulsion and was utterly grateful for not being the poor soul trapped inside the cage.

The animal unsheathed the full magnificence of its body, a wealth of tawny, glistening skin dappled with brown shapes and black outlines. It fixed its kindling eyes on the kneeling man, flattened its neck, and spat its horrid tongue between its mouth, hungry.

'Seek, Juwairiyah!' Yazid goaded the snake with his voice. 'Seek him, my beauty! Show us your power, Juwairiyah!'

Juwairiyah was breathing hoarsely as if sexually aroused. She inched herself to her victim, and the man sank lower on the ground, gabbling weakly. 'My sultan, forgive me!' he cried in pleading. 'Save me!'

They were the last words he ever spoke.

Juwairiyah sprang out and seized him by the collar of his haik, fastening her teeth into the thick wool. He screamed and tried to fight free, but her sheer weight pulled him to the ground, where she lumped herself on top of him.

Within seconds her long, serpentine coils had wound themselves around his chest like a grotesque swaddling. He gurgled and choked, using his free hand to beat at the beast's head, but his efforts made Juwairiyah's muscles tighten further. She squeezed him until foam seeped through his lips like water from a sponge, his eyes bulging.

'Enough of this!' Brannon cried, but his voice was lost as the guards bellowed their encouragement.

The man's struggles began to weaken, his lungs collapsing like paper. The air was rank with the stench of his voided bowels. Juwairiyah waited until he had stopped moving completely, and like a sated lover she slid herself off his devastated body. Her massive jaws unhinged themselves over his head, and she began to feed.

'Good, Juwairiyah,' Yazid chuckled. 'She is beautiful, no?'

Brannon thought he would vomit.

Yazid abruptly clapped his hands, and the room was roused from its hypnosis. 'The daughter will have had her punishment by now. I'll visit her later, kiss her wounds better.' He sneered at his own words, and the guards bowed their heads appreciatively.

Brannon averted his eyes, trying to swallow his anger. He knew that if he looked at Yazid's face one moment longer, he wouldn't be able to resist throttling the horrible bastard. And that wouldn't be a good thing.

No, not here.

He was biding his time.

They left Juwairiyah to digest her meal and went into the expanse of cultivated gardens circling the harem, where sprinklers tossed glistening mountain water over the close-cropped grass. By now Yazid was sufficiently stirred to see his wife. The display in the cage had amused him, but he soon reverted into impatience. He slapped a servant for standing too close, and when her face didn't register pain sufficient to his liking, he ordered her to be taken away and whipped. Walking up a pathway, he spotted a slave boy tending to the flowerbeds. Something about the youngster's appearance annoyed Yazid, and he commanded the guards to seize him. The boy was then subjected to a bastinading, an extremely cruel punishment where the victim is turned upside down and has the soles of his feet beaten until raw and bloody. The boy's screams seemed to put Yazid in a better mood.

Brannon quietly simmered, watching it all take place. His sense of outrage was steadily lending him courage, dispelling the last of his fears about killing the sultan. Yazid was a thug, a bully. Brannon had met thugs and bullies in his time, the wealthy ones, the powerful men. That Randall Whiteley was an example for sure, and there had been others—landlords, bailiffs, even some of the clergy. Abusive men, abusing positions, inflicting misery on the weak. Brannon liked to think that he had always stood up to them, but he had never stood up to Moulay Yazid. He had been afraid of Yazid until now, and this only stoked his temper even more.

He had to do this thing.

Yazid's wife was waiting for him at the bathing pool within the garden. The crystalline waters had been piped from a nearby well, and there were palm trees circling the tiles to give the lovers more intimacy. The guards, including Brannon, were directed to patrol the pentagon-line of covered passageways around the grass, distanced discreetly to allow Yazid's wife to remain unseen, but close enough to provide an effective watch.

Brannon subtly eased himself into a pace that allowed him at least thirty seconds between the nearest guards. Would thirty seconds be enough? He began to fret again. But Yazid wasn't positioned far away. Thirty seconds should be enough to get in there, cut the bastard in half, and run for it. If he kept his hood down, the woman wouldn't recognise him. He could be back patrolling the corridors by the time her screams had drawn attention.

There were loud noises coming from the garden now, splashing water and peals of female laughter. Brannon scowled at their frolics. He peered through the marble columns that bordered the grass, realising he was closer to the pool than he had estimated. Sidling carefully to the screen of a boxwood hedge, he studied the scene beyond.

Yazid was sitting naked, his back to Brannon. His wife faced him, a portly creature with big, pendulous breasts that Yazid was fondling with childish glee. She scooped up a handful of water and trickled it over his thin, hairless chest; he giggled in delight, pulling her forward and making her straddle him. She let out a low moan.

Brannon's fury rose. Less than an hour ago he had witnessed the sultan condemn a child's father to the most horrible of fates and send the child herself to have the skin flayed from her back. Now he sat cavorting in the water, blithe and blissful, with this obscene lump of a woman. Brannon had never wished death on another human being so much. With a deep breath he steadied himself.

Now or never.

It would be easy. None of the guards were in sight; Yazid was vulnerable. With his body turned, he wouldn't even spot Brannon's approach. The woman was busy putting on a show of sexual ecstasy with her eyes closed, and the chance was there.

He must act.

Subconsciously his fingers moved to the handle of his scimitar. Its smooth ivory grip had never felt so snug and convenient in his palm. With Yazid dead there would be freedom, there would be Dromkeen, there would be Orlaith. There would be everything—if he made his move now.

And so he could resist it no more.

The scimitar scraped as he pulled it from its sheath; he broke into a run down the length of the hedgerow, flexing his sword arm, and the world around blurred into insignificance. Fury and adrenaline blinded his reason now, and for brief moments he was invincible, like a god riding his cloud across the sky. He raised the sword and poised himself for a swing, a powerful swing that would sever Yazid's head from his shoulders and put an end to his malevolent influence for good.

The sentry pounced faster than a cat in ambush. From the shadows he attacked, deftly flicking his sword across to knock the scimitar from Brannon's hands so that it fell to the ground with a clatter. He grabbed Brannon's neck, spun him into a headlock, and bundled him behind the columns. Yazid didn't even notice the commotion, being too entranced with his wife's elaborate feats of sexual engineering.

Brannon fought back viciously, knowing he didn't stand a chance against all the guards together. He kicked and punched, and the sentry grunted with effort as he tried to restrain him.

'Stop fighting, soldier,' the man panted in English. He abruptly released his grip and stepped back, keeping the point of his blade at Brannon's throat. 'You fool. It is forbidden to approach His Majesty in the garden. It is certainly forbidden to approach him with your sword in the air.'

Brannon didn't reply. There was a sickening knot forming in his stomach now as he realised the trouble he was in. It had been a wild idea, ill-planned and foolish. And now he was going to die for it.

'Why do you wait, then?' he asked bitterly. 'Call your hounds. Finish me.'

'You seem to enjoy imperilling your life, soldier,' the sentry remarked with a smile. 'I wonder why that is.'

'What are you talking about?'

'Ah, let's just say your little whisperings with a certain slave girl have not gone unnoticed.'

'Slave girl?' Brannon said, feigning innocence, but the sentry had a shrewd glint in his eye.

'I have seen you with her myself. You are not supposed to mix with the female slaves. It is immoral.'

'You take your vengeance out on me, you coward,' Brannon warned him. 'The girl has done nothing.'

'I mean her no harm, soldier. Take my word for it.'

'So why watch us? What's she to you?'

The sentry's smile faded. He rubbed his jaw thoughtfully and let out a sigh. 'It's quite simple. She is my sister.'

The following day Brannon perched himself in a cramped alcove off the armoury workshop. The slaves were polishing gunlocks and repairing firearms, and the noise of three hundred clanking hammers and voices was thunderous. It was an ideal spot in which to hold a discreet conversation.

Ahmed stood by the alcove, his present temperament evident from the deep furrow in his brow. He had the same emerald-green eyes as his sister with long black hair combed back from a brooding but handsome face. Though smaller and slighter than Brannon, there was an air of stubborn strength about him, like someone shouldering a weighty grudge. Brannon didn't know whether to feel safe or not.

'She asked me to find you,' he said in his defence. 'That's why I mentioned your name around.'

'Asiya has been foolish,' Ahmed answered sourly. 'She has drawn attention to herself, to us both. You will warn her not to talk about me again.'

'Warn her yourself. Why haven't you made contact?'

'It was too dangerous. I didn't want to be seen with her. There are reasons why.'

Brannon rubbed his eyes. He was due for watch duty at the harem, and this conversation wasn't hugely enlightening. 'Very well, I will pass on the good news to her. Her beloved brother is still alive. It'll cheer her up.'

Ahmed raised a warning finger. 'Do not mention my identity to anyone but Asiya. Do not even speak of me. If you do, I will report your actions yesterday and have you arrested. I'm afraid I'm not as trusting as my sister.'

'Mention you? I'll have forgotten your name in an hour. I have my own problems to worry about.' Brannon scowled, piqued by Ahmed's admonition. But his curiosity couldn't remain idle for long. 'Come on, damn you. What's it about? Asiya wouldn't tell me anything either.'

'She was wise in that regard at least.' Ahmed glanced into the busy workshop. 'We have been talking too long. Tell my sister that I live, and that soon I will speak to her. Tell her that she has been strong so far and she must remain so.'

Brannon whistled. 'Very cloak-and-dagger, Ahmed. Yes, I'll pass on your message. Maybe one of you will eventually be polite enough to tell me who you really are.'

Ahmed smiled for the first time, briefly. 'Maybe we will, Brannon. Maybe.' Then he strode away and vanished skilfully into the throng of sweaty, labouring bodies.

⊕ ⊕ ⊕

Shards of broken sunlight fell across the cobbled alley like tiger stripes. The morning crept tentatively over the rooftops and warmed the streets as flies began to gather around midden heaps and meat stalls and the faithful followed the call to *fajr*, the first of the daily *salat*. Asiya stepped into the shade and peered about. She was alone here, the area bereft of voice or footfall.

The rubbish in the alley suddenly rustled as a shadow fell across her view. She spun around just in time to see an Arab man coming at her fast. With a shriek, she tried to bolt for cover.

'Shh!' He grasped her arm. 'Stay quiet, sister, or you'll have us both in trouble.'

She stared at him in stunned shock, recognising the timbre of his voice and the glittering jade of his eyes. She almost shrieked again and went to embrace him, falling into his arms.

'Praise Allah!' she wept. 'It's true—you are alive. For so long I have been waiting.'

Gently Ahmed pulled her arms down and touched her cheek soothingly. 'I am alive, Asiya. But I couldn't come to you. You know how dangerous it would have been.'

Kissing his hand, she said, 'So many times I gave up hope. I was weak. Now Allah has brought you back, and I am so happy, my brother.'

'I was never far away, Asiya. Even after that night, when we were separated, I knew where you had been taken. But it wasn't safe to follow you, not with Yazid's killers stalking the streets. He might not know what we look like, but there are others who would recognise us. So I hid.'

Asiya shuddered at the memories of that night. Even now she suffered from nightmares, her mind haunted by the images of blade-wielding assassins inside her home, the blood of her murdered siblings spilling across the floor. She should have been killed too, along with Ahmed. Only through the grace of Allah and sheer luck had they survived.

'I knew Brannon would bring you to me. He is an honourable man.'

Ahmed frowned. 'Reserve your judgements, Asiya. You shouldn't have allowed him into your confidence so easily.'

'I know, my brother.' She bowed her head. 'I was so lonely and so desperate. But I felt the goodness in him. He will not betray us.'

'Asiya, he's a renegade in whom I would place no faith. And if he does betray us—well, I need not tell you what the consequences will be.'

She reflected glumly on that for a moment. 'What is to become of us, Ahmed? I live in fear almost every day. When is all of this to end?'

'End?' Ahmed's eyes flashed with sudden anger. 'It will end when I have put right all the wrongs inflicted on us. It will end when I have avenged the deaths of our family, when I have put to the sword the butcher responsible for all of it. Mark my words, sister, when I say that Moulay Yazid's debauched days are coming to a close.'

She was bolstered by his resolve. 'And I will help you, Ahmed. I will do all that you ask of me.'

'For now, Asiya, I ask only that you keep your strength. You will need it before all of this is finished, Allah be merciful.'

❀ ❀ ❀

Brannon did not like Ahmed. And he knew that Ahmed did not like him. The Moroccan was condescending whenever they spoke, addressing Brannon like a child. Brannon, infuriated, resolved to return the same treatment, to show the stuffy little bastard just how little he cared, and if Ahmed's manners didn't show a marked improvement, then a perhaps a slap in the jaw might achieve better results.

To his surprise, however, Ahmed did soften over the following weeks. It was still evident that he was testing Brannon, appraising him, but he became more amenable in disposition, friendlier even. The icy barrier between them slowly thawed.

'You look troubled.' Ahmed grinned at him as they met one morning inside the throbbing markets of the Fez el-Bali. 'You're working too hard. Come, let me take you to a coffee house.' There was a smell from the bread ovens and the roasting dishes; the traders had lifted the canopies off their stalls, and the bargain hunters were streaming in.

Brannon nodded grumpily, too tired to object. They negotiated a path through an alleyway blocked by wheezing mules and their wheezing drivers and found a shortcut to the docks. A number of trade vessels were in the river, discharging timber, gum-copal, and spices onto the quay. Brannon followed Ahmed, ducking under a low awning into one of the noisy coffee houses.

Inside it was dimly lit and perfumed with mint tea, with a stronger aroma of herbs, sauces, and sweat wafting from the kitchen. A thick miasma hovered languidly, discolouring the sunlight that fell through the windows. This place didn't taste fresh air often, and the walls which had once been white were now stained a sickly brown by the smoke. Even at this early hour it was crowded with lean-faced soldiers and weary foreign diplomats, drinking out of brass thimble cups and smoking *kif*. Nobody took much notice of the Arab and the white soldier when they came in, and Ahmed directed Brannon to a table in the corner where they could talk in private.

Ahmed clicked his fingers, and coffee was brought. Brannon sipped a little and spat it out. 'You could caulk ships with that,' he said in disgust.

Ahmed smiled and sampled his own. 'Perhaps a little rich for European tastes?'

'What's on your mind, Ahmed? You didn't bring me down here to drink this shit and talk about culture.'

'Nothing's wrong. We are all happy. Certainly you must be?'

'About what?' Brannon's mood was rapidly souring. He tried to fan the pungent smoke away from his face.

'Here you are, one of the sultan's captains, and, I hear, a personal favourite of His Majesty. You have achieved so much in so little time. You must be happy.'

'Oh, I count my blessings every day. But why are you telling me this?'

'Making conversation with you, Brannon.' Ahmed nodded. 'Lucky Brannon Ryan. In time you will have a woman and a home, and after that you will have want of nothing.'

'Nothing but my freedom, Ahmed.'

'Ah!' Ahmed winked. 'So there is more to it.'

'Of course. I want to go home, back to my own country and my own people. And I will be doing so very soon, I can assure you.'

'Nonsense. Morocco is your home now. This is where the sultan wants you, and what the sultan wants he gets.'

'We'll see about that,' Brannon muttered. 'The sultan won't always be around.'

'Dangerous words, soldier. A man shouldn't use such words lightly.'

'You should have let me finish the bastard. I'd be a free man now.'

'My friend, don't underestimate Moulay Yazid. If it was that easy to get rid of him, somebody would have done it long ago.' Ahmed leaned closer. 'But don't think that my actions mean I love the sultan. I wasn't saving him. I was saving you from yourself.'

'Damned decent of you.'

'Well, in truth, I wanted to find out why you were spending so much time whispering to my sister. Otherwise I would have let you attack him.'

'I barely know your sister. She hardly ever speaks.'

Ahmed sighed. 'Yes, Asiya and I have secrets to hide, if we're to stay alive. But she seems to have taken a liking to you, and she does trust you. Perhaps I can trust you too. Why? Because our interests are in common. We both want to see Moulay Yazid removed.'

Brannon was immediately suspicious. 'Why would you want that?'

Ahmed ensured nobody was listening, and then he edged his seat closer. 'Let me explain my story. My father was Khaled bin Abdellah al-Qatib, the brother of Sidi Mohammed, who was the last sultan of Morocco. When Sidi

114

Mohammed died, a power struggle ensued between his sons, of whom Yazid was one.'

'No surprises there.'

'Yazid's first aim was to eliminate his rivals, but his brothers were protected by their own armies and beyond his reach. So Yazid turned on his relatives, members of the Alaouite dynasty. His uncle, my father, was one of the first victims.'

'Wait...' Brannon stalled him. 'Are you telling me you're Moulay Yazid's *cousin?*'

'Same extended family, yes. But every vineyard has rotten stalks. Yazid, anyway, decided to visit my home a week after the sultan died, and in a single night of violence he had my parents and all my young siblings slaughtered. Asiya escaped by disguising herself as a servant. She was captured and put in a slave pen, with no one wise to her identity.'

Brannon swallowed, trying to take it in. 'And you?'

'Just before they broke my door down, my bodyguard begged me to swap clothes with him. He wanted to fool them into thinking he was me, and he bravely sacrificed his life. Like Asiya, they took me for a house servant, and I became a slave, but later I earned my place in the army. To this day, only a few know that we are Khaled's children.'

'So you're royalty?'

'We once were. Perhaps we will be again.'

'Ah, I see now.' Brannon wagged his finger reprovingly. 'You're set on killing Yazid and jumping into that throne yourself, aren't you?'

Ahmed shook his head. 'Never. It wasn't mine in the first place. What I want, more than anything, is to avenge my family.'

'Open your eyes, Ahmed. If you kill Yazid, it simply leaves the road free for the next lunatic to take control. You'll have your revenge, but nothing will have changed.'

'You're wrong. Yazid has a brother, the only male sibling of his who is not a brutal killer. His name is Suliman, and he is a good man, a learned man. I am already in contact with him, and he has his people here, in Fez. I think he will make a just and noble sultan.'

115

Brannon took in the significance of this. 'Are you saying there's going to be some sort of rebellion?'

Ahmed peered around the room and motioned for Brannon to lower his voice. 'Yes. But when the time is right.'

'Hold on, Ahmed—'

'If we succeed, you will have your freedom. With Yazid dead and Suliman in power, no one will stop you. We'll do what whatever is necessary to get you back to Ireland.'

'Will you now? And for what in return?'

'Simple. You are a captain, so you have access to places I do not, and more importantly, you have the confidence of the sultan and his officials. This can be used to our advantage if you are willing to do as I say. We'll be in it together— you have your freedom, and I have my vengeance. And Morocco has a future again.'

Brannon blinked as he came to terms with it. His little friend Asiya the slave girl was of the royal dynasty, and Ahmed the secretive Arab was formulating a plot to topple the sultan. And Brannon, now, was being invited to land himself in the middle of it. 'And what if we don't succeed?'

'Then you will probably die in Morocco and never see Ireland again,' Ahmed reasoned.

But still he hesitated. It was madness. He wanted his freedom, but joining an Arab revolt wasn't exactly the solution he had in mind. Yet had he any other choice? With every passing day, his need for Orlaith burned more painfully.

He had to try. Even if he was almost certain to fail.

'Count me in then, Ahmed.' He grasped the other's hand. 'If this business will get me home, I'll do it. To be perfectly honest, though, I think I'll be doing well to see out the year with my balls intact.'

'Allah is kind,' Ahmed told him. 'Don't despair. Ireland will wait for you.'

CHAPTER TEN

Edmund Boyle, Lord Cork, Seventh Earl of Cork and Orrery, pushed aside the plate of venison pie and wiped the dribbles of gravy from his chin before belching loudly. He heaved himself around in the chair and undid the top button of his breeches, sighing at the extra space. Rain rattled against the windows and gathered in pools outside, a determined wind hunting around the eaves. It was a day for brandy by the hearth, smoking sweet Virginian tobacco, and he'd flick through Paine's newly published *The Rights of Man* for a chortle.

The maids had lit a mountainous turf fire inside the drawing room, and Boyle measured a drink before lowering into his favourite armchair, relishing the tranquillity of the afternoon. His wife, Anne, had taken their six children to Devonshire to visit her cousins, and he was glad of the few weeks of peace that this would allow him. Anne doted on the youngsters, but Boyle found them bothersome, always one of them crying or laughing or shouting. He wondered what sin he had committed for the Almighty to have sent him five boisterous boys and a girl within the space of just eight years.

There was a knock on the door, and he looked up with a sigh. 'Come.'

The door was pushed open, and a dour-faced butler appeared, hands clasped and head bowed as usual, like a perpetual bearer of bad news.

'Redmond?' Boyle inquired impatiently.

'Visitor, Lord Cork,' was the mumbled reply. 'A Miss Orlaith Ryan, my lord.'

'Orlaith Ryan?' Boyle shook his head. 'Never heard the name. Have her make an appointment—I'm engaged at present.'

'Very good, my lord.' The butler nodded and turned at his tediously slow pace back into the hall. As he moved through the door, Boyle caught a glimpse of the young woman beyond, dripping wet on the marble floor. *Good-looking piece*, he thought.

'Redmond,' he said, interrupting the butler's laborious progress, 'send her in to me, please. And fetch her some towels before she catches her death.'

The visitor was shown inside, and Boyle rose from his chair. 'Miss Ryan?'

Orlaith nodded and curtsied. 'Yes, Lord Cork.' She had given 'Ryan' as her surname out of caution. Randall would be furious if he ever heard of this. 'I'm sorry to trouble you unannounced, my lord, but I had hoped to speak to you on a matter of importance.'

'Must be quite important indeed, Miss Ryan, to have you travelling the roads on a wretched day like this.' Her accent suggested to him she wasn't local. West Cork perhaps, or Kerry. From her clothes he guessed her to be a woman of means, and his interest was roused. 'What is it I can do for you, my dear?'

'It's about my, um, my cousin. Brannon Ryan is his name. He's in some trouble, my lord, and I've come to ask for your help.'

'Trouble, eh? I'll assume it's cash, then. Cash is the only reason why anyone comes knocking on my door. As if I was growing the stuff in my back garden. So he's run up a rack of gambling debts? About to lose his shirt to the money-lenders?'

'No, my lord, nothing like that. He was victim to a most foul business last year, taken by pirates from over the sea. They'll not give him up without pay. That's why I need your help, my lord.'

'Ah...' Boyle let out a sigh and returned to his armchair. 'The raid. I should have guessed. Do you know how many people have come to me since that list of captives was produced, Miss Ryan? A lot. I've had every strain of tradesman and labourer and farmer's wife trudging up my driveway and tramping muck through my hall. And all for the same reason, of course. They want me to dig deep into my pockets and get poor John or Mickey or Maureen on the next boat home.'

'It's just, I heard you paid some ransoms already, my lord. And Brannon Ryan is a decent man, worthy of intervention. It would mean the world for me to have him back, sir. I would be so happy.'

'Such tender words, Miss Ryan,' he observed. 'I'd nearly have thought you his lover rather than his cousin.'

She blushed, and Boyle sat back, sniffing at his brandy. 'I paid only one ransom, two hundred pounds for my stable groom, grabbed in Dromkeen and enslaved by a nigger winemaker in Morocco. I've paid none else, and nor is it my responsibility to. I'm afraid somebody has misled you.'

'But I could pay you back, sir.' She stepped closer, clasping her hands. 'I swear I would. I beg you—Brannon will die if I don't get him home soon.'

'You're not listening. If I pay a ransom for him, I will be expected to do the same for everybody else. It would never end. So I'm sorry. I'm not in a position to help.'

Orlaith gazed about the oak-panelled room, at the damask curtains and walnut chairs, the wall sconces of burnished gold, the table of Venetian marble, the gilt-framed family portrait. The earl had a lavish mansion that dwarfed even Randall's, with innumerable acres of prime grazing beyond its walls. Local gossip estimated his personal fortune at something like one million pounds. Was there even that much money in the world? A few hundred would be a drop in the ocean, and she was piqued. 'With due respect, Lord Cork, you're a powerful man. Do you not feel any obligation towards them?'

'With due respect, Miss Ryan, why don't *you* pay the ransom?' He gestured to her attire. 'I can see you're not a pauper. Those linens must have set you back a pretty penny, and since you're not married, can I assume you are independently wealthy?' He raised an eyebrow. 'Yet you can't raise a few coppers to save your own flesh and blood?'

She wasn't sure how to answer that. 'But I...I'm not wealthy, my lord—'

'Come now, Miss Ryan. I feel you're not being honest. Do you reckon me soft-headed?'

'No, Lord Cork. I had reckoned you honourable. Clearly I was wrong.'

He flushed slightly. 'I think that will be enough, Miss Ryan. I indulged your company to hear you out, but you are a discourteous woman. I'll thank you to leave now.'

'I'll leave gladly,' she answered, her temper flaring before she could restrain it. 'You are too greedy to be of use, hoarding your coins in your fancy home while your countrymen languish in chains. You should be ashamed.'

'That's enough!' He burst from his chair, and the effort seemed to tax him, for he erupted into a fit of coughing. 'Out!' he spluttered.

Orlaith turned and stormed from the room, scattering raindrops in her wake. The old butler stared at her in astonishment and hurried to shift his decrepit frame aside. She made her own way out, slamming the front door and marching into the rain. The carriage was waiting by the driveway, and her driver, Jack Dunphy, was sitting inside. Jack had been a childhood friend of Brannon's, one of the few people Orlaith could trust. She had confided to him her plan, and he had agreed to drive her here so that she could seek the earl's help.

'He wasn't much good to you then, ma'am?' he asked, seeing the flagrant hostility in her face.

'No. He's a mean old pig of a man. Please take me home, Jack.'

'Aye, ma'am.'

They trundled back along the coastal highway, and Orlaith tried to push the disappointment from her mind. She had known that the chances of the earl helping her were never substantial. Like most of the gentry, he would sooner swallow fire than part with his precious pennies. The richest man in Cork was always worth a try, but it couldn't be helped. She would have to find the money elsewhere.

'If it's any consolation, ma'am,' Jack offered, 'Brannon Ryan is a tough bastard, pardon my language. Don't worry about him. If I know Brannon, he'll survive this and come out the other side with a grin on his face.'

She sighed in exasperation. 'Jack, do you even know where he is? In Africa, a slave in chains, probably starving if he's not dead by now. And you say not to worry about him—I've never heard anything so stupid!'

He blinked at the ferocity of her attack, and with a quiet shrug he turned his attention back to the road. She was immediately ashamed.

'Oh, Jack, I'm sorry. That was cruel. You have been so good to help me.' She reached out for his hand. 'I didn't mean to take it out on you. It's just—I'm so afraid. Every hour that passes could be his last one. If I don't get him home soon, who knows what will happen?'

Jack's face softened in sympathy. 'I know that, ma'am. But I meant what I said. He was always a strong fellow—he'd tackle anything. And he's clever. He'll be back, I know it.'

'I hope you're right,' she sighed. 'But I must do everything in my power to help. I owe it to him. And I love him. I'll get him home, Jack, whatever it takes.'

He smiled, seeing the firm resolve in her eyes again. 'I believe you, ma'am. There's a fever in you now. Brannon Ryan is a lucky man to have you standing second for him.'

It was nightfall when they reached Dromkeen Hall. Jack left Orlaith at the gate rather than drop her outside the door. Randall was in Cork City brokering a land deal for a Scottish friend, but she didn't want to be seen by one of the servants. All it took was prying eyes and a quiet word, and she'd be in the height of trouble.

She trudged up the flooded avenue where the oak trees thrashed and groaned in the darkness. She had left Sean in Kathy's care, telling the servant girl that she was walking into Dromkeen to visit a sick friend. When she reached the house, Kathy brought her a change of clothes and made her sip a hot whiskey by the fire. Sean was in bed, a relief, for she hadn't the energy to deal with him now. She was exhausted, and later, when she had dozed off in the armchair, Kathy wrapped a woollen blanket around her shoulders and left her to sleep in peace.

Two nights later winter abruptly tightened its grip as a bitter wind sheared down from the north, and temperatures fell to freezing. By the time Randall arrived home from Cork City, the ground was already hardened with frost and the trees stiff with ice. January's chilly embrace enveloped the land, the fields turned white, and the woodlands closed into slumber.

Sean gazed in wonder at the bed of snow that carpeted the lawn. He had never seen a snowfall before, and he was intrigued—how it glittered in the sun! Scampering over the grass like a puppy, he let out a squeal of delight. Never was a boy so lucky.

Orlaith had allowed him to play but warned him not to amble far. Randall had already hunted him off the steps, so instead he frolicked in the snow, kicking up white showers of it and grasping it between his fingers. Curious, he decided to taste it, rolling a tiny ball and placing it on his tongue. The snow was cold and flavourless, not so appealing. More fun to just belt it about.

A rumble of wheels distracted him from the driveway. Scattering slush, the mail coach rounded the flowerbeds and creaked up to the front door. A man climbed down, carrying a wide, flat parcel thickly wrapped in brown paper. Randall appeared after a few seconds and took the parcel, pressing a coin into the man's hand and waving him off. The coach trundled down the driveway, and Randall went inside.

Sean's interest quickened. A present? But for whom, he wondered. It wasn't like Randall to buy presents. Perhaps he had bought one for himself.

After a few minutes, when all was quiet, he slipped inside the house to investigate. The door of the library was ajar, but Sean didn't want to run into Randall. The latter left soon afterwards, however, dressed in his riding apparel and bellowing for the stable groom. Perfect, Sean thought. He would be gone for hours.

Discreetly he sidled up to the library door. Randall didn't normally allow him in here unattended, which was a considerable nuisance. It meant he couldn't enjoy all the exciting playthings that it housed, such as the antique swords or the ornamental duelling pistols or the spinning ball that displayed a map of the world. He resented this, being three years old. They treated him like a baby.

To his frustration the parcel was still unopened. Why hadn't Randall at least removed the wrapping? Sean was concerned. He knew that if he opened it himself, there would be trouble. On the other hand, if he didn't open it, he would never learn its contents. He gave the matter some thought. Surely it was Randall's fault for not opening it straightaway. If he had done so, then there would have been no need for Sean's curiosity. Sean thought this a reasonable argument, and he soon came to the decision that it was perfectly within his rights to open the parcel.

He knelt down. It was covered with brown paper and bound in string, and hard as he tried he couldn't undo the knots. When he attempted to rip it apart, the string cut into his soft hands.

Getting cross now, he searched for a tool of some kind. On the writing desk was a letter opener, and he used this to begin sawing across the string. It was a laborious task—the letter opener had a dull blade, and the string was unyielding. Eventually, after about twenty minutes of application, the string gave way. In his determination Sean accidentally sliced the knife through the paper and cut a deep rent. It couldn't be replaced now, so he ripped away the rest. When he saw what was beneath, he sighed in dismay.

Another painting. And not even an interesting one, such as a horse or a dog or a boat. It was a portrait of a rosy-cheeked man in a shiny suit of armour, one hand draped arrogantly on his hip. His wig was a wild cascade of curls down to his shoulders, and there was an air of smug indifference in his eyes. He didn't look like a nice man.

Randall wouldn't be happy when he saw this picture. It was a boring one, with no decent colours or animals in it. But even a slight improvement might make a difference. Sean decided that the man would look happier if he had a companion. A dog would do. Everybody liked dogs.

There was a goose-feather quill on the writing desk. Ideal. There was also a jar of indian ink, which was black and therefore not entirely suited to Sean's purpose of brightening the picture. But it would have to do.

In his mind's eye he could see the dog exactly as he wanted to draw him. But it wasn't so easy with the quill. His first attempt was clumsy, with too much ink dripping from the nib. It left an unattractive splatter mark on the canvas, which smudged when he tried to erase it. He made a second attempt, and this time managed a circle for the dog's body with four stubby lines as its legs. He tried to make the dog look as though it were smiling, but the effort was unsuccessful. Its mouth became a black hole, like it was choking on an old sock.

Sighing in frustration, he applied his next touch more carefully. He drew the ears, the eyes, and a big round nose. When he had made the animal look as realistic as he could, he stood back to admire his artistry.

The dog didn't appear any happier than its human companion. Its features were misshapen and disjointed, like the poor animal had taken an almighty beating. In fact, as he studied it a bit longer, it didn't look like a dog at all. It didn't look like anything.

Hindsight, late as usual, told him it might have been better to leave the painting alone. He put the quill and the ink back on the desk, already planning a story in which a cat had found its way into the library. The nearest cat would probably get kicked to death, but that didn't bother Sean.

He skipped to the door—and suddenly found himself confronted with two long legs clad in riding breeches. He fell between them.

'What the blazes—' Randall gaped down. 'You ferret! What are you doing in here?'

Sean tried to wriggle through his feet, but Randall held him easily. 'Stay as you are, boy. What devilry are you at now?'

He did a quick survey of the library, searching for the inevitable mark of destruction. Then he stopped in dread. 'Oh Christ above...' He moved towards the painting, one hand maintaining a grip on Sean's collar. 'The Duke of Marlborough. Tell me you didn't, Sean. Lord God, tell me you didn't...'

The painting lay amid its crumpled heap of wrapping. There was a hole in the canvas, just above the Duke's right shoulder, where the letter opener had punctured it. Near the bottom it had been grossly defaced, an untidy mass of blotches and crude lines sketched with indian ink.

It was destroyed.

Randall closed his eyes.

Sean realised the futility of his struggling. Instead, he tried a little persuasion. 'I made a dog. Look.'

'You made a dog.' Randall gave an evil chuckle of despair and mounting fury. 'Oh, by God, you made a fucking dog all right!' He lunged out, grabbing Sean's shirt and yanking him off the ground; Sean squeaked in fright as Randall subdued him with a clap to the ear and sat himself on the armchair, dumping Sean on his lap.

'You brat!' he snarled. 'This is the last time you'll provoke me!'

He hauled Sean's breeches back and slapped his bare buttocks with such force that the sound echoed into the ceiling. Again and again he beat him, goaded into it more by the youngster's screams. Sean thrashed about in agony but was unable to free himself, and the sting of every blow made his body jolt straight like a tautened rope.

'...nineteen, twenty!' Randall finally ran out of energy. He pushed Sean off his lap and stood up, using his handkerchief to wipe his brow. Sean fell on his tummy with his hands clasping his reddened bottom. He was crying inconsolably.

'Let this be an end to it, boy,' Randall growled at him. 'This is what happens when you disobey me!'

Sean bawled in response, his tears flowing so copiously that they clogged his throat. He rolled away from Randall and tried to stand, but his breeches were still around his ankles and they made him fall over.

Randall guffawed in contempt. 'What a damn fool you are, boy!'

It was a heart-stopping sound: the scream of an imperilled child, the voice that was instantly recognisable. It made Orlaith start and dash from the bedroom with animal instinct, a mother sensing a predator near her offspring. Randall, she realised in dread, had caught Sean where he shouldn't be.

The scene inside the library brought her up short. 'No!' Sean was lying on the ground, weeping pitifully, breeches down and bottom slapped raw. For a moment she was too horrified to take it in.

'You can have him back now.' Randall stood nearby, re-fixing his cuffs. 'A pretty penny he's cost me today. Look!' He pointed to the ruined portrait. 'That's the Duke of Marlborough—or at least it used to be. Thirty pounds it cost, and another small fortune to have it shipped from London. And your brat has reduced it to firewood.'

Orlaith's anger was so much that it threatened to overwhelm her. With steady breaths she walked over to Sean and picked him up, lifting his breeches back in place. 'Go to your room now, sweetheart,' she whispered. 'I'll come to you in a moment.'

Sean let out a traumatised sob and waddled painfully from the room.

'You stay where you are, Orlaith.' Randall stepped in front of her, raising a finger in warning. 'You're going nowhere until I explain the rules of this house again—'

He never saw the attack coming. Turning with the speed of a leopardess, she grabbed a candelabrum and smashed it across his head, hitting him so hard that the lumps of wax flew like hailstones. Randall flinched and reeled backwards, grasping for the mantle. Before he could balance, she came after him, sunk her nails into his cheeks, and drove a knee into his testicles. The impact doubled him over and made him retch. In the next instant the pain swamped his whole mid-region, a vicious, hot flood of agony, immobilising his body so that he could only slump into a ball and groan.

Orlaith stood over his crumpled form, cheeks pink with rage. 'Randall Whiteley, the next time you lay a hand on my son, I swear I'll kill you. With my own bare hands I'll kill you. Do you understand?'

He whimpered in anguish, too crippled to answer. She aimed a wild kick that snapped his head back and split his lip, completing the lesson. With a sweep of her hair, she marched from the room and left him sprawled on the floor.

She knew that retribution would not be long in coming. An arrogant man, Randall would never allow such an affront to go unpunished. She expected him to come to her bedroom that night, in the dark hours, and give her a beating or inflict some other brutality in revenge. She stayed awake for hours fearing the worst, but Randall never came, and the following morning she rose puffy-eyed and tired.

They crossed paths when she brought Sean into the dining room for breakfast. Sean stiffened when he saw Randall, but Orlaith sat him at the table, making a point of not showing fear. 'You must eat your food now, Sean, and then you may go out to play.'

She was surprised to see Randall, as he rarely ate breakfast. There was a dark purple bruise on his cheekbone and his lip was swollen, but he looked relaxed and unruffled. He even smiled when they sat down. 'Kathy's done some kippers this morning,' he told them. 'They're rather good, actually. Perhaps Sean would like some?'

'He can't eat fish so early in the morning. It upsets his tummy.'

'Ah.' Randall nodded in understanding and returned to his food. The three of them ate in silence for a few minutes. Sean had a bowl of oatmeal while Orlaith contented herself with bread and marmalade. Then Randall spoke again.

'Gus is back in the stables, by the way.'

Sean's ears pricked up.

Gus was an eighteen-hand thoroughbred, the offspring of an Arabian stallion and an English mare that Randall had bought some months previously. He had spent only a week at the estate before Randall loaned him to a stud farm in Tipperary, but in that time Sean was captivated. He had spent hours watching him strut around the paddock, tossing his silver mane arrogantly and blowing out his nostrils. Inevitably he was heartbroken when they took Gus away.

This morning's news already had Sean scrambling to finish his breakfast. He wolfed down lumps of it, almost choking in his haste, which drew a sharp rebuke from his mother.

'Slow down! Eat properly, or you shall not leave this table.'

Randall chuckled. 'Oh, let the boy be, Orlaith. He's excited. It will be a treat for him to see Gus again.' He was showing no ill feeling from the previous day's incident, and Orlaith didn't like this. Randall wasn't one to simply forgive and forget.

'He'll finish his breakfast first,' she said firmly.

Sean pushed away the bowl of oatmeal. 'Yuck, it's poo! I want to see Gus!' He was too agitated to eat now. She knew a tantrum was brewing.

'Finish it,' she warned, 'otherwise you'll see no horse today, and I'll—'

'Come now, Orlaith,' Randall intervened smoothly. 'He can eat later. Can't you see the poor boy is all in a tizzy?' He came round the table and beamed. 'What do you say, Sean? Will we say hello to Gus? Would you like that?'

All of Sean's animosity towards Randall evaporated in that instant. He clapped his hands. 'Yes, now, go now!'

Laughing excitedly, they departed the room together, Sean knocking a chair in his enthusiasm. Orlaith tried to stop them, but she was ignored as the pair of them headed off for the stables.

She fumed. Randall had worked that well. In a single manoeuvre, not only had he won Sean's trust back, but he had managed to spark friction between mother and son, which would doubtless work to his own advantage. Yet there had to be more to it than that. Ironically, she would have been relieved by a beating, for a beating was something normal. What wasn't normal was Randall playing the role of indulgent father around her son.

He had to be watched. He was up to something. The thought of it unsettled her stomach, and she pushed her breakfast away with a sigh.

Sean enjoyed his morning tremendously. Not only did he meet Gus and help to groom his coat, but Randall had another treat in store. He allowed Sean to sit in the saddle while he led Gus around the paddock on a halter, and Sean couldn't contain himself. He laughed and squealed as Randall coaxed the horse into a canter, and Randall had to hold him in place with his free hand to prevent him sliding off the saddle.

Sean had a hearty appetite by the time they were finished. Randall told the kitchen to send out a basket of cheese and biscuits, and they ate together under the oak trees, a shared blanket over their shoulders to protect them from the chilly temperatures.

'You're a good horseman, Sean,' Randall told him as they watched Gus nosing around the frozen clumps of grass.

The youngster's face lit up with pleasure. 'Can I ride him by myself? When I'm big?'

'When you're big, you may ride him on your own. But not just yet.' He lowered his voice. 'Your mother says you can't ride him alone. Promise me you won't?'

'I promise!' Sean nodded impulsively, anxious to please.

'You are very good with Gus, and I know he likes you, but your mother would only get annoyed. You know that, don't you, Sean?'

But Sean's eyes were already wandering to the open door of the stables where the saddles and bridles were stored. 'Yes, I know,' he said absently.

Randall saw the direction of Sean's gaze. He smiled and patted the boy's head.

⚜ ⚜ ⚜

For four days Sean perched himself on his windowsill and stared across the courtyard to where the stables were. Four torturous, trying days in which Randall never kept his promise to let him see Gus again. By now Sean was exasperated. He failed to see why he had to be supervised anyway. Gus liked him. Randall had said so. Randall also said he was a good horseman.

So why such fussing? He could manage Gus by himself, and even sneak him a few treats from the kitchen. Gus would love that.

'Sean?' His mother's voice hailed him from below. 'I'm going for a walk. Won't you come?'

He purposely didn't answer, and when she came to check on him, he pressed his face into the pillow, feigning sleep. She pulled the blanket around him.

'Sean is sleeping,' she told Kathy downstairs. 'I'm going for a short walk.'

The front door closed.

Sean peered out and saw her walking under the sculpted archway that led into the lawns. Good riddance. With a sly eye he turned his attention back to the stables. The horses were in their pens, awaiting the groom to set them loose in the paddock.

There was time for a quick visit, he felt. A dash over, a hello to Gus, and then he would leave. Where was the harm in that? He went downstairs and slipped past the dining room, where Kathy was polishing the mahogany, and in the kitchen he observed the younger servant girls preparing lunch. They paid him little notice, being used to his presence about the house.

Unseen by them, he opened the teak cupboard in the corner and rummaged through the shelves. He found coffee beans, tea leaves, cloves, syrup, pepper, and to his satisfaction, a half-full bag of sugar cubes. He stuffed some of the cubes into his pocket, replaced the bag, and scurried out before his thieving was spotted.

Gus would be delighted.

Coolly he trotted outside, palm clamped discreetly across his pocket to prevent the sugar falling out. On the steps he did a quick check. No mother, and no Randall. The way was clear.

The courtyard was slick with snow and trampled mud. He tiptoed across it and put his hand on the stable door. It creaked, and a nervous snort sounded from somewhere within.

'It's me, Gus,' he said calmly, stepping inside. Again the horse snorted noisily and stamped its hoof in agitation.

'I brought you sweets,' Sean said. 'Do you want them?'

Gus was inside his pen and backed away warily when he saw Sean.

'Don't be silly, Gus.' Sean tried to dismiss the animal's fears. 'Look, I brought you nice sweets, and you can eat them now.'

Gus was getting flustered, heaving his great bulk about like a caged lion. A skittish, distrusting animal by nature, he didn't like the presence of this stranger inside his space.

Slipping into the pen, Sean rummaged in his pocket, dug out a fistful of sugar cubes, and thrust them towards the horse's face.

'Here!'

This sudden movement startled Gus. He whinnied and reared up on his hind legs, his front hooves missing Sean's head by inches. Sean staggered back, losing his footing and landing on his bottom. He let out a scream, and the sound of his voice goaded Gus into greater panic. He kicked his hind legs against the stable panels with such force that the entire structure shook. Driven into a wild state now, he bucked and thrashed, desperate to distance himself from the intruder. Again he kicked at the panels, and there was an audible crack as the wood splintered.

Sean was writhing on the ground, the giant hooves impacting just inches from his body. A blow from one of them, driven by Gus's immense weight, would be enough to stave in his ribcage or split his skull in two. He tried to crawl to safety, but the maddened animal was throwing itself about, and Sean didn't know which way to move. He cried out, 'Stop it, Gus, please! Don't hurt me!'

Randall was smoking by the fire when he heard the patter of the little boy's feet in the lobby. Looking out the window he saw Sean ambling off towards the stables, and he grinned. The lad had finally yielded to temptation, as Randall knew he would. Children were so predictable and so easily manipulated. Taking a puff on his cigar, he hovered by the window and waited.

Within moments of Sean entering the pens, Randall heard an almighty clamour erupt. He knew Gus's character—he had all the strength and aggression of a thoroughbred stallion, and he was a volatile animal who would only submit under the most experienced of hands. The sight of this chattering little menace inside his pen was sure to inflame his temper.

The stable shook with the force of one of Gus's kicks, and Sean could be heard screaming within. Randall blew a wreath of smoke and settled down on the windowsill to listen.

CHAPTER ELEVEN

Orlaith was wandering the wooded banks of the lake when the noise reached her. She quickly tossed the flowers from her hand and broke into a run, hearing screams penetrate the thuds and bangs. The land below the house was on a gradient, and it was a testing climb to the top. She was out of breath as she searched for the disturbance; in the stables one of the horses was kicking up a furious racket, pounding the insides of its pen and whinnying in confusion. The screams, of course, were Sean's.

'I'm coming!' She dashed across the courtyard.

Suddenly the stable door burst open and the groom emerged, cradling Sean in his arms.

'Sean!'

'It's all right, ma'am,' the man forestalled her. 'I managed to get him out. He just gave old Gussy a scare is all.'

She scooped Sean from his arms and set him down, running her hands over his body to feel for injury.

'Mammy,' Sean wailed, 'I don't like the horse.'

'I know, Sean.' She turned to the groom. 'God bless you for that.'

He smiled and went on his way. Orlaith took a moment to compose herself. Once satisfied that Sean had escaped unmarked, she raised her tone reprovingly. 'What were you doing in the stables, Sean? You are forbidden—'

'Typical.' Before she could finish, Randall's voice interrupted them both. Orlaith turned and saw him strolling across, hands in his pockets. 'It's just typical. Tell the boy to do one thing, and he does the opposite. He's lucky he didn't get his brainless head knocked off there.'

Orlaith blushed. 'I'm sorry, I thought he was asleep. I didn't mean to leave him long.'

'Damned irresponsible. He could have been killed. Would have served him right, though—I've never known such a disobedient child.'

'I'm sorry. It won't happen again. He's safe—that's all that matters.'

'Well, he must be punished. He's upset my horse and probably the other horses too. I can't have it.'

'Your horses are fine, Randall,' she answered. 'It's Sean you should be worried about.'

'If Gus is hurt, there'll be hell to pay. I could hear him kicking the panels from the house. He might have damaged himself.'

'You heard from the house?' She stared at him, confused. 'But I had to run up from the lake. How did I get here before you?'

He smiled, saying nothing.

'Oh, you bastard!' Her face flushed with sudden anger. 'You bastard, Randall Whiteley! My son was in danger of his life, and you did nothing. What in heaven's name were you thinking?'

'Orlaith,' he said quietly, moving towards her, 'let this be a lesson. You saw fit to assault me in my own home, and you thought you could get away with it? You stupid bitch. This will remind you who is in charge. Your son is at my mercy every hour, every day.'

Her face paled at his words.

'That's right, accidents can happen on a busy estate like this. Especially with a child around. The worry is you can't watch them all the time. It's always that brief instant when your back is turned that something dreadful is likely to happen.' He nodded gravely. 'Yes, you might remember that, Orlaith.'

As he walked away, Orlaith slumped to her knees. Tears of exhaustion began to flow down her cheeks. 'Come here,' she whispered, embracing Sean to her chest. 'No one is going to hurt you, Sean. You're safe. I promise.'

She gave it much thought that evening. It was sinister. If Randall hadn't quite forced Sean inside the stables, he had certainly orchestrated the incident. This made one thing horridly clear—her husband was willing to see her child injured or even killed simply to enforce his authority. Orlaith knew she couldn't blind herself to it. She had to confront him.

Once Sean was asleep, she made her way down to the drawing room, where Randall was reclining on an armchair, brandy in hand.

'My dear, is something wrong?' he asked in mock surprise. 'Not like you to join me of an evening. May I pour you a sherry?'

She sat on the walnut chair opposite him. 'We must talk, Randall.'

'I see. Sounds intriguing.'

'Randall, your actions today prove how much you must resent our presence in your home. So I've decided to put your mind at ease. I will take Sean away from here, for good. We will trouble you no more. All I ask of you is a small contribution, enough to travel to Dublin perhaps, or England, and something to live on until we get settled.' She took a deep breath. 'Is this a reasonable request?'

His smile faded. Carefully he set his brandy down and leaned forward on the armchair. 'Do you take me for a fool?'

'What?'

'Do you think, for one moment, I'll let you humiliate me like that? Desert me in front of the entire county? Are you out of your mind?'

'Randall, I would be doing you a favour—'

'Damn your favours, Orlaith! I'll not have my own wife put me to shame. Your place is here, and it will always be so. We're married. You're mine.' The potential embarrassment of losing another wife was only partly the reason for Randall's refusal. Mostly he couldn't suppress his jealousy, couldn't stomach the thought of her ending up with another man, like his first wife had.

'Randall, you can't stop me.' She struck a defiant chord. 'If I choose to leave, there's nothing you can do. To hell with your pride. I am taking my son, and we are leaving this horrible place once and for all.'

He leapt to his feet suddenly, clenching his fists. Grabbing her hair, he thrust his face into hers and snarled, 'The only way you will ever leave this place, Orlaith, is in a wooden box. You and that brat of yours. By God, I promise it.'

'You don't frighten me, Randall,' she stammered.

'Two wooden boxes, Orlaith. A big box and a small box, side by side. I'll put roses on top of yours, the kind you like. What kind shall I put on Sean's?' When she didn't answer, he smiled again. 'There you have it, then. I trust things are now clearer? Good girl.' He pulled her face forward and kissed her roughly on the mouth. His breath stank, and she recoiled from him.

'Get off me!'

Wiping the spittle from his lips, he said, 'This is your home, Orlaith. Forever. Accept it and be grateful.'

She pushed past him and fumbled her way to the door. Randall grinned, pleased with himself. At last he had learned how to treat a wife. Orlaith would respect him for this in time; she would put aside her selfishness and become a more devoted spouse, and thus the marriage would not founder like before. He eased himself back into the armchair and returned to his brandy with relish.

Orlaith went instinctively to Sean's bed, her hands trembling as she lifted the eiderdown and climbed in. She couldn't let him sleep alone tonight.

Randall's threat was not a bluff. She knew he meant every word of it. It was time to escape—before it was too late. But to where?

Nowhere in the surrounding area would be safe. Randall's thugs would find them. Even in the next village they would be recognised, and word would filter back to Dromkeen Hall before long. They had to go further than that, as far as Cork City if they could reach it. It would be easier to hide in the city. In time she could arrange for passage to Dublin, and if they made it that far, Randall would never find them.

The messenger who brought news of the captives had also spoken of the people ransoming them, the order of monks in Dublin negotiating personally with the slave owners. What had he called them—the Mercedarians? She could seek them out. If anyone could help her with Brannon's rescue, it was them. But of course it wasn't that simple. She had no means of transport and no money to survive on. With Sean she wouldn't be able to move very fast. And if the escape attempt failed, well, the Lord alone knew what kind of wrath she would bring down on herself. Randall's retaliation would be merciless.

She tried to think it through step by step. Leaving the estate itself would not be difficult. They could do it at night, when Randall was in one of his drink-induced comas and everyone else was asleep. On the road in the dead of night, however, there was only so far they would get. She could have sought Jack Dunphy's help, but he was working in Limerick and wouldn't return until summer. Cork City itself was thirty-five miles away, too far to walk. Once their absence was discovered, they would be pursued on horseback, a chase that would be over very quickly. Walking was therefore not an option.

They needed a horse. Orlaith knew the horses on the estate; she had observed their handling and even ridden them on occasion. She wasn't an experienced hand, but she reckoned she could manage one. Sally, perhaps, the mare that Randall liked to ride in the hills. Sally was a docile creature, quick to submit and easy to control. She would recognise Orlaith's voice.

There was a carriage in the stable, light but big enough to carry both herself and Sean and whatever meagre luggage they brought. It was an elegant model, two wheels and an open top, referred to as a whiskey carriage because of its ability to 'whisk' along. She hadn't a clue how to harness it, but she could figure that out over the coming days. With a horse and carriage, they could make it all the way to Cork City in a matter of hours, before daylight came, before anyone knew they were gone.

Then there was the matter of money. Not only did she desperately need to raise Brannon's ransom, but she would also have to acquire food and shelter. Randall didn't allow her any money of her own, and without it the journey was hopeless. She had to have money. But how?

She thought about it hard. Randall was a wealthy man, but he kept little in cash. Estate bills were usually settled by promissory notes that could be drawn on any of his accounts in Cork, Dublin, or London. The bulk of his resources were tied up in business ventures, everything from mink pelts to pineapples. It would be impossible to get her hands on that. If she asked him for money, it would merely raise his suspicion and land her in even more trouble. Yet there had to be some way…

Then an idea formed.

There was the rent money. Percy Gray collected it from the tenants once a month, and then it was bagged at the estate and the ledgers updated. Randall normally stored it in a safe overnight, and in the morning it would be transported under armed guard to the bank in Cork City. Orlaith knew where the safe was—behind an oil painting of the Mourne Mountains inside the library. But she had no idea where he kept the key. It would never open without the key, not with anything short of a keg of explosives. But if she could find the key...

She could open it during the night, with the money all inside. She didn't know how much to expect, but perhaps as much as a hundred pounds. More than enough to survive on, and a substantial portion of Brannon's ransom too. The tenants wouldn't be robbed as their rent was officially paid once Percy Gray took the money at their doorsteps and made the mark in his book. It would be Randall's money she was stealing, and that didn't bother her conscience at all.

She began to feel a tingle of excitement. This was very much possible. With some careful planning and a strong stomach, she could pull it off. And it would mean so much—freedom from Randall's tyranny and, with God's help, Brannon's salvation, if she could find the Mercedarians. She was suddenly frustrated with herself, wishing she had thought of this all along. But it wasn't too late to try now.

❀ ❀ ❀

Padraig Welsh, Randall's stable groom, was feeling nicely puffed-up with self-importance. 'Horses is like children, you see,' he explained authoritatively. 'As in, you must have a care with them. But you must be firm too, so that they does what you tell them to do.'

Orlaith peered around the stable with appropriate awe. 'But they're so big and strong. Do they not make you nervous?'

He chuckled. 'Bless you, ma'am, you're only a woman. But a horse is easy managing—once you has its respect, like.'

'Oh, what's that?' she asked, pointing to the carriage as though noticing it for the first time.

'Ah, that's a handsome-looking yoke, isn't it? Cost the master a pretty penny, if you don't mind me saying, ma'am. But sure isn't he be-titled to ride in style?'

'Do you put it on the horse all by yourself, though? That must be hard work.'

'Not at all, ma'am, there's nothing to it. Anyway, do you want to go and see the other horses now?' He was warming to his new role, surprised but delighted by Orlaith's interest.

She pressed him on the carriage. 'I could never manage that by myself. How on earth does it work?'

He rolled up his sleeves purposefully. 'Allow me, ma'am.' He took her arm and led her to the carriage, reaching inside to pull out a bundle of links and leather straps. 'This is the harness. You slip it round the beast and fasten it to the carriage, then sit up in that seat, crack the reins, and you're off.'

'Could you show me?' she persisted, fluttering her eyelids hopefully.

'Of course!' Padraig brimmed with pleasure. With a spring in his step, he led one of the horses out of its pen and set about harnessing it to the carriage. It took him only minutes to accomplish the task, and Orlaith was relieved. It wasn't as complicated as she had feared.

'My goodness, Padraig, you're so clever.'

He nodded proudly. 'People does say I'm fierce smart, ma'am. I can make a duck sound with my voice for the hunts—do you want to hear it?' His mouth opened to commence a needling croon, but Orlaith stalled him.

'I'd love to sometime, but I've been such a nuisance. I will let you get on with your work.'

He was crestfallen. 'But there's more I can show you, ma'am. I'm terrible busy, of course, but if you really want me to…?'

She smiled at him. 'Next time, Padraig. I look forward to it.' She touched his arm affectionately as she left the stable.

'Any morning you want, ma'am,' he called after her eagerly. 'I wouldn't mind at all, like!'

She crossed the courtyard and went to the scullery where the laundry was stored, selecting a few items of her own and Sean's. Carrying them to Sean's bedroom, she then opened the rosewood cupboard in the corner and pulled out a canvas haversack half filled with clothes. There was nearly enough. She had to be discreet about it, otherwise the servants would wonder why so much laundry was going missing, and she was anxious not to draw attention. Sooner or later they would notice something amiss, but by then, hopefully, Orlaith and Sean would be long gone.

⊕ ⊕ ⊕

On Thursday morning Percy Gray arrived at Dromkeen Hall, his nose and ears red from the snow flurries and the blustery sea winds. Beside him rode Vincent Barry with a brace of pistols tucked into his belt, the normal safeguard when Percy was carrying Randall's rent money. In any case, the mere sight of Vincent's perpetually hateful expression was usually enough to ward off any would-be thieves.

Randall was in the drawing room when Percy presented himself. 'Ah, is that my good friend Percy Gray standing before me? It must be collection day, then. Dear Percival, you've brought a bagful of coppers for me to count, I suppose.'

Percy was feeling more relaxed than usual because this morning every tenant had paid up. That wasn't a regular thing; normally one or more families wouldn't have the money due to some mishap or misfortune or injury, which in turn would have Randall berating Percy for his ineptitude.

'A full debit this morning, sir,' Percy said with relief. 'There should be just over one hundred and fifty pounds in the bag, if my calculations haven't let me down.'

'Excellent, Percy,' Randall said, rubbing his hands. 'Now, a brandy before we start? That's nasty weather blowing out there.'

'Thank you, sir.' Percy moved towards the comforting blaze of the fire, letting it draw the January cold out of his legs. 'All is well, I trust? And Mrs Whiteley?'

Randall rolled his eyes. 'She's a woman, Percy. Since when was all well with a woman? You're a lucky bugger to have your Joan—a good, quiet woman who knows how to behave herself.'

Percy blushed. 'Yes, sir.'

'Oh, now, that reminds me.' Randall cleared his throat. 'I have a slight problem, Percy. Do you know that Slattery girl—Con Slattery's daughter?'

Percy cast his mind back. 'You mean Siobháin? That girl you had up here?'

'No, the younger one. Siobháin's sister. What's her name, damn it…'

'That's Mairéad. About sixteen, is she? What of her?'

'Well, she's kicking up no end of a fuss at the moment. It appears she's, em, up the flagpole, so to speak.'

'What? Pregnant?' Percy was appalled. 'I didn't realise you had Mairéad too, sir.'

'Now steady on, Percy, I don't even know if the whelp's mine. That little strumpet has probably bedded every lubber in Dromkeen, brazen trollop that she is. The point is, she's bleating bloody murder about it to me, and I can't have that. I've enough problems to deal with.'

'And what exactly do you want me to do, sir?'

Randall lowered his eyes. Even he felt embarrassed. 'The Slatterys are behind on their rent, aren't they?'

'No, sir. In fact, they have a superb record. The most consistent payers on the roll, to be quite honest.'

'Are they?' Randall sipped at his brandy. He took a moment to pace over the floor, but he quickly became agitated. 'Oh, just get rid of them, Percy. I don't care what excuses you use, just turf them out. I want Mairéad Slattery away from me as fast as possible—let her make her mischief elsewhere. Can you do that?'

'Evict them, sir? Even though they have paid their rent? Hardly a noble course.'

'Why not, damn it?' Randall's temper rose. 'It's my land, and I want them gone. Give them some money, and tell them go to Clonakilty or Skibbereen, or the city. Anywhere but here. Just get rid of them, man!'

Percy sighed inwardly. He knew that, despite his own protestations, he would inevitably go along with Randall's orders. Randall gave both him and his wife a nice living, and Percy was too comfortable with that to allow any moral objections to interfere. 'I'm sure it can be arranged, sir. If that's your pleasure.'

'Good.' Randall nodded and lowered himself into his armchair. 'I need to run a tight ship here, Percy. Things would fall asunder otherwise.' He recharged his brandy glass. 'Right, back to business. You start sorting those coins, and let me look through that paper of yours.'

It took just over an hour for Randall to satisfy himself that the money in the bag matched the records on Percy's ledger. Then they bagged the lot and sealed it.

'Nesbitt will be here at the usual time tomorrow?' Randall asked.

'Seven o'clock, sir. As always.' Bill Nesbitt was the bank official who collected the money and escorted it to the city with his armed protectorate. He was a stiff-lipped, punctilious native of Belfast who took his job very seriously and whom Randall trusted implicitly.

'Almost done.' Randall went to the corner of the drawing room, shifted the bookcase a few inches forward, and pulled up the end of carpet beneath. He picked at the wooden floorboard until it came loose, and with his other hand he reached into the hole and retrieved a large metal key. Then he replaced the floorboard and carpet, moved the bookcase back into place, and nodded to Percy.

'If you'll follow me to the library, please.'

Percy knew the procedure by now. He downed the rest of his brandy and closed the door behind them.

In the sudden quietness of the drawing room, the french curtains twitched and billowed as a figure emerged from behind them.

Orlaith took a deep breath, her pulse racing. She had been convinced she would be caught, that Randall would spot her cowering behind the curtains. In order to conceal herself behind them she had to release their holders, and it was only pure luck that Randall hadn't noticed this sign of untidiness.

She was giddy with relief now, and excitement. She had seen him open the compartment underneath the bookcase, his secret hiding place for the key. That meant tonight she could make her move. Quickly she fixed the curtains and hurried from the room. The hallway was quiet; she gathered her skirts and scampered up the stairs, smiling now with the success of her scheme.

Randall's money wouldn't be secure for long. She was one step ahead of him, and everything was going according to plan. In a matter of hours, they would have their freedom.

The air was sharp that night when she crept out to the stables. Padraig Welsh had gone home hours ago, and the estate grounds were quiet. She carried a lantern but didn't light it yet, not wanting to draw attention from the windows. A pale moon shone through the wisps of cloud as she crossed the wet cobblestone and undid the latch of the stable door. Inside she heard movement in the darkness.

'Good girl, Sally,' she murmured. The mare approached her tentatively. Orlaith lit the lantern, and a weak orange light fell over the damp stable. There was a smell of hay and oakwood. Taking a halter from a hook on the panelling, she slipped it around the horse's head and led her down towards the carriage.

Padraig had made it look easy, but alone in the dark it was daunting. Sally stood obediently while she fumbled with the links, trying to figure out where each piece went. After fifteen minutes of nervous effort, her hands trembling in the cold, she was satisfied that everything had been connected to something else.

'You must wait here,' she told Sally. 'I'll be back for you later.' The horse seemed to nod acquiescence, and Orlaith made her way back inside the house.

Eight o'clock. Bedtime for Sean. He had been lying by the fire and leafing through a picture book of African animals, but he was yawning now.

'Three more yawns,' he pleaded, trying to delay the moment of his bedroom banishment.

'Now, Sean,' she said firmly.

She didn't undress him but merely placed his shoes by the bed so that he could be ready to leave in a hurry. The bag of clothes was in the cupboard, full now.

Randall had been gone all evening, which was a relief. Hopefully he would be drinking somewhere, playing cards and enjoying himself enough not to come home. Yet she wouldn't dare open the safe until the small hours, when everyone else was asleep. She told Kathy that she was feeling unwell and going to bed early, which would allow her a few hours' rest before her plan swung into action. After that, she didn't know when she might have the chance to rest again.

⊕ ⊕ ⊕

The night was achingly long. The clock on the dresser ticked as tediously as a dripping tap, each sound amplified in the silence of the room. Orlaith lay on the bed and stared into the shadows, listening to the servants padding about on the wooden floors below. The last of them blew out the candles just before midnight and retired to their own quarters.

She let an hour slide by. Too early yet to risk it. She waited and listened and fretted, her mind already travelling the route she would take through the darkened house. One more hour should be enough. One more hour and she would leave the bedroom to execute her plan while everybody else slept in oblivion.

Then, to her profound dismay, she heard the front door open.

Randall was home.

She cursed her luck. If he went into the drawing room and started drinking, she wouldn't be able to get to the key. And the rent money would be gone in the morning. The thought of having to wait another whole month was unbearable.

But Randall wasn't alone. She heard a woman's voice, and by the sound of it they were both drunk. Orlaith wasn't surprised. She had heard herself his conversation about getting Mairéad Slattery pregnant. It wasn't unusual for members of the landed class to have several mistresses on the side, with the full assent of their wives. It was often the only thing that held their marriages together. And quite frankly, Orlaith was delighted for every minute that another woman might take him away from her.

Tonight, however, it was a huge inconvenience. They went to one of the guest bedrooms, the woman tripping in the doorway and then erupting into hysterics at the hilarity of it. The annoying laughter and moans of sexual rhapsody didn't let up for a long time, and Orlaith worried that they might last all night at this rate. But finally they tired of their games. After a while the laughter stopped, and she could hear the hacksaw sound of Randall's snoring. She stayed put for a few minutes and then tiptoed out on the landing.

Four o'clock. The night had passed quickly in the end. She crept downstairs and made for the drawing room. It was cold in here, the fire reduced to a few faintly glowing embers. Taking a minute to compose herself, she gazed around the room. Slowly her eyes adjusted. She moved to the bookcase and placed her hands around its edges; it looked heavy, but it yielded to her efforts, giving a slight creak that made her cringe in dread. But no one came.

She prised up the loose floorboard and retrieved the key. It was surprisingly big. Quickly she left the drawing room, crossed the lobby, and went into the library. Once she had removed the oil painting, she tried the safe. To her relief, it opened without fuss. The rent takings were there, next to some wax-sealed envelopes and a yellowing sheaf of documents. She took up the bag, closed the safe, and replaced the painting. Then she froze.

There was a light in the lobby, its flickering beam cast from the corridor that led to the kitchen. In the uncertain luminosity she saw the black shadow of a man, advancing this way with measured footsteps. Her throat went dry.

In panic she flew across the lobby, scampered into the drawing room, and crouched behind the furthest armchair with the bag in her hand. The wavering light grew brighter. He was coming this way. Where was she supposed to go? She bit her lip and crouched lower down, heart racing in terror.

The light stopped moving. He stood at the drawing room door and peered inside. From her hiding spot Orlaith could see his face—Vincent, Randall's big ape of a security guard. She feared him almost as much as she did Randall.

Vincent was an ugly man with a misshapen nose and sharp, beady eyes. He began his search of the room, checking the windows and curtains, under the tables and chairs, moving gradually closer to where Orlaith was only barely concealed. She held her breath.

Vincent stopped.

Someone had moved the bookshelf out of position. Devilry afoot, he realised. With his hand clasping the knife on his belt, he turned from the room, intent on summoning the whole house with a bellow to root out the intruder. Orlaith knew she couldn't let him go. He couldn't be allowed to ruin everything.

Unseen, she rose from the shadows. Lifting a large alabaster vase from a side table, she stepped out from the armchair, crept up behind Vincent, and smashed the vase down over his head. It exploded on impact, and Vincent stumbled in shock, his eyes spinning from the blow. He turned, for a moment unable to register his attacker. Then like a wounded beast he snarled and fought back, reaching for her with his massive shovel-hands. In that instant she knew she hadn't hit him hard enough.

He grabbed her throat and spat, pushing her to the ground with brute strength. She gasped, unable to breathe. 'Bitch!' he hissed as she clawed at his face. He gave her a hard slap and began to drag her across the floor. 'We've got you now, you double-crossing Taig bitch!' She couldn't break free. His strength was immense.

But the vase had done more damage than they realised. Vincent suddenly seemed to falter and lose his way; his grip on Orlaith slackened, his eyes rolled, and he spluttered once before collapsing like a rotten tree on the ground. In the lantern light Orlaith saw blood in his hair. He was out cold.

Shaken and out of breath, she gathered up the money and ran for Sean's bedroom. Those noises would probably have woken the house. Sean squealed as she bundled him up, and she pressed a finger to his lips. 'Shh!' She grabbed their clothes and hurried downstairs, almost tripping under the heavy load. Still no one challenged her.

It was bitterly cold outside. Reaching the stables, she tossed the money and the clothes into the carriage, and then she pushed Sean up. He was coming more awake and starting to complain vociferously, but there was no time to placate him. She flung the stable doors open, climbed onto the carriage, and cracked the reins. The horse kicked into movement, and the carriage rattled across the courtyard.

A howling sea gale battered them once they were past the gates. She followed the coast road, along the wild cliffs where the waves boomed in the darkness. The beach remained in shadow, but there was a long, shimmering strip of moonlight out on the water. The only other visible lights came from the ships in the bay. Orlaith glanced behind her, but no one followed. It was ten miles to the highway that would bring them to Cork City.

They drove on. After an hour's travel, a rim of pearl appeared above the eastern horizon, the first fledgling light of dawn. Gradually the light spread across the sea and gave shape to the dark hills and fields. The sun rose like a god from the waves, infusing the water with whorls of blue and gold and green, though the puddles on the road stayed frozen as the gusts raked the landscape with icy claws.

Then things began to go wrong.

One of the traces slipped and fell loose. The carriage bucked violently, swinging onto one wheel and tipping to the side. Orlaith screamed, thinking they would be thrown clear. It managed to correct itself but continued to bounce wildly as it was pulled out of balance. The horse felt the disturbance and slowed, but the whole carriage was slipping away, and Orlaith knew she hadn't harnessed it properly. She pulled on the reins, and finally everything came to a stop.

Sean let out a wail.

The carriage was detached on the right side. If they had continued much further, it would probably have toppled over, killing them both. She closed her eyes in exasperation, ruing the precious time lost. The traces needed to be reattached as fast as possible.

This time it took longer. The freezing air had rendered her hands stiff and useless, and her mind was groggy from tiredness. It seemed a monumental task to re-harness the horse. Half an hour slipped by, and still they were stranded at the side of the road.

'Just a few more minutes, love,' she told Sean. He was perched miserably on the seat, his face raw from the biting wind. She retrieved another blanket for him and folded it around his shivering body, making him lie flat so that the sides would shelter him. Then she returned to fixing the traces.

There was a sudden rumble of hooves from the hillside. She stared up, her mouth opening in shock. They appeared over a crest, three horsemen silhouetted against the pink sky, thundering down an old cattle track that sloped to the road.

'No!' she cried. They were no more than half a mile away. She grabbed the bag of money in one hand and took Sean in the other, and then she fought a path through the briars growing along the cliff. A number of paths meandered down to the shore, and she followed one, slipping in the mud on the way. On the beach the tide was advancing steadily, and the wet sand sucked at her shoes. Sean cried out at the salty sting of the wind.

'You must be quiet, Sean,' she urged him desperately. 'They're coming. Don't make a sound!'

A wave slid up the beach, sparkling in the pale sunlight as she splashed through the foam. Several craggy sea stacks stood out ahead, the only possible concealment on the exposed shore. She made her way between them, the freezing water surging around her hips and making her gasp. Sean buried his face in her chest and used her coat to wipe the spray from his eyes. She glanced back to the cliff.

Three men—she recognised them as Dromkeen's constable with his two subordinates—were descending the path. They spread out across the beach, calling to each other, though she couldn't hear them above the relentless crash of the waves. Two moved in the opposite direction, but one came towards her. She edged further behind the sea stacks, venturing perilously deep into the cold water. If she lost her footing here, she wouldn't be able to recover, not with Sean clinging on like a dead weight. She put a hand on the barnacled rock to steady herself.

The man gazed across the waves, shielding his eyes against the strengthening sunlight. The tide continued to advance and swirled around his legs. He shivered, disgruntled. 'Nothing!' he yelled up the beach.

One of the others gesticulated towards the sea stacks. '...behind those rocks!' His voice carried faintly on the wind.

The man blasphemed and waded deeper into the sea. He had a pistol in his belt, but he removed it now to prevent the powder getting wet. He peered behind one stack and then another, blinking against the coils of spray.

Orlaith held her breath. She was at the second-outermost rock and could go no deeper without drowning. If the man came this far, he would find her.

He seemed to be debating it. He stared at the last two stacks, balancing himself against the heave of the tide. Each lap of cold water against his skin was like a thousand pricking needles. He strained his ears, hoping to hear something.

Orlaith pressed herself against the far side of the rock. Even Sean kept quiet, as though sensing the very real danger they were in.

'Hell with it,' the man snorted. He turned and began to flounder his way back to the beach, and Orlaith breathed a sigh of relief.

Sean was rubbing his nose, the salt stinging the sensitive insides of his nostrils. His mouth opened slightly, and before Orlaith realised what he was about to do, he sneezed.

The man stopped dead in the water.

He wasn't sure what he had heard. Cocking the pistol, he hesitated for a minute. The sea was a myriad of noises, splashing and tumbling and bubbling. He gazed at the big stacks, standing solemnly like ancient guardians, eddies curling around their edges. The thought of wading back into that icy current did not appeal at all.

There's no one there, he decided. He moved back to the beach and scampered gratefully from the water, shaking himself off like a dog.

Orlaith placed her hand over Sean's mouth to muffle him. The three men were abandoning their search and making their way back to the cliffs. She waited a few minutes until sure it was safe, and then she struggled back onto the sand. Their teeth were chattering now. She needed to get them both into dry clothes soon. To her sheer relief, the bag of money was still clutched between her fingers.

Up on the cliffs she saw the carriage sitting abandoned by the roadside. The clothes bag was still inside, but they had taken Sally, and thus the carriage was now useless to her. She changed their clothes. It remained wretchedly cold, and Sean huddled inside his tiny coat, bewildered by the goings-on.

'Mammy,' he pleaded miserably, 'I want to go home.'

'No!' she said fiercely. 'We're not going home.' Then, a little gentler, she said, 'We can't go home, Sean. We must go on.'

He was too tired to complain. She wrapped him in the blanket and placed him in her arms, and then she turned to the road and began to walk. Mists followed them in the fields to their left where specks of sheep cluttered the hillside. She kept a vigilant eye up there, worried that Randall's henchmen would be combing the tracks. Her bones ached; Sean seemed heavier than usual, and after a half hour she had to stop. She rested for a while on a grassy bank and hugged Sean to her side. He cried weakly, but then he became quiet, as if the effort of crying was simply too much.

She wondered how much further they had left. It felt like they had made good progress during the night, before the carriage let them down. But it could be another twenty miles at least. She didn't know if she had the strength to walk that far.

A faint sound reached her ears.

She grabbed Sean instinctively, preparing to rise. It was the rumble of wheels, coming from around a bend in the road. Almost dropping Sean in panic, she searched desperately for somewhere to hide, but the beach couldn't be reached from here. The slopes opposite the cliffs bore only ragged vegetation, offering scant concealment, and the nearest trees were about a mile away.

She was too slow.

A large, canopy-roofed carriage came thundering over a hump in the road, pulled by two storming horses. It was headed to run them over, but at the last second the driver hauled frantically on the reins. 'Whoa, Jesus!'

The horses reared and protested but managed to slow their flying hooves. The carriage ground to a halt, hurling a cloud of dust into their eyes.

'God's bones!' the driver cursed. The quick stop had almost thrown him from his perch. 'Jesus, missy, I nearly knocked you down flat there. Good God, you've got a child too. Another few seconds and I'd have squashed you both.'

Orlaith let out a gasp. She had thought them dead for sure. 'I'm sorry, sir, I'm so sorry. I didn't see you coming.'

The driver gave a sigh and blessed himself. 'Very well, missy. You take care.' He nodded and made ready to strike off again, but then the carriage door opened and a middle-aged, well-dressed man leaned out.

'Madam,' he said in shock, 'are you all right? Oh my dear, I do apologise.' He seemed genuinely concerned. 'Are you hurt? Is there anything I can do?'

'We're both fine.' Orlaith smiled weakly. 'We were on our way to the city.'

'Walking? By yourselves?' He was appalled at the notion. 'Madam, I couldn't permit it. Far too dangerous for a mother and child on these highways. Please,' he said, gesturing for her to come forward, 'let us bring you the rest of the way. The city is not far.'

Orlaith hesitated. She had no idea who this man was. 'Um, that's very kind, but—'

'Come now, madam. Your son is blue with the cold. Climb inside, both of you.' He stepped out and held the door open.

Orlaith peered in. There was a woman in there also, presumably the man's wife, and she made way for them on the leather seating.

'You poor thing, do sit down. No sense in walking when we have the car, dearie. Now,' she said to Sean, 'I bet you like chocolate biscuits, no? All boys like chocolate biscuits.'

Sean licked his lips.

The driver cracked the reins, and the carriage moved off again.

CHAPTER TWELVE

The wind blew all that morning and buffeted the outside of the carriage, but within the sheltered confines of the cabin they were kept warm. Orlaith had a glass of wine with some cheese while Sean was given milk and biscuits. They laughed and chatted with their hosts, and the day sped by almost unnoticed. The man introduced himself as John Beadle. He was a garrulous sort, and he tried to engage her in a range of issues.

'Frightful business in France, isn't it? A bloodbath, according to the reports coming out. Mobs on the rampage and aristocrats being slaughtered in the streets.'

'Now, dear, not in front of the child,' Mrs Beadle hushed him.

Orlaith wondered what they made of her. Her attire, though crumpled, was of fine quality and looked expensive. They obviously believed her of genteel breeding, otherwise they probably wouldn't have offered her a lift.

They covered nearly twenty miles by midmorning, and now they were passing small farms and villages half sunk in reed swamps, which marked the outskirts of the city. Every time they encountered another coach or rider, Orlaith withdrew into the darkness of the cabin in case it should be Randall's henchmen scouring the highways. But no one stopped them.

They came up a long, climbing road, and here they had a view that stretched as far as the harbour. Cork City sat amid a patchwork of marsh islands, just beyond which the two arms of the river Lee converged into one broad channel that flowed eastwards into the sea. The carriage followed the winding track past old escarpments and sloblands until it reached the belching chimneys of the cotton mills where the city's pulsing civilisation began.

The streets were loud and stank of the city's meat trade, a tangy, putrid smell of carcasses and offal. In the city centre the buildings were green with lichen growth, people were gathering rainwater from low rooftops to drink, and beggars skulked in dark alleys. At the wharves there were ships moored, big ships that were able to travel right into the heart of the city because of the river's depth. Barrels of salted beef, pork, and butter were being hoisted into ship-holds to be transported to Great Britain, Europe, and the Americas. Exports to North America had fallen ever since the colonies were lost, but Cork thrived on being a chief supplier of provisions to the Royal Navy, particularly now with France beating revolutionary drums across the water.

Orlaith found the city a distasteful place. There were too many people, too much activity, and it was far too dirty. Red-faced women in moth-eaten shawls stood behind vegetables stalls and squawked at passers-by. Barefoot urchins frolicked in the murky marsh water that swamped the streets. On the footpath a drunken man staggered, swigging from a bottle of brown glass while trying to fend off a clergyman intent on saving him.

The Beadles were headed for Sunday's Well, a more affluent suburb to the northwest of the city, comfortably distanced from its smells and squalor. They owned a three-bedroom townhouse on the hill with a rear garden and a view overlooking the boat-cluttered river.

'Forgive me for asking, my dear,' Beadle said to Orlaith, 'but are you meeting someone?'

'Um, yes,' Orlaith replied hesitantly, 'I'm meeting my husband. He asked me to come here.'

Beadle concealed his disapproval. What kind of man would have his wife and child walk to the city? 'That's excellent, my dear. So where might he be now?'

'I'm not sure. I…I must find accommodation first. Then I will send word to him.'

He was surprised at such a loose arrangement. 'But have you not got some-where to stay already?'

'Yes. I mean no—I mean, I will find an inn and book us a room today.'

'I see. Well, if you don't have somewhere in mind, let me recommend the Stanley Arms. A clean, sober establishment, and Mrs Dempsey is a no-nonsense landlady. She'll fix you up.'

'Yes, that sounds fine.' It was better than trying to find somewhere herself. She already felt lost in this city.

The driver stopped the coach outside the inn. Beadle wanted to escort her inside, but she insisted that he continue his journey. She took Sean out and bade them farewell. 'You have been so kind to me. I will tell my husband of your hospitality.'

Beadle grinned. 'And you be sure to tell Mrs Dempsey that John Beadle sent you. She'll put an extra pillow or two in your bed!' They waved and closed the door, and their carriage rambled off.

Orlaith gazed at the inn, a smart, Tudor-style structure built out of an attractive combination of stone, stucco, and timber with mullioned windows and nearly a dozen chimneys. It looked like a nice place in which to lay her head down for the night. She peeked at the money, which she had kept tucked inside her coat for fear that it would arouse suspicion. There was than enough there to pay for a few days' accommodation and food. After that, she would find passage on a boat to Dublin. The longer she spent in Cork, the greater the danger that Randall would learn of her whereabouts. She was also anxious to make contact with the Mercedarians to tell them of Brannon. Time was precious now.

'Come on, Sean, let's go inside.'

A man had been idling at the side of the road a little further up. She hadn't taken much notice of him, but now, as she went to walk towards the inn, he began moving down the street. She quickened her pace, but he cut across her path.

'Beg pardon, ma'am,' he stalled her. 'Can I talk to you there a moment?'

'What is it?' she asked anxiously, taking Sean's hand.

'Just a word is all, ma'am.' He wore a tattered brown coat. His cheeks were unshaven and covered with open sores.

'You're smelly,' Sean pointed out, and the man let out a guffaw.

'By God, you're a smart lad. Never a truer word spoken.'

Orlaith pulled on Sean's hand, trying to quieten him. 'We have to go,' she told the beggar. 'We're late for an appointment.'

'What's that inside your coat there, ma'am?' the man asked.

'It's nothing. I don't have anything.' Orlaith tried to walk around him, but he suddenly lunged at her and yanked open her coat. The money fell on the ground.

'Don't touch that!' Orlaith screamed. 'Get off me!'

'Leave it, bint!' he snapped, shoving her in the chest. She fell backwards and landed with a splash in a puddle of water. The man plucked the bag from the ground and ran.

'Stop!' Orlaith cried after him desperately. 'Please!'

He sprinted down the street, promptly disappeared into an alley, and was gone.

Orlaith sat in the puddle, her lips trembling in horror, water soaking through her skirts. She stared hopelessly down the road.

'Mammy, you're all wet!' Sean said in alarm, indicating her sodden clothes.

'Oh God...' Every penny. Every last penny.

'Madam!' Another male voice hailed her, and she clambered up to face him, raising her fists to fend off another attack. But it wasn't a vagrant this time. It was a vicar, his boyish face flushed with concern as he hurried over.

'Madam, I saw the whole thing,' he said. 'Are you all right? Did he hurt you?'

There were tears glistening in her eyes. 'My money. He stole it!'

'Goodness, madam, I'm so sorry. These streets can be vicious. Is there anything I can do?'

'You don't understand—I need that money, I need it...'

'Come now, madam, you're upset. Let me offer you assistance. Is there somewhere you were going? Perhaps I can escort you.'

She gestured towards the inn. 'I was going in there. But now I don't have the money to pay for it.'

'Oh.' He shook his head in sympathy. 'That is a quandary all right.' He thought for a moment and then said, 'Maybe I can help you. I work at a foundling hospital nearby, and I might be able to find you a room for the night. It will let you recover from this ordeal.'

'Thank you, Reverend, but I have no money, as I said—'

'Oh goodness, I wouldn't charge you. We run the hospital on God's good grace and the generosity of private donors. What do you say? You can't wander the streets with this little one in tow, can you?'

She hadn't much other choice at the moment. The loss of the money was a dreadful setback. But the vicar seemed like a kind man. She nodded humbly. 'It's very good of you, Reverend. Thank you.'

⊕ ⊕ ⊕

The Protestant foundling hospital had been built by the clergy and local philanthropists, designed for the care and education of orphaned and abandoned children. It was located in Blackpool, only a short walk from Sunday's Well. It had two wings and a church built around an open courtyard, and before they even reached it, Orlaith could hear the deafening noise of about a hundred children all screeching or laughing or crying. She squeezed Sean's hand. There was a spring to his step now at the prospect of meeting other children.

They entered by the courtyard, where the hospital's clientele had been allowed out to play. There were dozens of them, raggedy little creatures with grubby hands and pinched faces, skipping and shouting and belting each other. The din was overwhelming.

Sean tugged on Orlaith's hand, frantic to join in. The vicar, who had introduced himself as Norman Johnston, laughed and said, 'He can go to them in a while, Mrs Doherty. But first let me show you to your room.'

She had given 'Doherty' as her name, not wanting to take any chances.

'I won't put you in the children's dormitory,' he said. 'Goodness, you'd never sleep. They can be a handful. No, you can both sleep in the nurses' quarters. I'm sure there's a spare bed there.'

It was a damp, draughty room with mildew on the walls and a leaking window. Three nurses normally slept there, but there was one spare bed.

'You're in luck then,' Johnston grinned. 'It's not Kensington Palace, but you'll have a roof over your head until you decide what you want to do.'

'Thank you, Reverend,' Orlaith said. She sat on the bed and looked around, already feeling lost in this cheerless room.

Sensing her discomfort, he said, 'We'll be having dinner soon in the main hall. You're both welcome to join us if you like. You must be hungry.'

She didn't feel like eating herself, but she knew Sean needed to have something. 'That would be lovely, Reverend. Thanks again.'

He nodded. 'Well, I'll leave you to get settled.' He smiled and closed the door behind him.

⊕ ⊕ ⊕

They ate an hour later, sitting at long trestle tables with the squawking children. They were each given a bowl of thin vegetable soup and some black bread. It tasted rotten, yet the children squabbled over the portions nonetheless. The nurses looked as gaunt and unhealthy as their charges, but the three of them were warm and friendly, and they were greatly distressed on hearing of Orlaith's ordeal that morning. She had to parry some awkward questions about her circumstances, for none of them could understand why her husband wasn't with her now.

'I must send word to him that we have arrived in the city,' she explained for the fifth time that day. 'He will be here soon to collect us.' If they didn't believe her, they were at least polite enough not to show it.

In the afternoon Orlaith wanted to go into the city to inquire about finding passage to Dublin, though she didn't reveal this to the vicar. She simply told him that she had a matter of business to take care of.

She was reluctant to leave Sean, but Johnston assured her, 'He'll be perfectly fine, Mrs Doherty. I'll keep a close eye on him. And look how eager he is to join the other children!'

Sean couldn't get away from her fast enough. He made for a group of boys his own age and within minutes had inveigled his way into their company.

'I shan't be long, then,' she told Johnston.

Cork was not a big city, and it was only a fifteen-minute walk to the quays where the ships were moored. Most were big cargo ships, destined for places far-flung from Cork, and they were of little use to her. But one of them she saw was a mailboat, much smaller in size.

She walked tentatively along the riverside, drawing admiring calls and whistles from the decks and rigging. In her distraction she almost tripped over a cable and instigated a great burst of raucous laughter right along the quay.

The mailboat was being loaded with parcels, which led her to believe that it would soon be departing. She approached a middle-aged, bearded man standing by the gangplank.

'Excuse me, sir, but are you the captain?' she asked nervously.

He turned his head to her, blinking in surprise. His eyes drifted over her body for a moment. 'That I am, lass. Can I be of assistance?'

'Well, it's a little embarrassing. I had been hoping to secure passage to Dublin for myself and my young son. Only I was robbed by a beggar this morning, and now I am at something of a loose end. I still need to get to Dublin.'

'This ain't a passenger boat, lass.'

'I realise that, but I was thinking that maybe if you were going to Dublin, I could for work my passage, or something like that. I am in some difficulty, and I would appreciate your help so much.'

The old captain appraised her hungrily. What pale skin she had. And such dark hair.

'Well, let me think now, lass. What is it you might do for me? You're not much of a sailor, I'd reckon.'

'Well, I can clean, I can cook…'

'We already have a cook. And I'm not in need of a cleaning lady. Look at those lads—do they look like a bit of dirt would worry them?'

'Um, but perhaps I could—'

'Ah now, I'm sure I can help you, lass. I'm a kind old heart myself.' He smiled, and there was a leering in his eyes that unsettled her. 'I'm in need for a sort of domestic maid, if you like. Just little bits of jobs that I might need doing. Do ye understand?'

Orlaith felt an unpleasant crawling on her skin. 'Cleaning?'

'Aye, cleaning. Cleaning and such. So are you in for it?' He ran a fat red tongue over his bristled chin.

'I…I must think on it.' But she knew exactly what he would have in mind for her on the voyage to Dublin.

'Don't take too long,' he told her. 'I'll be leaving tomorrow at sunrise. You make up your mind by then, lass.' He winked at her slyly.

She walked back along the quays, a little shaken now. She made more inquiries, but found to her dismay that the mailboat seemed her only likely means of reaching Dublin.

Could she suffer it? It would take several days to get to Dublin by sea, and she would be at the captain's mercy every moment. But what else was there to do?

She couldn't risk staying in Cork for much longer. Randall was closing the net all the time, and if there was anything less appealing than a perverted old sea captain, it was the prospect of being delivered back into her husband's malevolent clutches. More importantly, she needed to contact the Mercedarians. Hopefully they could still help her, even if her money was all gone. She would beg them, she would do anything. Brannon had to be brought home.

She took a deep breath, trying to steel herself.

We must get to Dublin, she vowed. *Whatever it takes. We must go all the way.*

Reverend Johnston was supervising the children when his superior entered the playground.

'Norman, a quick word if you don't mind.'

Johnston grinned. 'They're in spirited form today, Reverend. I'm worn out!'

'Yes. Norman, about that young lady you brought here this morning…'

'Oh—Mrs Doherty? I know I should have cleared it with you first, but she had a bit of a mishap. A beggar stole her money, and she got a terrible shock. I thought it the only decent thing to do—to bring her here.'

'No, no, I'm not questioning your actions. You did well. But has she told you of her intentions, where she is going?'

'Not really, but she did mention her husband. I think she's hoping to meet him here. If only we knew where to find him.'

'Ah, but I think I do know. Her husband is quite well known to me.'

Johnston looked at him. 'Why, Reverend Wheeler, that's wonderful news. She will be relieved. We can send word to him, and he can come and collect her.'

Reverend Wheeler nodded. 'Actually, Norman, I recognised her the moment I laid eyes on her, so I took the liberty of sending word to him then. He lives in a village called Dromkeen, out beyond Courtmacsherry, and my messenger is on the way there as we speak.'

'Then he can be here tomorrow.' Johnston was delighted. 'Wait until I give her the good news!'

'Norman, my dear fellow, I'd prefer if you said nothing for the moment. Just in case. We don't want to disappoint her, do we?'

'No, Reverend, but surely—'

'Just say nothing until tomorrow, Norman. It's for the best.' Wheeler narrowed his eyes to let it be known that he wasn't asking.

'Of course,' Johnston acquiesced. 'We should wait until he arrives, and then inform her.'

'Good man.'

Wheeler left Johnston to the children and returned to his office. He was still taken aback by this morning's sudden appearance of Randall Whiteley's wife. He had never forgotten her face, not since the day he married them. Here she was, miles from home, tramping brazenly around Cork City. Wheeler couldn't begin to imagine what she was up to. For certain, Randall wouldn't be pleased. So he had despatched a rider to Dromkeen within an hour of spotting Orlaith, informing Randall of her whereabouts.

He smiled, anticipating the impact his message would have. He knew Randall's character only too well. There would be an unholy hammering on the hospital gates by morning.

⊕ ⊕ ⊕

Orlaith had made her decision about Dublin before she woke up, and she resolved to stick to it. Time was running out, and they had to get out of Cork quickly. The captain had specified sunrise, so she dressed Sean and put on her coat. The room was empty, the nurses having risen from bed before dawn.

159

She packed their few belongings into the bag, though without the money. It didn't matter. She would think of something. In a few days they would be in Dublin; they would be free at last, and somehow she'd get Brannon home.

She hurried Sean downstairs. It was already late. The vicar would probably want to offer them breakfast, but she couldn't delay.

Johnston spotted them in the hallway and called out, 'Mrs Doherty!'

She stopped. He had been so good, he deserved politeness at least. 'Reverend, I was just making ready to leave. We've troubled you enough.'

He approached her slowly. He looked uncomfortable. 'Mrs Doherty, can you come with me for a moment?'

She hesitated. 'Is something wrong? We really do need to be on our way. We have an appointment to keep.'

'Yes, of course. You can leave by the back door. It's just as fast.'

'Very well.' She followed him down the hallway, confused by his odd behaviour.

Johnston opened a low door and bade her step through. She entered the room beyond, thinking it empty.

This isn't the back door, she thought.

The room wasn't empty. A man loomed in front of her, and Orlaith let out a cry of sheer and terrible anguish.

'Oh God, please no!'

Randall's fist flew with vicious speed. She was slammed against the back wall, and blood spurted from her nose. Her vision blurred, her eyelids closed, and she slid to the floor. She was unconscious as Sean began to scream.

CHAPTER THIRTEEN

Deep in the rugged, serene wilderness of the High Atlas Mountains, a messenger rode into the camp of Suliman bin Mohammed al-Qatib. Suliman's guards had intercepted him an hour earlier as he crossed one of the tumbling streams in the foothills and had resisted killing him only because of the personal seal on his letter. No chances were taken with strangers entering their remote hilltop enclave. Suliman had come under threat from spies before, men driven to treachery by force or the lure of gold. But this message was from a friend.

The rider studied his surroundings nervously as they led him in. There were tents pitched across the wooded slopes; silver smoke curled from cooking fires and blended into the alpine air; shifty-eyed tribesmen with leathery skin sat and talked. It was a good spot in which to camp. There was wild game in the forest, several freshwater springs, and an abundance of wood for the fires. Beyond these mountains were even higher ones, great towering creations whose peaks seemed to breach the very heavens. No one could touch the rebels here.

'Wait where you are.' One of the guards approached a tent near the banks of a stream. He ducked under the flap, reappeared moments later, and bade the messenger approach.

'He will see you now.'

The man fumbled within his djellaba and produced the letter, a small piece of rolled paper sealed with wax. Inside the tent it was gloomy, and he blinked a few times until he could make out the shape of the man sitting opposite. Quickly he knelt and bowed his head. 'Forgiveness, Excellency. I bring word from Ahmed bin Khaled of Fez.' Keeping his head down, he indicated the message in his hand.

'Thank you.' The man on the cushions inclined his head in gratitude. 'Please be at ease. It is a long ride from Fez.' He offered the messenger some tea and then took the piece of paper to read.

The messenger relaxed a little. He had met Suliman bin Mohammed before, and the latter was a gracious host. He was younger than his brother Yazid by several years, and even the dark beard that covered his cheeks couldn't diminish the boyish aspect of his countenance. But his eyes were like those of an older man, thoughtful, shrewd, and wise. He had a quiet intelligence and a calm manner, his every movement seeming the result of careful and considered planning. It was just another way in which he contrasted so strongly with his more impulsive and volatile brother.

Suliman folded the piece of paper when he was finished and sat back to absorb the information. According to his cousin Ahmed bin Khaled, Yazid's hold on the throne was already weakening. Yazid himself probably did not realise how brittle it was. They were plotting against him, palace courtiers, army officers, and influential city merchants, secret whisperings being passed from the teeming streets up through the corridors of power. Though they hardly dared to say the word, the imperial capital was now rife with the smell of rebellion. And Suliman was quietly pleased.

Yazid was a brutal ruler. Morocco had suffered greatly in his short rule with thousands murdered, entire villages wiped out, and the economy in turmoil. He had initiated a disastrous war with Spain, led a violent pogrom against the country's Jews, and made enemies of the European governments by enslaving so many of their subjects. Soon, if he continued in power, there would be nothing left to ruin.

Far up in his mountain lair, Suliman knew of the support that was spreading across Morocco for his own rulership. Yet the sultanate did not register heavily in his thoughts. He had no great desire for power, only a desire that Yazid should be removed as soon as possible. Once that was achieved, the matter of a successor could be addressed.

His brothers Hisham and Maslama were built from the same mould as Yazid, he felt, and if one of them seized the throne, then nothing would have changed. That was why the people looked to Suliman. They wanted him to take

162

the sultanate himself, to ensure the transition into a more peaceful and prosperous era for Morocco, one where people might live without having to watch over their shoulders. It wasn't enough to simply defeat Yazid. Morocco would need strong hands to guide and nourish it in the years ahead, to breathe life back into its blighted lands, to restore optimism to a people wearied by despair. Suliman said a silent prayer, daunted now by the monumental burden being presented to him.

'Tomorrow I will provide you with a reply,' he told the messenger, 'but tonight you must rest. We have plenty of food and blankets. Please make yourself comfortable.'

The messenger bowed to him and left.

Suliman went outside too, walking through the tall cow parsley that grew around his tent. A cold wind lifted the hair behind his shoulders, and a single snowflake alighted on his cheek, melting almost the instant it touched his skin. Winter was coming. In one month from now these mountains would be cut off, the passes adrift with snow. They had to push for the lowlands, back into insecure territory. But it didn't matter. The time for facing Yazid would soon be at hand.

That night, after a long and intense period of prayer, he composed a reply to Ahmed:

Dear Cousin,

It warms my heart to know that you are safe, and I am humbled by the brave efforts you have made on my behalf. Your words give me great cause for hope. My forces have grown in the time since I last wrote to you, and it seems your own have too. At present we are still encamped deep in the High Atlas, but I plan to see out the winter in the desert where my main army lies. In the spring we will drive north, and then all is in the good hands of Allah. In the meantime, please keep me informed of developments in Fez. All bodes well for us, and soon we will fight side by side.

Again, however, I urge caution upon you, dear cousin. There are those who will smile at you while holding daggers behind their backs. Do not trust in people, but use your own instincts to judge them. We have many enemies, including ones who would befriend and aid us, only to betray us at some further point. Be wise to this always.

The peace of Allah be upon you.
Your cousin,
Suliman

The wailing chants of the muezzins drifted languidly from the minarets over the haze-embalmed city. The sun had fallen to the horizon like a bloodied warrior, leaving behind an amber-red splendour above the mountains and a fading twilight sky. Weary guards walked along the walls and peered from the ramparts while in the streets the townspeople shuffled into mosques. It was almost at day's end.

Kaid Azedine Ben Hassi pulled up on his dusty mount and stopped outside the barracks. His beard was thick with dirt, his eyes red from fatigue. He handed his horse to a groom and went inside, desperate for the cool sanctuary of his bedchamber. The previous five days he had spent escorting Moulay Yazid's hunting party in the hills, providing an armed guard while the sultan and his palace friends hunted stag and leopard. Five long days in the saddle under the draining glare of the sun—he looked forward now to a night of well-earned sleep.

He lit the candles in his chamber and unrolled his sleeping mat. Ben Hassi had been a professional solider for most of his life and had never become accustomed to sleeping in a bed. He mixed a drink that would take the ache out of his abused limbs and lowered himself on to the mat, breathing raggedly.

There was a knock at the door. He shut his eyes in exasperation. 'Who is it?'

No one replied, and he felt a hot rush of anger. This was his time for relaxation; there should have been no interruptions.

He came to his feet with a grunt, deciding that in the absence of an extremely good reason for bothering him, he would throttle the life out of the person on the other side of the door.

'Azedine Ben Hassi.' The young soldier standing in the doorway had the neck to address him by his name and not his title. Ben Hassi felt like murder.

'Who do you think you're speaking to?' he snapped. 'You insolent whelp, how dare you!'

To his disbelief, the soldier actually laughed in response.

'That's exactly what you used to call me when I was a boy bouncing on your knee. An insolent whelp. Good to see you haven't changed, Azedine Ben Hassi.'

Ben Hassi held his tongue for a moment. 'What are you talking about, boy?'

'It's a few years since we met, so I can understand why you might not recognise me. My name is Ahmed bin Khaled al-Qatib.'

The name made Ben Hassi stiffen in shock. He peered into the other's eyes, searching for treachery. But recognition slowly dawned.

'Allah save us. Ahmed. It is you, isn't it? I don't believe it.'

'It's me, all right. A little older now, of course, but it's me.'

Ben Hassi struggled to control his emotions. 'But I thought you were dead. They said you were dead. How can you be here?'

'I'm not dead, Azedine. I survived Yazid's carnage, as you did.'

'But Yazid murdered your father. And all your father's children. How did you escape? The sultan will kill you when he hears of this.'

'He would have killed you too, if only he had realised how close you were to my father. You should be dead also, Azedine.'

Ben Hassi shook his head in denial. 'The sultan knows I am alive; he means me no harm. I am a simple soldier, not royalty. But you—well, he won't be pleased when he learns of your return.'

'I'm hoping he won't learn anything just yet.' Ahmed put his hand on the older man's shoulder. 'I need your help, my friend. You were a faithful servant to my father before his murder. Yazid may believe that you simply transferred your allegiances to him afterwards, but I don't think you could do that so easily.'

'But I did, Ahmed. It's my duty to serve the sultan of Morocco, whoever he may be. A soldier doesn't have the hindrance of conscience.'

'Did you not have a conscience when they came to slay my father? The man you were once proud to serve?'

Ben Hassi's eyes flashed with anger. 'I have not forgotten what happened to your father. You insult me.'

165

'Then how can you serve the man who killed your lord?'

'It's simple. If I had been there that night, I would have stopped Yazid. He wasn't the sultan then, just a rebel. But he's the sultan now. I have never forgiven myself for not being there when your father needed me, but nevertheless, I am bound to pledge myself to Yazid regardless of my personal feelings. He is the sultan of Morocco.'

Ahmed shook his head. 'I am disappointed. I would have thought you glad of the opportunity to redress the balance with Yazid.'

'What's this?' Ben Hassi narrowed his eyes and raised a finger in warning. 'Careful, boy. If you are hinting at what I think you are, then be careful. Valiant it may sound to avenge your father's death, but Moulay Yazid would brook no such treason. He will destroy you.'

'You're wrong. And I am not alone in this. Hear my words—Yazid's time in power is coming to an end.'

'I should have you arrested for saying that,' Ben Hassi growled. 'You forget that you are talking to a high-ranking officer in His Majesty's army. You were stupid to come here tonight.'

'Turn me in if you will, Azedine, but Yazid will not destroy us. We're too strong. You can be part of it if you want, or else you can fight alongside our great sultan. I hope you'll do what you think is right.'

As intended, this pricked sharply at Ben Hassi's already troubled scruples. 'Get out,' he snapped. 'Don't come near me again. Yazid would cut off your head if he heard what you just said. Get out, and if you're very lucky, I might just pretend we never had this conversation.'

'You can find me when you need to,' Ahmed said, and he walked away from Ben Hassi's door.

The sentry looked at Brannon suspiciously and refused to budge. 'I was told nothing of this. I can't let you in. Go back and bring me the proper authorisation.'

'I don't have authorisation because this only came to light now. I'm telling you, somebody has been stealing muskets. They've shown up in searches around the city, and Kaid Fadhl is spitting fire over it.'

'Kaid Fadhl should give you the proper authorisation. Then you can go inside to count the stock.'

Brannon raised his hands in exasperation. 'I don't have time to argue with you. I will tell him. He'll be furious, of course—you know the kaid's temper. And when he hears that his investigation has been held up by one lowly sentry, I shudder to think what his reaction might be.'

The sentry shifted uncertainly. It was true that Kaid Fadhl had a wicked temper. He was an impatient man, easily irritated by the constraints of formal procedure. Perhaps it would be wise to bend the rules on this occasion.

'Very well. But just this once. Next time, you bring the authorisation with you.'

'Most certainly.' Brannon waved him along. 'On you go.'

The sentry reached under his djellaba and took a key from the ring hanging at his belt. He stuck the key into the big, studded door and heaved it open with effort.

'We have much to do—this is a serious matter. Very serious.' Brannon prattled on, trying to distract the guard. 'We must hurry. Quickly now, quickly.' He ushered the guard inside, and his little ploy worked—the guard neglected to take the key back out of the lock.

Seconds later a man emerged from the outer corridor and moved to the door. In his hand he carried a candle, the side of which he had just melted over a brazier. He had to act fast before it hardened again.

Removing the sentry's key, he pressed it into the soft wax of the candle, holding it there while the wax slowly hardened around it. After a minute he worked the key back out and was left with a perfect impression of the key's shape embedded in the candle. Success.

He wiped the key and inserted it back into the door, and then he tucked the candle under his haik and vanished.

A while later Brannon reappeared with the sentry. The latter was grumbling. 'I could have told you that myself. No one can get into this place. You saw yourself how many outer doors you had to go through to get here.'

A quick count of the guns had revealed that the stock was intact. The sentry saw it as a waste of time.

'Never mind, we have to keep the kaid happy.' Brannon cast his eye towards the key, hoping that Daniel had managed to take the impression in time. 'Look at that!' he growled at the sentry. 'You left the key in the door. How foolish.'

The sentry gulped, realising his error. 'That was your fault. You were chattering too much, putting me off.'

'Well, don't let it happen again. There are devious characters out there. We don't want them taking advantage of us, do we?'

That afternoon Brannon made his way to the south of the city and climbed a set of stone steps to the ramparts. Up here the breeze tousled his hair and carried a rich fragrance from the olive groves and wheat fields. Outside the wall, trading stalls were scattered about the dappled shade. A constant traffic of pack animals and people moved through the gates, which as always were open. The guards patrolling the walls paid little attention to Brannon; he was dressed in their garb, and they recognised him as a captain. He was free to wander as he pleased.

It was the gates themselves he had come to look at. Each of the studded frames was built from solid oak, over thirty feet tall and three feet thick. When closed, nothing short of an array of artillery could bring them down, and even then it would take some time.

Ahmed's instructions to Brannon had been simple—find some way in which the gates could be prevented from closing. If Suliman's army managed to reach Fez, Yazid would be quick to close the gates and prevent an easy assault. For Ahmed's plan to succeed, however, they would have to be kept open.

He turned his attentions to them. They were too heavy to be moved by human hand alone, so a series of cables and pulleys had been attached to enable the operation. At each side of the gateway was an iron wheel, drawing on a steel cable that ran around a pulley. The other end of the cable was affixed to the gate. When the wheel was turned, the cable would unwind, the pressure would ease, and the gate would slide closed.

It was quite simple, really. An idea came to mind.

That night he returned to the ramparts with a bulky sack over his shoulder. He waited in the darkness of the alleys for several minutes, taking note of the guards' movements. Each patrol of the wall took about five minutes before an individual guard returned to the same spot. It didn't give him much time.

He crept between the buildings. The alleys were mostly empty, but as he moved along, he saw figures stirring in the shadows—a man and woman. She was naked below the waist, and her golden legs gleamed in the moonlight as she ground her hips against her lover's. Brannon gave them a wide berth and slipped into position below the gates. At the next lull in the patrols, he hurried up the steps.

Taking a quick check, he emptied the sack on the wall. It was full of small stones, each about an inch in length, ideal for his purposes. Near the top of the gate, the back post was fitted into a round stone socket. When the cable was released, the post would turn and the gate would move. Selecting a few of the flatter stones, Brannon used the heel of his hand to jam them between the socket and the post. It was a difficult job, and his skin was mottled with cuts by the time he had forced twenty or so of them inside.

He glanced up. Time was running out. Quickly he repeated the same procedure on the other gate, and then he tossed the remaining stones and the sack onto the heaps of rubbish outside.

The stones would inhibit the post from turning smoothly. It wasn't the most effective attempt at sabotage, but by the time the guards figured out why the gates weren't moving, it might already have made a crucial difference. That depended on how fast Suliman was.

He slipped back down the steps, praying that he hadn't been seen. He went to cross the street, but suddenly there was a noise behind him and a body lunged out of the darkness. Brannon cursed in fright. But it was a beggar, a blind man with white orbs for eyes, gibbering in a strange tongue and clawing at the scabs on his face. Brannon stepped away from him and continued on. Nobody stopped him.

Asiya hummed a light song while arranging the flowers in the vase, placing them under a curlicued window to let the sunlight bring out their velvety textures. She brushed the cobwebs from the walls, washed out the greasy food bowls, gave the mat a beating, and swept the floor. Soon she had the little room back in order.

'It's sweet of you to help me, Asiya,' the girl on the bed said. 'I would have done it myself, but my stomach aches so.' She made a face and clasped her belly in a show of infirmity.

'That's all right, Reema,' Asiya said. 'You should rest while you are ill. I am happy to help.' But Asiya wasn't fooled by her pretence of sickness. Reema was a lazy sort, always looking to pass her burdens on to others. She would gladly have had Asiya do her chores every day if she could. Secretly Asiya detested the girl, but she had her own reasons for being here.

Reema was a concubine, but no ordinary concubine. She belonged to Naseem al-Malek, a general in Yazid's army and one of its most powerful men. Round-bodied and buxom, Reema perfectly matched the general's predilection for larger women, but he might have reconsidered his choice of bedmate if he knew just how loose her tongue was. This was where Asiya sensed opportunity. Reema was not a clever girl and talked far too much. Valuable information could be gleaned if one was careful about it.

'You should rest tonight. Sleep will be good,' Asiya said, knowing full well that Reema would not be alone.

'But Naseem will come,' Reema lamented. 'He has come into my room every night this week. How can I sleep with him rutting on top of me?'

Asiya nodded sympathetically. 'A shame. But perhaps if he has business, you will have some time to yourself? I suppose that would depend on his orders.'

Reema brightened, remembering something. 'Actually, he does intend to leave for Marrakech in the near future. He told me so. I think the sultan must be getting nervous. He wants Marrakech secured before one of his brothers takes it.'

'Really?' Asiya inquired innocently. 'Such a long way, Marrakech. Does he take many men?'

'Ten whole battalions,' Reema said proudly. Seeing Asiya's quizzical look, she explained, 'A battalion is about one thousand men. I think.'

'But won't that leave Fez unguarded? His Majesty will be vulnerable.' Asiya feigned concern.

'No, Naseem says the sultan's enemies are far to the south. They'll never reach Fez. Don't worry, Asiya, we are safe from those brutes in the desert.'

'I do hope so.' Asiya went on with her cleaning, not wanting to show too much interest. Then she asked, 'When does Naseem leave?'

'Not until spring, I think. When the mountain passes have opened.' Reema sighed. 'Maybe in spring I'll get some sleep.'

'Ten thousand men,' Asiya declared. 'That means ten thousand less guarding Fez. Am I not right?'

They were sitting on stools in the garden of an abandoned house that had once belonged to a wealthy Jewish family. Moulay Yazid had launched violent pogroms against the Jews upon his accession to power, and ever since then this house had lain idle. The windows had been smashed by looters, the walls daubed with anti-Semitic insults. A few hens picked at the stubbly grass, and a stray dog sniffed at the piles of discarded cooking pots. It was otherwise quiet.

'Al-Malek tells her secrets in bed,' Asiya went on, 'and he shouldn't. Reema is a silly girl. She can't keep her mouth shut.'

Brannon gazed between his feet where a beetle had been ambushed by a column of ants. The beetle had toppled on its back and was kicking wildly. 'I guess it does make sense. If Yazid loses Marrakech, he'll also lose a whole heap of southern Morocco. Cramming the place with men is probably a wise move.'

'Ahmed will be pleased. He will also be pleased that you managed to take care of the gates. You are brave, Brannon.' There was a twinkle in her eyes, and Brannon chuckled.

'I'll do whatever your brother asks, Asiya, as long as he keeps his side of the bargain and gets me home afterward.'

Her smile faded. 'I will be sad when you are gone. I will miss you.' She went without thinking to reach for his hand, but then she realised what she was doing and withdrew in embarrassment. It was considered indecent for a Muslim woman to display such public affection towards a man.

Footsteps sounded from the street. Ahmed came walking across the grass and glowered in irritation when he saw how closely they sat, their knees almost touching.

'Good afternoon.' He stood pointedly between them so that they had to edge their stools apart. 'I got your message, Brannon. Is something wrong?'

Asiya relayed her information and said, 'It's good news, isn't it?'

'Perhaps it's good news for our assault on Fez,' he mused, 'but Suliman will have to move his army twice as fast now. We simply cannot afford to let Yazid take Marrakech.'

'What about those gates?' Brannon asked. 'We should have waited longer. Somebody is going to notice something wrong.'

Ahmed shook his head. 'I doubt it. Those gates haven't been closed in ten years, not since Yazid's last rebellion against his father. I think it's safe to assume they'll remain open until spring at least.'

'And Suliman will come in spring? You believe him?'

'Suliman will come.'

'And let me go free? I hope you were telling the truth about that.'

'Suliman is opposed to the slave trade—he means to abolish it once he assumes power. He will let you go free, Brannon.'

'Good. I won't be shedding many tears that day.' He didn't mean it to sound so callous, and he compromised. 'It hasn't been so bad here, of course. You have a fine land, if only you could get it in order. And I like the people.'

Ahmed smiled. 'We understand your wish to return home, Brannon. I would like to see your country someday. I think it would be a little different.'

He glanced around. 'You must excuse me now. I was slipped a message only minutes ago, which I believe has come from our brothers in the south.'

'Read it out,' Brannon said.

'Not here. Not safe. We'll meet tomorrow, the same place I showed you before. Come before noon, Brannon, and whatever you do, make sure nobody follows you.'

CHAPTER FOURTEEN

Ahmed opened the piece of paper to the flickering candlelight. He was crouched in the darkness of a dilapidated warehouse, its windows boarded with wood to screen the interior from the street outside. There were only a limited number of safe-houses available to him, and this place, abandoned by all but the spiders, was ideal.

'It's good news,' he said finally. 'Suliman's army has come out of the desert and is moving north. I will despatch a messenger and warn him of Yazid's intentions—and may it please Allah that Suliman can reach Marrakech first.'

The men he spoke to were his core council, the ones in whom he was obliged to place the most trust. Their various influences within the imperial power structure would be crucial to the eventual success of this rebellion. It was through them that he was slowly paving the way for an all-out strike on Yazid's regime while maintaining his communication link with Suliman to the south.

'If Suliman takes Marrakech,' one of them warned, 'what do you think Yazid's response will be? He will garrison Fez to the hilt, of course, and make it doubly hard to breach.'

'It's likely, yes,' Ahmed admitted. 'We will have to keep the city open in order for Suliman's army to get inside. Use a distraction, perhaps, something to lure Yazid outside the gates.'

'Yazid is not made a fool of that easily,' a kaid pointed out. 'How do you suggest we make him leave the safety of the city?'

'We need another army. One big enough to force Yazid into a confrontation. That way the city will be exposed.'

'Another army. Do you have one tucked away in secret somewhere?' the kaid asked with scorn. He was twenty years older than Ahmed and had yet to be convinced of the latter's ability to lead this stage of the rebellion.

'I wasn't thinking about regular soldiers,' Ahmed said. 'There are others who might join us. We want men who fight like devils, but who owe the sultan no loyalty.'

The kaid shifted uneasily. 'If I know whom you're referring to, it's a bad idea, Ahmed.'

'Who?' Brannon piped up.

Ahmed rose to his feet. 'I'm talking about the Berber tribes in the mountains. They're an army in themselves, and Yazid must have realised it. He persecuted them when he came to power, forced them to retreat into the wastelands. I know they'd relish the chance to settle old scores.'

'They're a rabble of warlords and bandits,' the kaid protested. 'They can't be controlled. We'd spend as much time battling them as we would Yazid.'

The others reflected on it. The Berber tribes of Morocco had always had an uncertain relationship with the sultanate. Under successive rulers they had been harried and victimised and driven into the hills and deserts in order to preserve their way of life. But under more tolerant leaders, such as Sidi Mohammed, they were allowed greater freedom and even a degree of autonomy. They had been able to come out of the sandy wastes and into the cities to live and trade and integrate. Yazid's accession changed all that. He couldn't abide the presence of these untamed warriors within his kingdom. Impossible to contain, they represented a threat to his security, and he launched a series of attacks against them. To escape his brutality, they again withdrew into the harsh lands of the south, where they lived as nomadic shepherds, beyond Yazid's reach.

'It makes sense. With their numbers and fighting skills, we would be able to hold Yazid down for weeks,' Ahmed insisted.

Brannon asked, 'How do you plan to find these people? Go wandering into the mountains, and you'll end up in a gully with your throat slit, I can promise.'

Ahmed smiled. 'I guess we won't know until we get there.'

'We?'

'I need someone to come with me. I'm not afraid to go on my own, but two or three of us would stand a better chance.'

'I'll go,' Daniel Jones offered. 'I've ridden as far as those mountains before. I know the way.'

'What about me?' the kaid asked.

Ahmed shook his head. 'The sultan would notice your absence, Abdul. And nothing must arouse his suspicion.' He nodded to the other two men present, a vizier and a bodyguard. 'For the same reason, you must stay in Fez also. A mere whiff of anything unusual could be enough to wake the tyrant's vengeance.'

That left only one remaining contender, and Brannon groaned. 'Wonderful. Thank the heavens. You'd better start saying prayers then, Ahmed, if you're serious about crossing wild Berber country. You do some praying, but I'll be shoving extra pistols into my belt.'

It was strange that a landscape that seemed so empty could emanate such hostility. The mountains south of Fez were unsafe, a dark place of gorges and cliffs and old tracks where bandits skulked and travellers died on lonely crossroads. It was the *bled es siba*, the land without law, baked to insanity by the sun and beyond the protective embrace of civilisation.

They rode on horses, carrying their accoutrements in their saddle-packs. Four days out of Fez they were traversing a barren countryside, through sombre valleys pocked with burnt-out farmhouses and fields that lay in silent repose like graveyards. The communities here had thrived once upon a time, before assassins came spilling down from the north and butchered the area to extinction. In their wake they left bodies and blackened tillage, punishment for the people's alleged support of Yazid's rivals. The three riders passed through settlements that were still heavy with the air of somnolent melancholy. Brannon stepped into one house for a look; cockroaches scuttled away at his approach, and the clay walls were festooned with spider-webs. Somewhere upstairs he could hear the loud, throbbing hum of a beehive, a noise that made his skin prickle. This should be a home of impish children and bedtime stories, with green pastures resonating to the industrious beat of prosperity, but instead the tools were rusting, the crop-fields were untended, and slowly the thick weeds were reclaiming the landscape.

After some days they reached the slopes of the Middle Atlas. Juniper and cork trees thickened on the foothills, and higher up the flaming sphere of the sun glared between limestone outcrops. A soft-tumbling stream ran through the bottom of a ravine where lavender and marigold scented the air, and after drawing lots it was Daniel who had to climb down and refill their flasks. In the shade of the ravine it was cool. Dragonflies skimmed the water's surface while snakes slid through the grass, hunting the small animals that sought to escape the heat above.

They rode on, climbing high on the slopes and then descending through gorges of baked rock that seemed to tremble in the heat mirage. The track narrowed for several miles, enclosing them suffocatingly between sheer bluffs of stone. Further on they saw a string of caves that peered from the hillside like the eyes of predators. Each of them wondered uncomfortably what sinister denizens those caves might contain.

'Keep your pistols at the ready,' Ahmed murmured, saying aloud what each of them was thinking.

The strange quietness of the hills was disturbed by the fluttering of a vulture above their heads. It alighted on a rock, folded its wings, and watched them going by. At a junction further on was a pile of human bones, bleached white by the sun. Travellers had been using these tracks for centuries, but many of them never completed their journey. There was a menace to the place, as unsettling as the heat, and they were all aware of it.

By late afternoon the sun was beginning its inexorable slide towards the west, and the shadows in the hills were lengthening. It would be dark soon, yet they were reluctant to stop. The night could bring evils as yet unseen.

'Starting to smell like a wild goose chase,' Daniel grunted. 'We haven't met a soul yet. We don't even know where we're going.'

He stopped.

Stones tumbled from the rugged heights. They heard them spinning and clattering down the mountainside until they came to rest on the track nearby. The immediate silence afterwards was deafening.

'Christ,' Brannon swore. 'Damned if I—'

'Stay quiet,' Ahmed warned.

They peered into the rocky surrounds. No one appeared. There were no more noises.

'An animal, probably,' Daniel said, though he didn't sound convinced.

'There,' Ahmed whispered, nodding towards a cave on their right. Two figures had slunk out from the rocks, men with long, greasy hair and beards. In their hands blades glinted.

Brannon and Daniel went for their pistols, but Ahmed hissed at them, 'Don't move. Or we're dead men.'

'We can tackle two of the bastards,' Brannon began, but he was cut short by a noise to his left. He quickly closed his mouth.

There were more than thirty on the opposite hillside, moving down swiftly to the path. Their leader was a hulking giant with braided hair and a welter of scar tissue around his face and chest. He waved a broadsword above his head and bellowed across at the trapped travellers.

'What the hell was that?' Brannon asked.

'It's Tamazight. They're a Berber tribe. He wants to know if we have money, and how much of it,' Ahmed answered.

'Tell him we're penniless, for heaven's sake. And diseased.'

'Do we fight?' Daniel wondered. 'Looks like we're up against it, boys.'

Ahmed shouted back to the leader, stating that they had little money but were willing to pay a small tribute for passage through the mountain. The leader growled. He wasn't satisfied with that. He gestured across the slope, and suddenly they were advancing.

With wild cheers they poured into the narrow track, pulling the three riders from their mounts. Brannon was aching to unleash a few punches, but his good sense prevailed. Such an action would probably have been an instant death sentence. Like the other two, they took his weapons and his purse and tore at his clothes. Soon the three of them were unarmed and half na-

ked, pulled to and fro like cuts of meat in a pride of lions. The Berber warriors began to jostle each other and squabble over the looted items. Brannon's
purse was ripped, and the coins tinkled over the stones, triggering off a frenzy
of action as men scrambled to seize the rolling monies. Angry voices filled the
chasm.

'What's going on?' Brannon cursed in alarm.

'An argument,' Ahmed panted. 'One side wants to enslave us, the rest want
to kill us.'

The situation became more heated. Brannon was hauled among the rocks
by one group, their knives out. As they were about to hack him to pieces, another group stormed forward and seized him back. He became the focus of a
wild tug-of-war. Daniel and Ahmed were shoved to their knees, blades placed to
their throats. The leader clobbered one of their would-be killers off his feet and
jabbed his sword at another; this aggressive move sparked outrage, and the track
was abruptly filled with dozens of brandished blades, each man making vicious
gestures and hurling insults at those around him.

'They're all mad,' Brannon gasped. 'We're done for!'

The shouting and blade-waving continued for some minutes, but neither
side actually went on the attack. After a while their voices slowly calmed, the
commotion subsided, and the leader managed to reassert his dominance. He
purposefully retrieved Brannon from a mob intent on killing him, and the danger passed. They were not given back their clothes and items, however.

'Lovely,' Brannon muttered to Ahmed. 'They'll not kill us here—they'll take
us home and cook us all up in a big pot.'

'Don't worry. If we reach their camp, I will talk to their chief. We'll get out
of this yet.'

'Ah, that has me reassured.'

They were bound together with a single hemp rope around their necks and
made to walk, their new hosts having taken the horses. It was dark an hour
later, but the motley group continued travelling through the night and for much

of the following day. The three captives were exhausted, yet the Berber men showed not the least sign of fatigue.

The camp, when they reached it, was set up beneath a steep, inward-sloping cliff. In the shade of the cliff were crude goat-hair tents and animal entrails sizzling on cooking fires. The camp's children tittered in glee when they saw the luckless trio coming; they ran out to prod them with sticks and thorn branches, encouraging each other with excited squeals.

'Get to your beds,' Brannon growled in ill temper.

Ahmed was relieved by the sight of the children. 'These are not mere bandits. A bandit gang would not be raising children in its midst.'

'Little angels, bless 'em,' Brannon said, and he grimaced as a child no higher than his knee jabbed a stick into his privates.

A tall, grey-haired man emerged from a tent and glared at the noisy group coming through his camp. He snapped a curt order, instantly stilling the childish laughter. The children obediently scampered back to their mothers. Though his voice was hoarse and his face weathered, he looked lean and fit, a craggy, robust physique honed by innumerable adventures under the African sun.

He took a seat at the communal fire in the middle of the camp and gestured to the ground before him. The three captives were pushed down on their knees. He gave Ahmed only a fleeting look, but Brannon and Daniel caught his interest. They were white men, valuable commodities in this wild land.

But it was Ahmed who addressed him first. 'My lord, I offer you my humblest gratitude for your hospitality. I come to you in peace, the peace that Sultan Sidi Mohammed promised for your people.'

The tribal leader sneered. 'The cockroach speaks the name of the lion as though they were kinsmen.' There were chuckles of contempt.

'But we *are* kinsmen, my lord. I am Ahmed bin Khaled al-Qatib from Fez, nephew and devoted servant of Sultan Sidi Mohammed.'

'From Fez!' The man glowered. 'Then you are a dog of Yazid.'

'No, my lord. I am the enemy of Moulay Yazid. I swear this before Allah, who sees all things.'

'Well, Ahmed bin Khaled, I am Tariq Chaker. This is my son, Bakka,' he said as he gestured to the grinning warrior-giant who had orchestrated their capture on the mountain, 'and I swear *this* before Allah: if a single word that leaves your lips should displease me in any way, I will cut out your tongue and feed it to my dog. No more will my people be tricked by the wickedness of Yazid.'

'It is your people I want to save, my lord,' Ahmed insisted. 'Yazid murdered your families, as he murdered mine. But I will avenge their deaths—I am not afraid. My hope is that you will find the courage to join me.'

Tariq Chaker bristled at the implication that his courage might be lacking in any way. 'I do not fear Yazid. But that does not mean that I must trust you. Why should I?'

'I will tell you why, my lord. I will tell you everything.'

An hour later, when the fire had burned to embers, Ahmed had explained the reasons for his hatred of Yazid. He told Tariq Chaker about his parents and siblings, stabbed to death in their nightgowns. He told him about Suliman's army which was marching north to do battle with the tyrant. He detailed their plans to eventually seize control of Fez and wrest Morocco from Yazid's grip. His only problem, he said, was that he needed help to do it.

Tariq Chaker's memories of Yazid were still fresh. The sultan had sent great hordes against them, the killers of the Imperial Guard who attacked their camps by night and forced them to retreat ever further. They had lost many. Much blood was spilled. And Tariq Chaker would never forget it.

He stared at the wilting flames and rubbed his beard. 'If you are indeed a kinsman of Sidi Mohammed, and you speak the truth,' he told Ahmed, 'then I think we must see a demonstration of your greatness.'

Ahmed bowed his head respectfully.

'A test,' Bakka elaborated, and his black eyes gleamed with relish.

'If it is my lord's pleasure,' Ahmed agreed. 'May I ask what kind of a test?'

When they had explained, Ahmed translated for the benefit of Brannon and Daniel. Their subsequent language was so abominable that Ahmed feared salvation for the three of them was surely an impossibility now.

'Jesus,' Daniel murmured uneasily, watching the Berber men comb out a long bed of burning coals that shone bright in the late gloaming. Their excitement was palpable as they grinned towards their champion; Bakka had removed his tunic and sandals and was tilting a jug of foul-smelling brew to his lips. He wiped the dribbles from his chin and let out a roar, and the young men crowded around him, slapping his back and yelling his name in hero worship.

'So if I'm correct,' Daniel said, venturing his understanding of the situation, 'one of us has to walk further across that stuff than he can—and if so, they'll help us. But if we can't, then they'll knife us up. How logical.'

Brannon sighed. 'Whose stupid idea was it to come up here anyway? Ahmed, as usual.'

'Can't we offer them some money instead?' Daniel asked.

'Of course we can. We just can't give them any,' Brannon replied.

'Hold up,' Daniel warned. 'Here he comes.'

Bakka stepped across to the starting mark at the top of the fire-bed. He took a deep breath, flexed his muscles, and shook out his colossal frame. With a smile he placed his right foot unflinchingly into the fire.

The skin of his sole immediately began to sizzle. Black tendrils of smoke wafted upwards, and the crowd held its breath. Bakka didn't so much as blink. He placed his left foot down; again the loud hiss and puff of smoke. He was now standing in the bed of fire, with ten yards to complete. He moved forward slowly, comfortably, resisting the urge to break into a run and end the pain faster. He seemed to relish it rather than endure it, his confidence natural to the point of arrogance.

'You're burning up!' Brannon yelled. 'Save yourself!'

He didn't understand Brannon's untamed Arabic, but even so he was in no rush to escape the fire. He carried on; three yards, then five, six, eight, and the Berbers drove him on with thunderous acclaim.

'He's not human,' Brannon said incredulously.

Bakka's challenge was nearing its end, but he was starting to sweat. The coals beneath his feet burned like a blacksmith's forge, and his blackened soles were losing thick peels of skin. He bit his lip as the pain mounted, quickened his pace, and covered the last few feet at a run. He crossed the finish line, and a deafening chorus of cheers erupted from the crowd. Two buckets of water were produced to douse his feet into, and his face twisted in relief at the cooling balm.

'You!' Tariq Chaker thrust his finger towards Brannon. 'You next.'

Brannon inclined his head towards Ahmed. 'Him?'

'You!' The Berber leader gestured impatiently. They offered Brannon a mouthful of the reeking brew, but he shook his head politely. 'No thanks. I'll have a drop at the finish.'

'You can do it, mate,' Daniel encouraged him. 'Steady up now. Close your eyes and think of Irish weather.'

Brannon stared out over the long, burning pathway. Hordes of grinning faces lined each side, goading him with malicious laughter. He scowled and tried to ignore them. Clenching his fists, he lowered his right foot into the fire.

The pain was instantaneous. It pierced his skin like a thousand blades at once, striking with the power of a lightning bolt right up his leg. He couldn't prevent himself from exclaiming aloud as thin wreaths of smoke swirled around his calf. It was sheer, ferocious agony. But he couldn't stop now.

He lifted his other foot in. The pain became all-consuming; it burned every nerve ending of his body, sucked the air from his lungs, made his vision blur. He staggered a little, and the crowd hooted its enjoyment. He forced himself to go on somehow, his anger sustaining him rather than his resolve. Three more steps. The stink of his own burning flesh was cloying. The urge to throw up made him gag.

'Go to hell, you bastards,' he snarled through gritted teeth. He wanted to wipe the smiles off their faces. But the torture was so unbearable that he could barely stand, and he hadn't even reached the halfway point. As he lifted his foot, he saw a strip of burnt skin peel away and remain affixed to the coals. The flesh beneath was red and raw, and when that touched the fire, the pain produced was the most horrific, intense beast of a thing he had ever experienced. Compared to this, his circumcision had been a mere pinprick. And it was simply too much.

With a howl of agony, he skipped to the side of the fire-bed, cursing bitterly. The crowd of Berbers had to cling to each other's shoulders in mirth. They jeered him even as they plunged his feet into the water and gave him playful digs in the stomach, riding on his humiliation.

With Brannon having failed to cross the fire, it was left to Daniel and Ahmed to match Bakka's triumph. At least one of them had to succeed. Daniel went first. He began swearing the moment the coals touched his feet, but he marched steadily nonetheless. Brannon, despite his physical discomfiture, yelled aloud in encouragement. 'Keep going, Dan! Show the heathens what you're made of!'

Daniel made it to the halfway point, and Brannon reckoned he was going to do it. 'Go on, Dan!' he cried excitedly. 'Don't stop!'

But the expression on Daniel's face was something awful. No sooner had he reached halfway than his strength finally went. Like Brannon, the pain was just too much. He faltered, stumbled to the side, and threw himself into the scrubby grass. His feet were quickly doused, and he had to run a gauntlet of scorn from the laughing Berbers.

Two down, with only Ahmed to go.

'Great,' Brannon muttered.

Ahmed stood at the starting point but didn't begin yet. He waited for several minutes, and the Berbers, believing him to be losing his nerve, hurled every manner of raucous insult at him. Ahmed stayed silent with his eyes closed, his lips moving gently.

'Oh, Christ, he's praying,' Brannon sighed in frustration. 'Look at him!'

Finally Ahmed opened his eyes again. He seemed barely aware of the boisterous mob. He stepped into the fire and began his challenge.

The abuse continued unchecked. They were sure he would fail. But Ahmed said nothing, and nor did his face betray any emotion. Within mere moments he was approaching the halfway mark, and despite the smoke coming from his feet, he showed no signs of discomfort.

Now the crowd was growing quiet. The jeering trailed off, and voices were hushed. Even Bakka stopped his boasting to follow Ahmed's progress.

Ahmed was three-quarters of the way there. He neither hurried nor hesitated, his pace remaining steady, his eyes focused.

'Go on, damn it,' Brannon whispered, yet he still expected Ahmed to falter.

Ahmed kept walking until he was just short of the finish line, and then, inexplicably, he stopped. Where Bakka had broken into a run to finish the ordeal, Ahmed simply stood there in the fire, his soles burning up.

There was complete silence. Nobody dared to even blink. Ahmed's pain must have been immense, yet he looked totally nonplussed, bored even. He turned his gaze along the crowd until he found Tariq Chaker, and then he spoke calmly. 'Well, my lord? What say you now?'

Tariq Chaker watched in astonishment. His son Bakka was the strongest man he knew, yet even he had been unable to resist hurrying the last few feet. This man, Ahmed, was still standing in there. And holding a conversation.

'Very well!' Tariq Chaker clapped his hands and beamed. 'It is done—get him out of there!'

The tension dissolved, and the crowd roared their appreciation. Ahmed was escorted from the fire and had his burnt feet tended to while Bakka, the erstwhile champion of the fire-bed, gazed at him in awe. 'You have my sword,' he assured Ahmed.

'How did you do it?' Brannon wanted to know, slightly miffed at the ease with which the Arab had beaten him.

Ahmed smiled. 'I prayed for Allah's help. He sent forth a cool wind to smother the coals, and thus I felt no pain.'

'Oh, I see.' Brannon rolled his eyes.

Tariq Chaker came pushing through the onlookers. He lowered his ancient frame to kneel beside Ahmed, and with a look of humble sincerity he said, 'Now that you have my respect and my ears, what is it you want me to do?'

So Ahmed told him.

CHAPTER FIFTEEN

Isach Sharraf had lived in the Taza Gap for most of his seven decades. As a boy his parents brought him into these golden-green pastures at the culmination of their journey from the coast of southern Spain, one of many families spearheading the latest wave of Jewish immigration into North Africa. Amid the combed furze grass of the valley, tucked between the Rif and Atlas Mountains, they had built a home of mud and pulped bark, dug a well from the ground, and sowed several acres of corn. Isach started breathing these airs when he was just five years old, had skinned his palms climbing the cedar trees that dotted the slopes, caught rabbits with his slingshot, and grown strong on the soil that nourished the animals that filled his belly. The Taza Gap was his flesh and blood.

Six decades later, their rugged patch of territory was tamed and cultivated and home to five more burgeoning families, Isach's sons having grown up, built houses, and raised broods of their own. It was to them that he entrusted the future of his small but beloved settlement. They were a close family. The wives visited each other daily with gifts of baked bread or to seek help with household tasks. They leaned on each other in the challenging times of childbirth or sickness or poor harvests. Their children played out the same games that Isach had done as a boy, chasing each other up the wild slopes and hiding among the strawberry trees. And every week on the Sabbath they gathered in Isach's home, where he said the prayers and offered the blessing and gave thanks. Out of his parents' humble beginnings, Isach had built a wholesome community.

This morning, like every morning, Isach looked to the rolling wooded hills that bordered the valley. He always did this nervously, as if afraid of what he might see. For four long years he had been watching those hills, watching to see what came out of them, but so far all that had come out were stories. Frightening stories, detailing the horrors and atrocities being carried out in the east where the mad sultan Yazid was pursuing his vendetta against the Jews. Stories had reached Isach of mass expulsions from the cities and the burning of villages in the countryside. Innocents were being slaughtered in the thousands, and not even the children were spared. If Yazid intended to remove every last Jew from Morocco, he had made a brisk start.

Every day Isach looked in fear, but every day the hills were empty. The years slowly passed, and Yazid stayed away. Seasons bloomed and died, birthdays came and went, the children grew, life went on, and all was quiet in the valley of Isach Sharraf.

This morning, however, the hills were not empty.

Out of the shadowed groves rode a line of horsemen, spreading wide across the valley to encircle the village. They wore black turbans and mulberry-coloured djellabas with sheathed swords on their saddle-packs. They were Arabs, from the east.

'Aaron!' Isach called his eldest son from the cornfield. 'Come here.'

'What is it, Father?' Aaron emerged sweaty-faced with a scythe in hand.

Isach didn't reply but indicated with his thumb the horsemen in the trees. Aaron's eyes widened. 'We should find the children.'

'Yes. Move them inside. And Aaron,' Isach said, gesturing to the scythe in his son's hand, 'bring that with you.'

The rumble of hooves grew louder. Aaron found all the young cousins playing hide-and-seek in the thickets behind his house, and he herded them into the byre, where he warned, 'You must stay here until I tell you to come out. And don't make a sound. Do you promise?' The row of little faces bobbed in assent, unsure whether they were still playing a game or not.

Isach ran to the other houses to warn them. The horsemen had now cleared the woods and were riding through the crops. Isach hammered on each door in turn, meeting three of his sons, though the fourth, Benjamin, was nowhere to be seen.

'Aaron has hidden the children in his byre,' Isach told them, so his sons instructed their wives to remain indoors, and they went to confront the visitors.

'Where is Benjamin?' Aaron asked them when they came outside his house. He carried his scythe and had concealed a pistol under his shirt.

'I don't know,' Isach answered worriedly. 'Perhaps he hunts in the hills.'

They had no more time for talk. The horsemen rode up by the fenced paddock, their steeds puffing heavily from the charge down the slope.

One of them cantered forward and regarded the five men coolly. 'Who are you?'

Isach felt his chest tighten. They were imperial soldiers, here doubtless on the sultan's business. 'I am Isach Sharraf,' he said, trying to smile. 'These are my sons. You are most welcome. May I bring you food and water?'

The rider looked around and sniffed. 'This is your farm?'

'Yes.'

'I am Kaid Saheed al-Kadel,' the man said. He waited for some moments and then raised his eyebrows. 'Well?'

'Kaid?' Isach said in confusion.

'I thought you were bringing us food and water.'

'Oh yes, forgive me.' Isach signalled to Aaron, and between them they retrieved some cuts of cold lamb and bread and filled several decanters of berry juice. The riders tethered their mounts and sat on a long trestle table with Isach and his four sons tending to them.

'Where are your wives?' al-Kadel finally asked. 'I see only men.'

'They wait inside, Kaid,' Isach said nervously. 'Your men are tired and do not need to be troubled by fussing women.' He grinned, trying to make light of the situation.

'And children? Where are all the children?'

Isach hesitated. 'There are none, Kaid,' he stuttered after an awkward silence, hoping his face did not look as red as it felt. 'I have not been blessed with grandchildren as yet. Someday, perhaps.'

The kaid peered around the farmhouse. By a side door he noticed a small, hand-carved rocking horse, a feather seat strapped to its back and bright eyes and a smiling mouth painted on its face.

He smiled, stretching his arms lazily. 'This is a good meal, Isach Sharraf. I thank you.'

'The honour is mine, Kaid al-Kadel,' Isach said, nodding in relief. 'Perhaps I can water your horses before you leave?'

'That would be a kindness indeed, Isach.'

With his sons helping, Isach led each of the horses in turn to the well and let them drink until their bellies were filled, and then they returned them to the soldiers. Kaid al-Kadel rose to his feet and took the reins of his horse. 'Thank you, Isach. They say the Jew is a greedy animal, but perhaps that is not true after all.'

'I am happy to offer you hospitality, Kaid,' Isach assured him.

Al-Kadel went to climb onto his horse, but then he paused. 'Just one more thing before we depart, my friend. Something that puzzles me.'

'Kaid?' Isach said uneasily.

'I'm curious. What would five grown men and their wives, without a single child to their name, be doing with one of those?' He pointed to the wooden rocking horse nearby.

Isach swallowed. He searched for an answer.

'It's mine,' Aaron interrupted. 'It belongs to me.'

'Yours?' Al-Kadel raised his eyebrows incredulously, giving a chuckle. 'Are you not a little old for such amusements? I would have thought your legs too long to sit on top.' The laughter spread around the ranks.

'It's just a fancy of mine,' Aaron said. 'I like to work with my hands.'

'Ah, we have something in common, then.' Al-Kadel smiled and raised his palms. 'You see these? I like to work with my hands too. I have a busy, busy pair of hands.'

Aaron nodded queasily.

Al-Kadel turned back to Isach. 'These are fine homes. I beg one more indulgence of you. Will you permit me and my men to take a look inside them?'

'Of course, Kaid, but I assure you there is little to see. It's a modest living we make out here.'

The kaid narrowed his eyes. 'How about that? May I look inside that?' He had indicated the thatched byre behind Aaron's house. Isach coughed as his throat seemed to constrict further.

'That's but a damp old cowshed, Kaid. Spare yourself the smell. Come, let me take you to my home instead.'

Al-Kadel ignored him and suddenly began to walk in the direction of the byre. Aaron intercepted him. 'My father is right, Kaid. Forget that filthy shed. Why don't you—'

'Get back, boy!' Al-Kadel snapped, placing his hand threateningly on the hilt of his sword. 'Stand by the wall. I shall look inside the byre.'

Before Aaron could protest further, the byre door abruptly swung open and the youngsters came spilling out of their hiding place with shrieks and squeals. In terror of al-Kadel's voice, they fled for cover into the stalks of the cornfield and disappeared. Al-Kadel spun around.

'So!' he snarled, eyes locking on the terrified Isach. 'You lie to me! Deceitful, lying Jews—I should have known!'

'No, Kaid,' Isach cried, 'you misunderstand!'

Blood mottled al-Kadel's face. 'Allah help me. Do you know *why* the sultan has ordered us to rid his kingdom of Jews, Isach? It's because they are a race of scheming rats and whores and thieves, plotters against His Majesty, parasites that feed on the blood of the righteous. I approached you in good faith, and you lied blatantly to my face. You think I am a dog, not worthy of your honesty?'

'No, Kaid, you are not a dog. Let me explain!'

'I am not a dog, Isach. But you are a pig. You and your entire family are pigs. You are lice on the sultan's holy back. You—' He was distracted then by a noise nearby. Isach looked too, and he recognised the figure that burst from the cornstalks.

'Benjamin, no!'

Benjamin, the second-youngest son, had been hiding in the crops and waiting for an opportunity all along. He charged from the greenery, cocked the pistol, and aimed it at the kaid's head. But Benjamin had never shot at a person before. His hand was unsteady, the aim too high. The pistol flashed, and the ball soared harmlessly into the air.

Al-Kadel reacted like a cobra. He pulled out a knife and hurled it, striking Benjamin in the chest. The young man lost his footing under the impact; he fell to his knees, gaping in horror at the six-inch blade protruding from his ribcage.

'Benjamin!' Isach's remaining sons howled in anguish. They saw the blood pouring from their brother, and they tried to go to him, but the soldiers pounced immediately. Swords were whipped out, and a vicious fight ensued, the trestle table sent toppling onto its side and Isach knocked to the ground. But it didn't last long.

Poorly armed and untrained, the young Jewish men were overcome one by one. Isach lay sprawled on his back, moaning in trauma. Al-Kadel wiped the blood from his sword and barked, 'Their brats have run into the fields. Find them! No one is to be left alive.' Five of the soldiers clambered on their horses and rode off. Al-Kadel peered down at Isach, shaking his head in perverse sympathy.

'Truly a pity, old man, that you had to be born a Jew.' He rammed his blade through Isach's throat and pulled it free with a sucking sound, and then he followed his remaining men towards the houses. They were hungry to find the women.

Isach's lifeblood gushed from the wound in his neck. He tried to speak, but his voice was gone. Slowly a swamp of blackness overwhelmed his vision. When he could no longer see, he closed his eyes. The last sounds he heard were the screams of his sons' wives as the soldiers found them.

High in the slopes, Kaid Azedine Ben Hassi swallowed the bitter bile that rose in his throat. He felt sick. Al-Kadel's men had caught all the children in the hills, and Ben Hassi flinched at the memory of what they did to them. It had become a game with the smallest ones, tossing them into the air and seeing who could slay them with a single sword-stroke as they fell. Some of them were no more than two years old. They didn't deserve to die like that.

The women had been raped and murdered in their houses and the farm buildings set alight. Thick black smoke rose over the valley as Ben Hassi gazed upon the scene of destruction. Their orders had been explicit—to remove all Jewish settlers from the Taza Gap using whatever means necessary—but Kaid al-Kadel had taken an undeniable pleasure in the killing. If it were possible, he loathed Jews even more than his crazed master in Fez.

Though they were of the same rank, al-Kadel had been given command of this mission, and there was nothing Ben Hassi could do about his tactics. Yazid would no doubt have approved heartily, would have applauded the sight of Jewish women lying bloody-legged amid their burning homes, their toddlers sprawled in the grass with their throats cut. Ben Hassi's veins swelled with the flow of his anger. He steadied himself, whispering a prayer to Allah for the souls of the victims. He was so ashamed.

How could he serve a man who would order such carnage? He had allowed his sense of duty to delude him as to what was right, but there was nothing in the world right about this. Rape and infanticide, Yazid's tools of the trade. Ben Hassi could tolerate no more.

He spurred his horse into movement and rode back over the hill to find his unit. In four days they would be back in Fez. He desperately needed to talk to Ahmed.

'I'm glad you changed your mind, Azedine,' Ahmed said. 'I would not have relished the thought of fighting you.'

Ben Hassi grunted in acknowledgement. 'Yazid is not fit to lead this country. I should have realised it a long time ago.'

'Can you be sure of your men's loyalty? If the sultan learns you have switched to the banner of Suliman...'

'My men will do whatever I tell them,' Ben Hassi said. 'They were taking orders from me long before Yazid arrived. You can count on them when the time comes.'

'Good. That time may not be far off now.' Ahmed went on to explain how Suliman's army was moving north to take Marrakech, after which it would continue towards the capital and face Yazid. He also told of the pledge of allegiance he had secured from the Berber tribes in the mountains, and Ben Hassi was impressed.

'Be wise, though,' he warned Ahmed. 'The Berbers will have to be strong, immensely strong, to take the brunt of Yazid's Imperial Guard. If they can hold

Yazid down long enough, then perhaps Suliman can indeed breach the city. When that happens, I will be there. We must seize strategic points—the palace, barracks, armoury, the cannon on the ramparts. My guess is that Yazid will put up the devil of all fights.'

'I'm certain he will. But he doesn't realise that the gates have already been sabotaged. He won't be able to close them in time. And I have a key to one of the armouries in my possession. Twenty men should be enough to get in there and clear it out.'

'Where is Suliman now?'

'Somewhere deep in the High Atlas as we speak, but he'll soon move into the desert and prepare for Marrakech. Yazid had planned to send battalions there in the spring. He would not be happy to know that he is about to lose the place to Suliman.'

Ben Hassi nodded. 'I will keep my eyes and ears open, then. As long as Yazid is unaware of Suliman's plans, hope lives. Let us keep it that way.' He rose up, clasping the younger man's shoulders. 'You have courage, Ahmed. Your father would have been proud. You should have been married by now.' He said the last sentence wistfully.

Ahmed shrugged. 'It wasn't to be. Yazid came, and everything changed.' He cleared his throat. 'I know she has since married…'

'Yes,' Ben Hassi said. 'And I am sorry. She would have been so much happier with you.' He reached down and strapped his sword back on his hip. 'Allah be with you, Ahmed. Indeed, let Him be with us all. From now on, it's death or justice we seek.'

⊕ ⊕ ⊕

Brannon awoke with a start and realised that there were guards hammering on his door. Imperial guards. He saw them through the window, and his blood chilled. Guards at a doorway meant trouble.

Pulling a haik over his naked body, he placed his scimitar by the bed within easy reach. The guards were armed. He felt like a snared animal.

Cautiously he unlocked the bolt and peered outside.

They were ordinary palace guards, Yazid's messengers. 'His Majesty sends for you,' one of them said. 'You must come with us.'

Brannon's pulse quickened. What did Yazid know? He glanced warily at his sword. 'But I must get dressed first.'

'Then do so quickly. But leave behind your weapons. You will have no need of them.'

No weapons. If something unpleasant awaited him at the palace, then he had to confront it without the assurance of a sword.

They escorted him politely but firmly through the pleasant Fez el-Djedid and on inside the regal gates of the palace. Instead of going to Yazid's chambers, they led him to a large, stone-walled courtyard beyond. Brannon now felt in serious danger. This courtyard was a place where Yazid was known to carry out executions, ones he wanted to observe in person. Its grounds had to be scoured every few weeks to remove the stains of blood.

But today the courtyard was crowded with people whose minds couldn't be further from hangings and beheadings. The palace guards had been busy, escorting dozens of the sultan's soldiers to this meeting point, though for what, Brannon still didn't know. Along with the soldiers, there was a substantial number of female slaves assembled. Both groups faced each other from opposite sides, a mixture of whites, blacks, and Arabs.

Then Yazid appeared.

He marched up the centre with his usual noisy retinue of servants and bodyguards, beaming broadly. He waved to the people and clapped his hands, clearly excited about what he had planned.

'My loyal warriors,' he addressed the soldiers, 'today you have been chosen to receive a special reward from me, your sultan, in return for the courage and devotion you have shown in my service. Each one of these women,' he said, indicating the females opposite, 'was hand-picked for her beauty and purity of body. They are to be given to you this morning, as your wives.'

A thunderous cheer went up from the ranks, and they bellowed Yazid's name in praise. But Brannon was aghast. A wife? He was up to his ears in a plot to topple the sultan—where was she supposed to fit?

For a few moments Yazid acknowledged the worship of the crowd, nodding imperiously. Then he rubbed his hands in anticipation. He would match up the couples himself, something he was looking forward to. A hundred men and a hundred women, to be paired off as he pleased. He began in earnest, picking out a man from the crowd, picking a woman, joining their hands, and sending them off. There was no prejudice as to race; white men were put with black women, black men with Arab women, Arab men with white women. The couples looked comically mismatched in some cases. Brannon saw a skinny little Turk, no more than five feet in height, being joined with a gigantic black woman with muscled arms who stood at least ten inches higher than him.

Brannon's own turn came eventually, and he was dreading to see what creature he would be gifted with. Yazid took his arm affectionately and led him out. 'My friend, for you I will find a woman so beautiful that you will weep when you lay eyes upon her.'

Brannon agreed he would probably weep, all right.

Yazid cast his eyes over the women, searching keenly, humming and muttering as he deliberated over the decision. The rows of blank female faces stared ahead. Finally Yazid spotted the one he wanted and exclaimed in satisfaction. The selection was made. He summoned the young woman from the crowd.

She was exactly to Yazid's personal taste: generously proportioned, big swinging breasts, wide hips. She came from the Bambara, the dominant tribe of Mali, and the rolls of flesh around her midriff quivered as she walked. Her teeth were large and very white, her hair was cropped short, and her ears were pierced with animal bones.

Brannon gulped.

She came only to his chest, but she was considerably wider and probably outweighed him. He saw that she looked as nervous as he did, and she lowered her head in mortification. Clearly she wasn't any more enthusiastic about this arrangement than he was.

'Ah, she likes you,' Yazid said, pleased. 'This is a marriage blessed.'

'Erm…' Brannon faltered. He couldn't spurn the girl, for Yazid had picked her personally. As he tried to avoid the sultan's eyes, thinking of a suitable answer, another face in the crowd caught his attention.

Asiya.

She was standing in the second line between two black women, gazing help-lessly at the ground. She was about to become a soldier's wife, too.

'That one,' Brannon blurted. 'Forgive me, Excellency. I would like that wom-an instead.'

A gasp of astonishment rose from the crowd. This was a gross insult. Not only had Brannon failed to thank the sultan for his kind gift, but he had actu-ally rejected it, asking instead for a replacement. A shudder of disgust rippled through the lines.

Yazid's expression was inscrutable for a moment, but he too was taken aback. He hadn't expected such bluntness—it was discourteous, to say the least. He glanced at the woman in question. She was a slight creature, thin-limbed—not at all what Yazid would have found attractive himself. He was aware of the hushed tension in the crowd—clearly they all expected some retribution to be inflicted on Brannon for his insolence.

He smiled. Killing the Irishman would give him no pleasure. They were brothers, after all, and such bold spirit was at least a change from all the fawning and drooling that Yazid was used to. For once he decided he would indulge it.

'So be it!' he announced magnanimously, dismissing the black woman and summoning Asiya forward. He took her hand and joined it with Brannon's, and then he raised an eyebrow. 'I trust the arrangement now meets with your ap-proval?'

Brannon nodded gratefully, aware that this unusual display of patience from the sultan was not to be tested twice. 'Thank you, Your Excellency. May Allah bless you always.'

Yazid declared them married, and it was done. He turned to the crowd and began his search for the next coupling.

Asiya held Brannon's hand as they walked away. Not until they were clear of the crowd did they speak. 'I don't know whether to be flattered or insulted,' she said. 'This I didn't see coming.'

'Likewise,' Brannon muttered. 'I was expecting to lose my head, but instead I gained a wife. Yes, Moulay Yazid is a somewhat unpredictable man. I wouldn't advise we forget that anytime soon.'

CHAPTER SIXTEEN

Asiya cast her eyes over the untidy one-room chamber that was Brannon's home, the last in a block of tenements to the east of the city which housed an assortment of soldiers, artisans, and freed slaves. There were food bowls on the bed, unwashed, some leaves on the floor that had blown in from outside, and a mangled lump of wax on the window which served as a candle. It was easy to tell, she mused, that he had no wife.

About to sit on the bed, she changed her mind, thinking it a little too familiar. Instead she opted for the single stool. Brannon stood in the centre of the room, scratching his head. He looked like he was searching for something to say, but he came up with nothing and began staring out the window as if there were suddenly a scene of extraordinary interest out there.

'You don't have to be so embarrassed, Brannon,' she said, trying to diffuse the stark awkwardness in the chamber.

'What?' He glanced at her. 'Oh. Sorry.' He scratched his head again. 'Um, are you hungry? I can prepare food. I have—'

'Brannon,' she said, smiling sweetly, 'now you are making me extremely nervous. Will you please sit down?'

He perched himself on the edge of the bed. 'It's a good thing Yazid doesn't know what you look like, or he might have recognised you. But don't worry, we're not really married. It was just a whim of his.'

'You want to return me already?' she asked with mock indignation.

'Goodness, no. It wouldn't be smart to insult Yazid twice in one day.'

'So tell me, why did you pick *me*? You had a whole choice of us out there.'

'Be glad I did, Asiya. Who would you have ended up with otherwise? Some lecherous old warthog with a potbelly and bad breath, no doubt.'

Her skin crawled at the thought of it.

'And more importantly,' he said, 'I could hardly take on a wife myself. Here I am, plotting to swipe the sultan's seat from under him—imagine what gossip the damned woman would be armed with. No, Asiya, you were the only sensible choice. Practical reasons entirely.'

'I'm impressed with your thinking.'

'That's not all. You won't have to work in the harem any more, not if they think you're my wife.'

That was a relief. Asiya hated the harem, hated those spoilt women with their petty feuds and schemes. She had had no voice in there but was merely a scratching-post for their claws and their wicked tantrums, indulging their whims and placating their self-pity. 'If I never set foot in the place again,' she assured Brannon, 'I'll not mourn.'

'Good. You're safe in this house, Asiya. It's a refuge, for both of us.'

'But where will I sleep?' she asked, and then she blushed for she hadn't meant to raise it so abruptly.

Brannon gazed around the cramped chamber. It offered no obvious solution. 'Well, you can sleep in the bed, of course. I'll sleep on the floor.'

There were problems with that. 'What about, um, privacy?'

'I can sleep on the road if you like. But I'll need a blanket to keep the insects off.'

'No, Brannon,' she said in haste. 'There's no need to do that. Stay with me.'

He stood up. 'Don't worry about your privacy, Asiya. I know a lady likes respect, and I do have a sense of discipline, believe it or not.'

'Yes, Brannon.' But the conversation had made her uncomfortable. It wasn't *his* sense of discipline that she worried about.

'That's ridiculous,' Brannon scoffed. 'What a thing to say. Nothing is going to happen.'

'It had better not.' Ahmed was greatly perturbed at this new domestic arrangement. He had lately begun to suspect Asiya of harbouring feelings for a certain Irishman, the kind of feelings a young girl would never discuss openly but would hoard within herself like treasured gems in a jewellery box, manifested only in gestures and nervous smiles and gazes. Feelings that could cause all sorts of trouble. He knew how attractive his sister was. He knew that most men, in this situation, would be unable to resist taking advantage.

'She's my flesh and blood,' he warned. 'If she comes to any…complication, under your care, you will answer to me. And I won't make it nice.'

'Enough of your threats,' Brannon said reprovingly. 'Didn't I just give you my word?'

'She's not your wife. This is not a proper marriage.'

'Well, the sultan of Morocco seems to think it's all right. And he's the one who married us.'

'Yazid has no authority to marry you,' Ahmed fumed.

'Ahmed, not that it's your business, but you should know that I am promised to somebody else. Her name is Orlaith, and she is beautiful. I won't be bothering your sister.'

'Orlaith—I hope she *is* beautiful.' Ahmed sighed. Protecting Asiya from male attention was one thing, but protecting her from the snares of her own affectionate nature was another. He would simply have to trust Brannon.

'What other news?' Brannon asked, trying to distract the Moroccan from his woes. 'That noble cousin of yours is taking his time in liberating us, isn't he?'

Ahmed glanced warily at the guards around the coffee house. 'Kaid Ben Hassi came to me yesterday. He wants to join us. This is good, for Azedine is a great man. I was right to put faith in him.'

Brannon remembered Ben Hassi. He was the kaid who had rescued him from the fight with the guards at the wall, back when Brannon was still a slave. That seemed a long time ago now.

'He has men,' Ahmed explained, 'and he is willing to commit to Suliman's campaign. We will need loyal troops in the city when the battle begins.'

'You make it sound so simple. But I'm getting tired of waiting, Ahmed. When will—'

'Soon, Brannon. Soon. Just stay sharp, keep your wits about you.' Ahmed's eyes narrowed as he rose up. 'And keep your hands to yourself, too. You know what I mean.'

Brannon guffawed at that. Ahmed glowered at him and turned to head into the streets.

❀ ❀ ❀

Asiya soon found that, ironically, a married woman enjoyed far less freedom than a slave did. When she worked in the harem, she was able to move about with relatively little restriction as she attended to her chores, but now, as a Muslim wife, she was limited in the places she could go without her husband being present. The law was strict for women. It was frustrating, particularly given that they weren't even man and wife in the fullest sense.

The end of Ramadan came as a blessed relief. For that whole month Muslims everywhere had carried out the religious fast, denying themselves food and drink in the hours between sunrise and sunset, and attempting to more closely follow the teachings of Islam by refraining from violent actions, lustful thoughts, gossip, greed, and other such ungodliness in general. Asiya eagerly awaited the end of Ramadan, for it brought the traditional festival, the Eid al-Fitr, which celebrated the breaking of the fast. After some initial grousing, Brannon agreed to decorate the house with ribbons and lights, and once he was caught up in the mood, he went out and bought her a new headscarf and himself a pair of shoes. In the evenings they joined in the revelries taking place outside, following the crowds through the streets where there was music, acrobats, snake charmers, puppet shows, and fireworks. It was loud and colourful, full of infectious cheer, and they enjoyed themselves immensely.

'No more!' Brannon begged as yet another swarm of grubby urchins surrounded his legs and began tugging at his wrists. He had been plying them with sweet treats and indulging their games all night, but he found to his dismay that their energies far outstretched his.

'Make them race again,' Asiya encouraged him gleefully. 'The one where you pick up their ankles and they run on their hands. They like that one!'

'You're supposed to be on my side,' he tutted. 'It's a good thing this party happens only once a year.' Grumbling, he allowed himself to be led back into the street to continue the competition.

As Asiya moved through the crowd, a voice hailed her.

'Asiya! What a surprise!'

She looked across and sighed inwardly. Somebody she had no desire to meet. 'Reema.'

'I thought it was you,' Reema said in delight. 'But what are you doing here?'

'I'm married now, Reema. I won't be working in the harem any more.'

'Married!' Reema blurted the word so loudly that several looks were thrown in their direction. 'Married, oh that is so exciting, Asiya! But where is your husband?'

'He's somewhere around.' Asiya had no desire to indulge the girl.

'And where do you live?'

'Nearby.'

'That's so wonderful. You are lucky, Asiya, to have a husband. I, alas,' she said, putting on a mournful face, 'I'm still only a plaything for Naseem al-Malek. Life can be so unfair. He barely even lets me go outside.'

Reema's closeness to Yazid's notorious general was another reason why Asiya was reluctant to encourage her company. 'I'm sure it will turn out well for you, Reema. Now I hope you'll forgive me,' she said as she glanced up the street, 'but it's time I returned home. My husband is a strict man.'

Reema kissed her cheeks like they were sisters parting. 'Oh, I do hope to see you soon, Asiya. Perhaps I can visit you? I'm sure Naseem would allow it...'

'Um, yes,' Asiya mumbled awkwardly. Brannon would have a seizure at the thought of al-Malek's concubine inside his house. 'I really must go, Reema. I'm sorry.' The youngsters were still frolicking with Brannon, but Asiya suddenly wished to be indoors. She slipped through the crowd. Bits of coloured paper blew across her path as she hurried along, taking a brief look back once she reached her door. The sounds of wild carousing echoed across the city. Their small house was in darkness, eerie candlelight shapes gleaming in the window. She opened the door and locked it carefully behind her.

A little bit up the street, Reema had followed at a discreet distance. She was hugely jealous and unable to contain her curiosity—what kind of house did Asiya live in? She was relieved to see that it was nothing too elegant but a modest tenement room with a back garden. Still, it was a house, and Asiya had a husband. Reema was anxious to get a look at the husband, too. Who was he? What was his trade? She would have to meet him. Now that she knew where Asiya lived, it shouldn't be too difficult.

The Eid al-Fitr came to an end within the week, the decorations were taken down, and the streets returned to teeming normality. Brannon continued his long spells at the harem, almost wishing for trouble to break the monotony, but all was quiet. Yazid closeted himself within his palace. Sentries watched from the ramparts. Nothing stirred for many days.

On Friday evening he plodded off through the twisting turmoil of the medina, an early scattering of star-lights twinkling in the sky. A rare tranquillity rested over the city as tired peddlers dragged their carts home and shopkeepers shuttered their doors, loath to leave so much as a toothpick behind. Around here beggars would steal anything not nailed down.

Brannon's back was aching. He didn't relish another night of sleeping on the floor, its surface of close-packed earth as hard as teak. Yet he hadn't much other choice, given the situation. It was a strange, strange set of circumstances. They were married, but not quite. They shared a house, but not a bed. He looked after her, but he couldn't kiss her. It left his head in knots.

She greeted him as he arrived, and not for the first time he felt a pang of desire when he saw her. She was truly beautiful, her eyes glittering amid the dusky complexion of her face. Smiling in welcome, she said, 'I have a meal ready. You made good time.'

'Welcome words. Let me clean up first.'

Asiya had earlier prepared a couscous of granulated millet flour soaked in a broth and flavoured with cuts of smoked lamb. To the granules she added butter, garlic, dried peas, and raisins and garnished it with eggs, and then she served it up in a large stoneware bowl. Once it was sufficiently heated, the smell wafted pleasantly in the room.

While Brannon went out the back, stripped off his upper clothing, and filled a jug of water, she lit candles and placed them around the chamber to lift the evening gloom. She caught a glimpse of him as he splashed the cold water over himself, droplets sparkling on the sleek contours of his chest. Her breath quickened, and she returned to her tasks with a nervous diligence.

When he was washed and had changed his clothes, they sat on cushions around the food bowl and scooped a plateful each. The stew was delicious, and Brannon helped himself to a second portion, which pleased Asiya. After dinner they sat in the back garden and watched the last slivers of light submerge into the black sky. This was the most peaceful time of the day, and they were comfortable enough to enjoy it without the need for trite conversation.

After a while the candles began to attract insects into the house, so they shut the door and retired inside. Brannon closed the curtains and placed the candles by the bedside. He searched for his sleeping mat.

'It's here,' Asiya said, retrieving it from under the bed. He turned around and, so small was the room, almost knocked her over.

'Sorry.' He grasped her arm to steady her. 'You'll have to excuse my big feet.'

She laughed as a light colour flushed her cheeks. 'It's all right. I don't think this house was built for two people.'

'No.' They stood facing each other for a moment, a little longer than was necessary. When Brannon spoke, his voice was husky. 'I'd better lock the door.' He did this every night, making a laborious task of it and thus giving her ample time to slip into her nightdress with privacy. When he heard the rustle of her bed-sheets, he came back and blew out the candles.

'Good night, Asiya.'

'Good night, Brannon.'

She shut her eyes, determined to settle herself. It was late now. She pulled the blanket to her chin and tried to drift off. She wanted, needed, to give herself over to peaceful slumber. Yet she couldn't. It was so quiet. She listened to Brannon's breathing, wondering if he was asleep. But he was awake too. An hour slid by. Nothing moved as they both stared into the darkness of the low ceiling.

'Brannon?' she whispered eventually.

Silence for a moment. Then, 'Yes?'

'Can I ask you something?'

'Yes.'

'I was wondering—is the floor uncomfortable?'

Another silence.

'It's not so bad.'

'No? All right then.' She looked into the shadows where he was lying. 'Good night, Brannon.'

'Good night, Asiya.'

They lay for several minutes, the only sound being the drumming of insects against the window. Then Asiya spoke again.

'Brannon…will you lie next to me?'

He let out a sigh. 'I can't.'

'Please, Brannon.' Her voice dropped a little. 'Please.'

He didn't move for a while. She could almost hear him struggling inwardly with his conscience. Then he said, 'No, Asiya. Go to sleep.' He turned on his side and didn't speak again. Nor did she.

Brannon slept only fitfully during the night, his mind tormented by nightmares. He dreamed of frost-hardened soil, of black crows on the thatch, his father's withered hand rising from the grave. He dreamt he saw Orlaith, her body and face as clear as the daytime sun. One moment she was before him with her arms spread in embrace, and the next she was far away, in the sea, being swept out by cold waves. He tried to swim to her, but she was dragged down by unseen arms and he couldn't save her. He screamed with the agony of it, sobbed with effort. 'Orlaith!' he cried.

'Brannon.' And suddenly she was beside him again, clasping his hands, soothing him. 'Brannon, it's all right.'

'Orlaith,' he said in relief. 'Thank God.' He was out of breath, his heart thumping.

'Don't be afraid,' she murmured, her face only an inch from his. He kissed her deeply, ran his fingers through her hair, and looked into her eyes. God, but she was so beautiful.

Slowly the room came into focus around him. Orlaith's face altered slightly; he became aware of his senses again, of the hard floor underneath him, the woollen blanket covering his legs.

'Orlaith?' he stammered, his heart sinking with impending loss.

'Brannon...' She went to kiss him, but he withdrew weakly.

'No.' He tried to turn away. Gently she touched his forehead and cheek and lips, and he felt a shudder of pleasure at the sensation. He wished her so badly to be Orlaith, so much so that his resistance began to crumble. 'Asiya, no.'

She kissed him softly, like a mother's kiss on a sick child's brow, tender yet powerful with emotion. Brannon's need struck him like thunder rolling in from the sea; he needed physical contact, he needed comfort, solace, love. He needed this woman in a way he couldn't fully understand. And she was there for him.

They kissed again, and it became a thing of urgency. He pressed his lips so hard against hers that she whimpered in pain, yet she wrapped her arms around his body to pull him closer, terrified that he might change his mind. He ran his hands under the light muslin of her nightdress, seeking out the warmth of her skin, grasping the roundness of her breasts and feeling the pert arousal of her nipples. She panted with the feel of his hands and clasped his head to her chest. Gently he turned her over onto her back, and she lay there, waiting in emotional and physical agony for it to happen. 'Please hurry, Brannon,' she begged him. 'Please...'

The sudden sting when he entered her was a brief pain only, quickly banished as an unexpected warm feeling flooded her lower body and was washed up along her belly and breasts to the base of her throat. She gasped for breath, lifting her legs around him and trying to cocoon them both together. She closed her eyes and surrendered herself completely, and he carried her off to distant worlds of bliss, worlds that she never even knew existed. 'Brannon, I love you,' she moaned, almost in delirium. 'I love you, I love you...'

Later, much later, the nightmares returned. As a pearly dawn light crept under the curtains, Brannon was shuddering in his sleep and trying to fight away demon dreams, seeing in the deep recesses of his mind that Orlaith was in trouble, and he was gripped by the horror that he was unable to help. He was losing her, and he was failing her, in so many cruel and terrible ways.

CHAPTER SEVENTEEN

Just after eight o'clock in the morning, as grey clouds replaced the black empti-ness of the night, a coach rolled through the gates of Dromkeen Hall. The frost crunched under the wheels, and the driver pulled to a stop outside the front door. It was bitterly cold. He blew through his hands and hopped down from the coach. Opening the narrow side door, he grinned wryly.

'Been a good girl for you, has she, Vin?'

Vincent was seated uncomfortably on a straw cushion, his pallor ashy-blue from the ceaseless draughts that had been hounding the cabin.

'I swear, McGurk,' he grumbled, 'that you managed to hit every poxed rut and stone over that whole poxed journey. Didn't you, you bastard?'

McGurk chuckled. 'I got you here in one piece—exactly what I was paid to do. How's her ladyship?'

Vincent glowered across at his fellow passenger. Randall had ordered him to escort her back to Dromkeen Hall in a hired coach while Sean was taken off her and put in Randall's own coach. Randall said he couldn't bear the journey home sitting next to her. Not without strangling her. She had finally fallen asleep in the last few miles, exhausted from crying. There were dark tear smudges down her cheeks.

'She'll be a damn sight worse in a while,' Vincent said. 'Mr Whiteley is wait-ing for her. And I hope he'll have more than a slap for the back-stabbing little bitch.' Reaching across, he gently squeezed her nose so that her breathing was interrupted. Nothing happened for a moment, but suddenly she shot forward and erupted into a fit of spluttering and coughing. Both men laughed.

'Rise and shine, my lady,' Vincent sneered. 'Time to face the beautiful music.'

Orlaith blinked, momentarily uncertain of her whereabouts. Vincent's barbarous features were the first thing that loomed into view, and she wanted to weep. 'Leave me alone,' she pleaded. 'Where are we?'

'Hold your sauce, you thieving mongrel. You're lucky to make it this far. If it was up to me, I'd have drowned you in the Lee, you and that snot-nosed runt…'

Sean—her thoughts immediately turned to him. But Sean would already be home, taken from her by Randall back in Cork City, a taste of the punishment he must already be brewing. God alone knew what would come next.

'Up!' Vincent grabbed her arm and dragged her from the coach, purposely releasing his grip suddenly so that she stumbled to the ground. 'Up, I said!' He stood on her leg, pressing down viciously until she screamed in pain. 'Hit me over the head, would you? You cow, I should have—'

'What's going on here?' The house had opened without their realising. Randall appeared on the front steps.

'Sir!' Vincent jumped back sheepishly. 'Sir, she was giving us trouble again. I was trying to restrain her.'

'Trouble, eh?' Randall descended the steps. 'Yes, trouble seems to follow this girl around like crabs on a whore. More's the pity, we all get infected by it.' He peered down at Orlaith. 'Hello, my dear. You took your time—we beat you here by a good hour. Aren't you going to give me a hug and a kiss?'

With a brave effort, she hauled herself to her feet and faced him. 'Where's Sean? I want to see him.'

Randall chuckled. 'Oh, but you're in no position to be giving demands, Orlaith. Sean's fate is in my hands. As is yours. And I've been making plans.'

'Randall, I can explain what I did—'

'Oh please, Orlaith. It's getting tiresome now. And I'm getting cold.' He snapped his fingers. 'Bring her into the library. I wish to have a private discussion with her.'

Orlaith was bundled up the steps by Vincent, and they disappeared into the house. Randall turned to McGurk the driver. 'Thank you, my good man, and I hope the journey wasn't too taxing. You've been reimbursed?'

'Yes, sir. The money what you gave me in Cork, sir.'

'Good. Then get the hell out of here.'

❀ ❀ ❀

It was so cold inside the library that Orlaith saw mists of breath in front of her face. She hugged her arms to her chest. 'I want to see Sean.'

Vincent stared back at her. He didn't reply.

The door opened.

'Thank you, Vincent, that will be all,' Randall said, ushering the estate hand out. He rubbed his hands briskly. 'Goodness, I should have had Kathy light the fire. Then again, I thought a warm welcome might be out of place.'

'I want to see Sean,' Orlaith repeated.

'Kathy's looking after him. I haven't beaten the lad, if that's what you're worried about. I don't care if I never see the squealer again. Squeals like a piglet, he does! All the way back from Cork, my ears were—'

Orlaith felt dizzy. She placed a hand on the armchair to balance. 'Randall, what is it you want? Please let me see my son. He's innocent.'

'As I said, I don't care to ever see him again. Nor you, for that matter. My own wife! A dose of poison.'

She hesitated. 'Do you mean…do you want us to go?'

'I do, by God. I do.'

She felt relief. 'It's for the best. I should never have been your wife. I will go, and Sean. We won't bother you again. Thank you, Randall.'

He grinned. 'Hold on a moment, Orlaith. You misunderstand. You think it's as simple as that?' He laughed. 'Oh, my dear, your audacity is breathtaking. No, it's not quite as smooth.'

'Go on then.' She braved herself. 'You will thrash me again, won't you? Blacken my eyes and burst my lip. Have your vengeance, Randall.'

His smile faded. 'In a moment—I will.'

She took a step back.

He walked to the decanter and poured a drink. 'Your real punishment, however, will remind you for the rest of your life that you should never have betrayed me. Your price will be eternal.'

Orlaith felt the cold reach into her deepest organs. 'Where's Sean? I want to see him...'

'I will allow that—so that you can say your goodbyes.'

'My what?'

He swallowed the glass in a single gulp. Slowly he removed his coat and shirt and began undoing his breeches. 'But first of all...'

'No, Randall...' She fell to her knees. 'Please! Is there no compassion in you? Please not now, Randall, I beg you—'

He kicked off his shoes. They clattered against the hearth's brass rail.

And he advanced.

CHAPTER EIGHTEEN

Grunting with effort, Brannon banged his sandals against the clay wall, trying to remove several days' worth of dirt. The Moroccan mud clung just as hard as the Irish stuff did, he reckoned bemusedly. Once he was done with the sandals, he turned to his djellaba, and the clouds of dust raised by his efforts shone in the morning sunlight. Asiya was in the house washing the food bowls, humming a quiet song to herself. The night before hadn't been mentioned since.

Brannon dressed himself, secured his belt, and strapped on his sword. He felt a loneliness today. He was in a cold place, an empty place, more troubling to his soul than he would ever have imagined. It was remorse, he supposed. Remorse and guilt. And regret, certainly. It had been an act of desperation; he hadn't meant it to happen. He hadn't hoped for it, yet no amount of inner excuses could take it away. What makes a man do what he knows is wrong?

Asiya appeared at the back door then, and her whole demeanour seemed to be the polar opposite of what he was feeling. 'Do you need help?' she asked, smiling sweetly like the angel she really was. 'I can clean your uniform before you leave.'

'No. I can manage it on my own.' *Christ, Ryan, what a bastard you are*, he thought.

Asiya didn't notice his brooding frame of mind, and she went about her chores, sweeping the dead leaves from the yard and rearranging the flowerpots.

'I'm going to the barracks this morning,' Brannon said, anxious to divert himself from his melancholy. 'Ahmed may be there. Do you have any messages for him?'

211

'Send him my love. Tell him to visit me when he can.' Her skin glowed with particular radiance. She looked happy.

'He might not be able to,' Brannon warned. 'He's watching his back carefully these days. If anyone recognises him, we're in trouble.'

'So when will I see him next?'

'I'm not sure—a lot is happening at the moment. Once Suliman has taken Marrakech, he will drive his army up to Fez. The Berbers will lure Yazid's forces outside, Kaid Ben Hassi will launch an attack from within, and Suliman can march right through.' He grinned for the first time that morning, reminding himself of what they were planning. 'Yazid won't stand a chance. He's finished. We'll put a noose round the bastard's head and hang him off the city walls.' He tied on his sandals. 'Now, I must go. The kaids are strict on time.'

'Brannon?' She stalled him before he could leave. 'Brannon, I just wanted to say, last night—'

'I'll be late, Asiya,' he said, cutting her off. 'I'll talk to you later.' *Yes, later*, he thought. *A very careful discussion.*

'Goodbye, Brannon.' She waved and blew him a kiss, but he had already turned his back. Nonetheless, she couldn't suppress a shiver of pleasure. She was indeed happy. He was a wonderful man, brave, handsome, and strong. Perhaps out of a bleak life she might finally know brighter things.

Reema swung the fruit basket in her hand as she cast a distasteful eye over the scrawny cats and children that loitered in the street. It was not an affluent area, she observed. Asiya might live in a house with a husband, but she could not lord it over the rest of them just yet. That was a relief to Reema, who was prone to frequent and sometimes crippling bouts of jealousy, particularly in relation to the other slave girls.

She knew where she must go now, and her curiosity was starting to niggle. The fruit basket was ideal as a present, a convenient excuse to be invited into Asiya's home. Reema intended to examine every inch of its interior. She was desperate to see the husband, too. Was he wealthy? Hardly, considering his tiny house. Hopefully not too wealthy, anyway, for Reema couldn't stomach the notion of Asiya having a more comfortable lifestyle than her.

She spotted the house at the end of its row. The back garden was not small, she noted with irritation. It had been recently swept clean and was prettily arranged with a number of clay pots holding tall green plants.

She sidled up and peered over the low wall. When she heard voices, she took a step back; Asiya's husband must be home. Unable to resist it, she indulged herself in a few moments' eavesdropping. What kind of conversation would they be having? Something romantic, no doubt.

The conversation lasted only a few minutes, but she heard every word. The front door opened, and Asiya's husband stepped out, taking a quick look around. Reema ducked below the wall. He didn't see her, and he turned to walk up the street.

Her hands trembled with shock. She couldn't believe it. She couldn't believe what she had just heard.

Asiya, sweet Asiya, involved in a murderous plot against Sultan Moulay Yazid? It was too incredible to swallow. Asiya and her husband, both knee-deep in a rebellion with the sultan's wicked brother Suliman. And Reema recognised the husband, too. He was an army captain, an Irishman, known to be a personal favourite of Moulay Yazid. A personal favourite, yet only just now he had spoken of hanging the sultan from the city walls! This was the most sensational thing Reema had heard in years.

She had to tell someone. She would burst. Scandal didn't come any more delicious than this.

There was only one obvious choice—someone from whom she would be guaranteed keen attention and, hopefully, would receive a generous measure of gratitude in return. General Naseem al-Malek, the sultan's most ruthless general, who counted Reema as his favourite of the concubines. This piece of information could be worth a lot to him—and to her, if al-Malek was in a good mood.

She tossed the fruit basket on the road, where it was snatched at by the gabbling urchins, and she hurried off to the general's private quarters, a lavishly furnished riad with an interior garden adjoined to the soldiers' barracks. It was a ten-minute walk, no more. And what a story she had to tell him.

When he had finished speaking, General Naseem al-Malek bowed his head in regret. 'Forgive me, Your Excellency, for being the bearer of this ghastly news.'

He was alone with the sultan, the bodyguards and attendants having been ordered outside. Moulay Yazid's breathing was rapid, his temper was soaring, and spittle flew from his lips as he pranced around the room. 'Dogs!' He pulled out his sword and began waving it about. Al-Malek kept his head low, fearing that the sultan might misdirect one of the wild swings.

'I'll not forgive you, General,' Yazid hissed, 'because you have done nothing wrong. But as for those snakes who have joined my treacherous brother against me...' He let out a profanity which made al-Malek flinch. 'Give me their names again!'

'As I said, Excellency, I have only two names for certain. Azedine Ben Hassi and—'

'Ben Hassi,' Yazid snarled. 'I should have killed him long ago. A curse on his soul! I'll strip the skin off his back and feed his innards to the lions. I'll put his head on a pike and leave it there for the next two thousand years. I'll...' Yazid recited the list of horrors that he had in mind for Ben Hassi, and when he was finished, al-Malek continued.

'And Brannon Ryan, the young Irish captain.' Al-Malek swallowed nervously. 'I know this must be a grave disappointment for you, Your Excellency. After all the kindness you showed him. And he turns against you like this. He's no better than a sewer rat.'

Yazid closed his eyes for a moment. He was indeed disappointed. He had liked the Irishman. He had liked him a lot. He had believed that some form of brotherhood existed between them, due to their shared Irish blood. Clearly Brannon Ryan had not seen it that way.

'The third man I don't know,' al-Malek admitted. 'My source heard him referred to as Ahmed, though this is not hugely helpful. But it seems he is in league with Suliman, and Suliman is on his way to take Marrakech. They must know that you planned to send me there, Excellency. I can't imagine how they discovered this information.'

'Ahmed,' Yazid murmured. Who was Ahmed, he wondered. There must be a thousand Ahmeds in Fez alone. 'We will act fast,' he said. 'Decisively. We will crush this little rebellion, cut off the poisonous limb before it infects the rest of the body.'

'A wonderful idea, Excellency. I will move to recall our troops from the countryside. We will garrison Fez and then send an army south. Suliman will be stopped long before he can threaten our walls.'

'Wait,' Yazid cautioned him. 'Recall the troops, but do it discreetly. Our enemies must not know that we have uncovered their plot. Warn your source to speak to no one.' He came forward and sat down beside al-Malek.

'Listen to me carefully. Here's what we will do.'

Saleem al-Harid was Moulay Yazid's most efficient spy. Short, slight, and chinless, he could move about as unobtrusively as the shadows and possessed probably the sharpest set of eyes and ears in Fez. Whether threading through the babbling crowds in the markets or sitting inside a smoky coffee house, Saleem had the kind of bland and forgettable face that never merited a second glance, never invited even the slightest curiosity. It would hardly have been that way, of course, had the passers-by realised how close in proximity they were to one of the most dangerous men in Morocco. It was Saleem's job to gather information and expose potential enemies of the sultan, thereby preserving the security of his reign. Countless numbers died because of what he did for a living.

This morning Saleem shuffled about with an affected limp, dressed in a tattered djellaba which was stained brown with the dust of the city. He loitered among the vagrants who congested the street, their begging hands thrust out to the merchants who walked by in silken robes. Saleem held out his palms to plead and was satisfied to see that he was completely ignored.

His eyes moved across the road. There was a house at the end of the row, its door locked. Both its inhabitants were out. Saleem waited. He had learned patience in this game. Patience was the surest means of outwitting a hasty enemy. It was a European, a blond-haired Irish captain whom he sought today. Earlier he had pushed a short, handwritten message under the door for the Irishman to find, part of Saleem's plan to snare the one they knew only as Ahmed. The Irishman was not to be arrested yet, Yazid had warned. Not until he'd served his purpose.

Saleem's thoughts were distracted as he glanced up the street. The European stood out clearly in the crowd—he was over six feet tall, and his blond locks shone like spun gold in the sunlight. He was returning from the harem, Saleem knew, heading for home. The Irishman brushed away the pawing beggars and took a quick look around before unlocking his door. Saleem adjusted his hood and settled down to watch.

Paper rustled as Brannon kicked off his sandals. He picked up the message in surprise and saw that it was written in neat Arabic script. His literacy skills were still poor, so he puzzled over the words for a time, but eventually deciphered their meaning.

We must speak urgently. Do not delay.

Ahmed

Brannon groaned. Was this something to do with Asiya? Surely she hadn't been stupid enough to tell him…

Swearing in frustration, he re-fastened his belt and put his sandals on. He knew Ahmed would be at the barracks at this time, spitting fire no doubt, heart set on bloody vengeance. Protective older brothers were never easy to placate, and Ahmed didn't like Brannon at the best of times.

Locking the door behind him, he turned into the crowd and made his way up the street. The barracks were not far, but there was a busy traffic of people and donkeys. He cursed silently, trying to curb his impatience. This was a matter that had to be nipped in the bud.

To his left, unseen to him, a small figure emerged from the rabble of beggars and slipped discreetly into the crowd. He remained a few paces back, his face concealed under the shadow of his hood, and with watchful eyes he followed the trail.

Ahmed was tackling a plate of pigeon breasts stuffed with tomatoes when Brannon entered the otherwise empty dining hall. He frowned in consternation and with great difficulty forced a mouthful of fatty chunks down his gullet. 'Brannon, something's wrong?'

The latter smiled tentatively, like an errant child. 'Now, whatever you've heard, let me explain. It was just a mistake.'

'What are you talking about?'

'I got your message.' Brannon tossed the piece of paper on the table. 'And I can guess what it's about...'

Ahmed stared at the words on the paper and felt a chill run down his spine, as though they pronounced his death sentence. 'Where did you get that?'

'It was left under my door. You didn't write it?'

'No. I didn't write it.' Ahmed's hand moved for his scimitar as he looked uneasily to the corridors. 'Are you alone?'

'Of course, why do you—'

Brannon's sentence was cut short by the sound of footsteps in the passage. Two figures appeared in the archway, a tiny goblin-man alongside a tall, bearded officer. The little man pointed towards Brannon and Ahmed, and the officer nodded.

'Shit,' Brannon whispered. He recognised the taller man.

General Naseem al-Malek approached them without hurry, his eyes seeming to glow like hot embers, and when he was a few feet away, he stopped. 'You fools,' he said quietly.

'General?' Brannon inquired, eyebrows raised.

Al-Malek clapped his hands once, and suddenly the corridors were echoing with dozens of charging feet. A long line of armed soldiers trooped into the hall, spreading out along the walls to seal off the exit points and snare their victims.

'Run!' Ahmed yelled at Brannon.

They clambered up and sprinted for the last passage at the end of the hall, but moments later a second line of soldiers burst in and cut them off. They hesitated, trapped on both sides. The two groups of soldiers advanced. Brannon didn't bother to unsheathe his sword, for they were outnumbered by about forty to one.

'Two rats have been caught in the pantry,' said a voice, and the soldiers parted to allow al-Malek through. He grinned at the two fugitives. 'Chop off their heads and boil their tails, I say.'

'You're quite the poet, General,' Brannon said. 'Perhaps your graceful tongue can explain what on earth is going on.'

'Don't feign innocence, Captain,' al-Malek growled. 'Your treachery has been exposed. You know exactly why we're here.'

'I have no idea, General.' Though he maintained a calm façade, Brannon's mind was racing. Who had betrayed them? Daniel? Asiya? Surely not.

'And you,' al-Malek said, turning his eyes on Ahmed. 'I know who you are. You're the architect of this foul scheme, are you not? I know you're in league with that murderous rebel Suliman. I know of your plans. Well, today, Ahmed, you are going to die a death more horrible than anything your worst nightmares could conjure up.'

Ahmed stared back at him coolly. He didn't reply.

'Hah! You don't even deny my charges!' al-Malek snarled in contempt.

'He's very shy,' Brannon intervened.

'Quiet, you Irish dog.' Al-Malek thrust his finger at Brannon. 'You have betrayed the trust of the sultan, he who is beloved of Allah. You have stabbed him in the back and wounded him most grievously. For this, you will—'

'—die a death more horrible than anything,' Brannon finished the sentence. 'Yes, I can imagine.'

Al-Malek chuckled, a coarse, malevolent sound that made Brannon's skin prickle. 'No, Irishman, you will not die today. You will take many, many weeks to die, and in that time we will teach you a whole new understanding of the concept of pain. You will scream for mercy, you will beg for the release of death, but we will kill you only one inch at a time. That is the reward for the man who chose to turn his back on his sultan.'

Brannon felt his mouth go dry. He had heard of Yazid's infamous torture methods; a man would be forced to die over a period of weeks, a slow and lingering death during which he would be driven to the point of insanity by the cruel horrors inflicted on him. Brannon had experienced in person the screams of such men. He would not have wished the ordeal on anyone.

'It's nice to be made a fuss of,' he quipped, concealing his fear. 'But there's no need to go to all that trouble.'

Al-Malek ignored him. 'And now, you will be brought before His Majesty. The sultan has been terribly vexed by this whole business. He wishes to meet the traitors.' Al-Malek's eyes gleamed. 'And he is not a happy man.' He turned to the soldiers. 'Go ahead, seize them!'

Before Brannon could react, Ahmed suddenly bolted to the side and drove his shoulder against one of the tall braziers that illuminated the room. It toppled over, slamming across the path of the soldiers and scattering coals between their feet. As they held off momentarily to avoid the flow of hot coals, a tiny gap opened in their line. It was enough for Ahmed.

'Go!' He grabbed Brannon's arm, and they dashed into the gap, ducking under the swing of a broadsword and charging onwards. The passages were still blocked, and they found themselves up against a large window that overlooked the street below.

General al-Malek laughed scornfully. 'A clever little move, but rather pointless, wouldn't you say? You're still trapped.'

'He's right, Ahmed,' Brannon muttered. 'I'm not sure what you were planning there. We've got no way out.'

'Yes we have,' Ahmed whispered, winking at Brannon. 'Do you trust me?' He jerked his head towards the window.

Brannon stared at him. 'Are you mad? Look at the drop. We'll be killed!'

'Just trust me, Brannon. Turn around and jump.'

The soldiers quickly surrounded them, baying like hounds on a cornered fox, determined not to let the pair escape again. Ahmed thumped Brannon's arm. 'Jump!'

They spun about and launched themselves through the open window, into the yawning void of air. From this height, the people below looked as tiny as ants. But Ahmed remembered something Brannon didn't. The floors below the dining hall were designed as sleeping quarters and therefore had awnings covering each of their windows to block the sunlight. They hit the first one with tremendous force; its wooden supports snapped instantly, and they kept falling. The second canopy held briefly, enough to slow their fall, and when they struck the last awning just twelve feet above the road, it caught and enfolded them, making for a relatively comfortable landing. They slid off and hit the ground at a run.

'Get out of here!' Ahmed roared. 'Every soldier in the city will be hunting us.'

They pushed through a mob of onlookers and scampered down an alleyway, heading in the direction of the quays. Beyond the alley was a noisy market thronged with people, and in their haste they accidentally knocked over a stall, sending an entire array of clay pottery hurtling to its death all over the stone ground. The vendor came angrily to his feet and shook his fist. 'A pox rot your balls!' he yelled, followed up by a list of similar calamities which he hoped would soon befall them. Ahmed and Brannon kept going, vaulting over a mule's back to reach the narrow street that led to the quay.

There were barges moored in the river, and slaves were unloading their cargoes under the close supervision of several armed guards. 'Cover yourself,' Ahmed warned, and Brannon slipped the hood of his djellaba over his head. They wandered into the throng. The guards saw that they were soldiers and paid them no heed.

'We must hide,' Ahmed said urgently.

Brannon watched one of the barges. There were slaves at the oars, and it was preparing to disembark. 'I have an idea.'

Moments later the barge set off downriver, slipping into the light current that carried past the banks and under a succession of stone bridges until it exited the city. Its crew never noticed the two men clinging to the stray mooring rope dangling at the stern, their heads just above the waterline. Shortly afterwards a swarm of soldiers came pouring onto the quay, searching the boats and interrogating the guards, but despite their efforts, no one was able to tell them of the white man and Arab who had escaped from their custody just twenty minutes before.

Ahmed retched in the acacia trees, trying to purge his stomach of the unclean river water. Beside him Brannon climbed up the sandbank and peered over the landscape ahead. They were in the countryside several miles outside Fez, a grand vista of dry golden hills and terraced vineyards lying indolently in the midday sun. He rubbed his forehead, wiping away the sweat. They would be hunted soon. There was no refuge on these sunburnt slopes from mounted soldiers.

Ahmed climbed the bank unsteadily, his face a shade lighter after his vomiting episode. 'We must go south,' he grunted. 'Head for the mountains. It's not safe here.'

Brannon stared dubiously at the miles of baked terrain. 'We'll have to move fairly fast to outrun them.'

'Yes,' Ahmed agreed. 'Let's go.'

An hour later they were crossing a broad valley through banks of reeds fringing cool lapis pools where plovers hunted insects on the shallow water. They drank to fill their parched bodies but had no flasks with them. In this heat their thirst would not remain at bay for long.

'We'll find water again,' Ahmed reassured Brannon, and so they left the valley and crossed a gently rippling plain of golden grass where the snowy peaks of the Atlas loomed in the distance. The sanctuary of those mountains was still a long way off, however. On the skyline west of the plain they spotted shapes, a faint line of them silhouetted on the horizon, and in alarm they threw themselves to the dirt for cover. But it was merely a goatherd, moving his animals between pastures, and they breathed in relief.

'Yazid won't be far away,' Ahmed warned. 'We must reach the Atlas where he can't find us.'

'And then what?' Brannon asked.

'We'll find the Berbers, explain what has happened. They will bring us to Suliman's army.'

'Oh, will they? Have you told them this?'

'Joining Suliman is their only hope of defeating Yazid now. Our plans for a surprise attack on Fez are ruined. I only wish I knew why.'

'We have to go back for Asiya,' Brannon protested. 'We can't just abandon her.'

Ahmed looked unhappy. 'We will return when we can. She has been strong all this time—she will survive.' He said the words only because he desperately wanted to believe them. 'She'll be safe.'

That night they slept on a wooded hillside, sheltering among the thick cedars where the darkness concealed them. The sun rose with a fury in the morning, its rays blazing across the landscape until the heat was as thick as treacle in the air. Brannon woke first, brushing the insects out of his hair. When he heard the sound, he gave Ahmed a shove.

'Wake up!'

Ahmed came awake quickly. 'What is it?'

Brannon motioned for him to be silent, and then they both heard it: the sound of horses nearby. Brannon put a finger to his lips, warning Ahmed not to speak, and then he moved slowly through the trees until he had a view of the valley floor.

They've found us, he realised in dread.

There was a group of riders in the valley, imperial soldiers, letting their horses drink from a stream. They were dusty and dishevelled as though they had been riding all night, and Brannon didn't have to guess why. He crept back to where Ahmed waited.

'Imperial troops,' he said. 'Yazid must have units scouring the entire countryside. We were bound to run into one of them sooner or later.'

Ahmed closed his eyes, mouthing something wordlessly. Brannon realised he was praying.

'You might need more than a prayer to survive this, Ahmed,' he said in irritation. But to his surprise and relief, the horsemen eventually moved on and rode away from the valley, still oblivious to the fact that Brannon and Ahmed were hiding in the trees.

Ahmed smiled in satisfaction. 'Allah watches over us,' he told Brannon.

The latter gave a noncommittal grunt, and they pressed on.

Their good fortune seemed to stay with them after that, for there were no further signs of soldiers over the next few days. They continued their furtive journey south, eventually reaching the low hills that marked the boundary of the Atlas Mountains. They drank out of streams and fed on taloe, a pleasant onion-shaped root which they dug in ample quantities from the ground. Up in the hills, however, the water was scarce, and their thirst returned like a fiery beast. It was another scorching hot day, and they faltered in the heat, sweat pouring through their clothes. Without water the journey was impossible.

'There are farms,' Ahmed sighed eventually. 'In the lowlands. We must turn back.'

Brannon was reluctant to go back the way they had come. But they needed water. Soon it would be a matter of life or death. He nodded his assent, and they left the mountain path down a rocky slope, travelling west over the next twenty-four hours until they reached the verdant low altitudes where tiny hamlets and mud-walled kasbahs clung to the hillsides. They were panting with thirst by the time they found the first settlement. It had several thatched clay houses and an old well in the centre, and it was a welcome sight.

There was a strange silence in the area. No animals picked at the ragged grass, no childish voices broke the sombre peace. 'Abandoned,' Brannon mused aloud. 'Like every other sorry village in these parts.'

They rounded a house and moved cautiously towards the well. Both were desperate for water now, so much so that they failed to notice the pair of legs sticking out from the side of the building. Brannon trod on them and tripped, inducing a startled yell from their owner.

'What—' The man, disturbed from his sleep, stared wordlessly at them for a moment. There was a sword by his side. He was wearing an imperial uniform.

'Tahar! Hassan!' he suddenly yelled, scrambling to his feet. 'Help me!' He plucked the sword from the ground.

Brannon sprang forward, drove his fist into the soldier's face, and managed to stab him in the stomach. The man gasped and reeled away, unable to shout any more. But in the distance they heard the sound of hooves.

'Run, damn it, run!' Brannon spluttered. They darted back through the village and followed the rough slopes into the mountains. There was uproar behind them, yelling men and stampeding horses. They found shelter within a thicket of scrub and peered back. The soldiers were on the wrong track.

'It won't take them long to realise their mistake,' Ahmed panted. 'They'll be back on our trail in no time.'

'Then keep bloody running.'

The climb up the slopes was steep. The sun rose higher, the sweat blinded their eyes, and soon they were approaching exhaustion. Once sure that the soldiers were far off, they risked a short rest. Swarms of mosquitoes harassed them, biting into every exposed patch of skin and raising angry blotches. 'The insects are loyal to Yazid,' Brannon decided miserably.

Ahmed didn't reply. He had been quiet for some time, his forehead creased in thought. Eventually he spoke.

'What did you mean? Back in the barracks. You said something about making a mistake.'

Brannon shifted his eyes. 'Um, nothing. It's not important now.'

'But what were you talking about?'

'It's not important, Ahmed. We've got about a dozen horsemen searching those lower hills—'

'You thought I had sent you that message. But why would I have? What did you do?'

'Nothing, I said.'

'Well, something must have happened. Was Asiya involved?'

Brannon didn't answer immediately, which was enough to stoke Ahmed's suspicions.

'So she *was* involved. What happened? Speak, Brannon. She's my sister. What did you do?'

'It was a mistake,' Brannon offered humbly.

'It was *what*?' Ahmed snapped, his composure giving way. 'What mistake, Brannon? Tell me!' He breathed slowly. An image flashed in his mind. 'You bastard. I warned you not to harm her. Did I not? And you gave me your word...'

Brannon blushed. He had no answers, none that would sound credible. 'It was a mistake, Ahmed. I didn't plan it, I swear to God.'

'Don't!' Ahmed snarled. 'Don't pull His holy name into your sordidness. I was wrong about you. I convinced myself to trust you. But you are no more trustworthy than any cut-throat rapist on the street.'

Brannon's countenance darkened. 'I am not a rapist. It was a mistake, I told you, but believe me, the girl was willing...' And even as he said that last line, he knew he had crossed the mark.

Ahmed pounced with a roar, locking his hands around Brannon's neck with every intention of killing him. They fought for dominance, Brannon gurgling as Ahmed squeezed down on his throat in an effort to choke him. He was spitting and snarling, driven into a frenzy of wounded rage.

Brannon, gritting his teeth, managed to use brute strength to force Ahmed's arms apart, and then he jolted his body and heaved the Arab clear. Ahmed rolled back on his feet. He swung a punch; Brannon blocked it with his arm. 'Calm down, you stupid Moor bastard...'

But Ahmed was far from finished. He hunched his shoulders, lowered his head, and charged like a battering ram. Brannon couldn't move fast enough and wheezed in pain as Ahmed's head piled into his stomach and drove the wind from his lungs. They both fell and wrestled furiously, trying to subdue each other with wild fists and elbows. Brannon, the stronger of the pair, soon won the upper hand and forced Ahmed onto his front, pinning his face to the ground.

'Stop this,' he panted. 'You don't have to kill me, Ahmed. We'll both be dead soon enough.'

And his words, it seemed, were prophetic.

At that precise moment they heard the loud whickering of horses and the thumping of hooves. Brannon glanced up the track in horror.

The soldiers were back. They had cornered their quarry, and a dozen of them now advanced with bared swords. They howled in triumph.

'Christ!' Brannon swore, rolling off Ahmed. 'Get up, damn it! Get up!'

Ahmed looked punch-drunk with the weight of his own anger, but now the haze slowly lifted as he saw the horsemen riding up the track. He blinked. 'How did they find us?'

'I don't care. Just run!' Brannon gave him a shove.

They clambered up the sloping track, and Brannon pulled Ahmed between two flat rock faces into a narrow path that meandered off the main one. The horses passed by, their riders still ignorant. 'Where are you going?' Ahmed demanded.

'I've no idea,' Brannon said, 'but hurry it up!'

They heard the horses whinnying in confusion as the riders realised they had been duped. There were roars of frustration, and threats were hurled around the mountainside. Brannon and Ahmed kept going; the path lowered into a gorge directly underneath the soldiers' position as they screamed for their prey.

'Step lightly,' Brannon warned with a whisper. 'They're still in earshot.' They covered several hundred feet and held their breath, but no one challenged them. The path meandered between brush-choked gullies and high cliffs. Deprived of their chance for water, they were now struggling, heavily tolled by thirst. They made awkward progress along the track as the sun continued to climb, and within the hour it had reached its blistering zenith. Brannon was the worse afflicted; his skin was lighter than Ahmed's and bore the brunt of the searing rays. But Ahmed was suffering too. The very air seemed to boil around them, their muscles throbbed in protest, and their throats were as dry as sand. The further they travelled, the sparser the vegetation became. Soon they were travelling across bare rock which had been stripped of its soil and moisture. They searched for springs or streams but found none, and every step was a grinding test of endurance.

'We have to find water,' Ahmed panted.

Brannon nodded weakly.

After that they walked for a long time without talking. The track dipped below a sharp ridge of rock where they cast their eyes down the slopes, listening for the blessed tinkle of a mountain stream. The sun had moved behind the peaks, stalking them like a predator. They knew it wouldn't let them go for much longer, not unless they could drink.

They covered five miles through the mountains before temperatures made progress impossible. Ahmed, weaker of body than Brannon, succumbed first. He staggered as they rounded a corner and would have fallen had Brannon not grabbed his arm and eased him down. They sat together, each breath a labour. There was no shade, and they could barely keep their eyes open against the blinding heat.

Then, less than a mile away, they heard the horses.

'No,' Ahmed whispered. 'We cannot die.'

'Call for Allah,' Brannon suggested bitterly, staring in the direction of the sound. With an effort he hauled himself on top of a boulder to get a better view. And he saw them clearly. He was surprised that it had taken them this long to catch up. 'Come on.' He hopped off the rock and pulled Ahmed to his feet.

They half ran, half fell towards the way ahead. They reached the cusp of another gorge and staggered downwards, slipping on the scree. The sound of horses grew louder. On the far side, the climb out of the gorge was steep. Too steep. Yesterday they might have managed it. Not today.

'We cannot die,' Ahmed whispered again.

Brannon pulled out his sword. The run across the gorge seemed to have burned away the very last vestiges of energy within him. He could barely stand. Even as he realised it, he heard Ahmed slump in a heap on the ground.

'Ahmed, get up,' he pleaded. 'We'll fight them.' But Brannon couldn't fight either. His vision swam into haze as his legs began to give way.

Ahmed was already unconscious, his mouth open, his dried lips splitting in the sun. Brannon stared up the path and almost willed the soldiers to appear. And then he got his wish. They spread out along the track and drew their swords, bellowing in unison when they saw their prey lying helplessly on the ground. There would be no more escape.

Brannon was too feeble to confront them. He blinked as he watched them charge up the path and saw the sunlight glinting on their blades. Stars flickered in his vision, and the rocks wavered and danced; the soldiers appeared like black flying ghosts, their roars echoing through the gorge. He realised his sight was failing.

Something confused him. The first rider seemed to disappear, but the shape of his horse continued on. The other riders were thrown into an untidy cluster, milling about in noise and commotion. Their shouts became a deafening cacophony in Brannon's head.

Dozens of figures came out of the slopes as suddenly as a landslide, fuelling the chaos. So many voices were erupting that was impossible to know what was going on. There were clashes of steel and screams of agony. Some vicious battle was being fought out there in that heat-baked gorge.

Brannon groaned, unable to see. Before he could fight it, a blackness washed over him and drowned his senses. He toppled back, hitting his head on a stone and slipping quickly into a void of unconsciousness. It was dark now, and mercifully silent.

CHAPTER NINETEEN

'Open this door, bitch, before we break it down!'

Asiya breathed in panic. There were at least a dozen of them outside, crowding the roadway, swords gleaming in their hands. She thought about making a dash through the back garden, but that route was already blocked. Two of them rapped on the window and leered in at her.

Again the door rattled, and a voice shouted, 'This is Captain al-Hameed. Open up immediately!'

With Brannon missing and soldiers pounding on her door, she knew something had gone horribly wrong. Cautiously she released the bolt and peered out. 'Who are you looking for?'

'Traitors,' the captain said with relish, 'and we'll begin with you.' Without warning, he grabbed her by the hair and yanked her into the street. 'Take this little whore to the barracks,' he ordered, bundling her into the arms of the other soldiers. 'There are some people waiting to have a word with her.'

As she was dragged up the road, Asiya saw that the city had been overrun with troops. Gunfire erupted in nearby streets, doors were smashed down, and children screamed in the chaos. Yazid's work. He had proved cleverer than they expected, and tears of despair filled her eyes. Where were Brannon and Ahmed? Were they even alive?

One of the soldiers slapped her across the head. 'Too late for that, witch. You and your rebel husband have earned your fates.'

But she couldn't stop the tears. When they reached the barracks, she was led down a stairway into the deepest bowels of the building. The soldiers shoved her into a lamp-lit cell that was filled with giant moths and smelled of excrement. They promised to return before very long.

'But what is to happen to me?' she pleaded. 'What are you going to do?'

One of them chuckled. 'You have a long night ahead of you, wench. Save your breath and get some sleep.' He sneered and slammed the door shut, pushing the heavy bolt into place. Asiya shivered in the sudden cold.

❀ ❀ ❀

Azedine Ben Hassi smiled defiantly through the streams of blood on his face. Despite a thorough beating, he hadn't yielded them the slightest morsel of information, nothing that would prove useful in tackling the nascent rebellion being plotted against the sultan. And General al-Malek was running out of patience.

'Bring me the material,' he grunted, and a soldier carried forth a tub of dark, wet tar. Al-Malek stirred it with a horsehair brush. A sly grin curled the corners of his mouth.

'Put him down.' Two guards shoved Ben Hassi on his knees and strapped his hands behind his back. He glanced warily over his shoulder.

'Now listen to me, Azedine,' al-Malek said. 'I am about to hurt you more than you have ever been hurt in your entire life. For the last time, will you not tell me what you know about Suliman's rebellion?'

Ben Hassi stared stonily back at him.

'Where is the Irish captain?' al-Malek asked. 'And who is Ahmed?'

No response.

'Very well, Azedine. You leave me little choice.' Al-Malek dipped the brush into the tub and streaked a wet mass of tar over Ben Hassi's head. It slid around his bald pate and dripped into his face, cold and sticky, but otherwise it caused him little discomfort.

Al-Malek stayed silent for several long minutes. Eventually he ran a finger over the tar to feel its texture. He nodded.

A guard to the left, out of Ben Hassi's view, stepped forward and placed a lighted torch to his shiny, tarred scalp. It ignited with a puff, and the flames shot up a foot in height. Ben Hassi screamed, an inhuman, demonic scream of pain so horrible that some of the guards felt their bowels loosen. He writhed on the ground and thrashed his head about, trying to put out the searing fire, but he couldn't undo his hands. The flames slicked down his face, and he felt his eyeballs shrinking in the heat. Already a stink of burning flesh filled the room.

'Hear me, Azedine,' al-Malek implored him. 'Let me extinguish the fire with this pail of water. Let me help you, Azedine. Will you then talk to me?'

He received no answer, for Ben Hassi was now in a place where he was beyond reasoning. Al-Malek had gone too far; the immense pain had driven the old soldier off the precipice of his sanity, and he couldn't reply even if he wanted to.

'It's no good,' a voice complained from the back.

Al-Malek bowed apologetically. 'Your Majesty, if I put out the fire, perhaps he will talk.'

'How can he talk?' Yazid snapped. 'You've burned the tongue out of his skull!'

It was literally true. The heat had made Ben Hassi's tongue swell through his mouth and drape over his chin, as if it were trying to wriggle free. Too much tar had been used, and the flames had engulfed his entire head, burning away his lips and skin. He didn't resemble a human being any more.

'Enough of this.' The noise and cries began to grate on Yazid's nerves. He took a pistol from the nearest soldier and shot Ben Hassi in the face, killing him instantly. Then he pinched his nose in disgust. 'Put him out, damn you—the stink is foul.' They doused the body until the fire died. Yazid turned on al-Malek.

'What good was that to me? I need answers, General, not smoking corpses. Get me answers, or it will be your own head in flames very soon.'

Al-Malek bowed as Yazid swept from the room. He was nervous. Time was running out, and Yazid was still furious with al-Malek for allowing Brannon Ryan and Ahmed to escape. Al-Malek needed that information on Suliman, and he needed it fast. But from where?

Then he remembered something. They had arrested the Irishman's wife that morning, whatever Reema said her name was, and right now she was being held in a cell underneath the barracks. She was bound to know something. As Brannon Ryan's wife, she would surely know his whereabouts and, more importantly, his secrets. And as a woman they probably wouldn't have to beat her very hard either.

Yes, she would do.

He ordered two of the soldiers to go below and fetch her. He would start on her promptly, and if the bitch had any sense, she would co-operate and spare herself the appalling fate which they had bestowed on Azedine Ben Hassi.

Asiya trembled when she entered the dark room. There were torches on the walls, and the shadows flickered eerily like goblins dancing a ritual. The man standing in the centre she knew, and she swallowed hard. Naseem al-Malek—Yazid's chief general, a ruthless, violent man. There were a number of soldiers in the room also, lean-faced individuals who stared hungrily at her as she walked inside. She tried not to show fear.

On the ground she saw what she thought was a crumpled sack, but on closer inspection she realised it was something else, and then she felt her stomach wrench with nausea. It was a man, quite dead, his head blackened and his scalp melted away in grotesque strips of flesh. Grey smoke drifted from his remains.

Al-Malek saw her reaction and smiled thinly. 'He was a stubborn old man. And a foolish one. Look at him now.'

She choked down her tears. 'What do you want of me?'

He studied her more keenly, realising that she was an extremely attractive woman. It would be a shame for her to end up like Ben Hassi. His men, he knew, would enjoy sampling a little piece of her, and indeed he wouldn't mind trying a piece himself. Perhaps, if she did as she was told here, he would be able to put her to better use afterwards.

'Young lady, you know exactly why you're here. His Royal Highness the Sultan of Morocco is hopeful that you might assist us in a delicate matter, namely the apprehension of a core of wicked rebels who have been plotting to turn the country over to that vile dog Suliman. Help us find them, my dear, and you will be very glad that you did.'

'I know nothing of such things,' she replied. 'I am innocent.'

'What's your name?' he asked.

She hesitated, and al-Malek knew then that she was far from innocent. Reema had been right; this girl was as much involved as Brannon Ryan. 'Come now. Be sensible. If you co-operate, then perhaps I can be lenient with your punishment. If you choose to be imprudent, however, then you have only yourself to blame.' He inclined his head towards the charred corpse of Ben Hassi in reminder.

'But I have done nothing wrong. I am—'

He stepped forward suddenly and struck her. She stumbled backwards, tripping over Ben Hassi's body and landing on top of him. His flesh was still hot, and she screamed in revulsion, trying to clamber free. Al-Malek seized her arm and dragged her up.

'You're a liar! I know you're hiding information. Tell me where Brannon Ryan is. And tell me who his friend Ahmed is. Either way, I'm going to kill them both.'

In a brief moment of relief, she realised that Brannon and Ahmed must still be alive. 'You'll never kill them,' she hissed defiantly. 'They are a thousand times cleverer than you, and a thousand times stronger.'

'Hah!' Al-Malek laughed with genuine amusement. 'Is that so? So you admit you know of this rebellion they have been planning? Who is Ahmed? Tell me.'

'I won't tell you. You can do whatever you want to me.'

'Tell me!'

'Never!'

'I'm going to find Ahmed, and I'm going to boil the skin off his bones. I'm going to hurt him so bad that even his corpse will scream.'

'No!' Asiya nearly wept at his words. 'You won't find him!'

'He's a coward, a devious little snake. He's—'

'My brother is the greatest man ever born of this country,' she screeched at him, 'and he will make Yazid pay dearly for the murder of our family!'

And in the very next instant, she realised what she had said.

'Your brother?' Al-Malek stepped back in surprise. 'Well, well. This is suddenly interesting. You say he's your brother? And Brannon Ryan your husband.

My word, a close-knit family of traitors and rebels we have. How interesting indeed!'

Asiya blinked in shame. She had said too much.

Al-Malek took a moment to digest it. 'Who were your family?' According to Reema, the girl's name was Asiya. Ahmed and Asiya. Where had he heard those names before?

Then he stopped. The significance was suddenly apparent.

'No,' he gasped in astonishment. 'I don't believe it! You couldn't be. Not Khaled al-Qatib's children…' It wasn't possible! He had led the raid that night himself, had personally supervised the killings to ensure that the entire family was dealt with. Yet the brother and sister had got away?

He shook with fury. 'You poisonous whore. So you made a fool of me? Allah witness, I'll punish you. I'm going to kill you tonight, one bloody little bit at a time, and scatter the pieces to the crows when I'm done. And I swear before the heavens, your brother will not escape my vengeance long. He's a dead man!'

Asiya could take no more. She collapsed in anguish, covering her face with her hands. Brannon, Ahmed, Suliman—she had let everyone down, and now she faced the wrath of al-Malek and Moulay Yazid. What brief flare of hope remained was now thoroughly snuffed out.

Al-Malek needed to report the revelation about Ahmed's identity to the sultan, and thus he delayed the pleasure of torturing Asiya to death for an hour or two. 'I'll be back for you in a while,' he told her. 'Be patient. I must first discuss with His Majesty how we are to dispose of that cowardly brother of yours.' He flashed her a smile and left the room.

The soldiers brought Asiya back to her subterranean cell and flung her inside. She heard their feet clomping down the corridor until silence fell again. It was pitch black in here. She was weak with trauma, unable to think, unable to plot a way out. Al-Malek wouldn't be gone very long, and there was nothing she could do to thwart the inevitable. She hoped for a quick death, but under his lingering hands, she feared it would be a slow one.

The truly heartbreaking implication, however, was that now she would never know whether the rebellion triumphed or not. As long as Ahmed and Brannon evaded capture, there was hope. But perhaps they were already dead. Even if by some miracle they survived, Asiya would never hear about it. She would be long gone.

The hours in the cell dragged by with cruel tedium, like a noose slowly tightening around her neck. She listened for footsteps in the corridor, knowing that the sound of them would mean her time was up, but it stayed quiet. She wondered if they were deliberately drawing it out, enjoying the agonised mental state they had put her in. She wouldn't be able to bear it for much longer, locked in this infested pit, waiting for the footsteps that would herald the beginning of her end. To distract herself she prayed, silently at first, but then louder as her lips worked frantically and her voice filled the tiny room. She was almost shrieking the verses when she realised what she as doing, and she stopped herself. It was the fear; it could so easily unhinge one's mind. She tried to relax herself. She closed her eyes and dreamed of brighter things, of brighter moments, wishing for a place that was far from here.

And then the footsteps came.

She bit her lip and huddled into the furthest corner of the cell, making a pitiful attempt to distance herself. But there was no escape in here. The bolt was unlocked, and the door swung open. A short, stocky-shouldered guard stepped inside. 'Get up,' he told her. 'You're leaving now.' His accent sounded strange to her—foreign, yet somehow familiar. He had a black, bushy beard and bronzed skin like an Arab, yet his eyes were pale blue. An incongruous combination.

Once outside, she was surprised to find him all alone. 'What is this?' she asked uneasily.

'We haven't much time. They'll be back soon.' He took her arm and began to lead her down the torch-lit corridor.

'Who are you?' She was completely bewildered now. 'Where are you taking me?'

'I mustn't have made much of an impression on you, miss, but you've met me before. My name is Daniel Jones; I'm an Englishman. I've been helping your brother and your husband these past months.'

'Yes!' She finally recognised his face. 'I *have* met you before. But I thought you were white?'

He touched one of his blackened cheeks with a grin. 'Henna leaves, miss. They make an effective skin dye. I knew the soldiers would come looking for me, so I had to make a disguise. I've got a notion my luck won't last forever, though.'

'What are you planning to do?'

'I saw you this morning when they brought you here, and luckily my captain's uniform allows me access to delicate places, so I lifted a set of keys for the cells. I'm here to take you away, miss.'

'But there are guards at every gate. We'll never get out of here!'

'Never say never, miss,' he tutted. 'A most uninspiring word.'

They passed a row of empty cells, listening for voices and scouting the way ahead. It was cold underground, but that wasn't the only reason Asiya shivered. Once they had rounded a dizzying series of bends, they came into a network of passages that ran deep under the barracks. The route was only barely illuminated, and the stone floor was awash with puddles. Asiya wondered if Daniel even knew where he was going. If someone got lost down here, they wouldn't be seen again.

To her relief, she caught a glimpse of daylight. An opening had been knocked in the wall and led out to the river where a tiny makeshift wharf had been built. 'This has been here a long time,' Daniel told her. 'It's used to smuggle alcohol and other contraband into the barracks. European craftsmanship, of course.'

There were three battered and ancient ferry boats moored at the wharf. Daniel untied one. 'This will have to do,' he said uncertainly. 'I hope it stays afloat.'

'Won't we be seen in the river?' Asiya was reluctant to enter the boat.

'Probably. But they're not looking for us—not yet. They think you're still in your cell.' He picked out a discarded blanket from one of the other boats. 'Here, cover yourself with this. Keep your head down.'

They climbed into the rickety vessel, and Daniel pushed off. The current was sluggish, and he used an oar to hasten progress. They drifted alongside the high walls of the barracks, under a stone bridge, and passed close to the streets where they could hear the markets in busy swing. Slaves working in the barges peered down at them, but they commanded little interest. Daniel was merely a soldier, while Asiya resembled a beggar under the cover of her tattered blanket.

They held their breath. The boat continued its laborious journey. Not until they had passed under the last bridge through the south walls did Asiya relax a little. 'I should tell you, Daniel, that Brannon is missing. And I don't know where Ahmed is. Have you heard anything?'

'The report I heard was that they had been captured by General al-Malek, but then managed to give him the slip. I'm afraid I have no idea where they could be now.'

'But they're safe?'

'Hopefully.'

'And what of us? Once al-Malek realises I'm gone, he'll tear the city apart. He knows who I am now.'

'That's why we have to get you out of the city. Fez is not safe any more.'

She sighed gloomily. 'It's all my fault. They didn't know who Ahmed was, not until I let it out. Now they will hunt him down to the ends of the earth.'

'Your brother is a resourceful man, Asiya,' Daniel assured her. 'Have faith in him.'

Sunlight blazed on the water's surface so that the river shone like a runnel of molten copper. They continued downstream, slipping past the outlying fields and banks of burnt furze where the countryside was somnolent and golden. Beds of papyrus bent under the passage of the boat, and after several miles Daniel plunged in waist-deep. He pulled the boat towards a shingle beach where the pebbles gleamed and a heron stared haughtily at their graceless intrusion. 'That's enough sailing for the time being.'

'Where now?'

He stood up on a rock to get a view of their surrounds. 'Well, let's see. My reckoning is that Brannon and Ahmed, if they made it out of Fez, will have headed south. Suliman is in the south. He's their only hope at this stage. And that's where we must go, too.'

'But Suliman's army is hundreds of miles away!'

'He's not that far any longer. And I know where we can get horses. It's only about a week's ride, providing Yazid doesn't catch up with us.'

'And if he does?'

Daniel stared grimly in the direction of Fez. 'Let's hope that doesn't happen. Yazid will be swift on the move. We must be swifter.'

CHAPTER TWENTY

It was a cold courtroom. Its oak panelling was cracked and mildewed, its floors scuffed with the indelible stains of rough country feet. But there was a tangible excitement within its normally dour confines, for today it seemed that all of West Cork had turned out to watch the proceedings, and those who hadn't gained a seat in the gallery were jostling outside, straining to hear every word. The judge, a frosty-faced man in his mid-fifties, wasn't used to working amid such bustle, and he glowered at the spectators, banging his gavel down to bring them to order. There were seven other cases to hear this morning, and he was impatient. A hush descended as the last of the people squeezed into their seats, and the matter was allowed to proceed. A young clerk stood up, pushed the spectacles back on his nose, and began to read the charge.

'Orlaith Whiteley was indicted for that she, not having the fear of God before her eyes, but stirred by greed and the instigation of the devil, on the twenty-seventh of February last, did steal from Randall Whiteley, gentleman, the sum of one hundred and fifty pounds, six shillings, and six pence, and on the said occasion, with malice aforethought, did also make an assault, with a vase made of alabaster, upon Vincent Barry, labourer, giving to the head of him, the said Vincent Barry, a wound of the length of two inches...'

A gasp of awe rose from the gallery. They stared at the defendant, deliciously scandalised by this sweet slip of a girl committing such wicked acts. And Randall Whiteley's own wife, too! It was fabulous stuff.

To the right of the bar where Orlaith stood was a table at which the jury sat. They listened to the charge impassively, each keeping his eyes on the defendant. As was standard practice, a mirror had been erected above her head to angle the light from the windows and thus allowing the jury to scrutinise her facial expressions more closely. Though they didn't show it, several of the jury were as surprised as the spectators. Those accused of "theft with violence" were usually male, usually habitual criminals who thought nothing of pulling a knife or a gun on an unsuspecting victim. This girl looked nothing of the sort. Appearances could, of course, be deceptive.

Orlaith tried to mask her fear. Her legs were weak, her stomach churned, and she thought she would faint. The whole scene was like a nightmare: ranks of leering spectators up in the gallery, a table full of cold-faced jurors, and an old man with a grey wig who now fixed her now with a probing stare. The prosecution counsel sat directly before her, a middle-aged man but with a youthful spring to his movements. His eyes darted about, and his fingers drummed impatiently on the mahogany table as he waited for his turn to speak. Beside him were her two antagonists: Vincent, sullen-featured and with his head cleanly shaved to display the scar that her attack had marked. Next to him sat Randall, his palms placed on his lap. Far from looking the aggrieved victim, there was a gleam of triumph in his eyes. She had known all along that his vengeance would be harsh.

She took a breath, trying to invoke some sense of inner strength, but she had never felt so powerless in all her life. It felt like every pair of eyes in the room bore down on her, like everyone hated her and wanted her to suffer. She could hear the cackling in the gallery, could hear the conspiratorial whispers being passed between the officials. She hadn't been able to afford a defence counsel, and as a result she was entirely alone, her wits now the only thing between her and whatever hideous fate these people could concoct.

Again the judge banged the gavel with such force that his wig came loose, and he snapped at the crowd to remain silent. The prosecution counsel rose with a flourish of his black robe. He cast his eyes over the courtroom and smiled, allowing himself a moment to bask in the warmth of their admiration, and then he turned his attention to the jury. Orlaith had already pleaded not guilty to the charge, hoping that the jury might take her side over Randall, but her plea of innocence simply had the counsel relishing his task even more. From memory he recounted the charge but this time elaborated on the cold and calculated nature of her mindset at the time, and he drew a chorus of indignant exclamations from the crowd when he described how she had involved her young son in the fiendish plot, an innocent child who could not have known any better. '*Shame!*' someone cried out, and Orlaith quailed. She was not given the chance to reply, but instead the first witness was called to the stand. Vincent shuffled up; his head was down, and because he was embarrassed, his countenance seemed even more ferocious than usual. He read aloud the oath and then stood with his fists clenched by his sides. He didn't once look at Orlaith, but she could almost smell the hatred emanating from him.

'Mr Barry,' the counsel addressed him, 'you were at Dromkeen Hall on the night that the alleged offences took place, were you not? Can you please explain to the court your version of the events that occurred?'

Vincent cleared his throat, embarrassed at being the focus of attention. 'Well, I had gone to bed already. It was the noise that woke me.'

'The noise?' the counsel asked.

'Footsteps, it was. In the lobby. Unusual for that time of night.'

'And what time was that?'

'About four, I think. So I got up to have a look, and I saw the drawing room open and the master's things disturbed.'

'What things do you speak of exactly, Mr Barry?'

'Well, his bookshelves, like. I shouldn't like to say…'

'Come, Mr Barry, you may speak freely, as Mr Whiteley has already given his consent.'

'The master used to keep a key hidden there. And I knew someone must have been at it, with the shelves out of place. So I suspected devilry afoot, and I went to call him straightaway.'

'And what happened then?'

'I didn't know what it was at the time, but someone gave me a fierce bloody crack on the head. I tried to grab them, but I couldn't. I didn't recall stirring for a time.'

'So you were struck on the head, and you lost consciousness. Mr Barry, the person whom you believe carried out the assault, is that person present in this courtroom today?'

'Yes, sir.'

'Can you point the person out?'

Vincent turned and fixed his eyes on Orlaith; his face flushed with sudden anger, and it seemed to take him a wilful effort to maintain control. 'There she is,' he growled. 'There's the one what hit me.'

'And she was gone when you regained your senses? She had simply left you there?'

'Yes.'

'Thank you, Mr Barry.' The counsel dismissed him and then called for his second witness. Red-faced and looking deeply ashamed, Reverend Norman Johnston took the stand, as though he would rather have been anywhere but in that courtroom. He glanced once at Orlaith, and immediately his cheeks burned bright with guilt.

His testimony took less than two minutes to complete.

'So when you found her on the street, Reverend, she told you that someone had just stolen a sum of money from her?' the counsel summed up. 'You're quite clear about that?'

'Yes,' Johnston said, nodding in regret. 'That's what she said.'

'Thank you, Reverend.' The counsel dismissed him and looked back to the bench. A murmur of anticipation sounded from the gallery.

Randall rose up, watching Orlaith. He mouthed something wordlessly to her and smiled. Taking his place at the witness box, he abruptly assumed a look of solemn dignity for the benefit of the jurors, the injured look of a decent man wronged.

'Mr Whiteley,' the counsel began, 'you were also at home on the night of the twenty-seventh of February. When did you first hear of a disturbance taking place?'

'Not long after four in the morning. I was woken by a servant to say that Mr Barry was lying in the drawing room in a pool of blood. Naturally, I was greatly distressed and went to ascertain his condition.'

'And where was your wife when this happened?'

'I had assumed her to be in bed.'

'But do you not sleep in the same room as each other? Forgive me the in-delicacy of the question.'

'Normally we do, of course. But on that particular night I had arrived home late, and not wishing to disturb Orlaith, I contented myself to sleep in one of the guestrooms.'

'I understand. Can you explain what happened next, Mr Whiteley?'

'I found Mr Barry as the servant had described. He was unconscious, and I called for assistance. Thankfully we were able to stifle the flow of blood, but he was in a desperate plight. I fear a weaker man might not have survived such an attack. We put him to bed, and I sent for a doctor to address his wounds.'

'In your written account of events, you say that you then noticed something unusual in the drawing room.'

'Yes, I did.'

Randall, in fact, had noticed the displaced bookshelves straightaway, and he had ignored Vincent on the floor for the best part of an hour as he ransacked the house searching for the key. 'Yes, once I was assured in the knowledge that Mr Barry was being tended to, I then saw that someone had been in the drawing room and had moved the bookshelves. Upon closer inspection, I was alarmed to find that a safe key was missing.'

'So you did what?'

'I checked the safe. It was open, of course, and a substantial amount of money had been taken.'

'What did you do then?'

'Well, knowing that an intruder had been in the house, my first thought was for the safety of my wife. I went to her bedroom to ensure that she was unhurt. It was a huge surprise to find that both she and her son were gone.'

The counsel nodded sympathetically. 'It must have been a shock to learn that the theft of the money coincided with your wife's untimely disappearance.'

'It was.' Randall lowered his head in disappointment. 'I have since realised that my wife is a woman of many wiles and secrets. I need not tell you how distressed this has made me.'

'Yet you had not noticed this behaviour in her before?'

Randall chuckled, trying to sound embarrassed. 'I was in love with her. I would have done anything for her. I guess I allowed myself to be blinded to her ways, wanting her to live a decent life with me, to uphold the same Christian values that I myself had been raised with. I feel quite the fool now—I can't help sensing that much of this is my fault.'

The counsel tutted. 'You are hardly to blame for this whole business, Mr Whiteley. It is a tragedy in itself that she was able to beguile you with such cunning and to have made you suffer like this.'

'May I remind you,' the judge intervened, 'that the guilt of the defendant has not yet been established. Until it has, you will refrain from expressing any such presumptions as to her behaviour.'

'Very good, Your Honour,' the counsel said cheerfully. He continued his questions, drawing from Randall a detailed description of how Orlaith had eventually been apprehended in Cork City, though with the money now gone.

'She put up quite a struggle when we found her,' Randall said, warming to his lies. 'It was at that moment that I became convinced of her guilt, however much I had wanted to believe that she was innocent. As you can imagine, I was deeply upset.'

'I certainly can imagine,' the counsel agreed. 'Thank you, Mr Whiteley. I have no further questions.'

Randall stood up, and as he passed the bar where Orlaith stood, he whispered to her out of earshot from the rest of the courtroom, '*They're going to take Sean away…*'

Orlaith was the only one who heard his words, and as Randall walked on, he gave her a quick, smug grin. 'No!' she cried in anger. 'You bastard!' She lashed out at him, but two constables pinioned her arms and restrained her while Randall scurried down to his seat, exclaiming in fright and mopping at his brow in a show of alarm.

'Mrs Whiteley!' the judge barked. 'I will not hesitate to have you manacled if you don't conduct yourself with propriety. You will respect this courtroom, or I will have you thrown in gaol without further warning.'

Orlaith took her place reluctantly, tears of frustration on her cheeks. How badly she wanted to kill him. Even in this room full of witnesses, she wanted to kill him. Randall, once he had demonstrated his shocked state for the jurors to take in, smirked across at her.

At last it was her own turn. Defendants, when lacking a defence counsel, could rely only on their answers to help their case, unless they had witnesses to call. But Orlaith had no witnesses.

'Mrs Whiteley,' the counsel asked her, 'why did you attack Mr Whiteley just there? Did you want to hurt him?'

'That incident is not the subject of these proceedings, Counsel,' the judged warned, so the former changed tack.

'Mrs Whiteley, have you ever before had wish to physically harm or otherwise cause trauma to your husband, Randall Whiteley?'

She was unsure of what to say. 'Sometimes. But that's because he—'

'Yes or no will suffice, Mrs Whiteley. And I will interpret your answer as a *yes*.' He went on. 'You have been married to your husband how long?'

'Um, over a year now. I'm not fully sure, I—'

'And can you describe to the court your circumstances before you were married, by which I mean your manner of lifestyle and domestic conditions?'

'I lived in a cabin outside Dromkeen. Me and my son. I had a farm.'

'A prosperous farm?'

'No,' she admitted. 'It was hard work. We hadn't much food.'

'So when Mr Whiteley proposed to you, it must have brought about a dramatic change in your fortunes, wouldn't you agree?'

'Yes,' she said. 'But not for the better—it was a huge mistake to marry him.'

'Nonetheless, he must have given you a good life, compared to the one you had been living. You never wanted for food or clothes or shelter after the wedding, did you?'

'Randall provided all those things, it's true. But he's a wealthy man.'

'And did you love him, Mrs Whiteley?'

She blushed, and the judge murmured a caution. 'Is this line of questioning leading to somewhere, Counsel?'

'It is, Your Honour. Please bear with me.' He gestured for Orlaith to continue. 'Well?'

'No,' Orlaith said bitterly. 'I didn't love him. But no woman could love him, he's a mean—'

'Please confine your answers to the questions asked, Mrs Whiteley. So, since you did not love him, I will surmise that you married him for money. Correct?'

Orlaith shrugged. 'I suppose it is. I had a child. I couldn't bear to see him starve.'

'You agree that your primary motive regarding your husband was money, not love. Do you not see the troubling implications of that?'

'What do you mean?' Orlaith asked.

'Think of a woman who doesn't love her husband, who is unbound by any sense of duty to him, but who wants to get her hands on his wealth. She may be driven to certain acts for the sake of that very wealth. An act such as, for example, assaulting one of his servants and stealing his money in the middle of the night?'

'No,' she reacted, 'I didn't steal the money—I really didn't.' But even to her own ears the denial was pathetic and unconvincing.

'And so why did you flee the house on the night that the incident took place?'

'I had wanted to escape Randall for some time. I was unhappy living there, so I left.'

'Yes, you had tired of him at this point, but since he had accustomed you to a lavish lifestyle, it wasn't enough for you to simply leave. You had to steal his money too, in order that you could continue to enjoy the luxuries which you were doubtless now quite fond of.'

'No,' Orlaith said quickly. 'I didn't mean to—I mean, I didn't steal the money, and I didn't hurt anyone. I...'

'In that case, Mrs Whiteley, can you please explain just what you *did* do that night?'

She tried her best to, and she carefully recounted the story that she had formulated in her head, admitting her part in taking Randall's carriage but avoiding the issue of the money and the attack on Vincent. 'I only wanted peace for me and my son. A woman is not breaking the law by leaving her husband, is she? I cannot be blamed for that.'

'Theft with violence *does* break the law, however, Mrs Whiteley. I thank you for your time. You have given the court a much clearer understanding of your mindset and motives, I think.' He turned away from her. 'I have no more questions for the defendant, Your Honour.'

The judge nodded and then asked Orlaith, 'Do you wish to call upon witnesses of your own?'

Orlaith shook her head in dejection. 'I don't have any.'

'Very well.' He signalled to the jury that they should begin their deliberations. No one in the gallery stirred. A guilty verdict was surely a foregone conclusion, but they all waited to see what kind of sentence she would be given. Randall conferred with his lawyer, who in turn conferred with the judge. Orlaith couldn't hear what was said.

After approximately eight minutes, the jury had a verdict.

'We find the defendant guilty, Your Honour,' said the foreman. Cheers sounded from the gallery, with urges of '*Hang her!*' being shouted out. The judge banged his gavel and cast a ferocious look in the direction of the noise. Once they were quieted, he removed his spectacles and turned his gaze on Orlaith.

'Mrs Whiteley, in a case like this, involving deliberate and cold-blooded violence, I would normally have no hesitation in applying the maximum penalty provided for under the law, which is death. The seriousness of your crime, too, is only compounded by the fact that a young child was embroiled in the plot from the outset. However, taking into account your gender, and appreciating that you do not have a prior record of convictions, I am prepared to allow a degree of leniency.' He cleared his throat as he mentally prepared his next words. Orlaith's head swam with dizziness. She felt sick suddenly. She gripped the wooden rails to prevent herself from collapsing.

'It is the judgement of this court that you be sentenced to twelve years' hard labour in His Majesty's colony of New South Wales.'

Orlaith reeled under the blow. Twelve years? Twelve years was a lifetime. She felt her stomach heave. And where was New South Wales? Somewhere in Britain? Surely they wouldn't send her so far. 'You can't!' she begged. 'I have a son!'

'Your son, Mrs Whiteley, I am about to come to. His part in this business was in no way his own fault. He is a child, entirely innocent, but he was no doubt corrupted by the wickedness of his mother. It is my feeling that had he remained in your custody for much longer, his course in life would already have been turned awry, and it would probably be only a matter of years before he appeared in this courtroom himself. Therefore, given your husband's reluctance to assume full custody of the child, which is understandable seeing that they are not blood-related, I am ordering that Sean Downey be given into the care of the Brothers of Christ School for Orphans in Dublin City, where he will be amply nourished and educated and redirected onto a Christian path.'

'No!' she screamed, and she would have stormed from the bar had the constables not held her. 'You can't take Sean from me. I'm his mother! I'm all he has, for the love of God!'

'Mrs Whiteley!' the judge snapped. 'It is not common practice for defendants to speak during sentencing. Hold your tongue, or I may have to rethink the lightness of your punishment. Now,' he said as he glanced towards Randall, 'I must address the practicalities of the sentence I have just delivered. Those intended for transportation to the colonies are usually housed in the city gaol until a ship arrives, which I understand is not for some months yet. I had felt that you should be brought there today, Mrs Whiteley, and prompt arrangements be made for your son's relocation to Dublin. However...' Again he looked at Randall. 'In an act of benevolence which I deem extremely saintly for a man who has endured what Mr Whiteley has endured, he has insisted that you instead be passed into his custody until the date of your transportation. Your son will remain there too until then, thus allowing you whatever time remains to make amends to the child and hopefully to undo the damage you have caused. Use this opportunity wisely, Mrs Whiteley, as it will be a long time before you see your son again, if ever. It goes without saying that armed constables will guard the premises day and night, and if you make the slightest infringement upon this arrangement, your temporary reprieve will cease to be in effect and you will be taken without further warning to the city gaol, there to await your redemption in New South Wales.'

It was too much for Orlaith. She stumbled over the bar and vomited, her legs giving way. The people in the gallery roared their approval, and Randall stood up, rubbing his hands briskly.

By God, he would take his dues from her. It would be several months before she was taken to the ship, and he was going to enjoy every moment of it. After that, let her rot in New South Wales. A fitting end, a hostile country of savage tribesmen and poisonous snakes and terrible heat. No one ever came back from New South Wales.

Ah yes, you'll pay dearly for your betrayal, Orlaith, he thought. *The last one made a fool of me and got away. But you haven't got away. I'm going to make you suffer.*

CHAPTER TWENTY-ONE

Ninety miles south of the city of Fez, in a pool of shadow cast beneath the mouth of a cave, Brannon was coming slowly awake. He blinked, turning away as torchlight pierced his eyes. The smell of woodsmoke was thick in the air, wafting in pungent coils around his head, and he coughed, instantly feeling a ripple of pain through his abused limbs. A hand grasped his head and placed a cup of water to his lips. He drank it gratefully, gulping it down and spluttering as it burned his lungs. A voice chuckled.

'Slower. Or it will come out as fast as it goes in.'

He opened his eyes fully. The hillside was in the cloak of dusk, wispy silver smoke drifting from campfires. Men were smoking outside their tents, and dogs lay at their feet. Brannon had no idea where he was. He looked into the face of the man tending to him. It was Bakka, the big Berber warrior who had ambushed them in the hills, whose fire-dancing skills had been legendary until Ahmed spoiled his show.

The man smiled, sensing Brannon's recognition. 'Bakka!' he declared just in case, thumping his breast in introduction. He had a friendlier disposition than the last time, though there was a recent and rather nasty-looking knife wound across his cheek. 'You were a fortunate man yesterday.' He didn't speak in one of the Tamazight languages, but in Arabic. It was just as well, for Arabic was the only language they shared.

'Bakka.' Brannon grinned weakly. 'Nice to meet you again. We're not going to be jumping in any fires today, are we?'

Bakka laughed heartily, enjoying the jest. 'No, no. You're *Bannon?*'

'Brannon.'

'The Englishman.'

'I am not,' Brannon said with a scowl.

'You're lucky, Brannon. Why were the soldiers chasing you?'

Brannon remembered it then. The fight in the gorge. He had lost consciousness just when it all erupted. 'Was it you who saved our lives, Bakka?'

'We didn't even know you were there. We spotted the soldiers coming into the mountains, so we followed them. And killed them. Only after that we found you.'

'You killed all of them?'

Bakka stroked his knife affectionately. 'Yes.'

'Where's Ahmed?'

'He sleeps. He will live. So, again,' Bakka asked him, 'why were the soldiers chasing you?'

'They found out we were plotting against Yazid,' Brannon explained. 'They wanted to kill us, but we escaped. We came here because we hoped you would help us. I'm afraid our original plan seems impossible now—we'll have to think of something else.' He remembered the lengths he had gone to in acquiring a key to the armoury and sabotaging the city walls, triumphs that would be in vain if this rebellion were to falter.

'A pity,' Bakka said ruefully, touching his knife again. 'I would have enjoyed a fight with Yazid.'

'You can have your chance yet. We're not finished. Suliman still marches at the head of an army.'

'Perhaps,' Bakka said. 'But Yazid will strike first. Do you think he intends to simply wait for Suliman? No. He will confront Suliman instead. And what then? Either way, many men are about to die.'

Brannon sat up and edged himself closer to the warmth of the fire. The small amount of liquid he had taken was already having an effect; he felt more clear-headed, and the pain of his parched throat eased a little. Night was falling softly on the mountainside, and children were called in from the high surrounds. The hours of darkness were a time for young ones to be closeted inside tents, safe from animals and other predators that roamed these hills. Tonight Brannon would sleep too. He needed rest. Tomorrow, refreshed and sated, he would turn his mind towards rescuing whatever remained of this shaky enterprise.

'*Allahu Akbar*,' he said wryly, grinning at Bakka. 'Or at least I hope so.'

After a week of arguing, the Berbers agreed to drive their numbers south and join the greater force of Suliman's army which, they hoped, was heading for Marrakech. They traversed the foothills of the High Atlas on a bright, cloudless morning, a long column of riders threading the sandstone gorges along tracks sprinkled with yellow gorse and shaded by carob trees. Skylarks and cuckoos scattered from their passing, and the sun beat down from above, bouncing against the sides of the canyons and sparkling in the waterfalls. The more Berber villages they passed the more their ranks were swelled, with every male capable of wielding a sword eager to play his part. But it wasn't just brash youngsters taking up the challenge; the older men, the hardened veterans with wrinkled faces, sat confidently on their mounts, invigorated by the prospect of battle. The fact that the sultan was currently amassing an army to destroy them was wholly undaunting.

Near the head of the column, Brannon and Ahmed moved in a pair. The conspicuous silence between them was making Brannon extremely uncomfortable, but he was struggling to find things to say.

'Those mountains,' he tried eventually, 'what name do you give them? They're big, actually. As mountains go.'

Ahmed looked at him.

'We don't have them as big back home,' Brannon said. 'Quite impressive, really.'

'I see.' Ahmed sniffed and turned his eyes back to the trail.

Making little progress, Brannon decided to risk a more direct approach. 'Look, Ahmed, about what happened before. I just wanted—'

'Don't waste your breath,' Ahmed said, cutting him off. He stared at Brannon, his expression like granite. 'You and I have unfinished business to settle. And it will be settled, I assure you. Until then, however, we have a war to win and a tyrant to defeat, and you would be wise not to irritate me with these ridiculous overtures again.' He didn't wait for an answer but spurred his horse on. Brannon fumed.

Arrogant bloody bastard, he thought. *Yes, we'll settle our business all right. I can't bloody wait. Keep it up and I'll break that snotty nose of yours...*

Ahmed carried on to the top of the column. He had already resolved to put Brannon's reprehensible behaviour out of his mind, for right now his focus was needed elsewhere.

'Bakka.' He saluted the Berber leader respectfully. 'The journey is long, no?' He wanted to ensure the other knew where he was going, but without seeming to question him.

Bakka smiled. 'Long? Perhaps. If you need rest, we can stop.'

'That won't be necessary.' Ahmed swallowed his misgivings. If Suliman was out there, he would be found.

Their chances of success had been substantially lessened, he realised. If they had been able to get their forces into Fez, he was sure they would have triumphed. The element of surprise would have won the day. But the surprise was ruined when an unknown person betrayed their plans, and now it would come down to speed and might. Who would reach Marrakech first? Who would win the inevitable battle to follow?

If Suliman took Marrakech, Yazid would come to take it back, and then they would fight. Whether inside the stifling streets or out on the breezy plains, it would be brutal and bloody, and only Allah could know its outcome. Yet Ahmed felt confident. These Berbers were warriors down to the adolescent boys, and once coupled with Suliman's forces, they would be capable of a mighty assault on the hordes that Yazid would send their way. And only the other night he had had a dream in which he found a serpent lying beneath his pillow, something he was hugely encouraged by. It was believed that a serpent in a dream was sent by the *moualin al-ard*, the masters of the earth, to be interpreted by the dream's recipient as a herald of good fortune.

Yes, Ahmed thought, *we shall succeed. Suliman marches, and our forces are strong; Allah is on our side. Before the month is out, we shall succeed.*

In the north, Yazid's legions were sharpening blades.

They made camp that night in a valley where the rocks smouldered amber in the twilight, sheltering under a copse of sweet-smelling thuya trees and cutting branches to throw on the cooking fires. The Berbers shot pheasants in the hills and roasted them on spits, producing cuts of smoky-flavoured meat for everyone. They slept until dawn and then moved off again, intending to cover as many miles as possible before the sun fully stoked its furnaces. The countryside remained oddly quiet apart from shepherds on distant hills. It was as if the land braced itself for the carnage to come.

On the sixth morning, they reached a rolling limestone escarpment that bordered the southern plains. There were several tracks crossing the hill, sunlight glinting between the weathered peaks. Then, high above, they saw riders.

They were a quarter mile off, their attire indistinguishable. They were the first people the travellers had seen in days, and their sudden appearance precipitated a commotion of scraping swords.

'Calm down, everybody,' Brannon growled. 'They're probably just lost.'

Ahmed gazed worriedly up the hill. 'It can't be imperial scouts,' he said, though he sounded uncertain. 'Yazid is not that fast. Is he?'

'Only one way to find out.' Brannon kicked his heels and rode off for the slope.

'Don't be a fool,' Ahmed snapped, but his voice was lost as Brannon began priming his pistol as his horse negotiated a path to the summit. There were four riders that he could now see. He suddenly found his eyesight blinded by the sun, and he cursed. The riders began moving along the crest.

'Wait,' he yelled, and he drove the horse faster until its scrabbling hooves sent clouds of dust rolling across the hillside. Both man and animal were panting by the time they reached the top. There was no sign of the four riders—but suddenly Brannon no longer cared.

'Good God,' he murmured in amazement.

Spread across the plain below was an army, a big army of men covering the ground for miles like a deluge from the sea. They had tents and wagons and horses and dogs, and they had left a vast swathe of churned-up ground in their wake. Brannon couldn't begin to imagine what their numbers might be.

'My word,' he breathed, and he grinned to himself. 'Suliman has done well.'

❀ ❀ ❀

A mob of raggedy Arabs came flooding out to gape at the Berber horseman, from skinny teenagers to gummy old men, all keen to greet the new influx of blood into their camp. The atmosphere was like a street carnival; voices cheered, dogs barked, and some of the more excitable men were firing their muskets in the air.

'Waste of ammunition,' Ahmed muttered, surveying the blusterous horde that was Suliman's army. They were peasants, as expected, yet they looked lean and strong. But could they fight? Time would tell.

'Easy now, fellows,' Brannon said bemusedly as they pressed around, clapping his back and tugging playfully at his blond locks. He could barely follow their speech, such was the rapidity of their babbling, but their mood was infectious. Soon a group of them had taken jealous ownership of him and bade him to come and sit at their cooking fire.

Suliman's army had ample livestock, and later that evening Brannon's new friends cut the throat of a camel and gathered its blood in copper kettles, which they boiled over the flames. The congealed blood became as thick as calf's liver, and they added the animal's intestines, with their contents still inside, as well as the lungs and the slippery green liquid that oozed out of the rumen. The end result was both nourishing and surprisingly appetising. The air grew chilly on the exposed plain, and so they piled up the fires and sat around shoulder-to-shoulder to talk and to smoke. Brannon enjoyed their banter and high spirits, and after a while he managed to get a hold on their fast-flowing Arabic. They asked him where he was from, and he told them he was from Ireland. They asked who his king was, and he explained that his king sat on a throne in another country. They were perturbed at this. Why not an Irish king for Irish people?

'Maybe one day,' he said, smiling.

They became even more excited when they learned that he had no wife, as he didn't attempt to explain his confused arrangement with Asiya. Several made offers of their sisters or daughters, with the bride prices ranging from a goat to six cows to five hundred Spanish dollars, the latter being requested by a shifty-eyed old man who claimed that his daughter's beauty was akin to Troy's Helen. When Brannon said that he could not afford her, the old man shrugged and admitted, 'It's just as well for you. She has as much charm as a nest of wasps, and she is so ugly that my camels cannot digest their food around her.'

'Where do you all come from?' Brannon asked them, and he regretted his curiosity later for it took several hours for every man present to relay the story of his background. Each rambling tale had one thing in common, however. They had all felt the mark of Moulay Yazid on their lives, in one way or another, be it through imprisonment or confiscated property or the murder of loved ones. Even the younger males, the ones with unlined faces and hairless chins, could tell stories of Moulay Yazid that made Brannon shudder. As much as any, they were determined to spill the tyrant's blood and end his power for good.

'And you'll have your opportunity,' Brannon assured them. 'You'll have it soon, probably sooner than we imagine.' And he wondered then just how many of these eager faces would be cold and lifeless before the month was out.

⊕ ⊕ ⊕

Suliman bowed his head. His eyes were closed in the soft lantern-light of the tent, his lips unmoving. It took him a moment to absorb the news, and then he said quietly, 'It is not your fault.'

Ahmed couldn't bear to look at that noble, trusting face. 'Of course it is, my lord. I should have been more careful. I put faith in too many people. You warned me of this, and still I failed you. Now Yazid knows everything.'

'Yazid knew all along that someday someone would come for him. We may have lost the initial surprise, but that is a small thing.'

'But now we cannot march on Fez. Yazid will send his armies south to stop us.'

'He will,' Suliman agreed, 'and we shall not run. We will prevail. Allah is on our side.'

Ahmed looked at him hopefully. 'You truly believe so?'

'I do. Allah's ways are not for us men to understand, but His love ensures the triumph of good. That is what I believe.'

Ahmed clasped his hands in reverence. '*Allahu Akbar*. There is no god but He, and Mohammed is His messenger.'

Suliman nodded his acknowledgement and stayed silent in respect. Then he poured some tea and moved the conversation on. 'About your sister, Ahmed. My beloved cousin Asiya. It makes me happy to know that she still lives.'

Ahmed blinked in dread. 'Forgive me, my lord, but there is something which I haven't told you. Asiya is not with me. I was forced to leave her behind in Fez, when Yazid's soldiers chased me. I feel so ashamed—'

Suliman smiled. 'No, you must forgive me, Ahmed. I shouldn't have made you wait.' He called through the tent flap, and seconds later it was lifted to admit a young woman.

Ahmed gasped in shock. 'It's not possible!'

Asiya burst into tears the instant she laid eyes on him. With careless joy they hugged each other, weeping unashamedly, weak with relief at finding the person they had both given up for dead. It was several long minutes before either of them could speak, and Suliman watched them with a fatherly patience. This very moment, at least, was a happy one. And a rare one, because he knew with a sense of foreboding that there would be precious little of such moments ahead.

'You sly old English dog,' Brannon blurted in astonishment. 'Where have you staggered out of?'

Daniel smirked as he eased himself into the company of men and picked a skewer of mutton from the fireside. 'When you've been raised on the streets of Peckham, matey, you learn fast how to keep your balls off the block.'

'I don't doubt it.' Brannon laughed. The last thing he had expected to see was Daniel Jones sauntering blithely into Suliman's camp. 'What's been going on, Dan? You look as black as a Moor! What happened to your face?'

'I've been tidying up a mess—the mess you buckos left behind. Bloody rude of you to leave without a goodbye.'

'We were in a bit of a hurry, as I recall. But how'd you find us?'

'That was easy. I knew Suliman was coming up from the south. Getting out of Fez was the hard part. And I had to collect your little wifey along the way, too.'

'Asiya? Jesus, Dan, you've been busy.'

'I have. Didn't I beat you here, even with your head start?'

'Aye, well, I was on foot. No boasting.' But Brannon was chuffed. Not only did he have his old mentor back, but Asiya was safe too. Brannon had feared the worst for her, knowing what Yazid's fury might be, but now through the grace of God and this resourceful Englishman, she was safe in good hands.

'Shame this lot aren't partial to a drop,' Daniel said wistfully, gazing across the ranks of sober Arabs. 'What I'd give for one night to get roaring, falling-down drunk...'

'Well, my friend,' Brannon quipped, 'someday you can show me around all the taverns and sin-pots of London, and we'll stay up all night and drink foul brew until our eyes pop out of our heads.'

'Sounds all right to me. If we ever make it home.' Daniel pursed his lips doubtfully. 'You really think these lads are up to tackling Yazid?'

'I don't know,' Brannon admitted. 'They're farmers, nomads, not soldiers. Yazid has some of the most ruthless fighters in the whole of Africa. So I don't know. As my father always pointed out, *claíonn neart ceart*, which means force overcomes justice.'

Daniel smiled. 'No fool, your father. He waits for you at home?'

'No. He's dead. Yours?'

'Never knew the chap.'

'What about your mother?'

258

Daniel shrugged. 'Dead these last thirty years. Hardly have a memory of her now. She used to cough a lot. And curse. That's about all I remember.' He looked at Brannon. 'I hope you had it easier.'

Brannon sighed, gazing into the fire. 'My father died a weary man. He buried four children one after the other, and then he had me, his only surviving one. He nearly broke his back lifting stones out of the field, building a farm for me.'

'He sounds like a good salt.'

'Shy fellow. Didn't speak an awful lot, though he'd get lively after some whiskey, whenever he could afford it. He'd come home merry-eyed and insist on hugging us to suffocation, but he'd nod off quickly afterwards, and my mother would wrap a blanket around him. They died within two months of each other. Him first and she after. I lost myself with grief for a while. I went into that field and dug up every last stone that his old arms hadn't managed, and I hurled all the bastards into the sea.'

'Must've been lonely up there without them,' Daniel said.

'I got through it.'

'Course you did, by sniffing round the local rosebush. That would take your mind off things.'

'Aye, it would,' Brannon chuckled. 'And I hope she's still there, Dan.'

They both were silent for some moments. Then they gazed back to the camp.

'Yazid will wipe the floor with us, won't he?' Daniel said.

'Not without a struggle,' Brannon answered. 'Damn it, if I have to kill the bastard myself, I'll do it.' He slapped his fist against his palm.

'I'm sure you will, Brannon.' Daniel gave him a pat on the shoulder. 'Christ, there's nothing more dangerous than an Irishman with a cause.'

His belly full of smoke-blackened meat, Daniel dozed off by the fireside shortly after midnight. Brannon was still awake; he left the Englishman to his slumber and wandered between the smouldering campfires, past the rows of peaceful faces glowing in the amber light, and headed for the scrubland beyond the camp. He wished now for some minutes of solitude.

Out here the stars glimmered like tiny paint spatters on a giant black canvas. He gazed at them in wonder. How far away were they? It seemed like a vast distance. He knew little of such matters. They were a long way off—that was all he knew. Like Dromkeen.

Dry leaves rustled. He turned around to see someone approach. As always, she surprised him with her near-silent movements, passing soundlessly like cloud shadow on a distant meadow.

'I saw you walking alone,' she said nervously. 'I disturbed you?'

'Of course not.' He smiled. 'How are you, Asiya?'

'I'm relieved to know you're safe. I never knew what happened to you, not until Daniel explained.'

'And he told me what happened to you. Thank God, Asiya, that you were not harmed. I would never have forgiven myself.'

His words brightened her. 'It comforts me to know you care.'

'I'll always care.' He stepped across the narrow space that separated them and placed his hands on her shoulders. 'You're a wonderful person, very special to me. You will always have a place in my heart.'

'I love you, Brannon,' she whispered, and her emerald eyes filled with helpless tears. 'I love you.'

'I know that,' he said gently. And I'm a lucky man to have your love.'

'But I missed you so much. After that night we had together, I felt as if the sun would shine on me forever. And then, in a single morning, you were gone. I just wanted to know...to ask the question—do you love me too?'

He hesitated, touching the smooth, beautiful skin of her face. 'Asiya, I do love you. It's not a romantic love. A romantic love can shrivel up and die just as fast as it comes. My love for you is much greater than that.'

'Oh, Brannon, where will you be when all of this is finished? I need to know.' She looked into his eyes, searching for the true meaning of his words.

'One day, Asiya, you'll be with a man who is noble and good and strong, a man who deserves to be with you. You will be happy. And you will be thankful, for it is a happiness that I could never have given you.'

She swallowed a lump, battling her tears. 'You don't want me. I was wrong. You've never wanted me.'

'Any man would, Asiya, any man with eyesight and a heartbeat. But I cannot be that man. Our paths were thrown together, yet they don't belong together. Mine belongs in a place far from here. Where my people are.'

She gazed at him, and despite her pain she began to comprehend the heartache he was suffering. Woman's intuition—it suddenly laid bare his torment.

'There's someone waiting for you, isn't there?' she said softly. 'There's a girl.'

'There is.' Brannon sighed, feeling guilt at the memory of her. 'Orlaith. That's her name. It's been so long.'

'Do you love her?'

'I do. And it's strange, but the first time I saw you, it made me think of her. There was a resemblance.'

She smiled at that. 'She looks like me?'

'Yes.' He nodded. 'She is beautiful.'

Asiya bit her lip, and a tear slid down her cheek. 'How I wish I could be this Orlaith. I wish it so badly. But I believe you will see her again, Brannon. Allah is kind.'

'Perhaps Allah is kind to the good. I don't know if He includes me in his favour.'

'Brannon.' She took his hand and kissed it. 'What happened between us was not wrong. We were two people who needed each other that night, who took strength from each other in our loneliness. I wish it could happen forever, but I can see now that Allah has not chosen that destiny for you. You are right— your path lies in a place far from here.'

He cleared his throat and rubbed his eyes. 'I'm sorry if I've caused you upset. It was never my intention to hurt anyone—not you, not Orlaith, not myself for that matter. The only person I wanted to hurt was Yazid, and where is he now? Sharpening a stake somewhere and reciting my name, no doubt.'

'Ahmed says that Yazid will soon be dead. We must pray that he is right.'

'What will you do?'

She came forward and rested her head against his chest. Her tears began to flow as she let herself drift into the warm reassurance of his body. This was goodbye. This was the moment where those paths must part. And the moment, she thought defiantly, was hers alone. Orlaith could never take that from her.

After a while she released him and stepped back, creating a space between them never to be bridged again. 'Ahmed is sending me under escort tomorrow to the village of our grand-uncle in the south. He does not want me to be with the camp when Yazid's army comes.'

'It's a sensible decision,' Brannon said, though his heart was heavy.

'So goodnight, Brannon. And goodbye.' She gave one last wistful look into his eyes, and then she turned purposefully and headed back towards the camp.

'Goodbye, Asiya,' Brannon whispered.

Behind him a kestrel flew off, uttering a shrilling cry as she scanned the twinkling lights of the camp for food. She saw only men, chewing on mutton chops or snoring in slumber, and behind them a cluster of tents inside which were older men, talking and making plans and plotting the downfall of a tyrant. The kestrel glided on, carrying herself on the warm nocturnal airs towards the city of Marrakech and over its walls into the barren plains and black mountains. Up there nothing stirred, like a glassy, tranquil sea before the first ominous rumble of the storm.

'Brannon Ryan?' Ahmed shook his head dubiously. 'No. Definitely not. He can't ride very well; don't put him with the cavalry. But he's a brave fighter, so give him an infantry unit to lead.'

Suliman nodded warily. 'You'll forgive me if I seem to wonder about these new friends of yours. You say both are army-trained?'

'Yes. The Englishman too. He's a little older, perhaps not as fast as Brannon, but he's a natural leader. I think, if we can take Marrakech, you should put him in a position of command with the city garrison. He'll look over Marrakech while we push north.'

'Very well,' Suliman agreed. 'I'm grateful for anyone with military training. It's an army of peasants we lead, Ahmed, not soldiers. Yazid will throw all his powers at us, so we must use our wits.' He raised an eyebrow. 'And where will you be, my cousin?'

'By your side, my lord,' Ahmed answered devoutly. 'Always.'

'I thought as much.' Suliman grinned. 'And I am glad.' He unfurled a map on his knees. 'Marrakech is but a few days' travel. Our scouts say that Yazid has not yet reached it—indeed, the devil himself could not move his minions that fast. So we will take Marrakech, garrison it, and then carry on north until we meet the sultan's army. We will pitch untrained farmers against Yazid's Imperial Guard and hope for victory.' He smiled bleakly at his own words.

'We have the Berbers too, my lord,' Ahmed reminded him. 'They will not be cowed by Yazid's Imperial Guard, nor by anyone else.'

'And we have Allah's benevolent hand to guide us,' Suliman said, 'and so we shall triumph.'

He stood up to address the other men present inside the small tent. They were a mismatch of garrison officers and tribal leaders, the ones to whom he entrusted the command of his army. 'Go to your respective battalions tonight. Speak to them. Tell them that tomorrow we leave this plain and there will be no rest until we are inside the walls of Marrakech. The devil does not rest, and nor shall we.'

'*Allahu Akbar.*' They bowed to Suliman and one by one left the tent. Their orders had been explained long ago, and each knew what was expected of him.

'There will be much violence soon, my lord,' Ahmed said delicately, mindful of Suliman's character. Suliman was not a natural warrior, not a killer of men, not a butcher of innocents like his brother. He was a man of books and peace and quiet contemplation, and sometimes Ahmed couldn't help but doubt his lust for battle.

'Much violence indeed,' Suliman reflected. He gazed at Ahmed. 'Dear cousin, the very turning of this world is lubricated by the blood that we men spill. That is the way it has always been. If by a kind heart and a gesture of love I could rescue our country from the grip of Yazid, then I would do it. But I cannot. And so you are right. There will be much violence soon.'

Ahmed nodded and rose up. He kissed Suliman's cheeks, left the tent, and walked out into the black night.

CHAPTER TWENTY-TWO

A dusty evening wind swept the ramparts, teasing the blood-red flags that stood like grave markers above the walls. An air of foreboding hung as thick as the stench of a corpse, permeating every last orifice of the tensed city. But this was good, it was appropriate, for soon there would be many such corpses, bodies rent by blades, blood soaking the innocent ground over which this army would pass. The time had come.

Moulay Yazid cast his hooded gaze over the panorama of men and steel that had gathered below the gates of Fez. Their numbers spread as far as the hills that hid the dying sun, a vast army of killers with swords forged from hellish furnaces, death in their eyes and brutal strength right to their fingertips. They uttered his name in one thunderous voice.

'*Yazid!*' And they stamped their feet as one and roared like lions. And Yazid was pleased.

'Forgive my impertinence, Your Majesty,' General al-Malek intruded, 'but are you sure you must join us? Perhaps it would be wiser to remain in Fez until the rebellion has been defeated. I can command this army in your absence.'

Yazid smiled thinly. 'General, this is my army, and I will lead it. And when we finally capture Suliman, it will be my blade that pierces his throat, not yours.'

'Of course, Your Majesty. I understand. Suliman will live to regret his cowardly actions.'

'He won't live long, General. I will kill him, cut off his head, and raise it high over the city walls. An example to all traitors. The people will see for themselves the price of rebellion.'

'A most excellent idea, Majesty. Truly you are beloved of Allah.'

'Tonight we will eat, and we will sleep. Tomorrow, we march for Marrakech. My brother cannot capture that city. We will take it and burn the lands around so that Suliman's men must starve. Once his will is broken, we will move in and crush him.'

'Praise Allah!'

'You, General, will then hunt down every last scrap of filth that ever dared to strike a foul blow against his regent. Every single traitor and rebel you will kill. My reign will prevail, and none will dare turn his hand on me again.'

'I will do all that His Majesty requires of me.'

'Yes, you had better,' Yazid warned. 'Do not think that your brave deeds in the past will win you my favour forever, General. My patience is not without limits.'

'Majesty?' Al-Malek spread his hands in a gesture of innocence.

'Four years ago, I now know, you failed to kill all of Khaled al-Qatib's children. Recently you captured one of them, but you foolishly let him escape. Then you arrested and interrogated his sister, a young girl—and she, too, made a fool of you!' Yazid spat in anger at the thought of it.

'It wasn't my fault, Majesty. Somebody betrayed me. I—'

Yazid pulled out his knife, seized al-Malek's neck, and placed the blade to his throat. 'Now listen to me, General al-Malek. You have served me well in the past, but mark this. If Suliman is not dead before this month is out and the rebellion dead and buried, you will discover exactly where the limits of my patience lie.'

Al-Malek gulped, a bead of sweat forming at his temple. He feared no man, except this one. 'Yes, Your Majesty. I give you my word.'

'Good.' Yazid released him and sheathed his knife. Then, incongruously, he flashed a smile. 'So let us begin.'

It was after dawn the following morning when the army rolled out of Fez. Yazid rode at the head of the Imperial Guard underneath their fluttering banners, followed by the cavalry and the infantry and the creaking artillery wagons. They were chased by a stream of excited children and yapping dogs while the townspeople stood and watched from a respectful distance. Great clouds of dust rose to choke the air as they rumbled southwards, and within an hour they had disappeared over the hills. The roads outside Fez, churned up by thousands of hooves and feet, lay quiet again.

Suliman knelt at the top of the grassy hill and peered through his glass at the clay walls where a phalanx of palm trees quivered in the breeze. For a while he watched in silence, studying the flow of people through the gates and the labouring of workers outside. Eventually Ahmed was moved to interrupt him.

'Well, my lord? Were our scouts correct?'

Suliman turned around slowly and nodded. 'I believe so.' He murmured a prayer of thanks and bowed his head. 'Yes, cousin, they were correct. We have beaten Yazid to Marrakech.'

Ahmed smiled in relief. 'Allah be praised. I will alert the battalion leaders.'

He went back over the hill and clambered down the slopes to where the main army sweated in a torrid valley. The news bolstered them. Yazid had not come, and Marrakech was theirs; their first major challenge had been successful. The artillery wagons were steered around the hills, but the Berber horsemen and the infantry approached the city directly, sending the field workers scattering in panic. However, once it was made known that the man leading the army was Suliman, cheers sounded from within the gates and the citizens came crawling back out of hiding to cry his name in praise.

The troops spilled through the streets, securing vantage points and manning the watchtowers. The city's tiny garrison, underequipped and overwhelmed, did not resist, and the pasha, the city's governor, was quick to pledge his allegiance.

'You are the true sultan,' he told Suliman when they met in his chamber, and he lowered himself in further submission. 'Whatever I have, I place at your disposal.'

'Get off your knees,' Suliman said, frowning in exasperation. 'We're not here to humiliate you.'

'Thank you, Your Excellency.' The pasha rose up and mopped the sweat from his brow, gesturing for his servants to bring food for the new arrivals. 'I had feared that Moulay Yazid would reach us before you did. There is much rumour. It is said that his army marches from the north—that it burns everything before it.'

'I suspect the rumours may be true,' Suliman sighed. 'But do not be troubled, my friend. We will stand up to the tyrant when he comes.'

The pasha looked anything but reassured. He glanced nervously through the window, at the horizon, half expecting Yazid's army to appear at any instant.

'What resources do you have for your defence?' Suliman asked him.

'Excellency, I have a garrison of five hundred men, though most are untrained and poorly armed. We have cannon on the ramparts also. Eight-pounders.'

'I see.' Suliman wasn't impressed; however, he knew he could spare only a limited number to stay behind to supplement the city's garrison. The bulk of his army was needed for the main assault on Yazid, whenever it happened. Numbers were crucial if he was to have any hope of success, for he knew he was already outclassed in terms of fighting prowess. He didn't like to imagine what would happen when he sent ranks of skinny peasants up against the sultan's elite.

'We shall have to stop Yazid before he reaches Marrakech,' he told the pasha with a smile. 'That is all we have to do, and then you will be safe.'

'Yes, Your Excellency,' the pasha said, and a fresh layer of sweat broke out on his forehead.

⊕ ⊕ ⊕

Moulay Yazid pushed his army at a flesh-melting pace through the vast ground that led to the south. They ate and drank on the march, sleeping only during the small hours of darkness, and in a few days they had covered over two hundred miles. In the African heat this effort would have killed weaker men, but Yazid's soldiers were strong, and they suffered only a few dozen casualties in all. To speed the movement, Yazid carried only small artillery with him and relied instead on General al-Malek, who managed to gather several cannon from a secret arms cache along the way. Given the circumstances of their hasty departure from Fez, the successful mobilisation of so many men was an achievement in itself.

However, it was not enough.

Long before he reached Marrakech, Yazid's scouts rode back with the news that he couldn't avoid any longer. The distance to cover had been too great.

'The flags of Suliman fly above the ramparts,' they confirmed with heavy hearts. 'Marrakech is taken by the rebels.'

He had expected as much.

Al-Malek entered Yazid's tent then, dourly. He knelt and bowed his head, and when invited to speak he said, 'Your Majesty, my officers have reported an outbreak of vomiting in the infantry units. Bad water, I fear, and there are already several hundred men infected. It is not good, Majesty. They are unable to walk five yards without fouling themselves.'

Yazid felt like killing someone.

'We should be able to contain it,' al-Malek added hurriedly, recognising the signs of mounting anger in his sultan. 'I will take care of the problem myself.'

'Shoot the sick men, General,' Yazid growled at him, 'and that will take care of the problem quickly enough.' He felt tension in his chest, a deepening anxiety which was fuelling his rage. Suliman's early victory had to be cancelled out. The balance had to be redressed.

'Go to every village in the surrounding area,' he went on. 'I want every man and boy drafted into service—I don't care how young. They mightn't be able to fight, but we'll put them in the front and let Suliman use up his cannon on them.' This smacked a little of desperation, but he had to keep his numbers up.

'Brilliant thinking, Your Excellency,' al-Malek said. 'I will despatch riders on the hour, and we will have the villagers rounded up in camp by nightfall.'

'Just hurry it up, General,' Yazid snapped, becoming more agitated. 'Suliman is laughing at me behind those walls—I can hear him. And I want him dead, General. I want Suliman and all his followers dead!' He let out a roar and swung his sword above his head, splitting the canvas roof and almost decapitating three of his servants. Al-Malek bowed and left the tent hastily.

⊕ ⊕ ⊕

The sun burned away the faint flecks of cloud as Suliman's army left Marrakech and ploughed north where the great savage peaks of the High Atlas towered like disgruntled gods. Mules dragged artillery carriages up the dusty road, and the infantry were forced to keep to a tediously slow pace as they negotiated a pass along the hilly terrain. Several times there were delays when a wheel came off a carriage and had to be repaired, holding up the entire line. The men sweated in the midmorning heat, but they didn't grumble too much. The Berber riders, however, were bored by the slow rate of progress and broke away into the hills to hunt deer. They returned some hours later, and still the main body of troops was negotiating its cumbersome passage. Ahmed fumed at the Berbers' failure to keep formation but was resigned to the fact that they couldn't be ordered about. Though their courage on the battlefield was renowned, they were impossible to discipline off it.

He rode on to where Suliman led the columns. He had taken it upon himself in recent days to maintain a near constant vigil over his cousin. Suliman's life was the only one which mattered. If he died, the entire campaign would collapse. Ahmed was determined to protect him.

Suliman endured this with a weary indulgence. 'I can look after myself,' he chuckled. 'You mustn't fret about me so much. Allah watches over me.'

'Even so, my lord, I would rather stay by your side.' Ahmed nodded towards the land ahead. 'It won't be long now.'

A few hours later they found that the main artery road through the hills narrowed as it passed between two high cliffs. The march was halted while the formation was rearranged to allow a smooth passage. The Berbers, bold as always, rode through on their own. Ahmed stayed behind to supervise the infantry, and precious hours slid by. It was only after they had negotiated the awkward route that he spotted Bakka, the Berber leader, riding back fast.

'I think you should look at this,' he told Ahmed, and there was a lusty gleam in his eyes.

Ahmed followed him up the escarpment ahead, climbing the heights until he had a view into a dusty plain, hemmed in by two steep sides of pebbled terrain. There were plumes of smoke rising from the plain, about two miles away. He could just make out clusters of men gathered by cooking fires, their horses tethered nearby.

'Yazid,' Bakka whispered in awe, and his fingers closed around the hilt of his sword.

Ahmed turned his horse around. 'Stay here,' he told Bakka. 'Don't attempt to approach them.' The Berber warrior raised his eyebrows innocently and gave Ahmed a wolfish grin.

'Bakka, I mean it,' Ahmed warned. 'We will send the scouts first.'

He rode back, forcing his way between the oncoming infantry. He found Suliman and gave him the news.

'Send scouts then, to investigate,' Suliman decided, 'but make sure they stay out of sight. In the meantime, let us discuss what we are to do.'

The scouts rode unseen behind the trees edging the plain. They returned an hour later, breathless and excited, and said, 'It is Yazid's standards which they fly, Your Excellency. They are the sultan's troops, it is true.'

Suliman formulated a hasty tactical plan. Battle tactics were new to him, and he had only a small handful of military-trained personnel to assist him, but he applied himself to the task with diligence.

'It's doubtful they know of our approach yet,' he said, 'otherwise they wouldn't be sitting around their fires unprepared. So we will take them by surprise, a quick attack. The Berber tribesmen are our best riders—send them to spearhead the assault, and the infantry will follow behind. If we are fast enough, they will be unable to react in time.' It unsettled him, even now, to imagine the violence that they were about to unleash. But Yazid would have done the same.

Once the orders were elaborated on, the infantry units were moved into position behind the cavalry. They would hold back until the Berbers launched the first wave, and then they would move in to clean up whatever remained. It was a decisive victory needed. Ahmed slipped in by Suliman's side, and they rode together.

Bakka led the Berbers. He was thrilled at the prospect of a proper fight at last. They assembled themselves across the ridge of the escarpment, a long line of riders, lances aloft in a forest of steel. Bakka acknowledged the nod from Suliman, and then he kissed his blade.

The Berbers roared. It was a blood-chilling sound, a thunderous booming of strength and murder. Their voices echoed around the plain, and their steeds lowered their heads.

And they charged.

The slope was obscured in flying dirt as thousands of hooves tore through the scrub. Resting birds were scattered into flight while the plumes of smoke in the doomed camp seemed to freeze in mid-air. It took mere minutes for the Berbers to cover the distance. Bodies scrambled to their feet when they saw the hills come alive with riders, weapons were seized in panic, faces turned white. But it was too late.

The Berbers fell upon them like savages. Lances glinted through the dust, and metal clashed, the sound ringing out in vicious melody. Men screamed and blood flew and limbs spun to the ground. The roars of the Berbers were thick with battle-lust, their eyes wide like madmen, and the plain was turned into a slaughterhouse. Yazid's troops were hopelessly outmatched. Anyone within reach of a sword-swing was cut down, and the bodies slumped in grisly heaps.

The infantry didn't waste a moment. They followed after the advancing Berbers and stormed into the plain, eager to join the carnage. In that first devastating sweep the Berbers had butchered almost a thousand men, and now the infantry would add their considerable weight. It was a scene of bloody mayhem.

Brannon ran at the head of his unit, determined to be the first of the infantry into the fray. He unsheathed his sword, and his months of military training seemed to return in a surge, flowing through his arms and right to his fingertips. This was it.

He searched for Yazid. That bastard had to be finished as quickly as possible. A man staggered out of the mêlée and thrust his pistol at Brannon's face, squeezing the trigger in panic. The ball flew by with a whine, and Brannon killed the gunman with a thrust to the chest. It felt good. One less of Yazid's minions left to plague the earth.

The battle was going well for Suliman. The enemy had been thrown into turmoil by the speed with which they were attacked, and there was barely any resistance offered. The Berbers seemed not to have suffered a single casualty, and now the infantry were inflicting their own heavy toll. It was too easy.

Something is not right, Brannon thought suddenly.

Yazid's troops weren't even putting up a fight. They were cowering in terror, hands over their heads, crying like children. Brannon held back momentarily, his ardour cooling. 'Stand off!' he yelled at his troops. But they were in the fever of battle and paid him no heed. He stared at the corpses piling at his feet. He looked at their faces. And he felt a touch of cold dread on his skin.

This was not Yazid's army. These were old men, boys, bewildered country peasants. They weren't even in uniform. Something was desperately wrong.

'Stop!' he yelled in horror, waving his arms back to the slope. 'Hold back!'

No one could hear him above the deafening noise of the battle. The infantry units continued to hack their way across the plain, and streams of blood were darkening the dust. The situation was out of control.

'It's not Yazid!' Brannon shoved aside the men in his way and ran for the slope. What was Suliman thinking? He had to be informed as quickly as possible before every poor unfortunate on that plain was dead. But then, mercifully, Suliman seemed to have realised.

He came tearing down the slope on his horse and rode into the thick of the violence. His agonised voice eventually restrained the wild troops. It took several more minutes to restore order, and by then the body count was immeasurable. The grounds of the plain were drenched in blood. Many of the victims had been decapitated.

Suliman couldn't speak for some moments, the colour drained from his face. He stared down at his feet, at the mutilated body of a boy, a boy no more than twelve years of age. It was too much for Suliman. He slumped to his knees, tears glistening in his eyes, and he began blubbering out a desperate prayer.

Brannon stormed angrily towards Ahmed. 'You fools!' he snapped. 'This is not Yazid's army!'

Like Suliman, Ahmed was dumbstruck. He gazed about at the horrifying scene as if seeking an answer amongst the piles of mangled corpses. A heavy silence descended on the plain. Already the skies above were flocked with hordes of carrion birds, lured by the sickly-sweet smell of slaughter. Suliman's army had prepared them a feast.

Ahmed picked a tattered flag off the ground. 'These are Yazid's colours. I don't understand. Where is he?'

No one could answer.

Then, in the unnatural silence of the plain, there was a sudden boom. It was followed by a ponderous rolling sound in the air, like echoing thunder, and a white arc of smoke trailed across the sky. Every man looked instinctively towards the north.

'Shit…' Brannon's mouth opened.

The shell crashed into the battleground, into the clusters of confused troops, and the terrain exploded in dirt and severed limbs. The men nearby were thrown off their feet, and the horses reared in panic. Brannon scrambled up and stared. He felt his mouth go dry.

A long, menacing line of cannon had appeared over the ridge, manned by scores of soldiers. They trained the weapons down into the plain, picked their ground, and lit the fuses. The gaping maws of the cannon burst into life. They fired in near unison, like a naval salute, a volley of shots screaming into the sky and then hurtling to the floor below. The shells pounded into the defenceless troops, blasting great holes through their ranks and killing them in dozens. The horses threw their riders and bolted for cover, stampeding over the writhing bodies in their way. The cannonade reached a crescendo, and the plain was swiftly churned into a grisly mess of mud and flesh and blood.

Suliman had walked blindly into Yazid's trap and placed his head between the lion's jaws. Now there was chaos.

CHAPTER TWENTY-THREE

High on the ridge of the hill, Moulay Yazid watched with relish as the blood-bath unfolded. 'How foolish my brother is,' he laughed. 'If I had known how easy this would be, I would have stayed behind in Fez.'

'He has no military experience,' General al-Malek agreed smugly. 'He over-estimated his own strength, and now he is doomed. It's like the pup challenging the wolf for rule of the pack.'

Yazid liked the analogy. It suited him. 'Move more troops to cover the southerly route. Look how the monkeys are already fleeing us. We'll put a little spring in their step.'

The rebels were indeed in flight for their lives, those who were still breathing. They made a scramble up the slopes and poured into the rutted tracks that led out of the plain. Marrakech was their only hope now.

'They're in disarray,' Yazid scoffed. 'Don't waste any more shot. Send the cavalry after them—cut down a few thousand of the dogs. We'll carry on at our own pace, and we'll have Marrakech in our hands by this evening.'

'It's useless, my lord. Leave them!' Ahmed pleaded with Suliman. 'We must go now!'

Suliman was torn by anguish. His army was being dismantled before his very eyes, and there was nothing he could do about it. Yazid was now firmly in control.

'Please, my lord,' Ahmed yelled. 'There's no time!'

As if to emphasise his words, a shell smashed into the ground, and the blast of flying debris knocked them both from their mounts.

'My lord!' Ahmed rolled to his feet, thinking Suliman killed. But the latter was merely grazed. He wiped the dirt from his eyes and grabbed the reins of his whinnying horse. 'Very well, cousin,' he croaked. 'We have lost this battle.'

Bodies littered the grass where they rode by. Already there was a stench, the particularly unsettling stench left in the wake of death and violence. The vultures had descended in malevolent packs, ugly, hunchbacked creatures with misshapen heads. They crowded in and began squabbling over the remains.

'This way, my lord,' Ahmed called, leading Suliman up a narrow game path to avoid the panicked horde driving the retreat. 'We will make for Marrakech.'

The moans of the dying could be heard from the valley now that the bombardment had ceased. Ignoring that haunting sound, Ahmed found a track skirting a field of wheat and waved for Suliman to follow. They could see in the distance Yazid's horsemen moving up the ridge, heading for the pass where Suliman's troops were trying to escape. Soon there would be another massacre.

'Hurry!' Ahmed shouted.

They galloped along the path, which was choked with decaying vegetation. It wound between cliffs and split into further tracks, leading them into dead-end gorges and sheer rock walls, but eventually it linked with the main mountain pass and they were through. They had bypassed the calamitous retreat, and they followed the main artery road back in the direction of Marrakech. The countless bodies they left behind didn't bear thinking about. The number, unfortunately, was rising fast.

⚜ ⚜ ⚜

Brannon ducked as a blade swung past his ear, two inches away from cleaving his skull in two. He twisted his body from the attacker and roared up the track where the rebels were fleeing from the oncoming cavalry.

'Don't turn your backs on them! Fight! Use your muskets!' But Yazid's horsemen were enjoying easy pickings. The command structure amongst the rebel infantry units had disintegrated, and now it seemed to be every man for himself. And in their desperation they had blocked the escape route.

Brannon picked a musket from the ground and checked its priming. He took aim at a charging rider, squeezed the trigger, and the rider took the shot in the chest, spinning backwards to the ground. Both groups of cavalry had engaged each other, and curses were being hurled as limbs were sliced off. Clouds of dust rose like tidal waves, and musket balls whizzed through the air, spattering off the rocks. There were screams, and the blood continued to pool around their feet.

Brannon reloaded and fired at another line of riders, but in the commotion he had no idea where the shot struck. The weaker soldiers were being trampled to the ground, and Yazid's forces were pouring through. Though the Berbers continued to fight, the infantry were trying to flee, and Brannon was dismayed. How had Suliman ever thought this rabble capable of defeating imperial troops? If it wasn't for the Berbers, they would all be dead by now. Yet even the Berbers weren't tough enough to rescue this calamity.

A roar distracted Brannon. Up ahead he saw a phalanx of black African troops advancing along the path. He recognised them as soldiers from the Imperial Guard, and his heart sank. He had observed these men in training, and he knew their ruthless strength. This battle was over.

The soldiers didn't charge blindly in. They opened fire from a distance, a burst of measured musketry that forced the Berbers to steer their horses to the slope where the rocks and uneven terrain hampered their manoeuvring. A second line of soldiers attacked, long pikes thrust out to spear the horses' throats and bring their riders to the ground. Once unseated, the Berber riders were set upon and hacked to pieces.

Brannon spotted Bakka in the mêlée, swinging furiously at the mob surrounding his horse. He half severed a head and then jabbed another in the chest while the rest swarmed forward, trying to unbalance him.

'Bakka!' Brannon yelled. 'Save yourself!'

The Berber leader didn't hear, or if he did he pretended not to. He continued fighting, bloodying two soldiers with a single swipe and then crushing them under the weight of his horse. The others surged around him, chanting, their teeth bared in carnivorous lust. Bakka could only hold them off for so long. Finally one of them found an opening, a chink in the Berber's flank, and he thrust his pike into the horse's neck. The horse bucked violently, causing its wound to tear on the barb of the pike, and it squealed in agony as a mess of bloody pink flesh was exposed. Bakka slipped and fell off. Swords flew at him, and he rolled under the rearing horse, scrambling up the rocky slope in retreat. He bellowed out, and moments later another Berber rider arrived; Bakka hoisted himself onto the saddle, and they escaped up the hill with the other Berbers following behind.

They were making a run for it. And Brannon couldn't blame them.

He looked around, searching for Suliman or Ahmed, but there was no sign. Perhaps they were amongst the victims scattered across the plain. If so, they were beyond his help.

It was time to go.

He ran for the track, taking the musket with him. Along the way he managed to pilfer some ammunition pouches from the dead men on the ground. With so many killed, at least the pass had opened a little, but it would be a tough sprint back to Marrakech with Yazid snapping at his heels. He caught up with the fleeing rebels and, having longer legs, soon overtook them. By the roadside he saw men panting for breath, white-faced with exhaustion. 'The sultan is coming, you fools!' he barked, and in despair they forced themselves to the trail again.

Along the winding mountain pass he ran, ignoring the protest of his battered muscles. Sweat blinded his eyes and his lungs heaved, but he continued to push himself at an almost suicidal pace. He saw where Suliman's artillery carriages had been left before the initial attack on the plain occurred. The artillery was now sitting untended, abandoned on the track. He was disgusted. When Yazid passed this way, he would get his hands on those guns and turn them on the city, pounding Suliman into the dust with his own weapons.

He ran for hours as the sun laboured across the sky. Yazid's troops followed at their own pace, moving their artillery through the mountains to position it for the assault on the city. Brannon came out of the hills, slipping on the scree and skinning his knees. He had almost reached the low-lying pastures where

Marrakech waited like a condemned prisoner, a sombre air of doom hanging above its walls like a noose. Brannon could see men fleeing in ragged groups through the scrub, seeking sanctuary inside the gates. It would be a temporary sanctuary at best.

The sun had climbed to its pinnacle, the time of the day when the city walls glowed in sunlight. Brannon was now staggering with fatigue. He reached the gates, and someone called his name from above.

'Is that you, Ryan?'

He recognised Daniel Jones's voice and picked him out next to a watch-tower. Daniel had been one of those selected to remain behind and garrison the city.

'Bad tidings, Dan. It hasn't exactly gone to plan.'

'I've gathered,' the Englishman answered, waving him on. 'Come on up.'

On the ramparts they stared out over the haze of dust and watched as a steady stream of beleaguered troops continued to flee into the city. As yet there was no sign of Yazid. But he wouldn't be long, and already he had his task half completed.

'We've got eight-pounders on the walls,' Daniel told Brannon, 'but I'll wager Yazid's guns are bigger and louder. He'll enjoy himself today. And by the looks of things, you lads have already taken a pasting.'

'We have.' Brannon nodded grimly. 'You're saying we can't hold the city?'

'I'm saying it's going to be bloody well difficult.'

'I lost sight of Suliman. I wouldn't be surprised if he's lying in several pieces back over those hills.'

'Suliman's alive,' Daniel assured him. 'He rode through the gates with Ahmed a couple of hours ago.'

'Did he, now?' Brannon smiled blackly. 'Then I hope the poor bastard is busy cooking up a miracle or two. God knows, nothing else is going to save our hides today.'

278

Suliman at that time was holed up in the pasha's chamber, thrashing out a plan with Ahmed and a number of other close advisers. The pasha was sitting at the back of the room, sweating himself into a damp mess. He had backed the wrong brother, and now he was going to pay for it.

'We must act with the assumption that Yazid will take Marrakech,' Suliman told the gathering. 'That looks certain now. We can put up a fight, but my instinct is that the city will fall.'

'Evacuate now,' Ahmed urged. 'Head for the hills and regroup. Once we are organised, we can return.'

'An orderly retreat is our best option,' Suliman agreed, 'but not just yet. We have a respectable force here in the city and cannon on the walls. Let Yazid come. We will take the wind out of his sails before we hand the city over to him. The more of his forces we deplete, the greater our chances next time.'

Ahmed looked optimistic. 'The fact that he hasn't arrived yet might mean he sustained heavy losses back in the hills. I'm sure those Berbers will have given a good account of themselves.'

'I hope so. We need every scrap of fortune we can get.'

They spent the following hour plotting their escape out of Marrakech. There were hiding spots in the hills, places where they could gather to count their remaining forces. Suliman didn't know how many casualties he had suffered. The number would not be small.

After the council came to a close, he went downstairs to the mosque. Prayer was needed now, for he didn't know when he would have the chance again. The mosque was empty, and he unrolled his prayer mat, trying to instil some sense of hope into his troubled soul.

Suddenly the door flew open behind him. Ahmed burst inside.

'What is it?' Suliman exclaimed.

Before Ahmed could answer, there was a low thump of cannon somewhere out beyond the city. They heard the shrieking flight of a shell and then a massive crash as it blasted through the walls. Mortar rumbled and collapsed, and dozens of terrified screams echoed through the corridors.

'It's Yazid, my lord,' Ahmed breathed in fright. 'He's here!'

'Jesus bloody Christ,' Brannon swore, watching the white thread of smoke unwind behind the shell as it came plunging into the city. It struck the front wall of a mosque and exploded in bricks and dust. The wall crumbled to rubble, the domed roof shuddering like a wounded beast.

Creeping over the rampart, he peered through a turret and looked for the enemy. The cannon were arranged above a low hill, and every time they fired there was a pulse of flame. Behind them the cavalry waited, alongside the hungry legion of the Imperial Guard. Brannon strained his eyes—he could just make out a cream-coloured canopy held above a tiny figure, shielding him from the hot sun. Yazid. He had come out of the mountains like Hannibal, bringing chaos and doom and pain.

Again a shell whistled into the sky, and the troops on the wall ducked. Again it exploded inside the city. The gunners were getting better. This time it was a coffee house reduced to a smoking pile.

'Don't worry,' Brannon assured the nervous men under his command. 'They haven't scored a hit on the gates yet.'

Another cannon fired, and the shell soared like molten rock spewed from a volcano, drifting levelly for some moments before dipping with malevolent intent. It hit the wall and, to their amazement, bounced away and failed to detonate. Rolling across the ground, it came to rest inside a cluster of market stalls before at last exploding and throwing the stalls high in a shower of fruit and wood and crockery.

'Poor craftsmanship,' Brannon observed. Before he could say any more, another shell hit the watchtower at the end of the wall. The tower was blown to pieces, and the men inside had their innards painted all over the ramparts.

The shells kept coming. The wall was hit several times, and another tower, and a tannery in the street. Then came the one they dreaded. The gunners hit the left gate, and the shell burst through, carrying much of the woodwork with it.

'What are those gates made of? Paper?' Brannon spat angrily. He looked to Yazid's troops, thinking this might give them the opportunity they had been waiting for. But Yazid didn't launch a charge just yet. The bombardment continued. The shells rained down, and much of the northern quarter was left in ruin.

Then they hit the second gate.

It seemed as if it would absorb the strike. Though it shook and groaned, it stood fast and the shell failed to penetrate its frame. But there was a squeal of tearing metal somewhere within, the sound of bolts and chains having been slammed out of position. With a baneful shudder and a snapping of wood, the upper side of the gate unhinged itself from the wall, and its sheer weight made the entire structure fall flat on its back. The ground quivered, and the dust leaped high to smother the astonished faces on the ramparts.

'Shit,' Brannon whispered.

There came a booming chorus of cheers. Yazid's troops raised their arms triumphantly and uttered his name in one thunderous voice. Their time had come.

'Muskets,' Brannon shouted. 'Prepare yourselves!'

A long line of cavalry spread out from the hills, like marauding ants bearing down on an enemy nest. They covered the ground swiftly, lances aloft in the sun, screaming war cries. The gunners on the Marrakech walls opened fire, but their cannon were smaller than Yazid's and could reach only limited range. The shells exploded around the advancing riders but inflicted little damage. It was nigh-on impossible to hit a moving target with a cannon.

'Outside,' Brannon yelled at his troops. 'Cover the front!' He secured his scimitar, loaded his musket, and ran down the steps through the splintered gates.

Yazid's cavalry cut a formidable presence out on the plain. They altered formation now, initiating a spearhead move to thrust their way through the gate. They looked invincible. They *were* invincible.

'Fire at will,' Brannon urged his men. 'Just shoot them, for the love of God!'

Those with muskets opened fire. Out of nearly a hundred shots, two hit targets. The advancing line of riders didn't so much as ripple. Brannon realised that with a few more volleys his men would be out of powder.

'Let them get closer,' he barked, cursing his own haste. But it was difficult to wait. With every yard of space that the cavalry covered, the sound of their assault became louder. The men guarding the gateway were unable to resist firing their guns, and within minutes they had spent almost their entire shot. 'Wait!' Brannon yelled angrily. 'Don't shoot yet!' But he realised it was useless. This was where the difference between experienced troops and untrained fighters was revealed.

The horsemen covered the remaining ground. Musket fire continued sporadically, but the gap soon closed. They rode at the line of defenders guarding the tumbled gate, and then they attacked.

Scores of bodies fell in that first blistering engagement. Brannon saw the men standing on either side of him receive fatal thrusts to the chest. He managed to parry a jab aimed at his heart, but the force of it knocked him from his feet, and he rolled perilously close to the horse's stampeding hooves. The ground in front of the gates was thrown into turmoil. Swords rang off each other, and the hills echoed with pulsing gunfire. So much dust was raised that the rebels could barely distinguish friend from foe and risked butchering each other in their confusion. The corpses began to gather.

Brannon fired his musket, and the bullet thumped into flesh; he reloaded and kept firing until there were too many of them around him. Then he used his sword, turning and ducking and thrusting and slicing until the blade ran red with blood. 'Shoot the horses,' he yelled at the marksmen on the ramparts. 'Bring the bastards down so we can kill them!'

But his efforts won minutes only. The superior strength of Yazid's troops began to tilt the balance in their favour, and the defence soon faltered. Several riders broke through under the arch and made it inside the city. Their lead was followed, and now all attempts at containing them collapsed. Some of the rebels broke and ran, tossing their weapons aside, and their panic was infectious. They began to scatter in greater numbers, seeking ignoble retreat rather than violent death.

'Stand your ground,' Brannon roared. He continued to fight, continued to kill. But it was hopeless.

To his alarm, another shell came hurtling towards them. Yazid was getting impatient, and he was willing to kill his own troops to sweep the remaining rebels out of the way. The shell exploded nearby and killed dozens of men on each side. It had its intended effect, however, and the last defenders now abandoned the struggle. The way for Yazid was clear.

Brannon had been standing under the shell, right in the path of the devil. With seconds to spare he dashed for cover, but the force of the blast lifted him off his feet and flung him through the air. He crashed into a shallow canal that ran into the nearby fields, bruising his body on the dry bed and lashing his forehead. He tried to get back up, but his legs wobbled and warm blood seeped down his cheek. He was barely able to see.

The cavalry were now inside the city, and Brannon heard the sound of Yazid's infantry charging across the plain. Marrakech was theirs. They would storm the buildings and slaughter the remainder of the garrison, including Suliman if they found him.

He stared at the wavering bank of the canal, trying to bring his vision under control. He took a few minutes to breathe and let his battered head settle. The rocks and plants slowly sharpened into focus. He touched the bump on his head; despite the blood dripping into his mouth, the cut was not too big. He took another breath to steady himself and then climbed out of the canal.

He was the only one left. The rebels were gone, and the infantry were almost at the gates. They had moved faster than he expected. There were several men on horses leading them—bodyguards and officers and, in the middle of them, Moulay Yazid, brandishing his gold-inlaid broadsword. He was shouting wildly, his face contorted in bloodlust.

Brannon delayed too long in staring at them. When he turned to hide around the corner of the wall, they saw him.

'*Hser!*' they ordered. 'Stop!'

Brannon grabbed his sword from where it had fallen, ready to defend himself.

Yazid was pointing to the broken gates, boasting about the power of his artillery, but now he spotted Brannon. Their eyes locked for a moment; a mask of rage darkened Yazid's features. Brannon could feel the hatred in those eyes, could feel it slice through him like an axe-stroke. He was afraid.

'Dimon!' Yazid kicked the shoulder of the bodyguard running beside his horse. 'Get him, Dimon. Kill him. Kill the Irishman! Bring me his head!'

The bodyguard was a Luluwa warrior from the jungles south of the Sahara. He looked to be nearly seven feet tall with a bald head like a cannonball and a scarred, tattooed face. He nodded devoutly, and his skin rippled with the coiling of his muscles as he unsheathed his sword.

Brannon was nearly sick at the sight. He had never seen a man so big, a man who so perfectly personified a killer.

'Yazid!' the bodyguard cried, and he charged.

Brannon knew he hadn't a hope. The man towered at least eight inches above him and had a body like a granite mountain. He did the only sensible thing—he ran. Vaulting over the shattered gates, he darted under the archway, seeking refuge inside the city. Most of the cavalry were spilling through the streets, and he sprinted for the steps leading to the ramparts. He could hear the panting growls of the guard giving chase, a sound that sent a chill down his back. He needed a gun, and he needed it fast.

The ramparts were empty, apart from bodies. Brannon searched desperately for a musket or a pistol. His sword was no good—it would probably snap in two if he tried to use it on that beast. As he looked around, the man came bounding up the steps. His teeth flashed as he lunged like a leopard, thrusting his sword out to pierce Brannon's belly and impale him. Brannon used his own sword to deflect the blow, but it was driven with such power that the sword was ripped from his hands.

The guard roared and delivered a backhanded smack, which loosened Brannon's front teeth and laid him out on the flat stone. He tried to roll clear, but the guard pounced on him, his immense weight driving the air from Brannon's lungs. He gasped and seized the man's wrist, trying to prevent him from driving the sword through his chest. Among his fellow slaves and soldiers, Brannon had been regarded as exceptionally strong, but now, against the might of this giant, he was weak as a child. The black man would tear him to pieces.

I'm a dead man…

As he thrashed about, frantically trying to wriggle loose, his head touched something—a rock, one of many blasted from the masonry by the shelling.

A weapon.

He reached back, seized it in his free hand, and smashed it into the guard's face. There was an audible crack as the man's nose fractured. He howled like a bull elephant, for a moment slackening his grip as the blood spurted out. Brannon reacted instinctively, arching his back and heaving the guard clear. With his nose mangled and blood filling his mouth, the man was disorientated. He staggered about, swinging his sword wildly.

Brannon launched himself and aimed a powerful kick into his flank, toppling him off the rampart. It wasn't a long drop, but the unfortunate bodyguard landed head-first. When Brannon looked down, he saw him lying motionless with his neck twisted at an impossible angle from his body.

The giant was dead.

Exhausted, Brannon got to his feet. To his annoyance, he spotted a musket lying close by. Where was it when he needed it? He picked it up and checked its priming. It was good still.

There were noises coming from the gates. He crept over and saw the invaders pouring in. Yazid himself entered under a flying banner, red-faced with excitement, the conquering hero.

Brannon crouched low on the rampart, musket in hand. The sultan was almost directly underneath him. The last time Brannon had had an opportunity like this was in the harem garden, when Ahmed had foiled his assassination attempt. But Ahmed wasn't around right now…

❀ ❀ ❀

Yazid dismounted from his horse and shouted, 'Sweep the city, bring out the Jews! We'll make a bonfire!' He rubbed his hands in glee. 'And bring the children first!' Yes, what an idea. He would build a roaring fire and gather a crowd and make the Jews watch as their children sizzled alive.

He looked around expectantly. 'Where's my bodyguard gone? Dimon! Show me the Irishman's head!'

He stopped then. There was a man lying below the shattered wall, his neck broken, flies crawling on his eyeballs. Yazid frowned in confusion. He turned around, and as he did so, he caught a glint of light on a metalled surface up on the ramparts.

'Hello, Your Majesty!' Brannon waved, lifting the musket to his shoulder. He closed one eye, picked his spot, and squeezed the trigger. There was a bright flash; a crack of gunfire echoed across the city.

Yazid was about to cry out when the musket ball struck him in the mouth. It smashed through his front teeth and deflected downwards before severing his spinal cord and exiting through the back of his neck. A fountain of blood spurted between his lips, and he gagged soundlessly before falling into the arms of his astonished bodyguards. They gaped around to see where the shot had come from, but the gunman had disappeared.

'The sultan has been shot!' They crowded around him, horrified, trying to offer assistance. But Yazid was in serious trouble. His lower body had gone limp, and his jaws were in a spasm, blood spilling over his clothes. He thrashed his head back and forth as he choked for air.

The guards heaved on his chest, trying to make him breathe, but these men were warriors and not physicians. Yazid's personal physician didn't reach the scene until some minutes later, and when he did, the guards were lamenting in despair. 'The sultan is dead! The rebel dogs have murdered our great sultan!'

The physician knew immediately how serious Yazid's wound was. His body below the neck was paralysed, and his mouth was a mangled mess from the bullet. Yet it was suffocation which ultimately killed him, caused by the massive amount of blood that clogged his throat and filled his lungs. The physician brushed Yazid's eyes closed and uttered a prayer for his eternal soul, while all around him the sultan's followers wailed in fury and anguish.

CHAPTER TWENTY-FOUR

Scores of women and children had fled into a mosque to escape the advance of the soldiers. General al-Malek was clearing them out when a breathless messenger arrived and blurted out the dreadful dispatch. His Royal Highness, gunned down by the rebels. Was he dead? The messenger could not confirm.

Al-Malek hurried back through the streets, his pulse racing. There was a throng of people at the gates. Yazid had been stripped of his garments, and a holy mullah was reciting the Qur'an while sprinkling water over his body.

Dead! Al-Malek couldn't believe it.

'Captain al-Hameed,' he bellowed at the nearest officer. 'Bring me the person responsible for this. Now!'

'We are searching the city, General,' Captain al-Hameed answered briskly. 'We will find the rat, I swear it.'

'Make sure you do.' Al-Malek looked at Yazid's bodyguards, who were still in a state of shock. 'Carry the sultan into one of the houses. The burial rites must be observed.' His hands were trembling, but he forced control on himself. This was an extremely serious situation. Without the sultan, who was in charge? He had to assume authority quickly, but the rituals must first begin. The body would have to be bathed, anointed with scents, and wrapped in a white shroud in accordance with Islamic code.

There were infantry units nearby, bemused by the developments and unclear as to what was required of them. Al-Malek summoned their captains.

'A great tragedy has befallen us, but we must carry on. Pockets of rebel resistance still remain. Move your men to seize all major aspects on the south side, and I will establish control here. And do not spread word of the sultan's death yet. It will cause confusion.' Al-Malek was desperate to avoid the uncertainty that a sudden power vacuum might create.

The captains nodded their assent and went to organise their troops. Al-Malek looked up to the ramparts. He wanted to conduct an inspection of the cannon to see which were still working so that a defence could be prepared against a possible counter-strike by whatever remained of Suliman's army.

A noise up the street distracted him. When he turned, he saw a column of soldiers tramping through the smoky rubble towards the gate where Yazid's body was being carried away. The soldiers were led by an officer on horseback, a chubby man with a combed beard and an imperious tilt to his chin. When he saw the corpse, he challenged the bodyguards holding it.

'Stand fast! What business is this?'

'General Husayn,' al-Malek hailed him hurriedly. Husayn was a distant cousin of Yazid's who had joined the sultan's army from Meknes and provided a formidable force of his own. Al-Malek neither liked nor trusted Husayn, but since they were of the same rank, he had to be careful here. 'General, I fear I have dreadful news. The sultan has been slain. I know not by whom, but I swear we will hunt down every last rebel wretch in the city and punish them for this outrage.'

Husayn's eyes narrowed. He didn't answer, but he climbed down from his horse and snapped his fingers at the infantry captains. 'Where are you going?'

'All is well, General,' al-Malek assured him. 'I have ordered them to secure the vantage points. The situation is under my control.'

Husayn smiled thinly. 'Thank you for taking care of matters until I arrived, General al-Malek. You may return to your own divisions now.'

Al-Malek flushed a little. 'With due respect, General Husayn, it is incumbent on me, as Moulay Yazid's right-hand man, to take command of the imperial army from here. I would, however, be very glad of your assistance.'

'General,' Husayn glowered, 'I do not doubt your ability to lead this brave army. But appreciate that since I am of the Alaouite line, a blood relative of Moulay Yazid, then it is my responsibility to assume full command until the matter of a successor can be addressed.'

That was a nonsense argument, al-Malek fumed. Yazid had thousands of distant blood relatives like Husayn across the land. They couldn't be allowed to claim authority as simply as that, not when al-Malek had been at the sultan's side ever since the day he took power.

'General Husayn,' he said, making an effort to sound reasonable, 'I was Moulay Yazid's chief commander throughout this campaign, his closest advisor. He trusted me above all others. Today the sultan is in paradise, and I would have been his choice to carry on his noble effort. And that, General, is the way it will be.'

He turned his back purposefully and spoke loud enough for every man to hear. 'You know your orders. You may proceed. I have assumed command of the imperial army, and I will be...'

His voice trailed off. He grunted in pain, his face turning white as a blade was thrust into the soft flesh of his lower back. He attempted to break free, but the knife was twisted viciously and a globule of thick, dark blood slid ponderously under the cover of his robe. The blade had penetrated right through and split his liver. He was a dead man even before he hit the ground.

Husayn pulled the knife free and spat on al-Malek's body. 'He's a liar!' he shouted at the stunned crowd. 'He killed the sultan and tried to seize power! Praise Allah, the traitor is dead!'

Al-Malek's captains looked on in shock. That was cold-blooded murder. They had all seen Yazid shot, so they knew that al-Malek had nothing to do with his death. Anger flared in their eyes.

'You will take orders from me!' Husayn snapped at them. 'I am of the royal line. I command right-wise!'

'Naseem al-Malek is our general,' Captain al-Hameed retorted. 'Our orders were given by him and no other.' His comrades grumbled their assent and fingered the hilts of their swords.

'He is dead, you fool!' Husayn snarled. 'He was with the rebels. This is my army!' Spittle foamed on his lip. He suddenly thrust an accusing finger at Captain al-Hameed. 'You're a rebel too! You were behind this, you rebel dog. You will be punished!'

Husayn's men had moved in to lend muscle to his words, resenting how these troops from Fez dared to show such disrespect. They focused their attention on the captain singled out by Husayn.

'I won't suffer your insolence!' Husayn screeched at al-Hameed. He waved his men on. 'Go and get him! Kill that traitor! Kill him!'

His troops gave a roar and charged across the open ground, ready to cut al-Hameed into a thousand tiny pieces. The young captain backed away. But he wasn't afraid because he had men with him too. He had a whole horde. And they weren't going to give in like that.

Like a spark to a powder keg, the scene exploded into violence. The two camps attacked each other with inhuman ferocity, abandoning in an instant the alliances which had existed between them until now. The fact that they had marched in the campaign side by side was now forgotten as simmering rivalries and old suspicions boiled to the surface and were manifested in the cold glint of steel blades. Pistols fired and swords hacked, and they began murdering each other with almost religious zeal. In the frenzy of commotion, it was unclear who was fighting whom. They mingled and fought like hyenas on a carcass, and all sense of order soon collapsed.

General Husayn, feeling a chill of dread, realised he had overreached himself. In his desperation to seize command, he had blindly ignored the fact that he was outnumbered by the soldiers loyal to al-Malek, placing himself in dire jeopardy.

But it was too late.

Captain al-Hameed came bursting out of the maelstrom, his sword bright red. 'For Naseem al-Malek!' He screamed and lunged at Husayn, swinging the sword under his shoulder. Husayn tried to turn and run, but his tubby body was too slow. He felt the blade rip through his right side, and the blood sprayed over his legs. Al-Hameed had cut him almost in half, and Husayn collapsed. He died even faster than al-Malek.

'Vengeance!' Captain al-Hameed cried out. With a clenched fist and a bellow of laughter, he ran back to join the fray. The bodies of the two generals lay slumped in the dust, and their men continued to wage an unholy battle all around them.

⊕ ⊕ ⊕

Oblivious to the wild scenes he had triggered off, Brannon ran through the streets towards the east of the city. With the garrison obliterated, he didn't want to be the last rebel to leave Marrakech. In a square he saw dogs snuffling at dead bodies with swarms of flies buzzing around them. Several Jewish-owned premises had been set ablaze, and the smoke billowed across the square, black and pungent. It was difficult to see through the miasma, and to his alarm he heard soldiers coming.

A mob of them appeared from a side-street, their arms laden with silks and jewellery. They were shouting and bragging to each other, struggling under the weight of their loot. Brannon crouched in the shadow of a doorway and let the smoke form a wreath around him. The soldiers passed by in ignorance. When it was quiet again, he scampered across the road into a tannery. There was a corpse on the ground and a dog chewing ravenously on its leg. The dog snarled at Brannon, thinking he was trying to join the feast, and he backed off.

'You enjoy it, boyo.' Slinking into the shadows behind the drums of lye he listened to the city's clamour. Yazid's troops were on the rampage, drunk with excitement, ransacking the opulent riads and firing off weapons. Fires raged from rooftops, and women screamed. As expected, the situation was out of control.

He hid inside the tannery for an hour. Soldiers stalked the streets, still hungry for slaughter. But something confused him. There was a furious racket coming from the north entrance, where Yazid's cannon had blown the gates apart. It sounded as though a battle had broken out, but between whom? Brannon had seen the rebels destroyed. He couldn't understand who was fighting now. The longer he waited, the more soldiers he saw heading in that direction. The gunfire became louder, the noises more calamitous.

He took the risk of leaving the tannery and moved up the street. The alleys were cleared even of beggars, and he covered his mouth against the smoke. Continuing east he reached another gateway, which had a handful of imperial troops manning it. Most of them had already deserted to join the ruckus taking place at the north gate. Some stood on the ramparts, but they were watching events unfold across the city, and they ignored the gate itself. Brannon slipped through unnoticed.

Outside there were trading stalls set up in a palm grove. He helped himself to some pomegranates, devouring the sweet flesh and sucking down the juices to ease his parched throat. This area was deathly quiet, the traders having run for cover the moment the bombardment began, so he stuffed some more fruit into his pockets and even found a gourd of water under a toppled stool. Then he faced east into the foothills of the Atlas Mountains and began walking.

'What on earth are they doing in there?' Suliman demanded.

The scout spread his hands. 'I couldn't see enough, Your Excellency. Yazid has trouble. His troops have turned on each other, but I don't know why.'

They were on the slopes overlooking Marrakech where Suliman's diminished army had fled. Despite the losses sustained, a sizeable number had managed to escape the city in time and were now regrouping. Up here they had a view that stretched for miles. They could see fires in the city and palls of black smoke drifting above the walls. Gunfire echoed out, and thousands of angry voices carried on the breeze. Where was Yazid in all this chaos?

Suliman caught sight of an approaching rider, coming fast through the trees. It was Ahmed, and he looked excited.

'Good news, my lord. I have found the bulk of the Berber cavalry in a valley over the hills. They were not destroyed as we thought. They say they're ready to strike again—' Ahmed stopped, looking towards Marrakech. 'What's happening down there?'

'I don't think Yazid is in control any more,' Suliman replied. 'How far away are the Berbers?'

'I can have them here within the hour, my lord.'

'Good. Tell them it's time to go back into Marrakech. The infantry too, whatever's left. Something has gone drastically wrong for the sultan, and we are going to take advantage of it.'

Hours later, as darkness fell, Marrakech was a city in turmoil. Yazid's untimely death had triggered a scramble for power, and now his army disintegrated into a greedy rabble of opportunists bent on plunder. Without his iron grip to maintain order, his highest-ranking officers reverted to what they really were—glorified warlords out to stake claims and settle old petty feuds. There were riches in Marrakech and throughout Morocco, and the man who emerged strongest from this could make himself very wealthy indeed. So factions fought each other in the streets and in the courtyards, and the bodies piled up in the dust. At one point several kegs of gunpowder had exploded inside a magazine, taking half a battalion with them. Fires continued to blaze, and much of the city was shrouded in smoke. Despite the violence and the fervour of battle, however, no one was able to take effective control, and by nightfall over half of Yazid's army lay dead.

The eastern gates were mostly unmanned, the sentries having left to join the fighting and looting. The only imperial soldiers there now were adolescent boys, terrified by what was happening and seeking refuge from the carnage being unleashed by their former comrades. They huddled on the ramparts, desperately wishing to escape but reluctant to abandon their posts. But their minds were soon made up.

From the east came the rumble of hooves, a thunderous sound of hundreds of charging steeds, tearing up the scrub and shaking the ground as they moved. In the darkling light it was difficult to see how many were there, but the noise they made was fearsome, like a great biblical flood engulfing the land. That was enough for the young sentries. They scrambled down the steps, ran through the gate, and fled in terror for the hills.

Suliman's Berbers surged unopposed past the walls. This part of the city was all but deserted, the only sign of life being a startled mule that broke from an alley dragging a cart behind it. The townspeople had barricaded themselves indoors. The ramparts were empty. Marrakech was open.

They poured through the streets, seeking their quarry, and when they reached the north gate, they finally found what remained of Yazid's army. Bodies lay everywhere. The buildings were on fire, flames groping lustily at the night sky, surrounding what earlier must have been a raging battleground. Men clutching bloodied wounds staggered out of the smoke and wandered into the path of the oncoming Berbers, who ruthlessly chopped them down. The pockets of troops still engaged in the fighting turned tail when they saw the Berbers come, horrified at this sudden brutal flood of horsemen. What little resistance remained soon crumbled, and the soldiers at the gates scattered into the wilds beyond.

Captain al-Hameed was busy hacking a swathe through his erstwhile allies and stuffing his pockets with their valuables. When he saw the Berbers coming, he gave a roar and sprang out to attack them. From their ranks Bakka burst forth. Without checking his horse, he brought his sword down in one smooth manoeuvre, sweeping it across and slicing al-Hameed's head from his shoulders. The body danced in a spasm for a moment and then collapsed on the bloody cobblestones.

Suliman's infantry followed the cavalry and moved to seize control of the governor's palace, the barracks, and the armoury. Gunfire rattled from the windows and dogged their progress, but street by street they began to retake the city. There was no sign of Yazid, and no one seemed to be commanding the imperial troops. The Imperial Guard, long feared for their prowess, were in disarray without a figurehead to lead them. They had been separated into isolated, ineffective bands of men holed up in buildings, clueless as to who was attacking them and why. The fires soon drove them outside, where they stumbled around in confusion and were then slaughtered to a man by the vengeful Berbers.

At about five o'clock in the morning, as dawn slowly lifted the eastern skies, the flag of Suliman was raised above the smoke-blackened ramparts of the city.

Will they not make up their bloody minds? Brannon fumed to himself. From his vantage point it looked, inexplicably, as though Suliman was heading back into Marrakech. He'd been thrashed to within an inch of his life, and he was going back in for more. Brannon cursed him. If it was suicide he wanted, then let him off.

But this time things went differently.

From the hills he watched the Berbers ride unchecked through the streets, heard them cleaving their way through mobs of bewildered soldiers and adding their own contribution to the catastrophic body count. Yazid's forces weren't even trying to hold the city. They seemed to have collapsed entirely, scattering like sheep through the gates. Brannon couldn't comprehend it.

He took refuge for several more hours as night enveloped the hills. The sky was bright with the light of the fires burning inside Marrakech, and soldiers continued to flee into the countryside. Towards dawn, when the noise had quietened and the fighting had ceased, he ventured back down.

The following morning the rebels discovered the body of Moulay Yazid in a storehouse where it was being prepared for burial. They wanted to strip it down and stick Yazid's head on a pike, but Suliman forbade this.

'He will receive a full Muslim burial,' he insisted. 'His sins were many, but it is for Allah to deal with that, not us.' So they afforded him the full rituals and later buried him in a tomb inside a walled garden. While his evil mark would scar the land for some time yet, Moulay Yazid's reign of tyranny was over.

'Perhaps we'll never know who killed him,' Ahmed remarked wistfully. 'One of his own, probably. Yazid had many enemies.'

Brannon wasn't sure. He remembered his shot from the ramparts. He had certainly seen Yazid fall. Was it possible? Not that anyone would believe him.

'Let's just be glad the bastard is dead,' he decided.

'Allah be praised,' Ahmed agreed.

There were many other burials to take place as the bodies were already decomposing in the heat. Brannon attended to one of them with a heavy heart, and he was unable to prevent the tears slipping down his cheeks. He had found Daniel Jones's body that morning, at the spot where he had been killed trying to keep Yazid's hordes out of the city. Nearly a dozen imperial troops lay around him—testament to how bravely the Englishman had fought before they finally brought him down. Brannon was deeply saddened. He had believed that the two of them would return home together.

'At least you're finally getting out of here,' he whispered to his old friend. 'Thanks for everything, Daniel Jones. You'll not be forgotten.'

That evening, in a brief ceremony presided over by the city's holy mullahs, Suliman was declared sultan of Morocco. Though it would be several years before his power could be consolidated over the whole of the land, the country had turned a long, difficult corner with the death of Yazid. The process of rebuilding and healing could begin.

The sun set into a splendour of golden-red above the hills, laying shadows of thousands of freshly dug graves on the pockmarked plain. Brannon was on the ramparts, gazing over the shattered stone fortifications. He could so easily have become one of those anonymous corpses, just another bloated pile to be dumped in an unmarked hole, the most ignoble of endings. But he had survived. Somehow, he had survived. And it was time now to go home.

The metallic snick of a pistol checked him. He stiffened, having thought himself alone on the ramparts. Slowly he turned around.

It was Ahmed.

He had a gun cocked, levelled at Brannon's chest. His mouth was closed, his eyes glazed, the blank, unperturbed expression of a killer.

'What the hell—' Brannon blurted in shock.

Ahmed held his aim steady. 'Before this battle started, I told you that we had unfinished business. Now it is time to settle that business.' He adjusted the muzzle of the gun slightly, fixing an angle for the bullet to bury itself in Brannon's heart.

'Come off it,' Brannon growled. 'Is this supposed to be funny?'

Ahmed was not laughing.

'Put that thing away, you clown. It's hardly a fair fight.'

'I'm not looking for a fair fight,' Ahmed replied. 'I'm looking for vengeance. You have only yourself to blame.'

Brannon swore angrily. 'But we made a bargain! I've earned my right to go home.'

'You have earned your own ending, Brannon.'

'Damn you!' Brannon stepped away, tensing himself for the bullet. 'I didn't rape her. If you don't believe me, just ask her. Why won't you listen to me?'

'Too late for talk. This,' Ahmed said as his finger tensed on the trigger, 'is for my sister. This is for Asiya.'

'Wait!' Brannon exclaimed in horror.

Ahmed fired.

There was a flash of flame, and the echo of gunfire rang off the stones. Brannon recoiled, his hand instinctively grasping the front of his chest to stifle the blood. At that range, he knew himself killed for sure.

When he drew his hand back up, it was dry still.

A small puff of dust rose from the wall where Ahmed had deliberately fired the shot. He looked at Brannon and smiled thinly.

'As I said, that was for my sister. Asiya would never recover if she thought I had killed you. So I spare you for her sake.'

Brannon blinked in confusion. 'What in the name of…'

'She spoke to me before she left camp. And she explained what happened. Perhaps you did not rape her after all.'

'I told you—'

'But this doesn't excuse your actions. What you did was still wrong, shamefully wrong. Do I not recall tender words spoken of a lost love in Ireland?'

Brannon reddened, Ahmed's words having their intended effect. 'I know it was wrong. It was a mistake.'

'Not a mistake you'll want to make around my sister again. And this does not mean that I forgive you. It simply means that I don't have to kill you.'

Brannon let out a breath to calm his frayed nerves. 'Well, that's good news at least. But you should have known that I wouldn't rape your sister. I'm not a monster.'

'Be glad you didn't, Brannon. For I would have killed you. Make no mistake.'

'Understood. Now will you put that gun away?'

Ahmed turned to rest his elbows on the broken battlements and watched the evening drift down over the hills. 'I should tell you that Suliman has spoken highly of your efforts in the fighting. He regards you as a friend of Morocco.

I think he would deem it a great service were you to stay on with us for a few more years.'

Brannon stared at him uneasily. 'You what?'

'Indeed, the new sultan will need strong men. And you've already convinced him of your worth.'

'But you said you would get me home—'

'A lot of things are said and done in time of war. They don't always translate back into everyday life.' Ahmed had a glint in his eye.

'You're a liar!' Brannon accused him angrily. 'Is that what a Moroccan promise is worth? A sultan's promise?'

Ahmed chuckled. 'Heaven help us. What an excitable creature you are.' He reached under his djellaba and produced a document. 'This is a letter bearing Suliman's personal seal. He will give you a horse and some money from the city's treasury, which belonged to Yazid. Ride northwest of here until you strike the Oum er-Rbia, and then follow that river all the way to the coastal town of Azemmour. Present Suliman's letter to the pasha of Azemmour, and he will help you from there. Consider our side of the bargain fulfilled.'

Brannon took the letter and placed it into an inside pocket. 'That's more like it.'

Ahmed regarded him for a second. 'You did fight well.' He reached across briefly and touched Brannon's arm. It was an unusual display of affection from him, and he withdrew his hand after a moment, but the gesture was not lost on Brannon. It was the Moroccan's way of saying thank you. Though they could never warm to each other, could never have been friends, there now at least existed a mutual respect between them.

Brannon cleared his throat. 'You're good people here, Ahmed. Worth fighting for.' He paused. 'You'll, um, you'll say goodbye for me?'

'I will.' Ahmed nodded. 'She'll miss you, though.'

'Take care of her, Ahmed.'

'I promise to.' Ahmed looked to the west where the sun had disappeared behind the horizon. 'Good luck on your journey tomorrow. I pray that Allah will watch over and protect you.'

'The peace of Allah be upon you,' Brannon answered.

'Goodbye, Brannon.'

'Goodbye, Ahmed.'

They turned from each other and walked their separate ways down the ramparts.

CHAPTER TWENTY-FIVE

The fifteenth of June, the fifteenth of June, the fifteenth of June…

It rang in Orlaith's head like the clang of a funeral bell. It was the day that her life as she knew it would cease to exist, and it was coming. She gazed at the French-made perpetual calendar on the wall in Randall's library, as if hoping it could somehow provide solace, but of course it could not. Time marched relentlessly, uncaring. She had two weeks to go.

Ever since the sentence was passed, Randall had had her imprisoned within the confines of Dromkeen Hall, with a troop of armed guards patrolling the demesne wall to prevent escape. At first she had puzzled over his decision to keep her at home rather than throw her in the city gaol. After all, he owed her no favours. But Randall had his own reasons. He had wanted to punish her himself before banishing her to the end of the world, to humiliate her and crush her spirit and to take away whatever shreds of dignity she might still possess. And he had enjoyed these past months.

The night-times were the worst. It had been bad enough before, but now he seemed to take extreme pleasure in the wanton and disgusting acts he forced her to partake in. Always late at night, when he was clumsy on his feet and reeking of whiskey. On the frequent occasions that he was too drunk for his manhood to rise to the challenge, he would simply pull her clothes off and beat her until he was someway sexually gratified. And afterwards, when dressing himself again, he would say something like, 'It's not even you I feel sorry for, Orlaith. What about Sean? He'll be raised by bent priests and sodomites; he'll not go a day without knowing the worst kind of suffering. Still, you should have thought of that…'

And each time Orlaith could only weep, powerless against his retribution.

She turned her thoughts to Sean now. It was wrong, but so far she hadn't been able to tell him. Where could she find the words for this? A child would never understand such things. She had delayed it, knowing that once he was told, his childhood innocence would be forever ruined. At three years of age he would have slept his last peaceful sleep, in future denied of a protector to comfort him when he awoke from bad dreams. And there would probably be many bad dreams.

Tears came again. She couldn't remember a time when she had known no troubles. Hope never seemed to last. Brannon was beyond reach, and soon Sean would be gone too. The fifteenth of June was coming.

Randall, ironically, was her only hope at this stage. Was it in any way possible that he would change his mind? Even Randall had to have humanity. She knew that his vengeance was pain-driven; she knew how wounded he had been. He had believed she loved him, and once his illusions were shattered, his wrath was terrible. Perhaps he could be made to believe it again.

If Randall had a change of heart, the court would surely bend to his influence. People like Randall *were* the law. He could turn this whole horrid business around; Orlaith could stay, and Sean could be saved. But would he entertain it even for a moment?

She wasn't sure.

An altered approach would be needed. She had made it plain just how much she loathed him, but that was inevitably her undoing. The more he was reminded of it, the more intense became his lust for revenge. She had to change tack, but time was now an ally she didn't possess.

She left the library and went into the hall. It was late evening and the house was in shadow, the summer sun fading to twilight on the lawns. She found Kathy and asked, 'Has Randall come home yet?'

'Yes, ma'am, he's resting. But I shouldn't go up there if I were you...'

'I must speak with him,' Orlaith said.

Upstairs she took a deep breath. She had to get this right. If only she had done it before now, they might have stood a chance.

Randall wasn't in the main bedroom. She sidled towards the guest bedroom where he sometimes slept. It was quiet. She pushed the door open.

The room was lit by candles, enough for her to make out two forms on the bed. Randall was naked, the woman next to him equally bare but for a pair of silk leggings. She had cascading blonde hair and was giggling as Randall pressed his lips over one of her breasts. Orlaith exclaimed in surprise, startling the two lovers.

'What the devil—' Randall blurted out. 'Orlaith! Jesus Christ, woman, you didn't knock.'

She didn't know what to say. An awkward silence filled the room.

'Orlaith!' Randall barked. 'You're being rude.'

'I…I'm sorry,' she stuttered. 'I didn't mean to be…' The visual impact of the scene had shaken her nerve.

He grunted in annoyance and climbed from the bed, pulling a nightgown around himself. 'Thank you, my dear. You have spoiled the mood now. I'm getting a drink.' He stomped off towards the stairs.

The blonde girl winked at Orlaith, rolling onto her side. 'Mrs Whiteley, I assume?' She spoke in a slurred voice. 'I hope you don't mind. Randall invited me here.'

Orlaith blushed. 'Ahem, no…I don't mind. I apologise for interrupting you. Randall is displeased with me.'

'Randall's a brute, sweetheart. But then all men are brutes. Only a woman can be gentle.' She parted her legs slightly, her hand sliding between them. 'You know, you're quite a pretty thing. Randall is a lucky boy. Why don't you lie down for a bit? Come, don't be upset. I am gentle, much gentler than Randall.'

Orlaith recoiled in disgust at the invitation, feeling a wave of nausea. 'No, thank you. I…I must go now.' She left the room. The girl's leering made her feel physically sick, and she hurried along the landing, shutting the door once inside her bedroom.

Randall's mind couldn't be further from forgiveness.

'We don't have a chance,' she whispered. 'We don't have a chance.'

She wiped her eyes and went to lie on her bed. The light faded in the room, the shadows grew, and night fell softly on Dromkeen Hall.

And Orlaith wondered who on earth could help her now.

CHAPTER TWENTY-SIX

'Whoa!' Brannon yanked on the horse's reins and was nearly thrown from the saddle as he tried to slow the animal's charge down the bush-stubbled slope into the Oum er-Rbia. The river was broad and brown-green in colour, its current pushing sluggishly between banks of stunted grass. Brannon made his way onto a shingle beach and let the horse drink while he refilled his water flask. This was his waypoint. Now he must follow the river to the coastal town of Azemmour, and if the directions given to him were accurate, he had roughly eighty miles to go.

The horse grazed for a while on the foliage that grew half-heartedly along the bank. Brannon dozed, allowing himself to rest into the cool night, and he took to the saddle again before dawn. He followed the course of the river for the next few days, stopping only for sleep and sustenance. Twice he saw bands of nomadic shepherds wandering through the mimosa trees beyond the river, but no one hailed him, and at the end of the week he found a road running alongside the riverbank to the west.

The river gradually widened into a deep blue channel with a pebbled strand before it was lost into the rolling waves of the Atlantic. There were structures here, high white walls and windowless kasbahs, seemingly built into the cliffs beside the river. Brannon tethered his horse and climbed a series of steps up the cliff, ducking his head under webs and vines until he emerged into a quiet, almost deserted road. There were two rows of flat-roofed houses either side of the street. A donkey drinking from a rusted trough raised its head and stared at him. He wandered on and found a man sitting on a stool at the corner of the street, an ancient fellow with skin as brown and tough as cedar wood. There was a dog at his feet, missing one of its ears. The old man was chatting while caressing the dog's single remaining ear. Their conversation was halted by Brannon's approach.

'*Salam!*' Brannon smiled and was about offer his hand in greeting when the dog emitted a low growl. He took a step back. 'I'm looking for the pasha's residence. Can you help me?'

The old man gazed dumbly at him. For a full minute no one spoke. Then abruptly he rose and walked up the street with the dog trotting at his heels.

'Where are you going?' Brannon called after them. Ignored, he sighed in annoyance and began to follow. There were more people in the street now, women carrying urns of water, children playing. The men sat in solemn pairs, white-robed and silent. Brannon knew he must have presented an unusual sight to them, wandering dirty and dishevelled through their sleepy town.

The old man led him to the end of the street, to a single house with lime-washed walls and a leafy garden. There was a middle-aged and grossly overweight man asleep in the lawn, sitting on a wicker chair under the shade of a canvas awning. He blinked and peered up when his name was called. With evident difficulty he heaved himself out of the chair, his cheeks red from the midmorning heat. When he came to the garden gate, he addressed the old man for a moment. Then he glared at Brannon.

'Slave?' he demanded. 'Are you a slave?' He didn't wait for an answer but shouted an order, and suddenly two guards appeared from the house. Brannon started at their appearance, his hand moving to the hilt of his sword.

'I am the pasha of Azemmour. Answer me,' the fat man commanded. 'Where are you from?'

'You're not giving me much of a chance to explain,' Brannon said hotly.

'You're a slave,' the pasha insisted.

'I'm not a slave. I'm a soldier.'

'A deserter!' The man became alarmed. 'You are not welcome here. Yazid will punish us for harbouring deserters. You must leave this town, now.' He signalled to the two guards, but Brannon interrupted him.

'But Yazid is dead.'

There was a brief silence. The man turned back to him. 'What did you say?'

'Moulay Yazid is dead.' Brannon rummaged in his djellaba and retrieved the letter bearing Suliman's seal. 'This is a message for you—from the new sultan of Morocco.'

The pasha swallowed. Nervously he took the parchment and began to read.

Ten minutes later Brannon was sitting at the man's table, eating a meal of hot, buttered fowl hastily prepared by the wife. The pasha was beside himself with excitement and couldn't sit for more than a moment without thumping the oak table with his paw, shouting Suliman's name and praising Allah. He made Brannon recount every last detail of the battle of Marrakech and how the former sultan's army had been destroyed. The pasha took particular delight in learning that the body of General al-Malek had been found amongst the corpses.

'He sent one of his armies here once,' he recalled. 'My father was the pasha then. He dared to withhold Yazid's tribute, so al-Malek had him killed along with several hundred of our young men. It gives me joy to know that he is dead.'

'There is a little more to the letter,' Brannon said, trying to curb his impatience. 'You should read on.'

The pasha did so, and when he was finished, he stared at Brannon in wonder. 'This is true?'

'Um, yes,' Brannon answered hesitantly, unsure what Suliman had written about him.

'In that case,' the pasha said, beaming, 'it would be a privilege to offer you my assistance. You are a brave man, Brannon Ryan, and Suliman's request will be given my immediate attention. So it's a ship you need?'

Brannon breathed a sigh of relief.

One week later he was balancing on the slippery deck of a schooner as the west coast of Morocco streamed by. They made brisk progress on their northerly setting, the boat gliding over the swell of the waves as the Spanish captain regaled his crew with an account of Brannon's part in the downfall of Moulay Yazid, so that he was afforded hero status for the remainder of the journey. It was with disappointment that they bade farewell to him when the ship docked at the port of Gibraltar ten days later.

Gibraltar was teeming with grizzled British tars. Brannon made his way into one of the smoky dockside taverns a little before noon and re-emerged several hours later, his balance decidedly unsteady. His new-found companion, an Englishman by the name of Jennings, declared magnanimously, 'To hell with it, Irish, even if you're not telling the truth, I still like you. You promised me a tale, and by God you delivered it. So what is it I can do for *you?*'

Brannon told him. And Jennings baulked at the idea. 'Hah! I'm not going nowhere near Ireland, matey. My lads will be steering that hulk home to London where I've a new young wife waiting for me. An angel she is, the sweetest, purest thing in England. Tits the size of melons.'

'I've got money, you know,' Brannon said, briefly lifting his djellaba to display the bag of gold guineas tucked beneath. The Englishman quickly sobered.

'Now on second thought, I'm thinking it my Christian duty to offer my fellow man a hand in his hour of need...of course it is. So!' His eyes gleamed. 'Exactly how much of that will it be worth to you?'

With Yazid's looted gold thrown in to seal the bargain, Captain Jennings agreed to stretch his homeward journey a small bit further to take in the tiny port of Dromkeen in southern Ireland. They took advantage of a brisk south-easterly that buffeted the sails and pushed them up the Portuguese coast and along the Bay of Biscay, where the seas rose and spray washed over the prow in great tumbling cascades. Brannon relished those weeks at sea, the grinding of the ship's timbers, the smell of brine, and the sharp bite of the Atlantic. Captain Jennings, mindful of the reward he was due to receive onshore, didn't scrimp on hospitality. Brannon was invited to dine in the officers' mess every evening, feasting on salt beef and Suffolk cheese and innumerable goblets of red wine. In the northern climes, the temperatures dropped and the clouds rose sullen and threatening. Rain fell in assaults, and grey banks of mists tumbled across the sea. The worsening weather, Brannon noted cheerily, was a clear sign that he was almost home. At last, free, returned to the bosom of Dromkeen with Orlaith and Sean to embrace and every good thing to look forward to. His troubles were over, he believed, and the illusion was comforting as the ship steered for the coast of southern Ireland.

The night sky was dark but for a sickly yellow moon resting between the clouds. On the road above Dromkeen's cove there were lights showing from the village tavern, where bursts of raucous laughter sounded within. In the doorway a drunken man was slumped against the frame, his head down as he blurted some disjointed verses of a song he had heard earlier. They had had a harp player that night, a rare treat for the denizens of Dromkeen. Alas, the drunken man had spent all his money on cheap whiskey, and when he had fallen against the window and knocked over the candles, the tavern owner had bellowed out, 'Will you not go away home now, Dessie Buckley, before that wife of yours comes down to box your ears. It's a sorry man you'll be when you present yourself to her, with your week's pay spent and you barely able to stand on your feet. Off with you!'

So Dessie Buckley left, shuffling down the cobbled road where candlelight glimmered in the puddles. Unsure of which direction he was travelling, he cursed and listened for the sea, using the method he normally used when too drunk to find his way. If the sea was on his right, he was pointed in the direction of home.

There was a sound from the cove. He stopped. The splash of oars and the bump of a boat onto the sand. He stared into the darkness, hearing voices and feeling a shiver of superstitious dread. What could be coming out of the sea at this hour?

He strained his eyes through the faint light from the tavern and made out a form in the gloom. A man came wandering over the sand and climbed the steps to the road. Dessie blubbered in fright; it was a ferocious-looking sight, a giant of a man with wild hair and sun-gilded skin, wearing a sword and the garb of a savage. Dessie dropped to his knees and began to wail out a prayer. The figure approached him.

'Don't I know you?' Brannon asked, grinning.

'Mary, Mother of God, pray for us sinners…' Dessie stammered in fright.

'Dessie Buckley, you're drunk,' Brannon admonished him. 'I'm glad to see nothing's changed.'

Dessie stared up at him in confusion. Because of Brannon's exotic appearance, he still hadn't recognised him.

Brannon didn't bother to introduce himself. There would be a huge fuss once news spread, and he wanted to find Orlaith first. Instead he said, 'I need directions from you, if you're still capable of sense. I'm looking for Orlaith Downey. Is she still living in the cabin out the coast road?'

Dessie's fear sobered him a little. 'Orlaith Downey?'

'Aye. Where'll I find her?'

'But there's none by that name any more, sir.' He gazed worriedly at Brannon's sword. 'Is it some class of a ghost you are?'

Brannon frowned. 'What do you mean there's none by that name? Where's she gone?'

'Ah, pardon me, sir, but my meaning is that she's not called that name any more. She's Orlaith Whiteley now.'

Those words didn't fully register. 'She's what?'

'She's married to Randall Whiteley, sir. She's not a Downey—that was my meaning.'

There was a brief silence. Brannon let out a chuckle. 'Are you making fun of me?'

'Sir?'

'Careful, Dessie. I'll ask you again, and this time answer me properly, or I'll wring your bloody neck. Where's Orlaith Downey?' He clenched a fist, and Dessie trembled.

'Honest to God, sir! Ask them all in there. Sure they knocked her cabin years ago. She became Whiteley's wife, and I'm not lying, please God!'

It landed like a punch to the gut, literally knocking the breath out of him. Worse, it made no sense. Randall Whiteley? Why on earth…?

He suddenly felt sick.

Never once had he considered the fact that Orlaith might not be waiting for him. He had assumed she would wait. She loved him. She had wanted to marry him.

Yet had she now fallen for another?

'Sir, my wife is waiting for me,' Dessie pleaded miserably. 'I have to go home, sir; she'll beat me rotten. She's—'

'Get out of here, you fool,' Brannon snapped. As the grateful Dessie staggered off, he returned to the longboat where Jennings was waiting.

'Well?' Jennings asked eagerly. 'Did you find—' He stopped, noticing Brannon's pallor. 'Are you all right?'

Brannon didn't reply but pulled out the bag containing Yazid's gold. 'How would you like to earn a little more than agreed?'

Jennings raised his eyebrows. 'How so?'

'I may not be staying here after all. But I need time. Can you wait?'

'I should have been in London last week,' Jennings protested. 'Wait how long? Are you coming with us?'

'Maybe. Just give me tonight. By tomorrow I'll know what I'm doing. Either way, I'll make it worth your while. Half now and half in the morning. You'll help me?'

Jennings gave a shrug. But the gold was tempting. 'You shouldn't be flaunting that stuff around so much, Ryan. My crew are scum, the lot of them. What if one of them decided to slit your craw and keep the lot themselves?'

There was a menace to Brannon's smile. 'Christ, they could try.'

'Oh, very well,' Jennings grumbled, 'but it's a bloody inconvenience. The lads will have to be paid for the extra days too.'

'Consider it done,' Brannon replied. He dished out a handful of the glimmering coins into Jennings's palm. 'And half again in the morning. It's just one night, all right?'

Jennings nodded. 'See you in the morning, then.'

Brannon tucked his djellaba around himself, scurried up the steps, and disappeared into the darkness.

CHAPTER TWENTY-SEVEN

Randall checked his timepiece. Half past ten. He debated whether to take up that offer at the Campbell estate. Card games, Willy Campbell had promised, and as well as that he had some girls down from Limerick to enliven the proceedings. Randall shuddered. Limerick? Still, he was bored, and Willy Campbell always threw a good shindig. He glanced through the window at the night. Padraig Welsh was gone home, but never mind, he could get Vincent to drive the carriage.

He had tired of Orlaith at this point. The fun of her torment had lost its appeal, and he was beginning to regret his decision to take custody of her. Yet it hardly mattered now. The prison ship was due to collect its motley clientele in four days, and he would be rid of the bitch after that. With Sean carted off to Dublin, he could then turn his attention towards restoring what life he had enjoyed before the treacherous Orlaith arrived to poison everything. And she *had* poisoned it. What a merry dance she had led him. He should have bloody well known, with a woman.

After Victoria he had sworn never to be made a fool of again, yet Orlaith had seemed so sweet, so essentially good and dutiful, that he had been unable to prevent himself from falling in love with her. In thanks for his kindness, he was stabbed in the back, and not even with the past few months of violence and rape had he been able to slake his thirst for revenge. It was not of huge importance, however. In the harsh colony of New South Wales, Orlaith would receive her just reward.

There was a knock at the drawing room door. It was pushed open hesitantly.

'Well, well, speak of the devil and he appears,' Randall chuckled. 'I was just thinking about you, my dear.'

Orlaith glanced to the whiskey bottle to see how much he had taken. If he was too drunk, then she would get nowhere.

'Randall,' she began, 'I've tried so many times to talk to you lately. But you won't even offer me the courtesy of a few minutes. Please, can you not listen to what I have to say?'

'My dear Orlaith,' he exclaimed in mock embarrassment, 'how unforgivably rude of me. Please, do feel at leisure. Speak.'

'I'm being serious, Randall. You must hear me out.'

'And what on earth could you want from me, my dear? More money, is it? Why don't you simply bash me over the head and grab it for yourself?'

'Randall.' She paused, preparing herself. 'Randall, I know what I did was wrong. And I deserve to be punished. But I need you to know one thing…'

'And what's that?'

'I always loved you, Randall. You are strong, and you were so good to me. I knew that, and I loved you for it. I've made such a terrible mistake.'

'Ah, but it's a bit late to realise that now, Orlaith. Amazing how you can suddenly find your manners again with the prison ship on its way.'

'I know it's on its way.' She hung her head. 'Perhaps in the penal colony I can somehow make amends for what I've done. Do you think God will forgive me?'

He hesitated. This was the first time that she had openly shown remorse, and he was surprised. 'I know not, my dear. I'm not entirely expert as to the whims of the Lord. But why would you care?'

'Because I need forgiveness, Randall. I was a fool. I was happy here, with you, and I spoiled it all. But I do love you.'

'Stop that!' he growled. 'You made me believe you once, with your lies. You'll not do it again. You're a damned harpy, Orlaith, and I'm glad you will suffer.'

'Yes,' she said in a small voice. 'That's the way it must be. I cannot hope for a second chance.'

'A second chance at what, exactly?' he demanded.

'At us, Randall. Here, in this wonderful home. I was not always bad. I made you happy once. We had nights together, many of them, safe in each other's arms. It saddens me that you have forgotten all of that.'

'You left me!' he blurted. 'You stole my money!'

'Because I was lost. I don't have the wisdom of your years, Randall. You should remember that you are a decade my elder. Perhaps I've made mistakes, but I need to learn.' She sensed that she was gaining some ground. She didn't want to push him too fast, however.

'Nonsense,' he said, shaking his head. But he sounded uncertain of himself. 'I could never trust you again, Orlaith. What we had is ruined. By you!'

'Love cannot be ruined, Randall. Forgotten, yes, but not ruined. I have not forgotten our love, but are you about to?'

He stared at her. For the first time in many months, he noticed her beauty again.

'Randall,' she whispered, 'don't send me away. We would be lost to each other. We would never have a single night together again.' Subtly she eased her fingers under the lace shoulder of her dress, displaying for a brief moment the pale skin underneath.

Randall's heartbeat quickened.

'Let me stay, Randall,' she coaxed him. 'Let Sean stay.'

'No!'

'And I promise, I will be yours forever. All of me, forever, yours alone. I love you, Randall.'

He blinked his eyes in a daze, his breathing made husky by his arousal. He took a step forward. 'No, Orlaith...'

'I want you, Randall. I love you.'

He couldn't resist her, couldn't resist the soft falling of her voice, the pearly sheen of her flesh. He reached out for her. She pulled the border of her dress lower to expose the bulge of her porcelain-like breasts. Randall panted with want. His fingers thrust their way into her cleavage while his other hand moved around her waist, pulling her towards him. He moved for her mouth, pushing his tongue between her lips. Orlaith lifted her head back, inviting him closer...

And then, abruptly, she could contain her revulsion no more.

She spluttered, her face turning red as she stumbled backwards. 'Wait…' she said, but she couldn't prevent herself from gagging involuntarily.

Randall flinched as if he'd been scalded. 'So!' he exclaimed in anger. 'I knew it! Your lies and wickedness at play again. You almost had me fooled!' He made quickly for the whiskey bottle and swallowed a thick draught, wiping his mouth and laughing. 'You should have been an actress, my dear. You're gifted! You should have trod the boards, some Shakespearean tragedy, the villain with the knife concealed. You could knife someone quite easily.'

'Randall, please!' she begged. 'You misunderstand. I do want you. I love you, Randall. Will you not—'

'Enough!' he roared, lunging out and slapping her so hard that she fell against the wall. 'Get out, you whore. Get out! Pray for the timely arrival of that ship, for if I set eyes on you one more time, I swear to God I'll kill you.' He grabbed her arm and bundled her through the door. She fled from him, tears streaming down her cheeks.

The dice had been thrown. Her chances were up. With fateful, weary steps, she made her way to Sean's bedroom.

'Sean?' she whispered. He murmured in his slumber, rubbing knuckles against his eye.

She wiped away her tears. 'Sean, you must listen to Mammy. I have something I must tell you…'

He blinked once, scowled, and turned on his side to return to whatever childish dream he had been engaged in: a field that grew chocolate, a wizard that lived inside a tree, a dog with wings who carried little boys off to fantastical worlds of adventure.

And Orlaith knew that all hope was doomed.

Doomed hope, it was a visiting cousin, familiar enough to drop by without invitation. So many stories of heartbreak she had heard in her young life, all the way from the west of Ireland to the wave-beaten south. People, her people at least, were always chasing shattered hopes. Dismal, luckless hope. A father gazing down on dead soil, with a brood of hollow-cheeked children sitting around a barren table. A lonely maid cleaning grates and waiting for a lover who by now wouldn't even recall her name. A weary labourer trudging miles between the hiring fairs, carrying his spade, clothes soiled from sleeping in damp fields.

They held candles to storms, her people. They saw their lights extinguished as cruel winds of fate blew. Orlaith was cold now, so utterly cold. The sun was frozen, and her whole world had turned to ice.

Brannon took the quicker route through the forests to reach Dromkeen Hall. Despite the time of year it was chilly, sea gales finding chinks in the mountain armour. He ran on. The trees were packed densely within the woodlands, the ground soft and moist. Brannon had heard as a boy of how these woods were known to be haunted, how no man would dare to travel them alone at night. Strange noises came from the forest at night. Some swore to having heard singing, others screaming.

He hurried his pace. The way was obstructed by gnarled briars, and more than once he lost his footing in the muck. If there was any sense to what he was doing, it wasn't entirely clear to him yet. Orlaith was a married woman. What was he hoping for? That he could simply march up to Randall Whiteley's front door and demand her back? He wouldn't even make it up the avenue without someone firing a musket ball into his belly. Yet he had to know for sure. He had to see for himself before he could believe it.

He pushed through the trees until he cleared the edge of the forest and reached a quiet meadow of tangled grass. There was an old pine fence bordering the meadow, separating it from the woods. This was Whiteley land now. He ran through the darkness, crossing a number of boggy fields where the faint shapes of cattle moved like spectres. After a mile he found the road that led up to the iron gates of Dromkeen Hall, the spikes black in the night like devil's horns. He avoided the avenue and instead crept along the demesne wall, searching for a spot from which to survey movements. He found an oak tree, heaved himself into the branches, and looked out.

The only time he had ever seen this house was when, as a boy, he had spent several days helping his father, who had been hired by the estate to clear a number of storm-felled trees. Brannon had been overawed by the size of the house then, and he was similarly impressed now. How many rooms must it contain, hidden nooks, lofts, passageways, cellars?

There were candles flickering in a ground window off the front door. The drawing room, he guessed, but to his alarm he saw three armed men patrolling the flagstones outside. Guards, and if there were three in front, then there must be more beyond. Whiteley was clearly taking no chances these days. It wouldn't be easy to get in there now, not without a fight. Instinctively he touched his sword.

She had to be found.

Quietly he eased himself over the wall and dropped soundlessly into the shadows. Keeping himself low, he moved past rosebushes and orchards, skirting a moonlit lake as he climbed the gentle slope to the house. After a few hundred yards he ducked behind a wall and lay in the grass to get his breath. There were earth banks and flowerbeds running along the east wall of the house, where the lights showed in the window. Waiting until the guards had moved on, he crawled like a cat past the banks of flowers and concealed himself in the gloom. Taking a quick check to ensure no one was watching, he moved to the window and listened.

A male voice sound from within, gruff and difficult to make out, and Brannon couldn't follow what was said. But then the next voice, feminine and soft and utterly familiar, made his heart stop in his chest.

'...and I promise, I will be yours forever. All of me, forever, yours alone. I love you, Randall...'

He flinched from her words, winced at the stabbing pain inflicted by their brutal clarity. Confused emotions assailed him—joy at hearing her voice again, despair at knowing she was definitely gone. She was here, just several feet away, but it could be another world to him, for she couldn't have made it any plainer. She loved Randall.

He backed away from the window, too sickened to listen to the rest of the conversation. There were footsteps rounding the corner, and one of the guards loomed into view. Brannon rolled behind the flowerbeds. He watched the guard ambling past and then sat in the soaking dew, his head in turmoil.

Why had she done it? He'd been gone a long time, but not a lifetime. She could have waited. She *should* have waited. But she hadn't, and he cursed the situation with bitter disappointment. All those months of toil and loneliness, of violence and danger, he had survived them only because of her. If he had only known all along that Orlaith was busy falling in love with somebody else…

He gazed around at the nocturnal calm of the estate. She must be happy in this place. Brannon certainly didn't belong here. There was nothing for him in Dromkeen any more, he realised. Nothing but a ship and an impatient captain at the cove. And that's where he should be now.

He got up and began walking across the grass.

CHAPTER TWENTY-EIGHT

The cupboard creaked within the darkness of the kitchen. Orlaith rummaged inside and located a bottle of brandy used by the servants for cooking. She swallowed a mouthful; the fiery liquid stung the back of her throat and made her eyes water. She didn't drink alcohol very often, and the taste of it made her nauseous, but she desperately needed something to help her sleep. It would be a long night otherwise.

It was no good. The brandy was too strong for her delicate palate. She replaced it and stood for a moment, listening to the rustling trees in the grounds. The night was cool, and for a moment it gave her peace, bereft as it was of voice and chastisement. She opened the kitchen door and stepped out, letting the airs sweep through the thin cover of her nightgown, not caring that the guards might see her in a state of undress. She closed her eyes. She would have cried at this moment, only that she felt there were no more tears left to shed. Everything was gone. Everything was dead.

Aware of the guards' presence, she nonetheless didn't expect one of them to be wandering so close. His footsteps startled her, and she stepped back. When he emerged from the shadows, she became deeply afraid.

He was a tall man with long hair and several days' growth of beard. He wore strange, flowing garments, caked in dust. He carried a sword. This man was not one of the guards.

She went to scream, but he raised a finger to his lips.

'Shh, Orlaith. You'll wake everyone. It's late.'

She stared in his direction, eyes widening in shock. Suddenly her hands began to tremble. His features were still unclear in the shadows, but that voice…

317

'Oh, my God,' she whispered. 'Oh, my God...' Her colour drained. She grasped the doorframe to steady herself. 'My good God...'

He took a step closer. 'I take it you weren't expecting me?'

It was too much. She stumbled forward and would have fallen had he not caught her in his arms. Her expression briefly glazed over as she slipped into unconsciousness, but he managed to hold her against his chest until she came around.

'Sorry, Orlaith. I didn't mean to scare you like that. Your husband will be annoyed with me.' He set her back so that he could look at her face. 'It's still nice to see you, though.'

'Oh, my God,' she whimpered again, seeing his eyes. They were about the only aspect of his physical appearance that hadn't changed. 'Brannon...' Tears of astonishment and joy began to flow down her face. She cried out and went to hug him. 'Oh God, Brannon!'

He stiffened, not returning the embrace. 'I know I shouldn't have surprised you. It's wrong of me to just show up. And perhaps I wouldn't have. If I had known...'

'Oh, Brannon, what are you saying—oh, I'm so happy!' Her eyes sparkled with elation, and she clasped his face. 'I can't believe this is happening. I thought you were lost—I thought you were in Africa!'

'I did pass through the place.' Gently he lowered her hands. 'And I must say I wasn't expecting to find this on my return.'

'What do you mean?'

He gestured to the grandeur of their surroundings. 'This, Orlaith. I'm a little taken aback.'

Her face dropped, suddenly aghast. 'Oh no, Brannon! No, you don't understand. You must let me explain.'

'Did you marry him, Orlaith?'

'Oh, Brannon, I did. But not for the reasons you think! Please let me explain.'

Brannon knew that no matter what answer she gave him, no matter what way she could ever treat him, he would love her always. And so he nodded. 'Very well, Orlaith. I will listen.'

Though she left out many of the details, it still took Orlaith nearly half an hour to explain her story from the moment when they had parted company on the mountain. It culminated here, in this landscaped estate, and Brannon swallowed a lump.

'New South Wales?' he breathed in despair. 'It's the other side of the world.'

'I know, Brannon. But Sean—he'll suffer more than I will. And he's just a child. God, but I hate these people.'

'Hate? It isn't strong enough a word.' He struggled to take it in. It was quite a story, and a tragic one. His own tribulations now seemed a distant memory. 'Jesus, I'm so sorry, Orlaith. I should never have doubted you.'

'I love you, Brannon,' she told him sadly. 'That never changed, even if everything else did.'

His countenance darkened. 'I won't let this happen. I won't allow it!'

She kissed his hand. 'Oh, my love, I wish they had never taken you from me. But this is how it is now. You can't stop Randall. Please, Brannon, don't do anything dangerous. You're free now. You have a life.'

'I have no life,' he declared, 'without you in it. And I will put a stop to this whole wretched business.'

'Brannon,' she said in alarm, 'you mustn't get in Randall's way. He's too powerful. And he has men. Men with guns. They'll kill you if you cross them. Do not—'

She stopped then, hearing voices from the garden. The guards were not far. 'Brannon, you can't stay here.'

His heart was breaking. He couldn't bring himself to leave, not after what he had heard. 'I'll come back,' he whispered. 'When do they take you away?'

'On Thursday morning the city gaol will send a coach. Sean is to be collected next week. But Brannon—'

'They'll never get their hands on you,' he vowed. 'Do you trust me?'

'Yes.'

'I must go. Be brave, Orlaith.'

'Wait!' She reached for him and pulled his head down to hers; she kissed him, her skin tingling with a lust that she had not experienced in a long time. His arms circled her waist, and she felt herself become weak with arousal. They kissed again, a deep, longing kiss, and she would have gone further had he not suddenly broken off.

'They'll see us,' he panted. 'We can't—'

'Come with me.' She led him by the hand into the trees, treading barefoot through the leaves. Beyond the pine groves there was silence where even the wind had stilled. He followed her uncertainly until they reached the ruins of a tower above a grassy hillock, the old crumbling Norman tower. There under the ancient stone and ivy they embraced. No words were spoken for a time, but eventually Orlaith released him and began hurriedly clearing the small rocks and brambles from the floor. Brannon watched her, bewildered.

'What are you doing?'

She didn't answer but made him lie beside her on the dead leaves, and then she sought him, pushing her tongue between his lips and rummaging at the ends of his djellaba. She managed to loosen it from his belt and pull it up over his head. In the darkness she explored with her hands and exclaimed in wonder at the feel of his bare chest, the whorls of hair and hard muscle, the sleek contours of his arms and the flatness of his belly. He was breathing heavily now, and when her hand touched his groin, she felt at once his desire. She started undoing the buttons of her nightdress.

'Orlaith,' he said, torn between confusion and aching need. 'What are we doing, Orlaith?'

She giggled nervously. 'I would have thought it obvious.'

'But we're not married. I thought you said—'

'Never mind what I said.' She kissed him and continued opening her dress. 'I made the mistake of waiting before, Brannon. And then you were lost to me. I will not make that mistake again.' She slipped out of her nightdress and heard his sharp intake of breath when he saw her pale breasts exposed in the moonlight. 'We may never meet after tonight. We don't know what is to happen,' she whispered. 'And so I will wait no more.'

She lay back.

In the darkness of the tower they came together, naked in body and want. Brannon thought he had slipped into a dream. He relished the very feel of her, the softness of her skin and the warmth of her legs, the comfort of her breasts,

320

the fragrance of her hair. He closed his eyes as her thighs parted to allow him in, feeling her fingers cling to his back as though she was dangling over a precipice and terrified to let go.

Orlaith had never realised before how beautiful a man's body could be, how wonderful the act of love really was. Seamus had been clumsy and hesitant, Randall usually rough and selfish. But with Brannon…

She felt herself melt with him inside her. She cried, but it was tears of bliss that flowed down her cheeks. She felt safe again, and protected and happy and loved. She wanted it to last forever in this new paradise of unspoilt beauty, of untouched treasures and long-craved delights. Lost together, they stayed in the tower for much longer than they should have, and it was with reluctance that they finally dressed and crept back through the grounds.

'I'll come back for you,' he promised when they said their goodbyes. 'You mustn't be afraid.'

Orlaith blinked away her tears, the memory of their love-making already beginning to recede as cruel normality returned to intrude. 'Yes, Brannon. But even if not, I want you to know—'

'I already know. We will be together, Orlaith. That's how it was always meant to be.'

She nodded, and she desperately wanted to believe him.

'Have faith. Randall Whiteley and all his minions won't stand in my way.'

She had to believe him. Brannon always made everything right.

'Now go. Go to Sean. And sleep.' He kissed her a last time and moved into the shadows, heading for the demesne wall, and within seconds he had vanished from view. Orlaith wiped her eyes. It was quiet again. Weary and with ominous thoughts, she made her way back inside the house.

'I wish you would tell me what you're up to.' Captain Jennings gave Brannon a reproving look, debating the latter's request of another few days in Drom-keen. Jennings should have been in London a week ago. The gold, however, was tempting as ever. 'Why do you need three more days? I really need to get out of here—half my lads have fallen in love with the local trollops. It'll be a job to get them all back aboard.'

'There's something I have to take care of,' Brannon told him. 'And after Thursday, I promise, I will keep you here no more. Will you wait?'

Jennings sighed. 'I'm only carrying tea and ivory. I guess it won't spoil. Yeah, I can wait.'

'Good.' Brannon shook his hand. 'Just be ready for me. I may be in a bit of a hurry.'

On Thursday the sea was calm, though the sun failed to make much of an impression on the grey banks of cloud that swathed the harbour. A black coach rattled past the cliffs, locating the north road in the direction of Dromkeen Hall. To the left and right the heather was dappled with bright bursts of summer flowers, mountain aven and meadowsweet and cloudberry, lorded over by stands of alder, birch, and spruce trees.

The driver of the coach, Bertie Brady, cared little for the colourful show. It was too early for him, this unnatural hour of seven o'clock, and his head throbbed from the bottle of whiskey he had drunk the night before. It was sleep he needed now. His hand hurt too, the pain more intense when he closed his fist. Had he been in a fight? He couldn't remember whom he had hit. His wife, perhaps, if she had got in his way. If so, it would serve her right, the fat bitch.

He belched and rubbed his belly. Sons of Satan, they were, sending him on this bloody errand. Bertie normally worked as a turnkey in the city gaol, but this morning they had been short of a driver, and thus Bertie was despatched instead, ordered to take the coach to Dromkeen Hall and fetch the prisoner back. He perhaps wouldn't have minded the fresh air if he wasn't feeling so sick. It was a seventy-mile round trip, the coach jolting over every hole and stone, hard on a man suffering from an upset stomach.

'Away out of it now!' he snapped at two girls picking berries by the roadside. They scattered before the coach, covering a safe distance into the nearby meadow before turning back to pull faces at him. He lifted a stout billy club and waved it threateningly; they giggled, calling him an *amadán mór* and remarking on the striking resemblance between his head and the contents of a latrine.

'Bugger off, you little witches,' he roared, 'before I bash the both of ye!'

One of them tramped brazenly back to the road, a bumptious little creature no more than nine years of age. She draped one hand on her hip and declared, 'You can't make us!'

'By Christ, and I can't...' Bertie's sullen mood gave way to outrage. He scrambled from the coach and went for the girl, wielding the billy club. She squealed in mock fright but ran easily from him, skipping over the dikes and bog-holes with the quickness of a rabbit. Bertie gave chase but was out of breath within a minute, and he bellowed after the two fleeing girls, 'Get back here and I'll skin your sorry arses, you—'

The ground suddenly seemed to move. A dark shape rose from the heather, a fist came flying like an artillery shot, and Bertie was turned upside down. He landed heavily, gasping as the air was forced from his lungs. He blinked once, gagged as the blood leaked from his nose into his throat, and then he fell into unconsciousness.

Brannon straightened up and rubbed the knuckles on his hand. He glanced behind. 'Good work, girls. Here!' He tossed them a gold guinea, a small fortune to them. 'Mind that and give it to your mother.'

They exclaimed their thanks and ran for the hills, racing each other home. And Brannon set to work.

❀ ❀ ❀

The door handle slowly turned. Daylight flooded into the bedroom as Orlaith came awake. She hadn't slept until about an hour ago. Her eyes were bloodshot, rimmed with swollen purple smudges.

'What time is it?' she murmured.

'It's time,' Randall answered simply. 'Get up.'

He left the door ajar and went downstairs. Orlaith climbed from the bed, her mind in disarray.

The fifteenth of June.

She walked across the floor and opened the curtains, gazing over the lawns to the distant shape of the Norman tower. The memory of that night returned, but she was worried now. He hadn't come back. Nor had there been any signal from him. Had he changed his mind? Perhaps he had realised the futility of it, after all.

The familiar despair returned, clenching on her chest like a vice. For a brief time, an all too brief time, it had seemed that the nightmare would end. Brannon made a promise, and Brannon never broke his promises. But that felt like a generation ago now, and today was the day that brought her perdition. Today she would be making her final journey out of Dromkeen.

She thought about Sean, and she felt her heart would break. Her few attempts to broach this matter, to somehow prepare him for it, had not been successful. He had been unable to comprehend it, all nonsense to him, Mammy's rambling. He didn't realise that she wouldn't be there tomorrow when he woke up.

Kathy came upstairs. Her eyes were puffy from tears. She sniffled and said, 'Ma'am, I've made you a hot breakfast. You'll need something good inside you, ma'am. Will you not come down now?'

Orlaith tried to smile, but her own eyes welled up too. 'I'm not so hungry this morning, Kathy. Would you be terribly cross if I didn't?'

Kathy stared at her like Orlaith had declared a blood-feud between them. She burst into a fit of sobbing and hurried out. 'I'm sorry, ma'am, I'm so sorry—'

When she was gone, Orlaith made her way wearily downstairs.

It was almost eight o'clock. Randall was in the lobby. He lifted his timepiece and tutted. 'You're not even dressed, my dear. This is a big day for you. I thought you might have made an effort.'

'Oh, be damned, Randall.' She made for the dining room, but he forestalled her.

'Didn't you just tell Kathy you wouldn't have breakfast? No point going in there now.'

'I'm taking breakfast up to Sean,' she snapped. 'I will feed it to him in bed. Even a monster like you won't deny me that.'

'Ah, but you're wrong.' He seized her wrist suddenly and yanked her back. 'I told you it's time. You should have got dressed.'

'What do you mean?' Her face paled.

'I mean, the coach is coming up the driveway. Your escorts are outside. Time's up, Orlaith.'

'No!' she cried in horror. 'I have to see Sean first!'

'Too late. Time waits not.' He began to pull her towards the door.

She screamed. 'Oh no, Randall, please! You must let me see Sean! Please, let me see him!'

'You should have said your goodbyes last night.' He chuckled. 'But then you were never one to get your priorities right, were you?' He squeezed her arm viciously and forced her to the door.

'Please, Randall!' she begged. 'Let me say goodbye to him. Oh God, please let me hold him!'

'Don't worry about Sean, my dear. He'll be on his own merry way this time next week. And if the brat stays out of my path in the meantime, he'll be the happier for it.' He smiled. 'Oh, console yourself. He'll have forgotten all about you within a month. Especially where he's going.'

'No!'

He bundled her through the door, and the coach was indeed just arriving. It had a canopy cover and two doors, driven by a man with a black cape over his shoulders and a cocked hat. She struggled wildly, but the two escorting constables took each of her arms and shoved her inside.

'It's thirty-five miles to Cork,' one of them grumbled. 'Is she going to keep this up all the way?'

'I have to see my son!' Orlaith pleaded.

'No, you don't, lass. Just keep your mouth shut, and the journey will pass quicker for us all.' He dug his nails into her arm, and the pain made her gasp.

Randall came forward once the doors were closed, and he peered through the small window. 'Don't let her give you any lip, Ned. I find the back of my hand usually stops that mouth of hers fast enough.'

Ned grinned. 'No fear of that, sir. We'll keep her in check.'

'Good.' Randall looked up to the driver and thumped the carriage. 'Off you go, my good man. Prisoner secure.'

The driver nodded and cracked the reins, and the carriage rolled across the gravel.

Orlaith cried out desperately, trying to see through the window. The house disappeared from view, and the last she saw was Randall's sneering grin as he waved her goodbye.

They left the estate and lumbered down the winding road through the hills. The clouds lifted briefly, but Orlaith was unable to see, pressed between the two brawny bodies beside her. The interior of the carriage was hot, and the smell of masculine sweat soon thickened in the air. She thought she was going to suffocate.

They covered a few miles until they reached the coast road where the waves lapped gently on the beach. The gravel was rough, and they bounced along. No one spoke for a long time. Then, suddenly, the carriage ground to a halt.

'What's going on?' Ned scowled. He leaned out but was unable to see the driver. 'What's wrong up there?' he yelled.

No reply.

'See what the matter is, will you, Liam?' he said to the other constable. 'If that driver has bent a wheel, I'll bend his head for him.'

Liam, the younger of the pair, climbed out and made his way to the front of the carriage.

'And tell him hurry, for Christ's sake,' Ned growled. 'We've got a bloody long drive ahead of us.'

There was a noise from beyond. A brief grunt, and the sound of something falling. Ned shifted uneasily.

'Don't you move,' he warned Orlaith, and then he took out his pistol and kicked the door open. 'Where are you, damn fools?'

The driver peered around the front of the carriage, grinning.

'Where's Liam?' Ned asked in confusion.

'He's here,' the driver replied cheerfully. 'Give us some help, will you?'

Ned cursed in anger. 'I knew it. You've damaged a wheel, haven't you? Useless sod. If we're late, I'll blame you.' He shut the carriage door, replaced his pistol, and stormed towards the driver.

But there was no sign of Liam.

'Where's the other constable?' Ned demanded.

'Down there,' the driver answered. Ned spotted Liam's unconscious form lying face down on the roadway.

'What the blazes—'

The driver swung a billy club round and smashed it across the side of Ned's skull. He reeled against the carriage, blood spattering across his cheek, before he collapsed in a pile beside Liam.

Brannon pulled off the hat and cape. He went to the door of the carriage and found Orlaith shaking inside.

'It's you!' she cried in relief. 'Oh, thank God, Brannon! Where did you come from?'

'Never mind that now. Stay here. I must deal with our friends.'

Ten minutes later he had both Ned and Liam tied up inside a byre for the farmer to discover in a few hours. He returned to the coach.

'We'll go back for Sean now, Orlaith, but then we really must get out of Dromkeen. I need to know—how many guards are still at the estate?'

She gulped. 'I don't know. The constables have left, but Vincent's still there, and he's dangerous. And Randall has a whole house full of guns. Oh, Brannon, how are we ever going to get Sean out?'

'I don't know. Something will come to us, I hope. Now hold on.' He yanked the reins and turned the horses so that they were facing back in the direction of Dromkeen Hall. The carriage took off. He pushed the animals hard, lashing the reins off their backs to squeeze every last ounce of effort from them. The carriage swayed and groaned under the pressure, its panels grinding so ominously that Orlaith feared the entire structure would disintegrate. It managed to hold, however, and within a half hour they were outside Randall's gates.

'Are you ready?' Brannon hopped down from the carriage. 'This is it. Let's just grab the boy and run like hell.'

'Where's Mammy?' Sean looked up from his bowl of oatmeal, only now noticing her absence from breakfast. Kathy came across and tried to wipe the cream from his mouth. He drew back in annoyance, growling at her like a chastened puppy.

'You finish your food now, Sean,' she told him. 'Mammy is…Mammy's not here now.'

He dug the spoon deep into the bowl, scooped up a dollop of the thick oatmeal, and flicked it across the table.

'Sean!' Kathy warned him. 'Don't play with your food, or you'll have nothing to eat for the day.'

He stared at her curiously. Why was it Kathy scolding him this morning instead of his mother? He hadn't even seen his mother yet today. It should be her telling him off.

'Where's Mammy?' he asked again, his limpid eyes widening. Kathy took a seat beside him. She was uncomfortable, not knowing what to say.

'Sean, Mammy's not here any more. She had to go away. But she loves you very much, and you mustn't be afraid.'

Sean looked anything but afraid. His fingers moved to the spoon again, a sly grin on his lips. That oatmeal would look funny on top of Kathy's head.

'Sean, please!' Kathy remonstrated with him. 'Don't do that. Listen, Mammy had to go away, but some nice people are going to look after you now. You'll have to go with them next week, Sean. Do you understand what I'm telling you?'

It didn't register at all. Sean hopped off the chair and turned his back on her, uninterested in her nonsense. 'Sean!' she called him, but he trotted on.

The hallway was quiet and the door open. Sean scampered outside. What had that servant been on about? Why, there was his mother now, coming up the driveway to the house. She wasn't gone away at all.

But she wasn't alone. Sean hesitated suddenly. There was a man with her— big, strong-looking. His hair was long and his clothes unkempt. Sean took a step back.

'Sean!' Orlaith exclaimed in relief when she saw him. 'Sean, thank God!'

But Sean was nervous now. The big man came closer. 'Is that you, Seany? Goodness, I've missed you, lad. How you've grown!' He smiled, spreading his arms as if moving in for an embrace. Sean wailed. He turned and ran.

'Sean, no!' Orlaith shouted. 'Don't run!'

But he was too quick. He ducked under her outstretched hands and made for the gardens, disappearing like a ferret through the hedgerow.

'Sean!'

Brannon glanced around the house. So far there was no unwelcome attention. 'Wait here, Orlaith. I'll get him.' He vaulted the hedge with a leap and began scouring the trees beyond. Within a minute he was out of sight. Orlaith fidgeted anxiously.

'Hurry, Brannon,' she whispered. 'Please God, just hurry.'

CHAPTER TWENTY-NINE

Randall swallowed a draught from his whiskey flask and wandered towards the house to fetch his riding apparel. A few hours in the hills, and by then he would have a handsome appetite for lunch. He was feeling good today. Orlaith was gone, and soon her brat would be, too. A turning point, he felt, the end of a rather messy and troublesome chapter. He would celebrate tonight, invite the fellows over, lay on a meal and some decent wine, card games in the drawing room and girls for fun. What finer way to begin the rest of his life…

And then he stopped.

What on earth?

He rubbed his eyes.

His imagination, surely. It couldn't be what it looked like.

Orlaith.

But that was impossible—he had seen her taken away himself. He had put two constables to guard her, for Christ's sake.

So why the hell was she now standing outside his door?

'Oh, for the love of Jesus Christ…'

Orlaith hadn't seen him yet. She was calling to someone. Randall walked up behind her.

'Brannon!' Orlaith shouted, oblivious to Randall's presence. 'Brannon, hurry up!'

Randall checked his footsteps.

What did she say?

No, he thought. *How could it be?*

Brannon Ryan…

But he was in Africa! He was supposed to be dead—and long forgotten. Wasn't he? Yet Orlaith was wandering free, and the constables were nowhere to be seen.

He closed his eyes in disbelief. Brannon Ryan. The one man Randall truly hated, the man whom Orlaith loved, the love that Randall had always wanted so badly. Brannon Ryan, penniless and ignorant, who had beaten Randall despite all the latter's power and money.

And he was back. He would merely snap his fingers, and Orlaith would run to him. Randall's own wife, about to be taken from him by a country peasant.

'No!' he shouted angrily.

Orlaith stiffened in shock.

'You,' Randall hissed, scarlet rising in his cheeks. 'I don't believe this...'

'Get away, Randall,' she warned, taking a step back. 'Stay away from me. I'm leaving, and there's nothing you can do about it.'

'Leaving, is it?' he snarled. 'With him? With that gutter rat?'

'Stay away from me, Randall.'

'You whore!' He felt the jealousies return, burning his stomach like an ulcer. The whole point in sending her to New South Wales was that he could rest easy in the knowledge that she would never be with another man, at least not in this country. But now Brannon Ryan was here, taking her for himself. And Randall simply couldn't handle it.

'You *whore!* He sprang at her and grabbed her hair, dragging her to the ground. She screamed; Randall went for her throat, the features of his face contorting into the mask of a monster. 'He won't have you! He won't!'

Orlaith fought back, digging her nails into his eyes. He howled in fury and drew off. She rolled clear, hitched up her dress, and broke into a run. He screeched after her like a demented banshee. 'Get back here, you bitch!' He clambered to his feet and gave chase.

She staggered through the pine groves, making for the demesne wall. There was a gleam of insanity in his eyes that she had not seen before, the gleaming, devil-eyes of a killer. She knew what he wanted to do.

As she reached the long rushes by the lake, he caught up.

'*Bitch!*' He flung himself forward, his momentum sending them both into the lake. They landed with a splash, and the water shot up her nose. She spluttered, choking as her throat clogged up. Randall seized her with both hands and forced her head below the surface. She kicked and writhed, trying to escape his lethal grip, but he was too heavy. 'I won't let you!' he roared. 'You can't!'

Orlaith couldn't get free. She tried to heave him off, but his strength outmatched hers. She screamed but made no noise, only succeeding in allowing another surge of lake water into her lungs. A full minute passed. Her movements began to weaken. He kept her head pushed down, placing his knee on her back to prevent her getting loose.

Finally, her struggles stopped.

Randall was out of breath. He released her and collapsed on the bank, panting with exertion. He glanced towards her body, but there was no movement there. Orlaith lay motionless, face down in the lake, the ripples lapping softly against her skin.

'Get off me!' Sean demanded indignantly as Brannon scooped him up. 'Leave me alone!' he cried, but it was still no good. Then he yelled, '*Bastard!*' He had learned the word from Randall, and it usually had the most profound effect on his mother. But it didn't bother Brannon.

'Hush now,' Brannon chuckled, carrying him easily through the garden. 'I can't remember your language being this bad before, Sean. It seems I have a lot of work ahead.'

Sean continued his threats and abuse and even tried pinching Brannon's arm, but to no avail. They reached the front of the house, where Brannon looked for Orlaith.

'Oh, what now?' he groaned, realising she was missing.

'Mammy!' Sean suddenly wailed.

Brannon stared off to the lake, where Sean was gesturing in panic. The sight made him want to cry out.

'Orlaith!' he yelled. He dumped Sean on the ground, and this time Sean didn't run.

Down the slope Brannon charged, leaping the paddock fence to reach the lake quicker. *Oh God, why did I leave her?*

Already the struggle had stopped. Orlaith was in the lake, Randall lying on the bank. Brannon roared, a blood-curdling roar that must have carried all the way to Dromkeen. Randall looked up, and when he saw what was coming towards him, his jaw dropped in horror.

There was an audible crack as Brannon's knee connected with Randall's nose. Blood spurted out, and Randall was sent spinning down the bank. Brannon stormed into the lake, pulled Orlaith out, and carried her dripping body to the grass.

'Orlaith,' he shouted. 'Orlaith, wake up. It's me. It's Brannon.'

She didn't respond. Her eyes were closed, her face bluish-white. There was no sign of life.

'Orlaith!' Brannon grasped her head in despair. 'Orlaith, please, wake up. It's me.' Surely not now. Not now. 'Wake up, Orlaith!'

But she wasn't even breathing, and he gritted his teeth. 'Damn it, Orlaith. Wake up. Wake up!' He clenched a fist in anguish and then hammered it down on her chest.

She shot up, spewing a gutful of dirty lake water over her dress, and gasped. Her eyes rolled in her head as she gaped around.

'Jesus Christ, Orlaith,' Brannon said. 'Easy now, easy. Are you all right?'

Slowly she focused her vision. 'Brannon,' she whispered. 'Oh my God...'

'Come now,' he said, helping her to her feet. 'We must get out of here. Your husband is a dangerous man.'

She looked to where Randall was floundering in the water. 'Sean—where's Sean?'

'He's all right. I found him. Come on.' Brannon led her back through the trees in the direction of the house. Randall was still sprawled in the lake, his nose bloodied and his clothes soaked.

'Bastard,' he cursed in despair. 'Bastard!' He crawled through the reeds to the bank, fumbling in the mud. He collapsed on his side and breathed for a moment in dejection. She was gone. With *him*.

He glanced up. They were making their way back, calling for their brat. Randall swore again.

'He'll never take her,' he hissed. 'He'll never have her!' He got up and broke into a run, heading for the house with rage and murder in his eyes.

Near the stables, Vincent stared in astonishment at the scene unfolding by the lake. Randall brutally assaulted, Orlaith fleeing with the attacker. It took him a moment to comprehend what he was seeing. His face reddened.

Her yet again.

Randall should never have been so lenient. He should have sent her straight to the gallows. She would be a torment to them forever if she was allowed. And there was only one way to stop it.

Vincent loaded his pistol and advanced.

Sean looked on, terror finally replaced by relief. The strange man had rescued his mother. Not a bad man after all.

There was a growl behind him.

Vincent's arm shot around Sean's body and plucked him off the ground. Sean squealed.

'Stand fast!' he snarled. 'Back! Or I'll kill him! He placed the gun to Sean's temple.

'Vincent!' Orlaith gasped in fright. 'Vincent, don't—'

Vincent bared his teeth. The scar on his head was still visible, and it seemed to inflame as his hatred boiled. 'I knew it. You bloody mongrel. And who are you?' He glared at Brannon, pressing the muzzle of the gun harder into Sean's head.

'Leave him!' Brannon backed away, lifting the drapes of his djellaba. 'Look, I have no gun. Only this sword. A gun will beat a sword; you're in no danger. Let the boy go.'

'Shut your mouth!' Vincent squeezed his nails into the soft flesh of Sean's tummy, making the child scream.

'Don't!' Brannon yelled. 'Don't do that. Please, just let him go.'

Vincent smiled then. Orlaith had never witnessed anything so ugly.

'I don't think I'll let him go.' He leered at her. 'You shouldn't have hit me, you mongrel. That was a mistake. I've always known you were trouble, and it's time to end it. Now? Now I'm going to kill all three of you.'

He steadied the pistol against Sean's head, cocked the hammer, and braced himself for the explosion of blood and brains.

Sean suddenly blurted out, '*Bastard!*' He sank his teeth into Vincent's wrist, and Vincent roared with the unexpected pain. He drew his hand up. Sean kicked his way free.

Brannon moved; he pulled the sword from its sheath, and it flew through the air, disappearing into a blur for a tiny instant, and then it struck its target.

'Fuck…!' Vincent staggered backwards, gaping in horror at the blade punching through his chest. The tip of the blade had managed to pierce his back.

He stayed on his feet still, stumbling back towards the house, trying to reach the door. But he didn't make it. Blood spilled over his lips. He fell, hitting his head hard on the ground.

Brannon came over carefully and peered down at him. He placed his boot on his chest and heaved the sword clear, and then he took the pistol and tucked it inside his belt.

'A pretty mess we've made here,' he sighed. 'We'll have to get some tracks behind us. Right now. Do you hear?'

Orlaith went to Sean. He was glaring furiously at Vincent, rubbing his stomach from where the brutish guard had hurt him.

'Bastard,' he said.

'Sean!' Orlaith scolded him. 'Don't use words like that.'

Brannon came across and touched her shoulder. 'Are you all right?'

She looked at him. 'It didn't go as smoothly as we'd hoped.'

'Don't worry. We can get away. A ship waits for me in the harbour. Will you sail with me? God knows, we can't stay in Dromkeen.'

'I'll go anywhere,' she smiled, 'but only with my two boys beside me. And I'll never let you go again.'

He kissed her, and they began to walk for the gate.

❀ ❀ ❀

Unseen by them, Randall had slipped inside the house. He opened the cabinet in the drawing room and retrieved a double-barrel flintlock pistol.

Two shots. Two bullets.

He primed the gun and then removed his shoes so that they wouldn't hear his approach. He made his way to the front door.

He'll never have her.

❀ ❀ ❀

'Well, they did far worse than that to me,' Brannon was saying. 'Jesus, it will take me years to tell you everything.'

'We have years. Many of them,' she assured him warmly, and she squeezed his hand. Sean trotted along beside them.

But they were no longer alone.

Randall crept across the flagstones. His pistol was cocked, their backs perfect targets. At this range he couldn't miss.

He smiled and raised the gun triumphantly.

Orlaith took her last look across the estate. The lake was quiet again. Where was…

She stopped.

Randall took aim.

She spun round. He was there. Reacting instantaneously, she pulled the pistol from Brannon's belt, cocked the hammer, and fired. Two shots echoed into the sky.

'Sweet Jesus.' Brannon gaped around in shock. He saw Randall, the latter standing with a pistol in his hand and a malevolent smile on his face. Smoke wafted from his gun. Slowly Randall's mouth tightened into a grimace as a dark patch of blood seeped through his shirt. He dropped the gun, stumbled to the side, and collapsed. His lifeless eyes turned upwards to stare vacantly at the sky.

'Sweet Jesus,' Brannon said again, spotting a graze on the branch by his head. The passing bullet had missed him by inches, its aim thrown off by Orlaith's faster shot.

'He's dead,' she gasped. Her hand shook, and the pistol slipped from her grip.

Brannon looked towards the fallen body. 'I think you may be right.'

Her face went hard, devoid of emotion. 'I don't even feel guilt, Brannon. I wanted him dead for so long. He will never hurt me or my son again.' She went instinctively to pick up Sean.

Brannon took her arm. 'We'll go now. We really *have* to go.' In an hour this place would be overrun by the authorities.

Sean was staring at Randall's dead body, and he was quiet. The body was that of the man who had been such a dominant influence on him, a foreboding presence for so long, a frightening figure, a bully and a tyrant. Sean's small face suddenly seemed that of a much older boy, for he had just witnessed the passing of an era in his young life. He turned from Randall and looked to Brannon. And he understood, looking at his mother's companion, that the new era had now begun.

'Let me go, Mammy,' he commanded. She set him back on the ground. He stood between them and reached for Orlaith's hand, then for Brannon's. And together they made their way down to the ship.

The End

ABOUT THE AUTHOR

Born and raised in Cork in the south of Ireland, Paul Reid has spent years trawling the Irish coast, searching out its history and lore. A former musician who also spent time in Australia working as a ranch hand in the Outback, Reid developed a love for story-telling while still very young. *A Cruel Harvest* is Reid's first novel and marries his fascination with the tales of his homeland with his love of imagination. He lives on the shores of the Atlantic Ocean in Cork Harbour.